Burnt Sunshine

Estelle Pinney grew up in Cairns and the tobacco town of Mareeba, North Queensland. She left school at the age of thirteen to work as a colourist in her grandfather's photographic studio. Estelle's eventful adult life saw her working during World War II in a hand-grenade factory, then as an ambulance driver for the US army. She's also been a beauty consultant and a registered deckhand on her husband's crayfishing boat in the Torres Strait. Estelle is the author of *House on the Hill* (2005), *A Net Full of Honey* (1996), *Time Out for Living* (1995) and co-author of *Too Many Spears* (1978) with late husband Peter Pinney. Estelle lives in Brisbane with her daughter Stella.

Also by Estelle Pinney

Too Many Spears (with Peter Pinney)
Time Out For Living
A Net Full of Honey
House on the Hill

Burnt Sunshine

Estelle Pinney

VIKING
an imprint of
PENGUIN BOOKS

VIKING

Published by the Penguin Group
Penguin Group (Australia)
250 Camberwell Road, Camberwell, Victoria 3124, Australia
(a division of Pearson Australia Group Pty Ltd)
Penguin Group (USA) Inc.
375 Hudson Street, New York, New York 10014, USA
Penguin Group (Canada)
90 Eglinton Avenue East, Suite 700, Toronto, Canada ON M4P 2Y3
(a division of Pearson Penguin Canada Inc.)
Penguin Books Ltd
80 Strand, London WC2R 0RL England
Penguin Ireland
25 St Stephen's Green, Dublin 2, Ireland
(a division of Penguin Books Ltd)
Penguin Books India Pvt Ltd
11 Community Centre, Panchsheel Park, New Delhi – 110 017, India
Penguin Group (NZ)
67 Apollo Drive, Rosedale, North Shore 0632, New Zealand
(a division of Pearson New Zealand Ltd)
Penguin Books (South Africa) (Pty) Ltd
24 Sturdee Avenue, Rosebank, Johannesburg 2196, South Africa

Penguin Books Ltd, Registered Offices: 80 Strand, London, WC2R 0RL, England

First published by Penguin Group (Australia), 2008

1 3 5 7 9 10 8 6 4 2

Design by Tony Palmer © Penguin Group (Australia)
Cover photographs: image of woman: MovieMaidens.com;
departing train: Bert Hardy/Getty Images; backwaters: Kelly Ryerson/Getty Images
Typeset in12/18 pt Fairfield Light by Post Pre-press Group, Brisbane, Queensland
Printed and bound in Australia by McPherson's Printing Group, Maryborough,
Victoria

National Library of Australia
Cataloguing-in-Publication data:

Pinney, Estelle.
Burnt sunshine.
ISBN 978 0 670 07196 8 (pbk.).
I. Title

A823.3

penguin.com.au

*To my darlings, Stephen, Genevieve
and the girls: Amy, Nicole and Bethany;
Emma, Brendan and their little ones,
Edan and Niah*

Good Lord above

Send down a dove

With wings as sharp as razors

To cut off the lugs

Of the wicked mugs

Who slash the poor man's wages

PROLOGUE

Summer was at its scorching best. A reluctant breeze inched its way across the room and did little to dry the sweat on the sleeping man's chest or cool the bare legs of the woman lying beside him. The tinny, scratchy voice coming from the gramophone was losing momentum and slowly dying in the afternoon heat.

Greta gave the sleeper a nudge. 'Your turn, Andy; either wind it up or change the record.' The response was a gentle snore. She sighed; easier to do it herself. Gently, so as not to disturb the sleeper, she inched herself to the side of the bed. The linoleum was cool under her feet as she padded across the room. Blowing a wisp of dust off the needle, she returned the tone arm back to its cradle and with careful fingers lifted the record off the turntable. Humming softly, she flipped through the small stack of records in the storage shelves of the machine, found one to her liking and grinned. This should wake him up with a bang, she thought. But before the record touched the soft felt of the turntable she paused, her eyes on the sleeping man and her grin softened into a wistful smile. 'Ah, Andy, what are we doing here? How the hell did we end up in this dusty little town? Who has given up the most – you or me?'

CHAPTER ONE

Three months earlier: December 31, 1935

Greta Osborne was living up to her reputation as one of the shining stars of Sydney's cabaret set. Tawny eyes that stopped men in their tracks sparkled, her wide smile enchanted and everything was swinging just the way she liked it. Music, champagne (the best of French) bubbled in Waterford crystal, silver salvers overflowed with caviar, and there was not too much competition, Greta decided, from the flock of beauties that had been invited posthaste to charm the officers of a British frigate anchored in the Harbour.

The unexpected arrival from Singapore of the British Navy had set the fashionable ladies of upper-crust Sydney into a flurry, and notables, debutants and the brightest of the entertainment world (including Greta) were begged – for King and country – to cancel all previous arrangements and come to the party. The invitation – more like a royal command – was intriguing enough for Greta to slip into her latest extravagance: a creation of turquoise and silver sequins with a dropped back line as low as she dared. Unlike the modish shingles and marcelled bobs that hairdressers recommended,

Greta's burnished waves and curls swung freely to the admiration of every male in the room.

The late arrival of a lone naval officer sent one of the doyennes of Sydney's society flying to the door with cries of welcome and an outstretched hand. Greta, close enough to hear the effusive dismissal of the officer's apologies over the chat of her own enamoured three (a politician and two bachelors of the town), raised an eyebrow. Lordy, what a fuss, she thought, for he was hardly admiral of the fleet, but it didn't stop her from noting in a flash that he was tallish, with straight sandy hair and a clear, light complexion. There was the touch of a Scot's brogue in his apologies. Handsome? Not really. But as he caught her eye and gave her a rakish grin it contradicted first impressions as far as looks went. Greta found herself surprised that fleeting contact could induce such pleasure; a new experience for her, she had to confess. She couldn't take her eyes off him and wondered why . . . Second discreet observations revealed that his profile was good, and an aquiline nose gave him an air of arrogance belied by the relaxed stance that the perfection of his uniform couldn't hide.

Up to this moment, Greta (who enjoyed every compliment from the many men who waited nightly at the stage door with flowers and invitations) had done little in her twenty-three years to encourage the next step into a serious liaison. There had been a lover or two, but ambition had kept her more or less on the straight and narrow towards a goal that she was now close to achieving. Her parents, thespians in a travelling company, had left Greta in her grandparents' care with instructions that dancing and singing lessons should begin on the day after her fifth birthday. A train collision in India had left Greta an orphan, but the dancing and singing lessons had carried on as requested.

Achieving champion or first place in every Eisteddfod that came along, Greta's clear tuneful voice, bouncy curls and tapping feet became the stepping stones that led her to Sydney at sweet sixteen with stardust in her eyes. Pantomimes in the City Hall, front-cloth acts in the baroque splendour of the city's picture palaces . . . it was vaudeville at its best. Greta had her part to play and already knew she played it well. Now a contract was waiting to be signed when the New Year's celebrations were over and strange men – even intriguing ones, she acknowledged with a tinge of regret – didn't come into the equation. She suppressed a giggle. But that don't stop me from lookin', she thought.

Madame Hostess, still fluctuating with gushes by the door, claimed the latecomer as her own. 'You must meet my daughter and her friends. Charming girls,' she warbled, her voice trailing in her wake as she swept the officer off, full-steam ahead. He gave Greta a wink as he passed. She winked back. Not giving a jot if her admirers had noticed the exchange, she gave a well-rehearsed shimmy of the vamp as she held out her glass. 'First one back with another of these and a plate of those devilled oysters shall have my blessings and more.' She gave a shooing motion with her hand and they galloped off towards the buffet, spurred on by hope and good intentions.

Now alone, Greta was ready to give her full attention to the late arrival who appeared to be perfectly happy with the company in the far corner of the grand drawing room. There was no denying that a navy rig of gold buttons, a white mess jacket and red cummerbund gave a dash and flair to any party. In a room full of such nautical glamour, Greta wondered why one man out of the blue should be capable of giving her the flutters with just a wink and a grin. She'd had more than her share of them over the years.

Aware that her three gallants were now bearing down at great speed with loaded plates and brimming glasses, she suddenly realised that champagne and devilled oysters were the last thing she wanted. The breeze coming through the long French doors behind her had died and the room with its noise and laughter, its smell of perfume and powder, body sweat and liquor stifled her. Without a thought for the approaching trio, she slipped behind the lace curtains and through the doors leading onto the balcony.

Outside the air, refreshed by a sea not so far away, cooled her cheeks as she walked over to the wide-lipped balustrade that curved around the mansion and lost itself behind a jungle of exotic blooms and potted palms. Now her head was clearing, and leaning on the cool marble Greta took a few appreciative deep breaths. Too much bubbly and caviar ain't no good for a dancing girl, she admonished herself.

Far below, stone steps led down to a sequestered cove and on a sliver of sand she could make out a group sitting around a small camp fire. Although it was already well after midnight, their 'Auld Lang Syne's joined in with the celebrations that could still be heard across the harbour. An occasional rocket lit up its share of the sky and from somewhere came the sound of yodelling to the accompaniment of saucepan lids. Distance softened the sounds of high revelry.

Greta's sigh was touched by a sadness that sometimes came upon her with the passing of another tired old year; a fleeting moment that could never be explained. But this time a flare of excitement swept away all thoughts of the blues and the sights and sounds of the festive night.

She flung out her arms, spinning around. 'Nineteen thirty-six,' she called out to the stars, 'here I am! Ready and waiting!' The lucky breaks that people yearn for had come her way, and a glittering future was ready to be snatched up with both hands. America and New York's Palace Theatre beckoned.

'And a Happy New Year to you, Greta Osborne.'

She snatched in a breath and came to a dead stop. He was standing no more than an arm's length away.

'And likewise . . .' She tried to conceal a ridiculous rush of happiness by giving him a brief, noncommittal nod. 'But you're one up on me, officer. How about an introduction?'

He gave a short, half-mocking bow. 'I apologise. Andrew Flight, at your service.'

'Andrew Flight,' she echoed, and left it at that. Never without a quip on her lips, she broached the gulf of silence growing between them with a laugh and pointed up at the moon, shining silver. 'Not a cloud in the sky. Oh, what a night and one hot, perfect summer's day coming up.'

'You could be wrong, Greta Osborne. Look over there.' He directed her gaze to a faint blurring of cloud low in the sky. 'Tomorrow, or should I say today,' a serious note had crept into his voice, 'it will rain. Three days of it.'

'With a sky like that?' A raised eyebrow mocked him. 'I very much doubt it, Mr Weather Man.'

'Of course, I apologise; you could never know that the old girl – my ship, pride of the royal navy – has a reputation. Three days of rain once she's in port and bedded down. Be it Hong Kong, Singapore or your own lovely city. She never fails us. It will rain.'

Greta felt the hair rising on her arms. 'You're joking.'

'Och, I'm dead serious.' She noticed that his smile, parenthesised by deep lines from cheek to chin, gave him a piratical air and it held her captive. 'Serious enough,' he continued, 'to take a bet on it.'

'With me?'

'Who else?' He made a pretence of looking around, enticing a chuckle from Greta as he carefully examined the underside of a broad-leafed Madonna lily and slowly shook his head. 'No one there,' he said, looking around again, 'not a soul. Only you. Only me,' he teased.

She couldn't resist his challenge. 'A bet, ay? I could be getting into big strife here. How high are the stakes? C'mon,' she stepped back, hand on hip, more at home now with his tomfoolery. 'What have you in mind?'

'If there is not a drop,' he spaced his words, 'before the last star fades from the sky . . .' Greta's eyes widened as she watched him take from a trouser pocket a stone that in the moonlight looked very close to a ruby and much larger than a sixpence. It was enough to promote a gasp of disbelief.

'This is ridiculous. You can't —'

'Och, but I can.'

Her head reeled. She'd had too much to drink and he was quite mad – even if it was in fun. And I'm just as crazy, so careful, my girl, she warned herself. I can feel trouble coming on, but at the same time she brushed caution aside. What the heck . . . It's probably a piece of glass, anyway. 'All right.' Greta's chin tilted. 'I'll take you on. And if it rains?'

There was confidence in the look he gave her. 'I'll pick you up after you've eaten your salt and porridge, then we'll walk. A whole day of it.'

'Salt and porridge! A walk in the rain? You're an idiot, Andrew Flight, and put that stone back in your pocket – it's making me nervous. Anyway, it ain't gonna rain,' she swung into an old music hall ditty, 'no more, no more.' Flashing a smile over her shoulder – an invitation for him to follow – she made her way though the balcony doors and back into the hubbub of a party in full swing.

A tango melody was throbbing its magic around the room. She didn't doubt for a moment that he'd appear and together they would take to the floor; for who could resist a tango? But the lace curtains behind her hung straight and still. She pulled one aside to take a peek, only to find that the balcony was deserted. Andrew Flight had disappeared. He must have followed the curve of the balcony and re-entered the room by another way.

Then, over the heads of dancing couples she saw him. He was in laughing conversation with the 'charming girls'. Not sure whether to be piqued or amused, it seemed as if their words and banter over a ridiculous bet had never existed. Greta shrugged. 'Maybe just as well,' she murmured to herself, determined to quash a tinge of regret that chances were poor of ever seeing him again. Visiting naval ships rarely outstayed their welcome and as far as she knew, Andrew Flight could be sailing over the horizon in a few days' time. Rain *or* shine.

'Will you honour me with this dance, Miss?' A young midshipman, so polite, so anxious, was standing before her, both hands outstretched.

'I'd simply adore to.' Without another word Greta fell into his arms, hip pressed to hip, her cheek close to his, her eyes closed in exaggerated bliss. 'Yes,' she whispered into his ear, 'let's show 'em.'

To Greta's surprise, this was no fumbling amateur that held her in his arms. The hand on her back was assured and firm, and as he guided her with smooth, long strides into a tango promenade, she acknowledged his expertise by matching him step by step, giving herself up to the rhythm of the music as he guided her across the room. Their staccato movements were perfection. It didn't take long for the dancers around them to realise that the gorgeous and famous Greta Osborne with partner unknown was giving them all a demonstration not to be forgotten. Gradually they formed a circle, silently admiring, while Greta, aware of the impression they were making, followed her partner in exquisite submission. The music stopped. Silence. Clapping and cheers lifted the roof as Greta, happy to share the applause, held high her partner's hand, her smile brilliant enough to light up the room. The young man, as if suddenly aware that they were the centre of attention and not sure how to handle such approbation, gave Greta an awkward bow.

'Thank you, Miss Osborne. I'll never forget it.'

'Neither will I.'

'I didn't realise —' he gulped down his embarrassment, 'until they cheered us – that you were the famous Greta Osborne we've all heard about.' By now the three-piece band had started up with a lively quickstep to the tune of 'We're in the Money'. The lad looked suddenly desperate as dancers milled around them. 'Afraid I can't do the quickstep.'

'So? She stepped back, ready to begin. 'I'll teach you.'

'No – no. That won't do. Won't do at all.'

With a stab of sympathy Greta was quick to realise that after such an exhibition of a flawless tango, stumbling around the floor under her guiding hand held no appeal. The midshipman

9

ducked to avoid a flailing elbow. She took his arm in a conciliatory gesture.

'It's okay, officer. Just take me back to where you found me.' She
held out her hand but his arms hung stiffly by his side. The situation
was turning farcical, and it seemed as if he was incapable of moving.
She couldn't walk off leaving him there nailed to the floor!

Weaving his way towards them, it took only seconds before
Andrew Flight was tapping the midshipman's shoulder. 'Ye canna'
have her for every dance, Thomas, m' boy. My turn, I think. And
there's a girl over there,' he pointed out a pretty blonde, one of a
cluster not far away, 'that one in the green dress, who is swooning
to have a turn around the floor with you. So go for it, laddie.' The
relief clearly expressed on Thomas's face as he hurriedly excused
himself was hardly flattering, Greta acknowledged, but easy to
ignore. Not so the thrill that surged up from her toes the moment
the naval officer put his arm around her waist, and drew her close
to him.

It took two steps only for her to realise he was no Fred Astaire.
But who cares? was the blissful thought floating through her mind.
She hadn't felt like this since the time when the kid next door – she
couldn't remember his name – had kissed her behind the lavvy in
her grandparents' backyard.

'Thanks for rescuing me, Officer Flight.'

'Not you I was rescuing, Osborne.' He leant back to look down
at her as she noted with pleasure that he was a good head taller
than herself; not often the case as far as men were concerned. 'It
was young Thomas,' the amusement in his voice was unexpected.
'Delayed stage fright with him. Seen it happen before.'

'Oh . . .' What else was there to say?

It was then she noticed that he was taking her in the direction of the French doors; a return to the balcony seemed to be his intention and a plan that Greta had no objection to. They would dance under the stars. And next? A few kisses between friends wouldn't go amiss, she told herself in happy anticipation, at the same time acknowledging that wine, dance and a man called Andrew Flight was a heady mixture to be careful of.

He didn't lead her through the doors after all, but stopped short of them, bending close to her ear. 'We have to leave.' Her hand was released although his arm lingered on her hip in a light caress. 'The skipper,' he nodded towards a naval man weighed down with gold braid and a chest of medals, 'is bent on making a night of it. Another invitation to attend and all hands on deck – unfortunately.' Lips downturned, he had the grace to look uncomfortable, then gave a shrug. 'As the Old Man would say, colonial hospitality cannot be ignored. However —'

'Flight!' The bellow of a fellow officer could be heard above the music. 'We're waiting for you!' Andrew gave a quick look around him. 'I don't think our departure is going to spoil things.' He sounded so unlike the man who had teased her on the balcony. 'Sorry, Greta, I have to go.' He gave a half salute and hurried away.

She could have killed him, then chided herself for feeling so deflated. So much for rain, salt and porridge. Damn it! She helped herself to a glass fizzing with bubbles as a waiter glided past. The night had lost its sparkle and Greta was ready to call it quits. It was then she noticed that the trio – the politician and the two bachelors of the town – were approaching, still all smiles and seemingly ready to forgive and forget her desertion of them. Greta lifted her glass, toasting them a welcome.

'Who wants the first dance?' she called out, a full bottom lip caught between even white teeth. 'Now. Let me guess . . .'

Falling rain on the shutters whispered that it was time to get out of bed. Greta gave a small moan. She heard the twelve tinkling chimes of the boudoir clock – a dainty thing of white xylonite and brass that stood among the creams and perfume bottles on her dressing table. Twelve o'clock . . . Noon or midnight? Carefully she eased herself out of bed and, stumbling over to the window, opened the Mediterranean shutters that darkened the room. Grey skies and the sigh of soft rain soothed a throbbing head and sand-blasted eyes. She drew back the curtain, grateful for the sweetness of the air, and allowed the mists of rain to cool her cheeks.

Raining after all. She'd lost the bet and what a joke *that* had turned out to be. Memories of the night washed over her. Memories of him and the wild hours of dancing that followed after his leaving. Her head! She moaned again as a well-aimed arrow split it open. 'Time for a strong cup of tea,' she whispered in deference to the throbbing that had taken over her brain, thankful that there was nothing to drag her away from a bed looking more attractive by the second. She leant out the window for one more deep breath of rain-cooled air.

It was then that she saw him.

Standing across the street, he made a dark figure in a heavy mackintosh with naval cap pulled down, the peak protecting his eyes from the rain. How long had he been standing there? Excitement brainstormed its way through her senses; a heavy night of partying instantly forgotten.

'Andrew!' she yelled, the street narrow enough for him to hear. 'I said you were mad, now I know it. Come out of the rain, you ass, first floor up and door to your left. Hell, no!' she shouted out to him again. 'Give me five minute. Five minutes only. Then come up!'

A sudden breeze tossed the curtain into her face and heavier gusts of rain blew in. Greta slammed the shutters tight, switched on the light and pulled up and straightened the crumpled bed sheets. Scanties, stockings and the sequin dress were kicked out of sight under the bed as she flung a quilt of Chinese silk over the top. For the first time she regretted that the tiny flat lacked a decent sitting room and a bedroom door.

Her scrap of a bathroom was given the once-over before she took the quickest shower she'd ever had in her life. A brisk towelling followed and flinging on a bright-green sleeveless shirt and a pair of matching shorts, her russet waves and curls damp from the shower, she was all-fresh perfection by the time he knocked. Breathless, Greta opened the door.

'Tea or coffee,' she asked him, 'or do you prefer porridge?'

CHAPTER TWO

That he was actually standing there, dripping water all over her doormat, looking quite at ease if anything, had Greta acting like a dumb cluck with a feeling of champagne bubbling helter-skelter through her veins. She stood aside as Andrew stepped into the flat, at the same time freeing himself of his raincoat and cap before hanging them on the rack by the door.

'Make yourself at home,' Greta said, and in spite of champagne bubbles it was hard not to avoid a touch of acid creeping into her voice. 'You seem to have had no trouble finding out my address.'

'The home of one of the most talented and famous performers in Sydney? Victoria Street, Pott's Point? And then there's the fact that your bosom pal, Flossie Stretton, known to wield a clever pen in the gossip columns, lives right next door.' He did little to hide his self-satisfaction. 'A touch of the old Holmes and Watson was all that was necessary, my dear.'

'Oh, *very* clever. And anyway, what brings you here?' Already Greta knew the answer.

'To claim a bet, of course.' Without hesitation he strode deeper into the room, bypassing the bed to reach the window shutters. He flung them wide open and the rain, as if to prove a point, spattered in. He turned, triumphant. 'I rest my case. And it's tea, thank you, strong, sweet and black.'

'Yes, sir!' Snapping a salute and with tapping side steps, Greta made her way to the kitchenette. 'At once, sir!'

The afternoon flew on wings as they sat over pots of tea and mugs of coffee and talked, taking time out while she cooked up the one egg in the ice chest and shared out a tin of baked beans. As if catching up on every day that had passed them by without each other's company, they talked all the while knowing that their time together was all too brief.

Sitting at the small dining table, they listened to each other's story, not touching, as if aware that surrender must wait until the full tale had been told. Andrew – Andy, as Greta called him as the afternoon lengthened – had lived in Aberdeen before joining the navy. He was the only son of a seafaring family that had travelled the seas, east and west, north and south, from sailing ship to sail and steam. He told Greta of his father, whose loyalties had been and still were with the P&O Company. But Andrew had gone one better, so he believed, and after naval training had become an engineer on the vessel 'that brought on the rain'.

In turn, Greta told him of the parents who had died and of the grandparents who only lately had followed them. 'I couldn't have wished for a better life than the one they gave me. And look at me now – best hoofer with a voice on the Sydney stage! But not for long.'

He raised an eyebrow. 'Tell me.'

Grinning, she leant back in her chair, thumbs tucked into the armholes of the green blouse. 'You, Mr Andrew Flight, are looking at the one Aussie girl in the chorus line of the famous Palace Theatre, New York, starring, of all people, Eddie Cantor – you must have heard of him – and I sail for the good old US of A via London in less than three weeks. How about that?'

'America, eh, lass? And we sail for Singapore the day after tomorrow.'

Greta, still leaning back in her chair, thumbs hitched into her blouse, gave a small shrug. 'Well, it is truly ships that pass in the night, isn't it?' she said quietly.

'Aye.' He gave his wristwatch a glance. 'And time's up.' The room had darkened; the rain still falling. Before she had time to feel regret, Andrew gave her the wink that could send reason into a tailspin. 'But don't forget, Greta Osborne, there's an IOU that must to be settled. Right?'

'Right!' was the no-nonsense response. 'This lady always honours a bet.' Still balanced on the back legs of the chair, she attempted to shake hands on it across the table – a wrong move that sent the chair legs sliding. With a magnificent display of shapely legs and a squeal of fright, Greta disappeared out of sight.

'Wha' she done now!' In a flash he was there, looking down at her spreadeagled on the floor, the chair balanced on her chest. 'Are you all right?'

Greta pushed the offending chair away. 'Think so, nothing broken.' Sitting up, she rubbed the back of her head.

'Here, take a hold.' Bending over, Andrew held out both hands. Was there a hint of amusement in his voice? Laughter under control? A swift flare of resentment was dismissed as she took his hands, feeling the strength of him as she was hauled in one smooth movement to her feet.

His touch lingered in the pretence of dusting her off and his amusement, imagined or not, seemed to have vanished. Brushing back a strand of hair, he replaced it gently behind her ear. 'Beautiful woman . . .'

Slowly his arms encircled her as she lifted her face. A soft lingering kiss followed, lips just touching. For a while, unmoving, they allowed the sweetness to flow over them, until as if in mutual agreement, they drew apart.

'Och, Greta, I didna' mean that to happen.' He drew a shuddering breath. 'To remember it would be too deep a hurt.'

Strangely enough, she understood. Whatever had passed between them, even from the first moment he had spoken to her – in spite of the tomfoolery – was precious and intangible; too precious for it to blossom and then wither away. And wither away it would, with the oceans soon to be between them. 'I know what you mean,' she whispered, accepting.

Once again he looked at the time, and said with a crisper tone, 'Duty calls.' Stepping back and holding her shoulders at arm's length, his eyes studied her. 'Until tomorrow, then.' He moved away to retrieve his cap and shrug himself into his mackintosh. It seemed to Greta that he was quite capable of pushing the tender moments they had shared aside, leaving her with no choice but to follow. She squared her shoulders. 'A bet is a bet, Officer Flight. Tomorrow. As early as you like.'

Now that he had left, the silence enveloped her. It filled the room, allowing everything that had happened – every word and every touch – to be remembered in minute detail; her lips moist, as if a trace of their kiss still lingered there.

She crossed over to the bed and stretched out full length, closing her eyes and allowing the dizzy elation that she felt and was still experiencing surge through her. Where did it all come from? she wondered. Had it been there all the time, lying dormant, waiting to explode into vibrant awareness the moment Andrew Flight caught her eye? But why him? A few brief moments on a balcony at midnight and an afternoon of his company, and that was all. Yet something told her that more than a kiss had passed between them; it was impossible to ignore that a bond so tight and strong had been created. Be careful, Greta warned herself. She was not much better than Flossie who fell in love, deeply and passionately (so she said) at least several times a month. Yet her heart sang at the very thought of seeing Andy again: to feast on his smile and hear the soft Scottish burr of his voice . . .

Suddenly, she sprung off the bed, strode across the room and scrabbled in the bottom drawer of her sideboard. Tossing aside programs, photographs, a tablecloth and serviettes, she drew out a fancy box of gold-tipped cigarettes, a gift from her agent.

Weeks ago, she had given up smoking and had hidden temptation out of sight. Now, lifting the lid, she selected one and took it over to the gas ring to light up. She sniffed the fragrance of cured tobacco before holding the slim cylinder to the flame. Then, inhaling deeply, she went to the window. The shutters were still open and in the empty street lamplight made pools of gold on the wet footpath. No one was in sight but imagination had him still standing there, waiting for her. Commonsense and a cold feeling in her heart said that she shouldn't be at home when he turned up in the morning. He was going away and she was off to America, with little chance that they would somehow meet again. Much easier now to cauterise any feelings that could wreck dreams and ruin the golden future that was waiting for her. Damn you, Andrew Flight!

Thoughts were shattered as the front door was flung open behind her and a cold blast of air hit the room. Greta spun around, half hoping that the naval officer had returned.

Flossie Stretton stood at the door, her mascara-framed eyes wide with curiosity, her blonde frizz completely out of control. 'Who is he?' Not waiting for an answer, she tripped into the room and came to a halt at the sight of the boxed cigarettes. 'Ooh-er, Virginia Triumphs.' She took one out for herself. 'Thought you'd given them up.'

'I have.'

'Nerves all of a jangle? Not surprised. All the nice girls love a sailor, all the nice girls love a tar,' Flossie began to sing. She raised an eyebrow and sucked in her cheeks. 'There must have been a lot of lovin' going on behind that closed door.'

'Shut up, Floss. You're making wild guesses.'

'Not so wild. All I know is that I've been waiting all afternoon for an intro, and not a word or a peep out of you. Not like you, Greta.'

'Since when have you turned chaperone?'

'Listen to her! You know you're a real prude if a male puts a foot inside that door. Usually can't get me in here quick enough for a coffee or something, making sure that said male don't get the wrong idea. Anyway . . .' She crossed to the window, taking Greta's cigarette from her lips and using it to light up her own. 'From what I saw, he's a bit of all right. Are you seeing him again?'

'No. I – there's no point. The navy leaves the day after tomorrow.'

'Well if you don't want him,' Flossie gave Greta a shrewd side glance, 'I'll have him.'

Greta knew that Floss would waste no time if she saw him walking up the street unattached. 'Nothing doing, Floss.' She surprised herself by the brisk rebuff. 'Changed my mind. I was fibbing anyway. Andy and I are doing the town over tomorrow.' The cigarette was tossed out the window and Greta bustled her protesting friend towards the door, deliriously happy that Flossie had made up her mind for her. 'Now outski, I have some beauty sleep to catch up on.'

CHAPTER THREE

As before, he was standing across the street, giving the impression that he had been there all though the night. Greta had no intention of him coming upstairs and into the flat. Lying awake half the night in tingling anticipation, she had decided that she was only honouring her part of the bargain. Merely playing a role in showing a stranger the delights of Sydney (even if it was pouring down cats and dogs) and at the same time asking herself, who was she kidding?

Already she had semaphored through the open window for him to wait and that she was on her way. High heels made a clatter down the uncarpeted stairs and before opening the door a last-minute check-up in the hallstand mirror told her that she'd never looked better. The head-hugging cloche and the matching yellow linen suit brightened up a rainy day, even if it had to be concealed by the drabness of a gaberdine raincoat. Never mind. The hat and yellow umbrella made up for it.

A whole day walking in the rain? Not on your life, Greta had said to herself over breakfast toast and a cup of tea. She had other ideas for the entertaining of Andrew Flight. A walk in Hyde Park certainly, even if only to admire its latest acquisition: the Archibald Fountain in all its flamboyant splendour of statuary and splashing water. Then perhaps a tram ride down to Circular Quay to view – if he hadn't already seen it – the mighty new bridge that straddled the Harbour from north to south. Greta gave a wicked smile envisioning her plans for the afternoon's entertainment. Andy was in for a rare treat, she hoped, flinging the door wide open to a gusting wind and a spattering of rain. Waving, she sprinted across the street to greet him.

'Whoa there!' Laughing, and with arms outstretched, Andrew broke her gallop. 'Such enthusiasm. I'm flattered.'

'So you should be.' She shook raindrops off her face, the umbrella no match for the wind whistling up the street. 'There was no point in meeting me over there,' she went on briskly, 'and getting soaked before we start. The awnings on this side will keep us dry more or less until we reach the Cross. It's not far from here.'

'How serious we are.' He held up one finger as if testing the direction of the wind, then nodded in satisfaction. 'It must be the weather,' he teased before releasing her. 'But am I allowed to mention you're looking gorgeous?' He stepped back to admire. 'Ah! Sunshine yellow. A bonny colour.'

It was then she gave him a happy smile. 'Compliments I can lap up night or day. Don't let me stop you.' Only for seconds he had held her, but it was close enough for Greta to smell a heady blend of sea and pipe tobacco and in a flash she knew that if he'd kissed her there and then, there would have been the taste of salt on his lips.

Andrew crooked his arm. 'The day begins. Lead on, Miss Greta Osborne.'

A wisp of blue could be seen in the clouds, and the rain, in competition with the splashing fountain, had eased to nothing more
than a soft drizzle. Andrew looked down at Greta sitting on the
fountain's rim, trailing her hand in the water; a bronze Theseus in
conflict with the Minotaur as her background and a chaste Diana
with bow and arrow close enough to be glimpsed. So far, so good,
he told himself, at the same time cursing fate's turn of the wheel
that had brought – swept, he conceded ruefully – them together.
For what? he asked himself. With the next morning's tide, he and
the rest of the crew would be leaving Sydney far behind.

It had been months, a lifetime, since a woman had charmed
him as Greta in her glittering body-hugging gown had done on New
Year's Eve. It had happened in the first moment when he'd heard
her laughter, matched only by a radiance that had seared him with
its brilliance.

Already armed by the disaster that had been London more
than two years ago, he should have stopped there and then before
attracting Greta's attention. But her smile had disarmed him and the
foolish action of a wink and her cheeky response had unravelled a
rigid determination to keep all emotions and involvements on hold.
What had followed the next day – only yesterday – had been the
pleasure he felt in her company and the easy rapport that had developed between them. To hold – if only for seconds – that strong,
lithe body in his arms had been enough to make the blood surge
through his own. Then a kiss that should never have happened.
And now today . . . A walk in the park? A few laughs? Harmless
enough, he assured himself.

It had been a morning of light-hearted enjoyment. Kings Cross
had much to offer: a cluster of laughing girls in the company of a

23

dandy in white tie and tails, and an excitable couple from somewhere east of Berlin toting a tray – a delectable melange of piled
cream and fruits – into a shop of miniscule proportions. Stalls and
wheelbarrows spilling over with roses and carnations contended
with overcast skies, reminding Andrew of the riotous banks of
blooms at the Covent Garden markets.

Greta had then led him into a dimly lit café, redolent with the
aroma of Turkish coffee, and there they shared a precious hour in
the company – so early in the morning – of a belly dancer and a
scattering of men crosseyed by Greta's vitality and carefree beauty
and the gyrations of the belly dancer with her tinkling ankle bells
and cymbals. The performance had come to an abrupt ending
when it became obvious that the dancer, charmed by Andrew's
and Greta's applause, had danced for them alone. Whispers,
glowers and frowns announced that it was time for them to go,
and concealing their laughter they had left the dancer and her
devotees behind.

'Now for the city, and . . .' Greta had arched an eyebrow,
'delights you have never dreamt of. Trust me. I think you'll enjoy
the experience.'

'I'm yours and ready for anything.'

'Well, c'mon, then!'

They had ambled along the leisurely slope that was William
Street, passing by second-hand shops with their racks of shabby
clothes cluttering the footpath, and cameras and watches, rings and
old books, looking tired and dusty behind bars in the windows of
pawnshops. The dreariness of it all was ignored by Greta, who had
explained that it was a street for poets to write about and had already
been enshrined in literary glory by a close and creative friend.

His musings about the morning they'd shared were scattered by her voice.

'Well, what do you think of it?' Greta, looking up at him, made a wide sweep of her arm, encompassing the whole glory of bronze sculpture and cascading water that was the Archibald Fountain. 'Isn't it just magnificent? Just beautiful?'

'Beautiful.' He looked down at her. 'I couldn't agree more.' She choose to ignore the steady gaze and, turning back, allowed her eyes to rest on the powerful nakedness of Theseus, dagger ready to thrust, and the fierce despair of the beast that was about to die. Giving a shiver as if feeling the dagger's plunge, she sprang to her feet, brushing raindrops off her coat and settling the yellow cloche firmly on her head.

'Well!' There was a forced brightness to her voice. 'We've done the things you *must* see. Kings Cross, viewed the Harbour, the bridge *and* seen the fountain. Now what?'

'Feeling peckish? Hungry? It's been some time —'

'Hit the nail on the head.' Greta clicked her fingers. The tenseness he had sensed in her suddenly vanished. 'And now . . .' She stood back, arms akimbo and a slow, sly come-hither smile parted her lips. 'Follow wid me to the Romarna and I weel show you, pretty boy, ze sights not often seen by strangers in this plaice. Very naice – very special.'

In retaliation Andrew closed his eyes into splits of devilment and curled a ghost moustache with one hand. 'Show me, my lovely one!' As if by magic there appeared in the palm of his other hand the ruby that Greta had seen at the New Year's celebrations. Keeping up the charade, Andrew went on. 'I 'ave the spondulicks to pay. No?'

'My God, do you carry that thing around with you?'

'Never leaves me.'

'Why don't you put it in a safe or a bank or something?'

'Not likely.' Andrew ran a finger over the ruby's smooth surface, a faint smile on his lips. 'Let us call it for the moment a lucky talisman.' He held up the gem to catch the light of an indifferent ray of sunshine. 'Not worth a fortune, I'll admit. But there'll come a day when this little beauty will serve me well.'

'It *is* a ruby, isn't it?'

'Burma has the finest, I've been told.' Leaving it at that, he slipped it into an inner pocket of his mackintosh. 'Now! Where's this Romarna? Seems a long time since we had that coffee.'

Only a short walk down Pitt Street and they turned into a lane, made unremarkable by a hardware store and a few shops selling unremarkable wares. With the drizzling rain and sullen clouds the lane had taken on a furtive air, relieved only by Greta's umbrella, bravely yellow in the afternoon's gloom.

'Here we are.'

They stood in front of a door that held no promise of cosy surrounds or the hearty dish of sausages and mash that Greta had promised. Without further explanation she pressed hard on the doorbell. It seemed as if the sound of it echoed down empty caverns, leaving only the silence behind.

'Good Lord, Greta.' The Scottish brogue intensified, his face comical with bemused puzzlement. 'Wher'r are you taking us? A brigand's den?'

With a twinkle in her eye, Greta grinned. 'You could call it that, I suppose.' Startled, Andrew suddenly found himself being squizzed at by a single eye attached to a peephole in the door.

'Do I know you, sir?' A pseudo-cultured voice demanded. 'Declare yourself, or be gone.'

'Eddie!' Greta elbowed Andrew aside. 'Don't be an idiot and open the door.'

Immediately it flew open and Andrew saw that the eye belonged to a tall, gangling young man with arms held wide in a greeting. 'Greta, beloved, you're back!'

'And you, Eddie, are drunk.' She gave him a slight push. 'Let's get upstairs before Andy and I starve to death.'

They followed a slightly swaying Eddie down the dimness of a hallway dank with the smell of ancient mildew until they came to a stairway. Muffled voices and an occasional burst of a song could be heard as they climbed into nearly total darkness, and on reaching a landing they were confronted, Andrew guessed by the feel of it, by a heavy velvet curtain. All the while Greta had remained silent but now and then a bubble of laughter, unexplained, had escaped from her lips. Now she was standing by his side and as Eddie began to pull back the drape, Andy heard her give a theatrical command, 'Wait!' Then without pause she herself pulled back the curtain. 'Voila!'

He was dazzled by an explosion of light from two large skylights and walls brightened by works of art, faded streamers and bunched balloons; a possible leftover from some gala affair. Vociferous with cries of delight, a group of men and a sprinkling of women bore down on Greta in welcome. Two of the party, one being Eddie, snatched her up and, placing her on their shoulders, paraded around the long plain timbered room, a line of rowdy celebrants behind them singing, 'Happy Days are Here Again!'

'Eddie! Ben! Put me down, you fools!' Greta ordered, a picture of happy abandonment, and with a show of silk-stockinged legs and lacy garters, she sent her yellow hat sailing through the air. There were cheers and clapping to a crashing of chords from a piano on a dais centred at one end of the room. Greta Osborne had arrived!

'Andy!' she called out to him, sliding off the shoulders of her two gallants. By now the line had dispersed and was returning to a long table cluttered with bottled beer, wine glasses and plates of spaghetti, pig trotters, notebooks, pens, indelible pencils and ashtrays full to brimming with the dross of discarded cigarettes.

Since the day his ship had left the port of Napoli years ago, Andrew had forgotten about the aroma of Italian cooking. The rich smell of it came from a larger-than-life enamel pot on the table and his stomach growled in anticipation. Already a place had been hastily cleared for them, but before sitting down, Greta held up Andrew's hand as if presenting the winner of a boxing ring.

'Brothers and sisters, good companions all, I want you to meet Andrew —' hearty clapping greeted her words, 'Andy by any other name —' more clapping and a few cheers, 'a stranger to our land,' she intoned, 'and I've promised to introduce him to the most brilliant, the most gifted scallywags, the brigands . . .' she gave him a droll side glance, 'and the *incomparable.*' Here Greta paused. 'Andrew Flight, meet the blue bloods, the shocking, the marvellous, the outrageous bohemians of Sydney town.'

The din was deafening as bottles, cutlery and open palms pounded the table. Frothing glasses of beer were thrust towards them, urging the couple to catch up with the afternoon's serious drinking.

'Are you flushed with the cash?' It was Ben, sitting opposite, who had carried Greta around the room.

Unfazed, the lines around Andrew's lips deepened. 'I've a bob or two on me.'

Equally unfazed, Ben gave a grin. 'Jolly good. The beer and plonk are getting a bit light on down this end of the table.'

Andrew gave a bark of laughter, obviously at ease with Ben's impudence and the garrulous company he found himself in, threw a pound note and some silver on the table and offered the next shout for everyone all round. If he knew, he didn't care that it was an over-generous contribution; he was delighted to find himself in one of Sydney's infamous sly grog hideaways. A fitting ending to a wonderful day.

Serving out sauce and pasta, Greta gave Ben's hand a flip with the serving spoon. 'Ignore him, Andy. One of the best-paid journalists in the business – and forever on the make.'

'Don't fash yourself lass, it's a bonny place you've brought me to.'

She handed him a bowl piled high with a generous helping. 'Sausages and mash are off the menu today.' She lifted her bowl to breathe in steam pungent with garlic. 'Umm . . . But I can vouch for the spag. Exotic!'

Lack of elbow room found them pressed hip to hip and thigh to thigh and although the morning had passed without so much of a hand clasp, they were aware of the accelerating excitement that the lightest touch – even of an arm reaching out for a crust of bread – was enough to make the blood race.

Impossible to eat . . .

A violinist had joined up with the piano player and as the music began, Eddie approached, tapping Greta's shoulder. 'Dance with me, m' darlin', before the rush begins.' Relief and desire made strange bedfellows as Greta, making a run for it, rose and practically threw herself into Eddie's arms.

A few couples had taken to the floor to the tune of 'Stardust'. Eddie danced well and Greta discovered that a dreamy foxtrot required little attention, leaving her to ponder over a situation that held all the hallmarks of trouble. And big trouble it would be if she allowed the barriers she had built up during the night to fall. Already she could feel the pangs of uninvited heartache; her future tainted by knowing that never again would success hold the same thrill, the same sense of achievement, after the encounter, brief though it was, with Andrew Flight.

And there wasn't a damn thing she could do about it.

What was it? Greta asked herself. It couldn't possibly be love. Lust? Or meeting for the first time in her life a man who had the power to electrify every nerve in her body?

Could it happen again with someone else? She doubted it.

Looking over to where Andrew was sitting, her mind went back to the night they had met at the New Year's celebration. She recalled their sparring and the bet made on the balcony, only later to find him completely absorbed with the company around him as if their moment under the stars had counted for nothing.

As she watched him there, a feeling grew that it was happening all over again. Roars of jocularity from Andrew and the men could be heard above the piano and violin, and like before, Greta had the distinct feeling that if she left the room, he would not even notice that she was gone. Much more disturbing was the sight of Flossie Stretton appearing from nowhere and acting the femme fatale.

Brandishing a cigarette holder a foot long, she was suddenly clinging to Andrew's arm like a limpet stuck fast on a rock. Greta quickly dismissed a mad desire to rush across the room and break up the party. Commonsense told her to stop acting like a twit, before she realised that the music had stopped and the foxtrot had ended.

Determined to ignore Flossie's flirtatious intrusion, she allowed Eddie to take her over to the head of the table, and accepting a glass of beer, she sat next to the woman who was holding court with wit and acerbic satire. Dulcie Deamer, 'Queen of Bohemia', as she was called, moved over, giving Greta a hug.

'Long time no see, Greta! And when do you leave for New York? God, we're going to miss you.'

A fervent 'Hear, hear,' by the Queen's courtiers had Greta flashing them a smile but she made no effort to outshine the star of Sydney's artistic and literary circles. Dulcie leant back as if to take a better view of the younger woman.

'You're lit up like a Christmas tree. Wouldn't have anything to do with that handsome devil – marvellous profile, by the way – escorting you oh-so-politely to our hedonistic wing-ding, would it?' She indicated to what now seemed to Greta an empty space. Andy was gone and Flossie was nowhere in sight. A stab of disappointment nearly robbed her of speech.

'No,' she managed to say lightly, 'just out to make a lonely sailor feel at home.'

'Looks as if Floss has taken over.'

'We all know Flossie, don't we.' Greta shrugged. 'It's no big deal, anyway.'

Suddenly, her heart gave an unexpected flip. Not only was Andy still in the room but surprisingly was in conversation with the violinist while the piano man played a few soft bars to Andy's nod of approval. Greta could only guess as to what he was doing there. Often people made special requests for a favourite tune or a dance number and Greta smiled to herself, remembering the song they had danced to on that first night. A few steps had been enough to tell her he was no great shakes at tripping the light fantastic.

For fun she made a guess as to what the request could be. Something old-fashioned and romantic? Somehow she couldn't see him up to date with the latest imports from Tin Pan Alley. A ballad, perhaps, like 'Annie Laurie', she decided, or some boisterous Scottish air that everyone loved to belt out, even at the Romarna.

Someone down the other end of the table was asking what the hold-up was and why the hell weren't they dancing? It was enough for the musicians to begin rattling off 'Yes We Have No Bananas' and for songsters to join in. Hardly a romantic request, Greta thought, but she was appeased to see Andrew walk over to join her. It was the smug satisfaction on his face that was puzzling.

Dulcie Deamer demanded that he sit next to her. 'Come here, gorgeous man, and tell us all about yourself,' she said, ignoring the objections from the disgruntled male forced to quit his place by Dulcie's side. She turned to Greta. 'And you, dear sister, have patience. I won't keep him for long.'

'You have my permission, majesty.'

'Och! The afternoon gets better and better,' Andrew said, at the same time favouring Greta with a grin before turning to Dulcie at the ready, giving her his full attention.

As if making up for lost time, the pianist increased volume and speed and the dancers and singers responded with enthusiasm.

Above the hubbub Greta could only make out snatches of what was going on between Dulcie and – yes, she had to admit it – *her* man . . . for the afternoon, anyway. By the look in her eyes, Greta guessed that at any moment Dulcie would be up on the table doing what she was famous for – the Dulcie Deamer Splits with a few high kicks to finish it off. Usually Greta found it a rollicking diversion, often joining in with a few high kicks of her own. But not this time, thank you very much. And, damn it, when was that racket going to finish? There were Andy and Dulcie with their heads together, and she couldn't hear a word they were saying!

As if in answer to her frustration, the dancing suddenly ended and 'Bananas' trickled away to a few weak arpeggios, as if the pianist was now incapable of playing even a five-finger exercise. Greta had already decided it was time to go, with or without Andy. What with Flossie and Dulcie, she fumed, maybe the Romarna hadn't been such a good idea after all. But she was gratified to notice that Andrew was already making a move to leave his company. As he bent over Dulcie's extended hand, her smile betrayed a delight in what he was saying. Greta wondered why. An assignation? With Dulcie? Impossible. No time. But *was* there time? How could she be sure that by tomorrow he'd be gone? She had no idea as to where his ship was tied up and he could still be in Sydney for days. When all was said and done, she hardly knew him. He had every right to see and do what he liked, and that last drink, she realised, was sitting queasily in her stomach.

By now, Andrew had rounded her side of the table and she felt his hand warm on her shoulder. No apologies, but a delicious tickling on her ear as he bent close and whispered, 'I have a surprise for you.'

Obviously, he was not planning to leave. Before another word was said he strolled over once again to the musicians' dais. They seemed to be expecting him. She was astonished to see the violin passing hands and its owner approaching her table, taking over the space that Andrew had just vacated. It was a neat swap executed without fuss and over in seconds.

Dulcie gave Greta a mischievous glance, raising her glass. 'Tricked you,' she chortled. 'Thought I was having him off, didn't you?' But the gibe passed unnoticed, for Greta's whole attention was now centred on the naval officer. In all their confidences, and their hours spent together, not once had the mention of music or musicians passed between them.

It seemed as if the world was standing still as Greta watched Andrew slowly tuck the violin beneath his chin, then raise the bow, drawing it confidently over the strings. He paused with a slight frown and plucked out a note or two before giving one of the pegs a twist. Again, he drew the bow across the strings. Appearing satisfied, he gave the pianist a nod. Greta held her breath. How well could Andy play? One may be able to fudge a few bars on the piano or strum three notes on a ukulele and sound an expert. But a violin? It could be a scratchy, pathetic calamity in the hands of a fumbling amateur.

The Romarna crowd, now exuberant with copious flagons and schooners, could be unforgiving with *poseurs* – not that Andrew was one, she was certain of that. She looked around the long table, noisy with argument, while others around her, not quite sober, were in serious discussion. Flossie was already whispering sweet nothings to a redhead with a beard and the face of a satyr. The one known as 'the Academic', in mortarboard and flowing gown (come hell or high water), prowled the floorboards, ready to enchant or bore captives into submission with his scintillating prose.

By the look of it, fisticuffs were threatening between two well-known journalists of competing newspapers. It was quite a gathering. Artists, poets and a smattering of the literati were in attendance that afternoon: Kenneth Slessor was sharing a joke with the brilliant Lindsay brothers. If she wasn't so distracted, she'd be inviting Slessor to entertain them with his latest. Then there was Dulcie herself. A clever wordsmith of articles and short stories, she was still celebrating her recently published book of verse, *Messalina*.

Greta sent over to Andrew a silent 'Do your best, darling', surprising herself at the involuntary endearment, even if it was only in her thoughts. But she groaned as the piano scattered the opening notes of 'Flapperette' up and down the room. Why hadn't they settled on something manageable – a slower tempo? But by now the violin had taken up the piano's challenge in perfect time, joyous in the race as neck and neck it outsmarted every trick that the piano tossed over.

Although engulfed by huge relief, it was obvious to Greta that conversation and rowdy guffaws were abating and all heads were turning towards the lean, tall Scot, his body swaying to the magic he shared with anyone who wanted to listen. 'Flapperette' was already coming to an end, but before anyone could applaud or acclaim, the pianist began a slow blues rhythm to Andrew's improvisation that held the room spellbound. Here was a maestro who could have held his own in any company, anywhere.

A feeling of tenderness swept over her and for the first time Greta acknowledged that she was headlong in love. Truly in love. The love that people read about; that troubadours down the ages have sung about; even the passion of love described in song from opera to music-hall ditties. What a wonder it was! But what a tragedy in her case, and hardly bloody fair. The sooner she was on her way to America the better. New faces. Hard work and enough excitement, she hoped, to banish every memory of Andrew Flight to perdition.

But not this afternoon!

The applause was deafening the moment Andrew ceased playing. There was a rush to clap him on the back, wring his hand, the women smothering him with kisses. To honour such a performance, Dulcie Deamer sprang to her feet. 'Clear the table, boys!' Bottles and flotsam flew in all directions as Dulcie, skirt hiked up high, sprang from chair to table top with a whoop, and to the gratification of all, launched herself with all the expertise of a can-can dancer into her famous act . . . the splits! Not to be outdone, she was joined by Flossie, whose high kicks matched Dulcie's own; their efforts not diminishing Andrew's musical perfection by one iota. As Greta watched, she chided herself for fearing cynicism and perhaps mild contempt from her Romarna cohorts if Andy's playing had not been up to scratch. Andrew Flight would never make a fool of himself. She should have realised that.

In spite of pleas for encores, the naval officer left the dais and returned to the table, handing over the violin to its protesting owner. 'Don't knock back the applause, man,' he said, and went on to invite Andrew to a beach-house that he shared with a few friends near Brighton le Sands. 'Come and play merry hell with us; you'll enjoy the company, I guarantee.'

Andrew shook his head. 'Don't tempt me. The boss would leave me balled and chained to rot quietly in the brig if I so much as miss out on a watch, which, by the way, is coming up all too soon.'

He gave the violinist a handshake and thanked him for the loan of his magnificent instrument, then shot a glance to Greta, who was already making a move to leave. He gave a short formal salute to the company. 'It's been a grand afternoon that I'll not forget in a hurry.' He then asked Greta if she would rather stay, but for him, time was running out.

'Thanks, but I'm ready to call it a day.' Greta Osborne had no intention of letting Andy leave without her. Every minute was precious now. How many minutes or hours did she have left to store memories? From the moment she had acknowledged her true feelings about him, wild thoughts and hopes had careened through her mind. The ways and means of seeing him again. She could picture them as a duo that any theatre manager would be proud to present on stage. But then, didn't the British Navy return to their base sometimes – Plymouth? Already she could see herself meeting him there. America was a lot closer to England than Australia . . . Each wild thought was swiftly followed by another and another, and just as quickly drowned by the tides of commonsense. She felt a gentle squeeze on her shoulder.

'C'mon, lass. We'll see you safely home.'

Too short was the tram ride to Kings Cross, its rain-washed streets ablaze with reflected neon colour and signs framed by flashing light bulbs.

'What time are you due back?' Greta made an effort to sound interested in a casual sort of way, giving Andrew no hint of the emotions that had engulfed her at the Romarna.

'That's a moot point.' Andrew made a show of examining his

wristwatch. 'Maybe now —' He paused, giving Greta a conspiratorial grin, 'or maybe later.'

'But you seemed so keen, so much in a hurry to leave.'

'Of course.' He looked mildly surprised. 'Did you want our day to finish in the company of merry fools? Wonderful fools, mind you, and I thank you for taking me there. But I thought a return visit to see what our dancing houri was up to would be a grand way to bring a perfect day to a fitting end.'

'Yes.' She smothered a sigh. 'Why not . . . then the circle is complete.'

She was not to know how his heart despaired at the thought of never seeing her again. One kiss. Was that all he was allowed? One taste of her lips when his body hungered to devour her? All day it seemed that between them they had arrived at some silent agreement to keep things at a light-hearted level. To forget about that one embrace. To ignore the raw magic between them – he was certain she felt the same way – which would ignite the moment they let down their guard. And he, more than anyone, had no right to inflame passions that could only end in regret.

Kings Cross was abuzz with commerce, pandering to shoppers and pleasure-seekers alike. Steamy air was infused with the smell of sugar and spice, of German sausage, strudels bursting with apple and raisins and the perfume of girls framed in doorways with flights of stairs behind, holding a promise for those who were game enough. But the Arabian coffee shop was closed, although movement and dim lighting could be seen behind lace curtains that backed a window display of enamelled platters and drinking cups.

'They might open up for us, they sometimes do,' said Greta,

giving the door a sharp rap, but it remained firmly closed. 'Well, that's that.'

'Any suggestions?'

'There's the Kookaburra, just across the road . . .' But the suggestion was half-hearted as she pointed out a solid, brick-red building that rounded off a corner where two streets converged. Even from where they stood they could see that the café was full to overflowing, with diners grouped on the footpath waiting for a vacated table. After the past few hours in the company of Greta's madcap bohemians, what the Kookaburra had to offer made for a colourless alternative. 'Do you think it worthwhile going over?' she asked.

'I think not.' The abrupt comment was unexpected. It was hard to gauge what Andy thought about the café, and even harder for Greta to interpret the flat dismissive tone in his voice. Here was a different side to the man she had so suddenly fallen in love with. His expression was sombre, his eyes not as blue as she'd thought, but nearly grey; eyes that could be as cold as a winter's sea. Slowly he shook his head. 'It's not to end like this . . .' Suddenly, he turned and cupped her face with his hand.

'There is a something I want you to know.' Her heart gave a jolt. 'Can you make us a pot of tea – coffee if you have it? There *are* a few hours left. Time enough . . . but then it's back to the ship by midnight,' he warned. 'And I canna' call m'sel' Cinderella. This great foot of mine is not for the wearing of a glass slipper.' It seemed as if sombre thoughts were whisked away on the breeze of a quiet chuckle.

Although his request to return to the flat was unexpected, and Greta had a good idea what he had to say, the Andy she thought she knew had returned, and she was more than willing to play the game of good companions if nothing else. The umbrella snapped open as the rain, after resting most of the afternoon, pelted down with renewed vigour. 'Coffee it is then. The kettle is already on the boil.'

CHAPTER FOUR

Her hand was a dead giveaway: impossible to hide its trembling as she tried to unlock the door, the key refusing to slide into its accustomed place.

'Damn!'

In the half dark of the landing she made another fruitless jab at the keyhole, knowing that in spite of the bravado evinced not more than a few minutes ago, Andrew would be well aware of the effect his suggestion had made on her. In her embarrassment she felt his hand, firm and warm, cover her own like a balm. Without fuss he took the key from her and unlocked the door.

Not saying a word, Greta switched on the light, removed her raincoat and the yellow cloche, leaving a spare peg on the rack for Andrew's mackintosh and cap. The silence lengthened and although the kitchenette was no more than five steps away, it allowed Greta time enough to take a few deep breaths. She gave herself a mental talking to while she went through the simple chore of spooning coffee and chicory essence into a pot. The banal unspoken question of whether he wanted milk and sugar seemed out of keeping with the charged atmosphere in the room behind her. It was electric enough to make her back tingle.

To her surprise, Andrew turned off the light and, giving a quick look over her shoulder, she saw that he now stood by the window, the gathering dusk keeping his face in shadow. 'Do you mind?' he asked, breaking the long silence.

'No – no, of course not.'

Sixth sense told her that what Andrew had to say was even more serious than she had imagined. She had taken a guess that he could be married and was all ready to assure him 'It's okay, Andy, it was fun while it lasted', and leave it at that. Forget about a splintered heart.

The light from the kitchenette sent a glow across the small round table in the other room; enough for her to take out an embroidered table cloth from the sideboard drawer, two of her late grandmother's best china cups and saucers and a tarnished, sugar-encrusted silver bowl. She gave a wry smile. The last supper? As she fussed and fiddled around, she realised it was only an attempt to delay the inevitable. She began pouring out the coffee, hot and sweetly strong. 'If what you have to say, Andrew Flight, must be said in total darkness, then for gawd sake come over and spit it out!'

Sitting down, he took a few quick gulps from his cup before taking Greta's hand. 'I have never spoken of it to anyone before, man or woman. None of their business. But you, Greta, should know it all. Everything. There is too much already between us. I canna' believe how and why it happened so quickly, but it did and you know what I'm talking about.' With his thumb he stroked the palm of her hand. That was all he had to do to send a shiver down her spine. As if he guessed the effect it had on her, he gently loosened his hold.

'When we kissed last night,' he continued, 'both of us knew that more, much more, should have followed. We made up silly excuses as to why it shouldn't happen – in part true,' he confessed. 'My ship was sailing off, and you were ready to leave for New York. The right thing for me was to go when all I wanted to do was take you over to the bed, feel every curve of your lovely body . . . But there was a grave reason why it never happened.'

'Why not?' she whispered.

What Andrew had to say next was too bizarre to be believable. 'Perhaps you have already guessed. I have a wife. There is a separation of sorts, but God knows when there'll be a divorce.' He then went on to tell Greta that years at sea and too-few returns to England had kept the marriage on a tenuous level. There had been bitter objections to his life in the navy, more than enough to feel relief when the ship took to sea again. 'It's been more than two years since Netty told me that she was having a child. I could only be pleased and happy. Happy for her – for myself. I thought – hoped – that things would finally come good. Having a bairn would bring her joy and comfort when I was at sea.' He shook his head. 'But it didn't work out that way.'

Andrew paused long enough to drain his cup, and even in half light it was plain to see the anguish etched on his face. She wondered if her own pain was as graphic. Not only married, but a child as well! If there had been a glimmer of hope that somehow a miracle was waiting to bring them together, it was now all too late. She was no family wrecker, even if there was a separation.

'You don't have to tell me anything more, Andy.'

Ignoring her words, he carried on. 'Ten months we spent in the East – the China Seas – only ten months, and although there was little mail from Netty, it wasn't surprising. Letters sometimes follow us around the globe then back home again. It happens. I couldn't wait to see her and the bairn. Boy or girl? How was she coping? Unanswered questions that had kept me in a fever of not knowing . . . wondering if she had received the telegrams I'd sent; regretting that we didn't have a telephone and making a promise I would see to it before the ship left port again.

'When shore leave finally came around I was surprised to find the front door of the house locked. It never was during the day, even if Netty was out. But the house seemed empty – *was* empty. Deserted. No one had lived there for weeks. Not a sign of the baby or the mother. I couldna' believe it, Greta.'

He spoke in short sentences between long stops as if he was still trying to recall every detail of his wife's disappearance. Greta, saddened by the pain on his face, in his eyes, witnessed a sudden change as his lips thinned in bitterness, ignorant of the images locked in his memory. How could she know of the frantic searching from room to room for clues, or some message of explanation? How could she possibly imagine the vice of fear clamping down on his heart as he'd opened cupboards to find them bare of anything to prove the existence of a child or a wife?

'Every day of leave I spent looking and asking.' His Scottish brogue was now so heavy that she could hardly understand him. 'Went to all the old haunts as well as everywhere else we'd been to, even before we married. Neighbours – not that we knew many – could not or would not help.'

'The police? Surely they —'

'Orr, they took a few notes, gave a few words of advice and left it at that.' Bitterness still etched his face in hard lines.

'So that means you still don't know anything. Don't know if —'

'If I'm a father? If there's a bairn? A wee girl or lad? If I even still have a wife.' Beads of sweat were forming on his forehead as a silence enveloped him; his mind turned inwards, delving back into the past.

But Andrew had not told Greta everything.

He could not tell her about the words, vitriolic with hate, that were seared like a brand into his brain. 'You'll *never* find her, Andrew Flight.' His nemesis, Netty's mother, had never accepted that her daughter and breadwinner was ready to marry. It had shocked him to learn that his mother-in-law had followed him all through the days of his searchings, keeping out of sight and obviously bolsted up by his anguish and her gin. Ties between the two women had been strong, and her ceaseless stream of innuendos to her daughter about male imperfections was given time to fester so that his precious time on shore with Netty was wasted, wracked by accusations and wild supposition.

The mother-in-law had turned up at the dock minutes before the gangplank was hauled in. Too late to find out the truth, his ship ready to leave. It was impossible to wring anything out of her as she repeated over and over again that Netty was in a place where he'd never find her and that the baby was gone. *Gone.* Gone where? Helpless, he had stood there while accusations had engulfed him in a tidal wave of emotional despair until in the end he turned his back on her to board the ship. Pent up regret and sadness expressed itself in a deep sigh.

'And there you have it, lass. The whole sorry story. As for Netty? Never a word. She could have written. She knew the ship's address.'

There had been revisits home over the following months and again he had spent the time looking for her. Results had been the same, except that one morning an old friend, in a pub he used to frequent, told of hearing that Netty had left London. He even hinted that another fellow could be involved. There was no talk of a child. Andrew ran his fingers through his hair, distracted by questions that had never been answered.

'Boy or girl. Dead or alive. I may never know.' He pushed himself away from the table, walking again to the window as if to distance himself from her, standing stiff and straight with hands clasped behind him, bracing himself against possible condemnation.

'Greta.' His voice was rough with emotion in the darkened room. 'Before I go, please believe me. Never in my life have I met a woman who could make a day,' the tone lightened a little, 'even when it rains, brighter than sunshine. You made me forget and I thank you with all my heart. Thinking of you will make the nights to come less lonely.'

Overwhelmed by love, Greta felt tears welling for him. He was such a decent man. Without a thought, she sprung away from the table and ran to him, clasping his body to hers, a cheek pressed hard against his back. 'Oh, Andy, I'm sorry – so sorry.' She held on, not letting go, trying to convey how she felt, trying to comfort. As if a spring had been released, Andy suddenly turned, holding her tight and bringing his face close enough to kiss her. Not the soft gentleness of the night before, it was a full-bodied embrace that smothered her, making up for all the hours and minutes they had denied themselves.

Locked together, they made their way to the bed, kissing and murmuring their love, feeling the mounting passion of their need for each other and not thinking of the consequences. He, wanting every part of her, was hardly aware as she removed each impeding garment that blocked his way. She, revelling in every exquisite moment as she felt his hand and lips on her breast and the steady, slow caresses that led to longed-for fulfilment. Again and again they made love. It was a bittersweet pact that left Greta breathless, her mind refusing to accept the parting that must come; storing one more memory to keep close to her heart.

Midnight passed and still they lay on the bed, their bodies cooled by rain misting through the open window.

'Time's up, Greta. I have to go.'

She rose and leant over him, kissing his throat and his chest, lowering herself down on him, not wanting the warmth and passion between them to end. 'Not yet, Andy. Not yet.'

She should have known better. As if she was something precious and fragile in his care, he moved out from beneath her and rolled over to the edge of the bed, picking up the uniform that lay heaped on the floor. There was enough light from the kitchen for her to see that there was deliberation in the slow way he dressed, smoothing away any betraying signs of the hours they had spent together. Gradually she found her lover replaced by a gentleman and officer of the British Navy, and through a haze of sadness she wondered how such a stiff and proper phrase like that came to mind. Andy had never given her that impression. Not once.

'I'll walk some of the way with you.'

She jumped off the bed, ran to a small wardrobe and pulled out a skirt and blouse but quickly felt herself swooped up into Andrew's arms and placed back on the bed. 'No, Greta, it's better for you to stay here. This is the place where I want to remember you. You looked so radiant then.' He stroked back her hair. 'And so beautiful now. You must know how I feel. How I want to love you and I shall never regret what has happened between us tonight. Forgive me. You must know that I canna' expect any woman, for God knows how long, to wait until this mess is cleared up.'

I would, I would, she silently pleaded, knowing that this was not the way Andrew Flight fought demons.

He bent over and kissed her, and in her misery she watched as he drew the bed sheet up and gently tucked it around her, as he would do for a child. A strange thing to do, yet it gave her a small measure of comfort. He kissed her on the lips again.

'Goodbye my love, my sweetling.' He turned away, and taking up the mackintosh and cap near the door, left the room.

She couldn't believe that she had slept. The last thing she remembered was feeling her pillowslip wet from tears. It was the quiet knock on the door that had her springing up from the bed, awake and alert.

'Can I come in?' Friend or not, Flossie sometimes knocked. 'Never know how you might find a girl,' she'd say.

'Go away, Floss, it's late.'

'I know. Three to be exact. And I can't wait a moment longer. Tell me all about it.'

Greta realised her sleep had not lasted that long. A few minutes, perhaps, and Flossie was already walking into the room, switching on the light.

'Kicked up the old heels tonight. Jeez, what a wild bunch. You and that adorable man of yours should've stayed on.' Strutting past her, Flossie reached the table and picked up a cup. 'Hmm, the best china tea set, I see, and guess who I saw going down the stairs when I was coming up?' She wagged a finger. 'C'mon, 'fess up that at long last you've been doing some serious hanky-panky.' Wheeling around and looking at Greta for the first time, her mouth dropped. 'Hell's wheels! What's happened?'

Flossie was beside her in a flash, arm around Greta's shoulder, leading her back to the bed. At the same time her shrewd eyes noted the crumpled sheets and the sodden pillow slip.

'Flossie, I'm stupid. Crazy! How many hours have I known him? Forty-eight to be exact.' For once it seemed that Greta was ready to confide, to share her misery with a sympathetic friend, but wrenching herself away from Flossie's arms, she paced up and down the room, tears rolling down her cheeks. 'Blame it on a bet, a ridiculous, silly bet!'

'What bet? What are you on about? Forty-eight hours before you fall into bed with a man? Why the tears? It's no record . . . I can do it in less than twenty.' She fanned herself with her hand. 'Whew! Getting hot at the thought of him. Have to admit, though; he's a real smasher – that smile!'

In spite of her airy response to Greta's tears, Flossie guessed that forty-eight hours had been time enough for her friend to be deeply affected. A casual night of hanky-panky, she thought, should in no way cause a girl to fall into such a miserable heap. In the six years she had known Greta not once had her friend made a commitment that could interfere with her quest for fame and, hopefully, fortune.

'Greta, m'girl, you need some sort of a cheer up and I know just the thing – never fails. How about tomorrow we join the gang at le Sands? Have a good booze up, take a swim – nothing like saltwater to chase away the blues – then dance the night away.' From her own experiences in love Flossie was sure that the whole thing would soon blow over and a new page would turn, ready to begin again. Wasn't Greta already on her way to an unbelievable and exciting future? 'Well?' Hands on hips, she confronted her friend, determined to stop her distraught pacing. 'Will we make a day of it?'

'Go away. Please, Flossie. Ask me in the morning.'

'Only trying to help.' Giving up with a shrug, Flossie made a quick exit.

Sunshine streamed across the bed. She couldn't believe that she had slept again; was sleep the antidote for overwhelming sadness? The bed was her refuge as Greta went over their lovemaking again and again; smelling the essence of him on the pillow and the sheets; trying to recall every murmured endearment. She closed her eyes against the brightness that told her he was gone. Three days of rain. Just as he had prophesied. Now sunlight flooded the room and his ship by now would have sailed through the Heads.

Greta dragged herself wearily out of bed. Her mouth was furry, her face tight with dried tears. Maybe she should take Flossie's advice and catch the train with her down to the shack. Music and wine, which was always there in plenty, could perhaps lighten the soggy lump lodged somewhere near her heart. She gave the idea some thought while making a pot of tea and as it brewed, removed a bottle from the kitchen cupboard and poured a good slug of whisky into her cup.

Sugar and plenty of it, she told herself, wandering back to the table and flopping down into a chair, deciding it would be too much of a bother to have a shower, let alone dress. Never in all her born days had she felt so shitty miserable.

The knock on the door was light. 'You know how to turn the knob, Floss – and no, I'm not going anywhere, so do the scram and enjoy yourself. I'm going back to bed.'

'Mind if I join you?'

Greta's head jerked around, eyes wide with disbelief. 'Andy!'

A different Andrew Flight was framed in the doorway. Gone was the impeccable uniform of a naval officer, replaced by a pair of dark corduroy slacks and a knitted pullover with a rolled collar touching an unshaved chin. He placed a violin case and a duffle bag at his feet, the grin on his face belying the strain he was trying to hide.

'What are you doing here?'

'I've missed the boat. You are now looking at a salvaged landlubber.'

'What are you talking about?' She felt wild joy that there could be another day, another night together. 'You're meaning the ship's still in port and . . .' Her voice dwindled as Andrew slowly shook his head. Realisation dawned as she sprang to her feet. 'You've jumped ship!' Running over to him, heart singing, her love was as bright and fierce as the sun spilling hotly across the floor.

'I had to come,' he whispered, burying his face in her hair, then standing back as if looking for assurance, searching for the right thing to say. 'I didna' want to toss away the best thing that has ever happened to me. I know, Greta darling, I'm asking a lot of you.'

'Don't say that.'

Crushing her close, he kissed her lips, her throat. 'My love, my sweetling. God, how I love you.'

Murmuring endearments filled her with exultation. He had come back to her! Never mind the consequences. Together they would work things out.

For Greta the rest of the day consisted of moments in heaven where memories are made. Never would she forget those first hours of ardent surrender as Andrew claimed her for his own. It seemed that they couldn't have enough of each other. On the bed as the morning and midday sun blazed over them, the pillow that earlier had been wet with tears dried. The very sweat of their bodies as they held each other close was an elixir to be shared and absorbed; the essence of love, Andrew claimed in jest as they later showered together in the skimpy bathroom.

Towelling her dry, he refused to talk about their future, only to say that all was well and tomorrow was the time for explanations.

'Meanwhile, my sweet,' he wrapped the towel around her and carried her back to bed, 'I'm not finished with you yet.' He dumped her down on the tousled sheets.

In a delirium of happiness, Greta held out her arms, laughing and remembering a nonsense thing sung in the schoolyard: 'Come to my arms, you bundle of charms and stick to my lips like chewing gum!'

CHAPTER FIVE

'What about the police? I can't believe – surely they're on the look-out for you. For us. Wouldn't the navy . . . ?'

It was a question that had been asked in many different ways from the moment they had opened their eyes, and only half believing the answers she had to ask again.

'The police?' Andrew gave a reassuring smile. 'Not a bit interested, and as I said, it is nothing to fash y'sel' over.'

They sat with the table between them. The morning and most of the afternoon had been spent in planning, and as for Greta, the timid doubts about an abandoned career were instantly dismissed. Nothing, come hell or high water, would separate her from Andy ever again.

'I'll put it right out of my mind, promise.' Crossing her fingers, she tried a different tack. 'But isn't it somehow breaking the law?'

'Jumping ship?' He shrugged. 'Maybe, but it happens more than you think. The United States is a popular choice if we drop anchor there, Canada another, and even sometimes Australia.' Devilment enriched his smile. 'But usually they return with their tail between their legs.'

'Then what happens?' This she had to know. In case . . . In case . . .

'Usually a reprimand, below decks for a time, perhaps, demotion if necessary.' He leant back in the chair, arms crossed, seemingly without a worry in the world. 'The days of hanging are over, m' love. It's forgotten I am, already.'

It was the past. A closed book.

Without giving a thought to her hard-earned success on the stage that she was more than willing to toss away, Greta had to voice her disbelief that a man so entrenched in navy discipline could in a matter of hours cast himself off from a career both satisfying and obviously enjoyable.

'It was surprisingly easy.' In the small pause that followed, the bravado Andrew had evinced before faded. 'And even if you kick me out – and I canna' blame you for that – it's too late now.'

'I guess I'm stuck with you, Andrew Flight.' But she blew him a kiss to make up for it.

In her heart, Greta knew that whatever lay ahead for her and Andy, it would always be an incredible adventure. Most of it good, and not that much of it bad. She was no fool. Life couldn't be so rich, so full of joy, so satisfying, without a glitch somewhere down the line.

And one glitch was already upon them. A matter of money.

Up to this point any discussion about it had been glossed over as Andrew spoke of plans and schemes, his optimism and enthusiasm sweeping her along with him into a future as outlandish as it was believable. He spoke of going to Far North Queensland. Who but madmen went further north than the border? she wondered with a shiver of excitement. But now there was tension in the air as he removed from his duffle bag a modest roll of notes and some silver. He placed them on the table. 'That is *it* for the time being.' There was an apology in his voice. 'Sailors who decamp canna' expect to collect back pay.' She glimpsed a wry sort of smile. 'It wouldna' have been that much but a something told me to stash away what I could and there's enough to cover my fare and a month with luck, before I start earning again. Then I'll send for you.'

'And leave me here? You're not going to fob me off that easily, Andy Flight. I'm not going to let you out of my sight.'

'In that case, we'll sell the ruby.'

'Not for me, you won't.' She gave a vigorous shake of her head. 'As you've said, it's a talisman and there might come a day . . . who knows?' She gave him a grin full of cheek. 'I've always wanted a man who owned a ruby as big as a football.' Her banter did little to erase his frown.

'I canna' ask —'

'Oh, yes you can. Anyway, I'm coming. There could be a hundred women up there ready to gobble you up, and you're not the only one rolling in cash. What I've got in the bank – and it comes out tomorrow – will stretch that month into a couple more.'

'I'll not hear of it, Greta.'

'I'm talking commonsense. You love me, that's what you've been telling me, isn't it?'

'You know I do.'

'Well, that means sharing. Good or bad, and that includes what I've got in the bank.' Words followed words until an argument threatened, with Greta's frustration on a collision course with Andrew's stubborn conviction that a man should support his woman above all else. It was the Scot who finally boiled over in masculine anger.

'Nothing but a besom of a woman ye are, Greta Osborne, and it's best for me to go before we do each other a mischief!'

'Go then!'

Pushing himself away from the table, he slammed out of the room, leaving a silence hot behind him. Stunned, Greta sat still, hardly believing that he was gone, her own anger abating as she wondered if he'd return. She sniffed, her mouth pursed. He'd return all right, for what sailor leaves his duffle bag behind? Not forgetting a violin in its case . . .

Afternoon melted into dusk, and there was still no sign of Andrew. Although certain of his return, a tiny worry niggled; the only assurance being the violin case on the chair where he had left it. Calling herself a fool, Greta had taken the step of opening it just to check if there really *was* a violin inside – which of course there was. Andy would never leave such a precious possession behind, of that she was sure.

She returned to the window to watch and wait as she'd been doing for the last hour. Street lamps shed light and shadows across footpaths. He has to come back . . . A spat, that's all it was. A stupid spat over money.

Obviously Andrew thought the same, and sweet relief washed over her as she saw him cross the road. She stopped herself from tearing out of the flat and down the stairs to meet him. No, better for her to be calmly spooning coffee into a cup . . . but taking the time for a quick peek in the dressing-table mirror, she snatched up a brush and attacked her hair.

The knock was hesitant as if it was for the first time he had stood at her door.

'Come in if you're a friend.'

Seconds dragged as she waited, wondering what was stopping him. It couldn't take that long to turn a knob! The answer was apparent when he finally entered. He had a basket of roses in one hand and champagne tucked under his other arm, a grin a mile wide and a wink that melted her heart.

'Glasses we need, my bonny darlin', it's time for a celebration!' Pushing aside the roll of notes still left untouched on the table, he placed the roses and champagne beside them. 'And look what we've got here.' Delving into the roses, like some magician pulling a pigeon out of a hat, he held up two railway tickets. 'There's nothing more I can say. You win!' Taking her up in his arms, he whirled her around. 'North Queensland, here we come!'

Victorious, she hugged and kissed him, breaking away, waltzing in happiness, singing for all the world to hear 'Every Nice Girl Loves a Sailor' and then rushing back to shower him with kisses again. On a second onslaught, she skidded to a dead halt.

'Andy, what's the matter? Why the frown?' He was patting himself all over. Digging into trouser pockets, his bottom lip was caught between his teeth and his face stamped with concern.

'My God, you've lost the ruby!' She watched as he searched again.

'Ah, here it is.' But she was puzzled as there was no sign of relief; he remained serious, his demeanour solemn. 'Come here, lass, and give me your left hand.' Her heart stilled, tears forming in her eyes. With reverence he gentled a ring along her wedding finger. 'This must do for the time, my Greta. Though be assured of my love, I swear to protect you, shield you and do my best to bring you happiness. You are my life, my precious own and with all my heart I hope from this day on you will never regret our first wonderful meeting.' His grave, tender gaze turned into a mischievous twinkle. 'And the day you lost a bet.'

Sydney was already a day and a night away, and Brisbane, the sleepy sprawling capital of Queensland, was almost five hundred miles to the south. Greta had not been impressed by the city, and after a day spent strolling along its main street, waiting for the night train to take them north, she had tried not to compare it with the bright glamour of her home town. Where was the wild jungle growth she had expected to find once their train had crossed the border? Andrew, forever buoyant, had kissed away a mild disappointment.

'Further north, my love, and we'll see paradise.' She wondered how far 'further north' was, admitting to herself that her idea of distance was all askew, never realising how vast the country really was. An expedition to the Blue Mountains had been, in Greta's reckoning, far enough away from Sydney for anyone.

After a morning of travelling through what she heard someone describe as a 'bush nothing', the train now steamed gently at the station of a large town smelling of dust, coal and cattle dung from a holding yard close by. Andrew flung open their carriage door and jumped lightly to the platform, holding out his hand for Greta to follow. She took his arm.

'Beer. Icy cold is what we need in this heat.'

'Ah-ah!' It was a sound of refusal as Greta shook her head, pulling away from him. 'We're not at the Romarna now, Andy Flight. Bars are verboten to respectable ladies – even disrespectful ones.'

'Good Lord! Fair maidens and lassies banned from bars in this outpost of the globe?' He could put on a posh accent if only in fun, Greta thought, but she shied away as he tried to take her arm again.

'No, I'm dead serious, Andy,' she said, giving him a push towards the bar, already rowdy as men jostled for pots of beer in the limited time they had before shunting off again.

She did not bother about a cup of tea but was happy enough to stretch her legs, walking up and down the long platform, her thoughts intent on reliving those first few days after Andy's unexpected appearance.

Since the morning Andrew had stood at the open door of Greta's flat, life for them both had been a hurdy-gurdy of emotions. She would never forget how he had taken her in his arms, burying his face in her hair: 'I had to come.' She could still feel how the coarse weave of his pullover felt rough against her cheek, and recalled her exaltation as he murmured endearments to her over and over.

There had been so much discussion about what they should do for the best. She recalled her surprise when north Queensland was mentioned. 'Cooktown, Cairns, a fellow could disappear up there . . . It's frontier country. Even New Guinea is only a hop, sail and a jump away.' It had seemed to her at the time that he knew her country better than she did. Now they were well and truly on their way.

There was no sign of Andrew as Greta pulled herself up on the high carriage steps, vaguely wondering how shorter people coped and grateful for the padded leather seat waiting to cushion her back. Andy had been right on insisting they take a first-class sleeper for the long train ride north. Each small compartment segregated from the others was designed for comparative comfort, with a washbasin and mirror, and a wall fan to combat the heat that seeped into every corner when the train came to a halt. An outside window funnelled breezes into the sleeper as the train sped on. Complete privacy, to Andrew and Greta's satisfaction, was provided by a windowed door with a roll-down blind. It faced a long passage leading into a miniscule shower room and WC, then on to a door giving access to the platforms of the many stations and railway sidings along the track.

Greta was still inclined to avoid meeting strangers, and although Andrew accepted his new role of traveller incognito, she still had to get used to the dramatic swerve she had taken in her own life. Entertainers, singers and vaudeville troops were known to tour far away from the southern cities into Queensland. She didn't want to meet up with any of them. Not yet.

But where was Andrew? People were starting to return to their carriages.

She poked her head out the window. Already the stationmaster's white pith helmet was bobbing importantly among the returning passengers. Any moment now he would ring the warning bell signalling that the train was ready to leave in a few short minutes. Responding to the sound, the train gave a jolt while couplings clanged and buffers clashed, impatient to be off and away.

By now the platform was nearly empty as the stationmaster exhorted all stragglers to get on board. Still no sign of Andy. The train began to move in earnest.

Where in the hell is he?

Suddenly, two men burst out of the bar room, a laughing Andrew making a beeline for the carriage while his companion scarpered into another further down the train. Greta tore down the passageway to fling open the door as the train gathered speed. 'C'mon!' she yelled. 'Hurry!' Andrew covered the distance between himself and the moving train with renewed effort and made for the carriage steps in a leap that would have done credit to a football tackle.

Missed!

He continued running alongside as Greta gave a wild grab of his outstretched arm in a desperate attempt to haul him to safety.

She did it! He lay in an ungainly heap at Greta's feet. Frightened and furious, she hauled him up. 'You idiot! Lucky you're not lying on the tracks cut to shreds. Never, *ever* do that to me again!' Andrew, still chuckling, headed for their compartment with a berating Greta in tow. Still more frightened than angry, she gave him a push on reaching the door. He tripped and once again his chest hit the floor. He rolled over, looking up at her as she took a stance over him, one hand dramatically covering her chest. 'You should feel my heart. It's —'

'Gladly, my darlin'.'

'Don't you darling me, Andrew Flight.' Greta gave the unfazed man a nudge with her shoe. 'Stop grinning like a fool! And leave my ankle alone.'

He gave a small growl. 'D'ye realise what a gorgeous sight you are from this angle? Long legs. A lovely face framed with a tousle of hair the colour of burnt sunshine. Burnt sunshine,' he repeated, stroking her leg, a glint of banter in his eyes. 'Robbie Burns couldn'a have said that better himself.' There was more than teasing in his voice as he caressed her thigh. 'Come down here for a wee while, woman, and let me make love to you.'

'If you think I'm going to get down on that gritty, sooty floor, you're making a big mistake.' But the husky timbre of her voice told him all he wanted to know. The train was now swaying in full racketing flight. Slightly off balance, her ankle still in Andrew's firm grasp, she managed to save herself from joining him and plopped backwards onto the sleeper's sofa bed.

'Why not here?' she coaxed, patting the rich padded leather. 'And pull down the blind while you're at it . . .'

Their love had never felt so good, had never tasted better, as they moved to the rhythm of the train, teasing each other to unbearable peaks; an incandescence that left them unaware of the gradual abating of the engine's speed or the sigh of steam as the train jerked to a stop. Its unexpected jolts and shudders were enough to send the lovers crashing to the floor. Passion was blown away by gales of laughter as Andrew, in spluttering high humour, kissed away a burgeoning bruise on Greta's backside.

CHAPTER SIX

Another night passed and the cool ferns and hanging baskets of the Townsville Railway Station were a sign that 'the tropics', as Flossie had described them, were just outside the station door. The platform was bustling with passengers leaving and others boarding. A Chinese man, his plait as black and glossy as a liquorish strap, kept a close eye on his diminutive wife and a clutter of children milling around him. Strident orders of porters, the rattle of luggage trolleys and the squalling of an outraged infant were drowned out by the verbal cacophony of a group of excited Italians.

Greta wandered through a waiting room and outside to a small overgrown garden flushed by a riot of crimson bougainvilleas. So exotic; the air hot. So different from Sydney. She was enchanted by it all.

This was no hick town, as Flossie had described it. From where she stood she could see a long avenue flanked by balconied hotels, handsome buildings of commerce and finance, many of them ornamented by columns of classical design. She had been told enough to know that the avenue led down to the sea and there was a large island not more than a few miles away. She regretted that there was no time to explore. In half an hour the train would be on its way to the last town and port of note – Cairns. A full day of travel still lay ahead. They were nearly as far as they could go by train and she wondered what tomorrow would bring. No turning back now.

She felt and stroked the smooth gold of the wedding ring on her finger. From now on she would be known as Mrs Greta Flight. Would she – they – get away with it? It was different on the train, where she had not spoken to anyone. But in a small country town where everyone knew what went on in everyone's kitchen? As a couple pretending to be married, they'd find out soon enough, she told herself. De facto relationships were the meat and spice of a gossip's cooking pot whether in Sydney or in the back-of-beyond, and Greta had no intention of skulking forever behind closed doors.

Divorce in the near future was out of the question; she had known that from the moment Andrew had returned to the flat. Five years of desertion was the normal wait for divorce proceedings. Adultery less. But since Andrew had no idea where Netty could be found, the chances of a legal separation, even if there was enough money to cover it, was remote. More often than not, it was left up to the court to decide the outcome.

She thought back to just a few days ago when Andrew had slipped the ring on her finger. It had been a time of sweet peace and quiet in the maelstrom of their ardour and speculations.

When Flossie had seen it the next day, she had nodded with a sort of grim approval. 'Well, that's something, anyway.' Flossie had soon known of Andrew's defection. It had been impossible to keep it from her. Horrified and fascinated in rapid succession, the sight of the ring on her finger had somehow modified her friend's admonitions and warnings. For Floss it was a good excuse for a festive shindig, and later on she burst into the flat armed with a shopping bag stuffed with bottles, a whole roasted fowl, sugared almonds and a Doboz torte from the new delicatessen at Kings Cross. The night had progressed into an unofficial send-off. Tenants of the apartment, on hearing the news (courtesy of Flossie) had shown up with food, liquid contributions and their well wishes. It had been quite a night, Greta remembered with a smile. Dear Flossie; she had cried into her bubbly while Flossie declared there had never been a friend like her darling Greta. She allowed a little twinge. A little sigh. Would she ever see Floss again?

'Ah! There you are!'

Thoughts of Sydney were banished by Andrew's quick hug. Just as suddenly he released her. 'There's someone here I want you to meet.'

Standing beside him was the man she had seen the day before when Andy had nearly missed the train. It was not the only time they had beers together at the many stops on the way. As far as she was concerned it was a 'blokey' thing to be dismissed with a shrug. Holding her poise, she looked him up and down, at the same time guessing that he could be close on fifty. Muscular arms were encased in rolled-up shirt sleeves and his trousers were crumpled with travel. His thinning hair patched a dome freckled by the sun.

'Samuel, old chap, meet the wife.' How smoothly 'wife' slipped off Andrew's tongue. Before she knew it her hand was covered in a calloused sweaty paw and vigorously shaken. 'Pleased to meet you, Mrs Flight. And forget about the Samuel. Sam's the name – Sam Riding.' He gave Andrew's shoulder a friendly slap. 'Right, Comrade?'

She forgave his yeasty smell, for the journey had been long and hot and second-class carriages didn't warrant showers, but there was so much warmth in his greeting that she flashed a smile guaranteed to dazzle a man into submission. Sam Riding might be a Communist Bolshie, but something told Greta that here was a new friend who could be depended on in the days ahead. She was guiltily pleased when he finally let go of her hand and, careful not to offend, she surreptitiously dried off his sweat in the pretence of smoothing down her skirt.

Andrew surprised her by saying he'd invited Sam to travel with them in their carriage to Cairns, 'And for a right bonny reason.' Greta found it hard to decipher the meaning of the gleam in his eye.

She couldn't help wondering who had paid for upgrading Sam Riding's ticket to first class, and dismissed a sneaky feeling that Andy had. Generous to a fault, he could be a little free with the pounds, shillings and pence, remembering how he had shouted the Romarna mob with drinks all round and not once considering the cost or counting the change. As for their first-class carriage there had been a moment of doubt whether they could afford such luxury, but it was easy to give in when Andy announced that a honeymoon deserved nothing but the best. Greta now admitted that she'd been thankful for every comfortable inch and mile they had travelled since leaving Sydney, and making love on a train was something else!

Hearing the station master's bell and his 'All aboard!' the three turned as one and hurried back to the platform. It wasn't the time or place to argue about sharing the day-long ride to Cairns with a complete stranger, and Greta was curious to know what the 'right and bonny reason' was all about.

––––––––

As the wheels of the train chewed up the miles along the track, Sam Riding's mouth organ and Andrew's violin kept up a merry pace – the right and bonny reason, as Greta found out, for Sam to join them. He was no slouch with the harmonica, and the music both men made helped the day to pass on wings.

Not one song was played with Greta conceding defeat. She egged them on to catch her out with another tune, old or new. It was a riotous competition between musician and songster as the hours flew, and the bottled lager that the men had smuggled aboard flowed. Fish 'n chips from a hamlet that was Cardwell; Tully where a cloudburst of solid rain drowned out every sound; mile after mile of sugarcane – fields of succulent emerald crowding close to the railway line. Innisfail, and Babinda behind them as the afternoon closed down.

Yells and shouts outside brought the train to a screeching, shuddering halt. What they witnessed through the window was enough to bring their shenanigans to an end. A scatter of men was fleeing into the safety of the towering cane with two policemen in furious pursuit. They all disappeared as the jointed stalks of sugar closed in on them.

'What the hell?' Andrew was the first to speak.

'Poor bastards.' Sam's voice was tinged with disgust.

'Law breakers, d' ye think?'

The empty fields outside were silent as the train began to move again. 'Nah.' Sam pocketed his mouth organ. 'Swaggies. Jumping the rattler, that's all.' He gave a brief smile in answer to the puzzled expression on Andrew's face.

'Swaggies?'

'I suppose you'd call 'em tramps where you come from. As for jumping the rattler – taking a free train ride, that's all. One town to the next for a feed and a plug of tobacco. Hoping to find a bit of work. Cane cutting, work in the sugar mill, anything that's going.' Suppressed anger wiped the usual look of benign humour off his face. 'It's getting bloody tough in the south, Comrade. Soup kitchens are in full swing in Sydney and Melbourne and wimmin and kids going hungry . . . It's a good time for exploitation and our brothers are going to feel the rough end of the pineapple before it all ends. Out-of-workers like them are coming up here in droves, and finding nothing. A depression, it's called.'

With the scene they had witnessed still vivid in their minds, Sam told them he'd been in Brisbane attending a union conference. 'Word is that things are not going to get any better.'

Just as Greta had reached the point of wondering if the afternoon was turning into a political rally, she was relieved to hear him say he'd done enough spouting for the day, and to please excuse an old Party gasbag. 'Can't help m'self.' With that he fished a tin of tobacco from his trouser pocket, stuck a cigarette paper on his lip and began teasing tobacco for a cigarette.

'Do you smoke?' He offered Andrew the tin.

'A pipe, sometimes.'

A companionable silence settled over them. In spite of what Sam said, it did little to dampen Andrew's optimism. Even before the ship had docked in Sydney he'd heard that Australia was the land of opportunities, and that a man could find work anywhere if he wanted it. 'Go north' had been the advice, and not necessarily the coast but further up and inland where a budding tobacco industry had the full support of an enthusiastic government.

Andrew admitted that he was no farmer, but farmers owned

tractors, trucks and generators that had a habit of breaking down and needing attention. He was convinced he could work up a nice little business; that he might fail had never entered his mind. The future held promise, and well aware of the sacrifice Greta had made by throwing her lot in with him, he vowed that he'd never let her down. Already the memory of London was fading, thanks to her. The malaria – a memento from the last visit to Bombay and something he had not mentioned to Greta – had disappeared. Quinine had been the answer to that.

Excitement of the unknown swept aside misgivings about the days ahead, and he knew that Greta felt the same now that Sydney was far behind them. A brand-new life for both of them was only hours away.

'Andy.' It was the first time Riding had addressed him that way. It had been 'Comrade' right from the start. Sam had claimed a corner seat next to the window. Andrew felt the thoughtful scrutiny of his gaze, and although Sam had been the first to speak, there came a distinct impression that the man was hesitant in what he wanted to say. 'Do y' know anything about boats?' he asked.

Greta was suddenly jolted out of the warm camaraderie the three shared between them. Why was Sam asking such a question – was he less than the genial stranger that Andrew had met in a bar? Had their rapid departure from Sydney not been quick enough? Was Andy wrong about repercussions after all? She held her breath, waiting for the axe to fall. But Andrew, with impassive calm, lounged with crossed legs against the silky oak panel hiding the washbasin.

'Boats? Aye, I know a thing or two about them.'

'Had a gut feeling you might. Don't ask me why.'

'And so?'

Greta felt tension creeping like some sickness into the cramped space of the first-class sleeper, then realised that the tension was in her own imagination. There was no sign of it between the two men. Andrew waited quietly for what Sam Riding had to say. And the Commie (as Greta thought of him), appearing more than satisfied, filled his glass from the last remaining bottle.

'Well, I'm needing a man, a deckie – deckhand – for a little venture of mine. In fact, more than a deckhand, and something tells me you're just the bloke.' He gave a bark of good humour. 'Even if you are a Pommy, you're one of the better ones.'

They listened, amazed, while Sam offered Andrew work as alternative skipper on a prawning boat he owned. Already he had told Andrew that he worked as a labourer, a wharfie, as he called himself, on the docks in Cairns.

Not for one moment had they suspected that Sam had anything more than his job on the wharves. A 'bachelor gay', as he called himself, he had Greta believing that his harmonica and a few possessions in a boarding-house room were the only things he could boast of. After Sam's impassioned talk about victimised workers it was hard to believe that Andy might possibly be an employee and skipper on a boat Sam Riding called the *Pelican*.

His enthusiasm washed over them like manna. When things were established and profit – even a modest one – was achieved, he'd give up the wharf lumping and the two of them would make an unbeatable team. 'The day is coming when every man dockside will be at the mercy of the agents – rotten bastards at the best of times – not forgetting the ship owners. But you and me, Comrade, will beat 'em all.' He paused, letting them catch their breath. 'Well?

What d' yer think?' He offered to go outside while things were talked over. He said he'd even wait until they had found digs in Cairns; recommending at the same time that the Railway Hotel across the road from the station was a decent-enough pub for a bed and a feed.

Greta's eyes were sparkling. She wanted to believe every word Sam was saying and there was no need to decipher what Andy was thinking. His grin was broad, and the laconic stance had been replaced by a jaunty straightening of his shoulders, at the same time giving Sam the nod to stay. 'Greta, darlin', what about it?' No need to say that here was opportunity without even looking. Many bridges had been burned, but luck and fate had shown them another solid enough to take them across to the other side where a new world waited.

'Let's do it!' Greta sprang to her feet and hugged him tight. 'Let's *do* it! The drums are rolling and strike up the band!'

There was enough left of the lager for a toast all round, and as the three raised their glasses they heard a triumphant whistle from the engine announcing journey's end.

CHAPTER SEVEN

An overhead fan stirred the humid air enough to cool the cotton sheet that covered them. Greta opened sleepy eyes, her gaze following the slowly twirling blades, and for a moment wondered where she was. Memory of a deal and a rough diamond of a man called Sam Riding had her jumping out of the bed. Lightly she ran across the floor and onto the hotel verandah that overlooked a street nearly empty, for the sun was just on the rise. A new day! A new life! She could hardly wait for it to begin. The thought of it sent her scudding back into the bedroom to share the moment and the sunrise with Andy.

'Rise and shine, lazybones!' It was the sight of him stirring awake and giving her his smile, open arms an invitation, that had her popping back to bed as quickly as she had jumped out of it. Oh, how she loved him. But the open arms were only for a cuddle and a loving kiss.

'Today is the day, my bonny dearr, for right-thinking men to get down to business.' It was said with a grin, but business, as Greta perceived, was far from the funny business she favoured at the moment.

'Okay, have it your way, Mr Flight – or is it Master Flight? Skipper Flight? Tell me, my bonny dearr.' She gave a good imitation of Andrew's Scottish burr that earnt her another kiss.

Andrew, accustomed to the tropics, had discarded his coat, taking on the casual wear of an open-necked shirt and slacks. Greta, more used to the formal dress that southern hotels demanded, wore the yellow suit that Andrew had so much admired on their first day together in Sydney. Having eyes only for him, she ignored the admiring if covert stares of the male diners in the room. It did not take her long to realise that fashion took second place in a north Queensland summer. Perspiring freely, she peeled off the coat, exposing a skimpy sleeveless top and a ravishing bust line that notched up more than one hungry glance, to Andrew's proud amusement.

'Uh-oh! Haven't I picked the right one? Every man in the room canna' take his eyes off you.' He attacked with enthusiasm a gargantuan steak smothered in onion gravy.

'Better get used to it, sailor boy.' Greta gave her shoulder a naughty shake. 'When I'm around it happens all the time.' She blew a damp strand of hair off her forehead. 'Even if sweat is wrecking my powder and paint.' Eyeing off Andy's breakfast, she pulled a face. 'Steak and onions in this heat? Not for me, thank you very much.' She helped herself to a platter of pineapple, passionfruit and soursop. 'Anyway.' Greta slurped on a chunk of pineapple. 'Where's that mud map Sam gave you?' She referred to a map hastily drawn as the train had moved into the station the previous night.

'Right here.'

Andrew shoved his plate aside and signalled for the waitress to refill his cup. He produced from a trouser pocket a piece of paper torn from a note pad and smoothed it out on the table. 'Looks easy enough.' A cross indicated where their hotel stood and a series of arrows took them down streets as straight as a ruler. Andrew's finger traced the route. 'Alligator Creek. That's where the *Pelican* is moored and not too far away, according to Sam, if we take the short cut through Malay town.' He took Greta's hand, fingering the wedding ring. 'Ready for a walk, Mrs Flight?'

It wasn't far away, Riding had told them when drawing the map, but Greta reckoned as she trudged along that he had a poor idea of distance; already they were an hour's tramp out of town. Thank the Lord Harry she had left her high heels under the hotel bed and had swapped them for her low-heeled dancing shoes.

If Greta's sleeveless blouse clung wetly to her back, Andrew hardly noticed the heat as he loped down one street after the other, ignoring a sky bulbous with rain clouds. In their stride they passed houses of faded paintwork and rooftops rusted by countless monsoons, their gardens brilliant with hibiscus and crotons. They skirted vacant lots where breathing space was lost to invading lantana and rampant weeds, the air rich with the smell of frangipani and the powerful sweetness of overripe and rotting mangoes.

A path of sand replaced a pockmarked street and ended in a clearing where pink and yellow cassias gave shade to a scattering of houses, neat and small – more like dolls' houses, Greta thought. Some were painted green with red doors and windowsills, others were pink and brightly blue, and each dwelling had a shell-lined path leading up to the door. Strumming a ukulele with his back against the base of a palm heavy with coconuts, a brown-skinned man gave them a casual nod as if they were no more than a passing breeze.

'This has to be Malay Town.' Andrew studied the minute map. 'And never a mention of what a charmer it is.'

'I'm in love with it all ready. We must come back sometime.'

Children, shrill in play, stopped to gawk at the couple, and they received a 'Ya war' in greeting from a man with a hibiscus tucked into a splendid crop of frizzy hair. Evincing mild curiosity, a threesome of women sitting on the steps of one house carried on with the importance of plaiting a pandanus mat. Another 'Ya war' of goodbye followed them as they left the small settlement.

'Can you smell it?' Andrew sniffed the air.

'Smell what?'

'Saltwater and mangroves.' Happy anticipation tinged his voice. 'The creek's not far away.' He quickened his pace then stopped in mid-stride. 'Whoa, there! What's the hurry?' And in a more conciliatory tone, taking in Greta's flushed and overheated face, 'I didna' expect the creek to be so far out of town. We should have taken a taxi.'

'Who is y' kidding, Andrew Flight? This gal has legs long enough and strong enough to take on Phar Lap.'

'Who?'

'Oh, never mind. Too hot to explain.' With a snap of her fingers she dismissed his concern. 'C'mon, let's find this boat and Comrade Sam. My watch says it's nearly one and we told him twelve o'clock.'

'That's my girl.'

Now closer to the creek and marauding mosquitoes, they could hear someone singing: not a happy sort of sound, and a tune that Greta – who thought she knew them all – didn't recognise. A clump of mangrove trees hid the singer from view but as they drew closer the words of the song became clear:

Good Lord above
Send down a dove
With wings as sharp as razors
To cut off the lugs
Of the wicked mugs
Who slash the poor man's wages.

The dirge was repeated over and over until they reached the end of the track and Alligator Creek was in sight. On a rickety wooden jetty they spotted the singer lying flat on his back and braying up to the sky. It was Sam Riding. Before they reached him it was easy to see that Sam was 'under the influence', and unhappily, it seemed to the pair. Empty bottles had been tossed into the mud beneath the jetty. Bleary eyes looked up at them.

'Ah! It's you two.'

He made an attempt to sit up and a more feeble effort to stand. He staggered. If Andrew had not grabbed his arm he would have joined the discarded bottles waiting to float away on an outgoing tide.

'Steady there, old chap.'

'It's all over, Comrade.'

'All over?'

'Tha's what I mean.' He waved a limp arm towards the creek. 'All y' gotta do is look out there. She's gone. Bloody bastards . . . Beggin' yer pardon for the language, Mrs Flight, but they're more than bloody bastards,' he slurred, turning to Andrew. 'Y' haven't got a drink on yer, ay? Mouth as dry as a witch's tit. Beggin' yer pardon again, Mrs Flight.' Greta looked away to hide a smile. Not that there was cause for smiling. Something had gone seriously askew.

With help from a whisky flask Andrew always carried in his pocket just in case, Sam did his best to sober up enough to explain why they had found him stretched out in a paralytic state.

He said that after leaving them at the hotel he'd taken the loan of a mate's utility truck and headed straight for the *Pelican* and the creek. 'When I got here the boat wasn't where she should've been; neither was the scurvy rat I was paying to look after her. More fool me, but that's another story.'

He went on to tell them that he had found the *Pelican*'s skiff tied to a jetty not far away from where they now stood, and had spent the next hours of the night searching for the missing vessel. 'Even the fellows from Malay Town were on the job – bloody skiffs and rowboats all over the place.' Sam held out his hand for another swig from the flask, took a gulp and shuddered, but it seemed to be effective enough to keep him on his feet. He wiped a hand across his mouth before handing it back. 'Yeah . . .' He heaved a sigh. 'We finally found her. As far upstream as they could take her. Holed and gutted. All bugger up.' As if the strength was leaving his legs, Sam slowly subsided onto the jetty.

'Here, mon.' Andrew took hold of his arm. 'Up you get.'

'Just leave me to die in peace, Comrade.' Sam gave a grunt. 'Anyway, a fella's too pissed to drive.'

'That's no problem, I'll drive us back.'

Sam's answer was to lie down and close his eyes. In seconds he began to snore. It seemed that nothing could be done but wait for a return to sobriety, enough to get him into the utility and back to town.

'We canna' leave him here to fall into the mud.'

Already the tide was creeping and lisping towards the jetty. Greta plonked herself down beside the sleeping man, refusing Andrew's advice to sit in the utility, half hidden by the mangroves and pandanus.

'You want me to be eaten alive by mosquitoes?' She patted the rough planks of the jetty. 'C'mon, make yourself comfortable. May as well.'

An hour slipped by and doleful cries from a seagull gliding overhead seemed appropriate for a day now shattered beyond repair. There was no denying that Andrew's hopes lay in shards about his feet and as a seaman he knew the pain a man must feel when his ship suffers a cruel and unnecessary end. No wonder Sam was drunk. He felt Greta's hand take his own. She gave him a jaunty smile as if she was still ready to take on the world.

'So we've lost out this time. Remember it was only yesterday when we knew nothing about the existence of a *Pelican*. So what's the diff? We'll just go back to square one. Okay? And the next step is to get the train up to this tobacco place – what's its name again?'

'Yunnabilla.'

As the three of them crammed into the front seat of the utility and drove back to town, a more sober Sam told them that he was possibly not the most popular man around. 'Mouth's too big for a start, and some galahs don't like me politicking on a Sunday.' He swerved to avoid a dog sound asleep on the dusty street. 'And there's a fella – owns a boat bigger than mine – who's not at all happy that one of my mates owns a fish shop. Thinks I'll horn-in on his deal with Alex the Greek.' He gave a chuckle. 'And when the old girl gets all shipshape again, I might do just that.' To the amusement of the Flights, this unexpected display of half humorous revenge could only be interpreted as evil anticipation. It left them in no doubt that Sam Riding knew who the real culprit was in the vandalism of the MV *Pelican*.

Although the boat's wooden hull had been savagely attacked with axes, Sam believed that all was not lost. It could be salvaged and repaired but it would take time and many pounds, shillings and pence. It meant that he would be a wharf lumper much longer than he had planned.

It was out of the question that Andrew could be involved in the work. There just wasn't enough cash to go around, Sam apologised, as he dropped them off at their hotel. Now there was nothing left for him to do but return the utility to its own backyard, see what was going on down at the wharf and try to find the dingo who had abandoned his ship to its fate. As he put out his hand to give Andrew a farewell shake, he was stopped by a slap on the shoulder.

'Not so fast, Comrade.'

Greta's eyebrows shot up to her hairline. What was Andy on about? Although not mentioned – there was no need to at the time – she recalled overhearing at breakfast about a railmotor leaving for Yunnabilla late afternoon. Time enough for them to pack up, have a bite to eat and get cracking! So as she listened it was hard to believe what Andy was proposing to Sam Riding's delighted approval.

A send-off! *And who'd be paying for that?*

She left them standing by the utility, happily unaware of her outrage as they made plans for an evening's entertainment. Be damned if she was going to make a scene in front of Sam 'Comrade' Riding, let alone mention a railmotor for Yunnabilla.

It was only minutes before Andrew followed her, and as if the disaster of the morning counted for nothing, he walked into the bedroom, humming in high good humour.

'What do you think you're doing?' Savagely she peeled off a damp silk stocking, letting it fall on the floor.

'Doing what?' The humming stopped.

'A send-off. Wasn't Flossie's farewell enough?'

She could see he was surprised. 'It's only playing a tune or two before —'

'But it costs.'

'Costs who?' He was genuinely puzzled.

Thinking about but not mentioning a wedding ring that had eaten into more than it should have, Greta replied, 'There's been enough spent. More than enough.' She couldn't help herself, and feeling a complete hypocrite had to say, rolling down the other stocking, 'And – and unnecessary . . .'

'Unnecessary? What are ye going on about?'

'Those first-class tickets. They —'

'Aye, and what a precious and wonderful time we had to remind us of our first days together.' He was over in two strides, taking her in his arms.

It had Greta beginning to think that Andrew's philosophy in life was to spend up on the luxuries and allow the necessities to look after themselves. He stopped further objections with his lips whispering in her ear that one night of merriment wouldn't break the bank.

On that reasoning, Greta gave up.

With no more to be said, they walked out to the verandah, their arms around each other, listening to the sounds of a town settling down for the night. A shunting train from the railway yards accompanied the irritable chatter of fruit bats as they attacked paw paws in a neighbouring backyard, and cheery whistling spiralled up to them as a cyclist peddled by, one of dozens they'd seen during the day.

They watched the evening star appear as Andrew assured her that things would go well for them in Yunnabilla. Already Sam had given him an introductory letter to a Mannie Coleman who, Sam had sworn, knew a thing or two. He could and most likely would smooth the way for the new arrivals to the tobacco town.

The regulars of the Railway Hotel had never had such a night. The sounds coming from the dining room had brought nightly strollers in from the street, the dedicated ordering 'one more for the road'. Mouth organ and violin had played in riotous harmony until closing time, and a lone policeman, investigating the goings on behind the now firmly closed doors, stayed on when informed that it was a private party.

All night she had sat proudly aloof among the drinkers, refusing offers of port and lemonade, 'or maybe a nice shandy?', happy to listen to Andy's violin and Sam's harmonica. But when the toe-tapping magic of 'Strike up the Band' began, Greta could stand it no longer. She leapt to her feet and in defiance of a spendthrift night and with a challenge to Lady Luck, she did a series of high kicks that inspired whistles and cheers loud enough to be heard more than a block away in the still night air.

Heedless of who thought what, she raked up her skirt and with hair bouncing and catching the light, took a graceful leap from a chair to a small table, the roars of approval music to her ears. There was a gasp and an intake of breath as they watched the dancer spring high and hit the table with a classic display of the splits; a clear announcement that Greta and Andrew Flight had arrived in the North!

CHAPTER EIGHT

It had taken the railmotor four hours to make an exhilarating, rattling gallop to Yunnabilla. Challenging a mountain range, its windows framed views of distant canefields and the crash and the pound of a mighty waterfall into a river far below. No more than sixty miles as the crow flies from the coastal port, Yunnabilla in Greta's eyes was the other side of the coin.

The verdant landscape they had expected to see was nowhere in sight. The extravagance of foliage and colour of the coastline lowlands lay far behind them. What they faced now was a town of sepias and ochres with an expanse of rock-hard soil held together by sparse and thirsty grasses and a scattering of mango trees leading down to the main street of a country town's commerce; not unlike the other townships viewed from carriage windows on their long haul north. Without looking, Greta knew (or thought she knew) what the main street of Yunnabilla was all about.

She was partly right.

Interspersed by a variety of small business undertakings were three hotels cut from the one blueprint, their commodious verandahs giving shade to the footpath below. From where the couple stood they could see that the undertakers and the Athena café standing side by side were undaunted by the superiority of a large produce and draper store next door. Its window featured two manikins, their belted floral dresses frowsy enough to be comical in Greta's opinion.

Eyes narrowed against the sun, Andrew placed an arm across her shoulder. 'Well, what do you make of it? Think we'll survive and still be friends?'

'Ooh-er, 'ow you go on, Mr Flight. Looks orl right to me, it does.'

Greta knew it was bravado at its best. Yunnabilla was a sister to the town she had been brought up in. She also remembered how at sixteen she couldn't get out of the place quickly enough. Sydney with its opportunities and neon lights had meant more to her than a pot of gold at the end of the rainbow. But just as her mind had already accepted the idea of leaving Sydney and friends for America and New York, it had been easy to take an alternative route with a man who could play violin and show her a love that she never knew existed.

Close by, the door of the railway refreshment room was open. Andrew hefted up the two suitcases they had allowed themselves, nodding in the direction of the tearooms. 'D' ye think they would mind these for a while?'

'We could ask, but there's a Ladies over there; you go ahead while I freshen up a bit.' She was too polite to say that she was dying for a pee. So far in their intimacies, bodily functions had never been discussed. As far as Greta went, they didn't exist.

His footsteps on the bare wooden floor echoed around the cavernous silence of the tearoom. Not a soul in sight.

'Hello, there! Anyone home?'

A head, followed by an ample bust, popped up from beneath the counter and as if caught out, the woman, closer to fifty than forty, began a vigorous clearing away of cups and saucers and swiping at crumbs with a dish cloth.

'Thought everyone'd left . . . Not much business when the motor comes in. All too anxious to get home – or to the pub, and I'm out of sausage rolls.' Without pause she gave Andrew a run-down on the perfidy of rail porters and their lack of appreciation of her cooking. Her stream of words came to an abrupt halt as if for the first time she had really noticed him standing there. Tucking a few strands of hair behind each ear, she gave him a look of instant approval. 'And what can I do you for?'

'Good afternoon, madam.' Andrew's tone was as smooth as silk and he gave her a light salute with a finger and a smile that could not be ignored. 'I have a favour to ask of you. I have two suitcases outside and I was wondering if you could —'

'Mind 'em for you? To be sure. It would be a pleasure. And a nice cup of tea?'

'Excellent. You wouldn't have a scone to go with it, would you? My wife —'

'Oh. And it's married you are.' Vague disappointment edged her voice just as Greta bounced through the door.

A thrill of pride swept through him. She looked radiant. He was amazed that in a few short minutes she could erase the rigours of travel and disappointment (and he couldn't deny her disappointment over the sinking of the *Pelican*) with a touch of powder and paint. Wearing the same green blouse and shorts she'd worn on his first visit to her flat – 'I'm damned if in this heat I'm going to dress up for a ride in a railmotor' – she looked delicious with her hair damp and curling about her face, walking towards him and beaming at the woman behind the counter.

'Did I hear mention of a cuppa and scones?'

'Out of scones. And if it's ports you've got, there's a cloakroom in the stationmaster's office.'

At this sudden change-around she then attended to the business of dealing with Greta. Mouth pursed, eyes raked her up and down, taking in the long legs in high-heeled shoes, the shorts and top. Her silence was audible. Greta kept on with a smile warm enough to melt the strange tension building up between them.

It was curiosity more than Greta's charm that eased the woman's obvious umbrage. She gave a sniff. 'Well, there might be a couple left in the oven. My scones come served up warm . . .' She shot a coy glance towards Andrew. 'Warm as a woman's heart.' But she didn't quite make it to the kitchen and instead leant on the counter with crossed arms. 'Is it visiting you are? Relations or something?'

Andrew was willing to go halfway. 'No. A business trip, Mrs – your name? I didn't quite catch it.'

'Rourke. *Miss* Ethel Rourke.' It was easy to see that Ethel Rourke considered Andrew a man of distinction, but she made it clear that his wife was another kettle of fish. It took Greta quite a number of days to learn why.

As Mrs Rourke seemed more inclined for conversation than for refreshments, Andrew made an effort to move on. 'Ah, Mrs Rourke. Do ye ken a gentleman by the name of Mannie Coleman?' Greta grinned to herself. Andrew fell effortlessly into his Scottish burrs and kens when it suited him.

'Are you meaning *the* Mannie Coleman?'

'Yes. He sounds a most important man.' It was the droll look with raised eyebrow that reminded Greta of their first meeting on New Year's Eve less than three weeks ago. It was a look she had found irresistible, and obviously it had the same effect on Ethel Rourke. It was enough to turn any woman into a simpering fool.

The scone-and-tea lady gave a fat chuckle. 'Important? He thinks he is. But go straight across the street from here, then round the corner and you'll see him in his office. Yer can't miss it.' With that said, she reached beneath the counter and produced two heavy china cups and saucers. 'Now, how about that cup of tea?'

But Andrew was already striding across the floor, gathering up Greta on the way. 'Sorry, Miss Rourke, no time.'

'What about yer ports? Still want me to mind 'em?'

'Not necessary, Miss Rourke. We'll worry about them later.' But Andrew took the violin case with him.

Greta couldn't resist stopping to deal Ethel a small shrug and a droll raise of an eyebrow in imitation of Andrew's own as she swept with him out of the tearooms.

Mannie Coleman was not hard to find. His office was snugged between a haberdashery shop on one side and a garage on the other. A large window announced in gold lettering that here was Mannie Coleman, Estate Agent, Tax man and Auctioneer.

With such a diversity of business Andrew was mildly surprised that apart from a few comfortable leather chairs and a small counter near the door, the office was furnished only with a single desk at which a lone man was busily typing. Hardly a Mecca of industry, was his thought as he and Greta walked in. Clanging, banging and the revving of an engine from the garage next door drowned out any chance of the typist hearing his rap on the counter. Andrew placed the violin case on a chair, then gave a second loud knock and his louder *'Hello!'* brought the typist to a sudden halt.

As he unrolled himself out of his chair, eyeing off the strangers, a look of incredulity crossed his face. He made it plain that they were nothing like the usual daily handful of clients that came seeking his advice. His gaze would have been piercing but for the pebbled lenses of spectacles perched on his nose as he hurried towards them, hand outstretched, apologising for the wait. The noise from the garage increased in ear-splitting decibels.

'Hang on.' With raised voice and long legs striding, he opened a side door leading into the garage. The noise was deafening. 'Stop that bloody racket,' he bawled, 'or it's out for the both of you!' A furious voice answered back that it wasn't his fault and 'Blame him!' The noise decreased to a manageable pitch. Shaking his head, the door was slammed shut. 'Now, sir.' His tone was business-like. 'Mannie Coleman at your service and how can I help you?'

'Andrew Flight is the name,' Andrew replied, dismissing a fleeting impression that Sam might have already been in touch with Coleman. He shook the outstretched hand, introduced Greta as Mrs Flight, then wasting no time handed over Sam Riding's note of introduction. Before opening the envelope, Coleman ushered them behind the counter with the invitation to sit down and make themselves comfortable. Still standing, the estate agent read Sam's letter in silence.

'You're a mechanic, Sam says.' He looked down at Andrew's

hands crossed lightly on his knees. Three weeks away from an engine room had removed the usual patina of grease and oil from his nails and skin.

'I know a thing or two about motors, tractors, engines, pumps. All depends what turns up.' Andrew rose to his feet; tall enough to look Mannie Coleman straight in the eye. He jerked a confident thumb towards the sound of the revving motor that still blasted its way through the door. 'And by the sound of that, the chappie who owns the car might be needing a new one sooner than he thinks.'

'That flivver just happens to be mine.' It was said without rancour. With a finger Coleman pushed back the spectacles taking a slow dive down his nose. 'Things are a bit quiet at the moment. However . . .' He removed his glasses, and with a starched handkerchief took his time to clean the lenses. Without the spectacles Andrew found himself looking into dark eyes, inquisitive and bright with speculation. 'Would you be interested in a little investment? I know of a farm that's just —'

'I'm no farmer, Mr Coleman. But I also have the right piece of paper for an electrician to have.'

'Not much use to you here.' There was irony in the look he gave. 'The town doesn't have the blessing of instant light. You go down to Cairns for that.'

A shock of disbelief made its rapid way through Andrew's mind. Even the poorest hovel in the wildest glen had a bulb to light up the night in Scotland! Good Lord, what was he bringing Greta into? Through his dismay he heard Coleman saying that the town did have a generator, but it was only good enough for the few shops who paid for the running of it, the council footing the bill for the churches and the School of Arts Hall.

Andrew began to wonder if they should return to Cairns and try their luck down there. Perhaps Sam could put a word in for him down at the wharf? It was a ridiculous idea, and he instantly dismissed it from his mind. He could do better than that. He turned to Greta but she sat silent, looking straight ahead. What must she be thinking?

Through a tumult of indecision he heard Coleman saying that he had an idea and it wasn't such a bad one at that.

'Sam says that you have a nice touch at playing the fiddle and your beautiful lady is quite a songbird.' He looked down at the seated Greta as if noticing for the first time – much to her annoyance – that she was actually in the office. Completely ignoring her brittle gaze and refusing to be offended by her terse, 'Yes! I *can* sing a note or two,' he carried on. 'I also know of a little lady who can tickle the ivories sweet enough to keep you dancing from dusk to dawn. As for myself,' pride added an extra inch to his height, 'I'm not too bad on the old accordion.'

'Bully for you,' Greta murmured, her sarcasm lost as another *brurrm brurrm* blasted through the closed garage door.

Coleman informed them that Yunnabilla folk had two passions: playing cards and dancing, the music supplied by himself and the piano player – his wife.

'A three-piece band *and* with a stunner of a singer,' he now gave Greta the benefit of his admiring approval, 'would have the district turning up in droves. Cards and euchre tournaments. And divvy up of the takings.' He banged his forehead with a clenched fist. 'Ideas, ideas where do they come from?' He spread his arms out in appeal.

Never able to resist a dramatist, Greta by now was laughing, her resentment forgotten. 'Well, that's Saturday night spoken for, I guess.' She sent Andrew a look, inviting him to take over.

Andrew studied the ceiling as if deep in thought, then took up the challenge. 'Aye, it's a bonny thought. But what about the rest of the week?'

'Ah, yes . . . that could be a problem.'

'Well, I have a proposition to put forward myself.' Greta's eyes widened: What was Andy on about? Before anything else could be said, Armageddon exploded in the garage and sounds of cursing and a howl of pain had Mannie sprinting once again across the office and flinging open the door.

They could see a car with its bonnet raised and a figure sprawled across an oil-stained floor, a buckled and dinted mudguard lying across his chest. Mannie gave a roar of outrage, rushed over, grabbed the mudguard and hurled it against a wall.

'Where the blazes is Arthur?'

'Gone.'

After the ruckus of the minutes before, the only sound that could now be heard was Mannie's heavy breathing and the spluttering demise of the vehicle's engine. With his nose bleeding, a youngish man struggled to his feet. 'I told yer he was no good. Doesn't know a piston from a duck's bum. As for panel beating, he knows bugger all.'

'Mind your language, there's a lady present; and by the look of it you're not that much bloody better than Arthur.'

A furious exchange ensued with Greta standing by the door, enjoying every bit of the show. Neither of the combatants noticed that Andrew had quietly crossed the floor and was studying the car's innards with interest. While Greta looked on, his head disappeared under the propped-up bonnet. It was impossible to know what he was up to. Seconds passed. By now, things had simmered down. The nose bleeder was ordered to go home and turn up again in the morning. Coleman apologised, and equilibrium returned. 'You had a proposition, Mr Flight?' he asked, as if nothing had happened. 'Tell me about it.' Returning to the office, he held up an arm to squint at a wristwatch that looked to be solid gold; a good eighteen carats, Greta guessed.

'Getting close to five,' Mannie said, opening a drawer under the desk and producing a bottle of whiskey. 'Time for a snort, you agree?' From another drawer he brought out three glasses and began pouring. 'Now, about this proposition.'

Andrew settled himself down in one of the chairs and Greta, sitting in the one nearest to him, felt his hand take hers and give it a squeeze. 'Forget about propositions, Mr Coleman, that will come later. For the moment I'd take a guess that ye'll be wanting a replacement next door. And, by the way, I hope the young man with the bloody nose knows a bit about tappets. They need care and attention sorely.'

'You're not suggesting I take you on, are you?'

'Yes, I am. For a wee time at least. Until Greta and I get a feel of the place.' He spoke with all the assurance of a transaction already sealed.

In answer to that, the estate agent pushed his spectacles up along his nose. 'Things are pretty tight around here.'

Andrew nodded toward the garage framed by the open side door. 'Tha's easy to see. Not much in the way of business there.' His audacity had Greta expecting that in seconds they'd be ordered out of the office.

'Ah . . .' Mannie's shrewd appraisal glanced off the steady gaze of Andrew's grey-blue eyes – now more grey than blue. 'You're right. Not so much in Yunnabilla, I admit, but tobacco farms are springing up all over the place, and what farm doesn't have its mechanical problems, eh? And that bastard Grimshaw with his Speedy Workshop is getting the lot.'

'And you're one good man short.'

Andrew's grin could only be described as predatory. Greta sat stock still while the sparring between the two men carried on. Tossing down the last of his whisky, Andrew stood up. 'Come on, mon, standing here before you is not only a damn fine mechanic, but a member of our three-piece orchestra with —' He bent down, swooping Greta up and pressed her close to his side, 'no other than our own Greta Flight, songbird extraordinaire! Ye canna' go wrong!'

Laughter settled the deal with another tote of whisky all round. At the same time the estate agent told them about a nice little house on his books that would be ideal for a couple and he would take them around for a look-see in the morning. 'Have you a bed for the night? I can recommend the Victoria.'

Greta wondered if Mannie Coleman just might be in cahoots with the Victoria Hotel; on commission, maybe. She wouldn't be a bit surprised. When they explained that there was luggage, hopefully standing intact on the station platform, Mannie offered to collect it and drive them around to the hotel. 'It'll be a bit of a squeeze,' he admitted, 'but we'll manage.'

'Are ye sure?' Andrew gave another look at the car, minus its mudguard, standing abandoned in the garage. Mannie pointed out a smart little Ford with a dicky-seat parked close to the footpath outside.

'That's my baby. Spanking new. But before we go, I'll close up the garage. Business is finished for the day.'

His absence gave Greta the chance she'd be waiting for. 'Can't believe what's happening. Not two minutes in the place and you've talked yourself into a job! But tell me, what's this proposition you're on about? What proposition? First I've heard of it.'

Once again, the predatory grin. 'Och, don't fash y'self.' Giving her a hug, he whispered, 'All ye have to do is mention a "proposition" and it stirs a man like Mannie Coleman into thinking ye're rolling in money.'

'But you're the one asking for the job!'

'Not a job. I have only offered my services. It's an agreement between gentlemen.'

Greta gave up. She couldn't deny that things seemed to be coming up roses for the Flights surprisingly fast.

CHAPTER NINE

Yesterday, by Greta's reckoning, could only be described as extraordinary. After the railmotor had dumped them on its clattering way to places unknown, followed by the strange encounter with the tea woman Ethel Rourke, her introduction to the town had seemed to be vaguely hostile.

Then came Mannie Coleman.

Andrew had accepted with aplomb a welcome akin to the return of a prodigal son; its outcome sweeping Greta along in a tidal wave of happenings over which she had little control. Andy bluffing – demanding, more like it – his way into a job, not to mention a house yet to be inspected, then of all things an offer for the two of them to join up with the estate agent and a wife – also unknown – to play on a Saturday night at the School of Arts. As newcomers, she had voiced her concern. 'It's too soon. Too fast. Why not wait until the town gets to knows us a little better?' It was a suggestion talked over and waived aside.

It seemed the Greta Osborne she once knew had disappeared. But who was this person taking her place? One thing for sure, the old Greta Osborne of Sydney wouldn't have been seen dead before eleven in the morning, let alone drinking tea at sparrow fart in a town that grew tobacco . . .

The squatter's chair she lounged in beneath the sloping roof of the hotel verandah was shabby but comfortable. The first surprise of the morning was finding at six o'clock a housemaid standing over the bed with tea and toast on a tray, while she and Andy lay stark bollocky under the sheet.

Unfazed, the girl had placed the tray on the bedside table with the suggestion that 'It's nice to have it on the verandah – with yer pyjamas on, of course.' Greta was left blushing and thankful that Andy had quietly snored through it all.

Before she even considered the busy day ahead, Greta took her time sipping the hot brew, enjoying the quiet of early morning. There was a tang in the air of eucalypt and wood smoke, and the clip-clopping of a horse unseen mingled with the liquid warbling of magpies in a large fig tree on a vacant lot across the road. She felt a hand tousling her hair and her heart filled as it always did at his touch.

'Today is a bright new day for the both of us.' He kissed her head as his hands slid down to her throat and found their way beneath her pyjama top. 'Let us have a wee celebration. A grand and wonderful way to begin it all.'

The magpies chortled in agreement.

They sat close together in the dicky-seat of Mannie's little Ford. Scooting down the main street at an exhilarating thirty-five miles an hour, Greta gripped Andy's hand, not because of Mannie's driving, but at the idea of seeing a house, rental or not, that they could call their own.

Shouting above the engine noise, the Flights agreed that Yunnabilla didn't look too bad at all. The shops had petered out in no time and the houses, some a ramshackle of rusted roofs and thirsty timbers, seemed not out of place between others bright with care and paintwork. Bougainvillea with careless largesse splashed its brilliance of royal purple, scarlet and orange over fences and water tanks, garden sheds and neglected shrubs.

Before the town was completely out of sight and buildings became more scattered, they swept by a sawmill with timbers stacked high. Not more than a ten-minute walk away, a small grey painted house with a red pitched roof came into view. It stood alone, away from what appeared to be the last line of dwellings that merged into paddocks for roving dairy cattle and herds of goats.

Greta knew long before Mannie pulled up that the little grey house was the one he had spoken of, rent thirty shillings a week and paid for in advance. There was a cosy look about it with its trio of mango trees in the backyard and a flush of honeysuckle and maiden's blush over the front fence.

'It's a bit on the small side,' she kept her voice down as the estate agent opened the front gate with flair and a sweeping arm that encompassed the house, the yard and the trees.

'Here it is. The sweetest little cottage in Yunnabilla, thirty bob a week and cheap at twice the price.'

Who was he kidding?

'A bit on the small side, even without a cat to swing.' This time she made no attempt to keep her voice down.

'You'll be surprised, Mrs Flight – Greta – once you get inside.'

Unfazed, his tone was brightly confident as he ushered her up the four steps onto a miniscule verandah. 'Two bedrooms, a sitting room and a kitchen large enough to swing *two* cats in, not forgetting the dog.'

It had been built to a simple plan, a verandah running the width of the house and leading into what had to be called a sitting room with a bedroom opposite, then a short hall that led to what Mannie described in a burst of high imagination as the second bedroom.

He was right about the kitchen, Greta conceded. Although it lacked a ceiling and had exposed rafters, it was large enough to accommodate a pinewood table and four Austrian bent chairs. 'They're brand new,' he pointed out, 'as is the stove.'

'A wood stove . . .' Her doubt did little to erode his enthusiasm.

'That's right – *THE VICTOR*.' He said it with capital letters. 'Nothing but the best. And we'll top up the woodheap before you move in.'

If she hadn't fallen in love with the funny little place she would have held out for an inspection of at least one other house. Apart from a seagrass sofa in the sitting room and a single bed that took up most of the space in the 'second bedroom', she found herself making up a list of necessities: pots and frying pan, a decent bed, plates, cups and saucers, and the most important thing of all – a gramophone.

'Well, what do you think?' Unlike the afternoon before, Mannie Coleman was giving Greta his full attention.

'I think I'm liking it.' Her expression was bland, not giving anything away. 'At twenty-five shillings a week?' Having in mind the few 'Up for Sale or Rent' signs she'd noticed on the way out, she guessed that there must be more than one estate agent in the town. 'Twenty-five shillings a week?' she repeated. 'Am I right?' She stood her ground, ready to bargain.

Mannie's hand went to his heart. 'It hurts, but twenty-five it is.'

Up till now, Andrew had not been drawn into the mild bickering between Greta and Coleman. He gave the impression that his mind was somewhere else. Greta had seen that look before and she knew it for what it was. Before they'd left the hotel Coleman had mentioned there was a farmer not more than a few miles away with generator problems. 'Your first job,' he had said at the time. At the moment Andrew's interest in the house was minimal. Greta understood that. He gave her a nod.

'I see you've decided to take it. Good. I agree.' It was his only input into the morning's proceedings; he was ready to move on. 'Now, Mannie old chap, let's away to this farmer and his generator.' With a quick kiss on Greta's cheek and a promise to be back in no time, he bundled the bemused estate agent out the door, leaving Greta quite happy to stay put, making lists for the shops waiting for her in Yunnabilla.

Every room, nook and corner had soon been properly examined, a task that took Greta all of five minutes. A walk around the outside revealed that apart from the mango trees, the backyard had all the charm of a jail's exercise quad; the ground hard and bald without the saving grace of a blade of grass. But this was no cause for concern, for the closest Greta had ever come to gardening was a flowerpot of jonquils on a windowsill. There was an open shed with a wash bench and a large tin wash tub and an outside copper encased in bricks. That was it for the washing facilities. The wood heap that Mannie had promised to 'top up' had Greta wondering just how good Andy was with an axe.

A big advantage to it all in Greta's eyes was that apart from a large house painted a sun-washed blue on the other side of a dusty, corrugated track – it could hardly be called a road, she thought – the little grey house stood by itself. Only one neighbour to cope with! The last thing she wanted was a street of nosy parkers peering over the fence asking questions.

Commonsense told her that Yunnabilla, as far as Sydney went, was unknown and of little interest. She remembered how she herself had once considered that life and living stopped at the New South Wales border, while conceding that Brisbane had some merit as a country town. Anything north of that was an unexplored vastness teeming with snakes, crocodiles and miscreants. Married or not, even if they lived in the wilds of New Guinea, they couldn't be safer from prying eyes and speculations about the past.

As Greta climbed the stairs into the kitchen a woman appeared at the back door of the untidy blue house. Pretending not to notice, Greta felt the spotlight of her gaze as she went inside. Time enough later on to make an acquaintance. If the plans of an orchestra went ahead, everyone in town would soon know all they should about the Flights.

Propped up against the kitchen table, she studied the handsome cast-iron stove. It stood in an extended recess that had been recently silver-frosted to hide the grease and stains of myriad fry-ups over the years.

Greta hadn't been near a wood stove since she'd left her

grandparents' home. For one who only knew how to boil an egg and heat up a saucepan of baked beans on a gas ring, the sight of its majesty standing silent before her, waiting for a stick of wood and a pot of stew simmering on the unblemished top, was daunting. Without thinking, she straightened up, folding her arms across her chest. What's wrong with you, Greta Osborne? she asked herself. You've a man to cut wood and light up the fire, and cookbooks to read in bed with his arms around you. The idea of the pair of them in bed reading cookbooks of all things hit the funny bone of absurdities, and sent her spinning around the kitchen singing, 'He likes potatoes and I like tomatoes; potatoes, tomatoes – let's call the whole thing off!'

As she twirled around she felt, more than saw, a movement. Something not quite right. Something alien. Something that made her look up. Nerves like spiders crawled over her body as she stared into eyes cold, black and malignant. Partly camouflaged by the dark-stained wooden rafters, the snake slowly rippled out of sight. She stood for moments terrified, knowing that it wasn't imagination. Carefully and quietly, not daring to turn her back on it, she moved towards the open back door, feeling for the top step with her sandal. Once outside she turned and ran down into the yard, avoiding even the shade of the mango trees. There was a kerosene box beneath the tank stand, and not trusting that it was as empty as it looked, carefully with her toe edged it well away from the house. Sitting down, she waited, determined to stay there until the men returned.

CHAPTER TEN

Marelda Larkin was boiling to bursting point with curiosity. Two strangers in the dicky-seat of Mannie Coleman's new car had been enough for her to leave the breakfast dishes forgotten in the wash-up basin.

There was only one reason why Mannie would have pulled up in front of the house that stood by itself next door. Too small for any family of decent size, it had been up for rental for more weeks than she could count. Behind the half-closed louvres on the back verandah, she'd been able to take a good squiz at the three of them before they'd disappeared into the house.

The man looked interesting enough: tall, fairish, and sort of posh-looking. Even from where she stood it was easy to pick up a touch of the Scot in his voice. It was the woman who held her astonished attention. Marelda could only describe her as beautiful. Without envy she admired the flash of red-gold hair and a figure so perfect in brightly coloured beach pyjamas that she could have stepped right out of the *Picture Movie* magazine, the one luxury Marelda allowed herself. They had to be, she guessed, the couple that Ethel Rourke had been talking about at euchre last night. Apart from saying that the man was a real gentleman, she could only gabble on about the wife's shocking display of legs, asking what was the world coming to when women wore shorts on the railmotor.

With one eye still glued to the louvres, Marelda remembered the dishes. Pouring in another kettle of hot water, she judged just how long it would take for Mannie to show them through, attacking the plates and pots with speed. Any moment the three of them should be coming down the back steps into the yard. She gave a hope that the couple would move in. The place could do with a bit of livening up, and the woman in her shorts or panama pants would surely do it. Already Marelda could see herself chatting over the fence and having morning cuppas with the new arrival.

Before she knew it, Mannie's car could be heard starting up and, rushing back to the louvres, she was in time to see it driving off. Feeling that the day was now not going to be any different to any other day in the week, Marelda rammed a few pieces of wood into the stove. A hot oven was all that was needed. Nothing like a good strong cup of Bushells and a hot scone, dripping butter, to chase away the blues.

With a cup in one hand and a scone in the other, she sat on the top back step, a favourite resting place at any time of the day or night. The second surprise of the morning was to see that the woman had not driven off with the men. Marelda waited, hoping she'd been noticed, but nothing happened as she watched Greta walk up the kitchen stairs into the house. Disappointed that no connection had been made, she munched on the scone and drained the cup.

———

It was impossible to make head or tail of it. Housework for the whole morning had been done in dribs and drabs as Marelda kept watch on the house next door. It had been more than an hour since she'd seen the girl sitting on that kero box in the middle of the backyard, hardly moving. Not even bothering to sit in the shade of the mangoes!

She began to wonder if everything was all right. It was getting on for twelve and not once had her neighbour (Marelda began thinking of her as such), made a move to get a drink of water or go to the dunny. It was there close enough for her to use it. She had always liked the next-door lavatory. The honeysuckle growing over it sent lovely smells into the kitchen when the wind blew the right way. What was the matter with the girl? Perhaps she should go over. Just in case.

Sitting there, the sun hot enough to give her a million freckles, Greta was wondering if she dared take a drink of water. There was a tin mug on the tank stand and so far no sign of the snake. Did snakes hunt? Would she suddenly see it sliding down the stairs, searching for a rat or something? Until the men returned – and why the hell weren't they back? – she damn well wasn't going to move an inch.

'Are you all right, love?' Concentrating on the snake's possible movements, Greta hadn't noticed that the woman next door was leaning on the back gate. She looked as untidy as her house, a few wisps escaping from a bun of greying hair and a body that had never known the restrictions of a brassiere or stays. Greta could see her curiosity was genuine and her concern sincere.

'Yes – no.' In spite of herself, it could only be described as a feeling of relief seeing the homely face and the sturdy bulk of the woman as she lifted the latch of the gate to walk in.

'I'm Marelda Larkin, but everyone calls me Relda. If I give 'em permission, that is. Now tell me, dear, what's the matter? You look as if all your silver has turned into match sticks.'

Greta tried to steady her voice. 'A snake. A black one, I think – I don't really —'

'Where?'

'The kitchen.'

'Nasty bugger, a black.'

The words had hardly left Marelda's lips as she made an about-turn and raced into her own yard. In a flash she was back, a Boadicea of a woman brandishing an axe. 'In the kitchen, y' said. Rafters, I bet!' She dashed up the stairs. The kitchen table stood in Greta's full view and she saw the woman with surprising agility scramble up on it.

'Where are you, snake?'

In what seemed like only seconds Marelda stood by the door, the writhing creature held by its tail. She cracked it like a whip and sent it flying across the yard, helpless with a broken back. Marelda followed, axe upraised.

Greta watched stunned as the axe came down and down again, cutting the reptile into pieces. Panting, Marelda finally stopped, blue eyes blazing and satisfaction beaming all over her face. 'That's the end of him! I'll get one of the kids to bury it for you.' But her self-congratulations were cut short by the sight of Greta in a spasm of retching, the cause of which was plain to see. Blood had spattered over her toes and one high-heeled sandal and a fair-sized chunk of snake had landed, twitching, beside her.

'Oh, you poor thing. You better come over to my place.' She took Greta's elbow. 'There'd be nothing in your kitchen to brew up a pot. And my kettle's on the boil every minute of the day. Come on and we'll clean up y' foot and shoe in no time. Messy stuff, blood.' With acid sour in her mouth, Greta allowed herself to be led through the gate and across the road.

Inside, the house was much neater than its exterior. The kitchen seemed to spill over onto the verandah. It was large enough to hold two tables with room to spare, and one, by the number of chairs around it, made its function clear. Soon Greta was sitting at the smaller table, her feet washed clean and the fresh odour of Lysol banishing all traces, imagined or otherwise, of the smell of snake. Already her silk stockings were pegged out on the clothesline, nearly dry, and for the moment she was happy just to sit, cosseted with sympathy, sipping tea spiced with some of Marelda's homemade chilli wine.

Still no sign of Andy or Mannie Coleman, though.

As Marelda fussed and consoled, Greta was learning all there was to know about her neighbour as if she had lived across the road all her life. It hadn't taken long to find out about her numerous offspring. 'Still on school holidays and home any minute for something to eat!' she told Greta with pride in her voice. 'I can hear them coming now.' They soon appeared one by rowdy one into the kitchen, eyes not quite staring at her. There were more important things in life, their sniffing noses told them as each one, lines well rehearsed, shouted, 'Hello, Mum! What's for dinner?'

Two boys from six up and a girl in between sat down at the table to heaped plates of cottage pie and pumpkin. 'And that's not all of 'em.' Marelda sounded cheerful as she slapped spoons of rice pudding into soup plates. 'The older lad, Spanner, works at the bacon factory, and the next one down, Tommy, works in the railways like his dad.' It was later Greta learnt that the husband and father was a fettler on the rail tracks and could be away from home for six weeks or even months at a time. 'That's why I'm real pleased to have a bit of company close by.' To Greta's surprise, Marelda's startling blue-eyed gaze held appeal. 'You *are* going to take the place, aren't you?'

'I'm not sure . . .' Snakes roaming around wild held no fascination for Greta, but in a matter of seconds her commonsense came into gear. This is a country town, for cryin' out loud! And where or when could you find a place without a flaw? Already there were good signs that their life in Yunnabilla – not perhaps the most exciting place in the world, and forget about the crawly things – was going to be okay. If the town turned out to be as dull as a Monday washday, the richness and colour that love had brought into her life made up for it.

Their hunger appeased, the younger Larkins disappeared in a boisterous helter-skelter out the door with promises to cut more wood for the stove. Before they were out the gate, Marelda went after them, yelling instructions. 'There's a chopped-up red belly next door. Take it down to those half-starved dogs of Barney's. Give 'em a treat.' It became a clamouring race to be the first into the Flight's backyard.

The quiet they left behind became palpable and the question of staying or leaving was still unanswered. The older woman took down a large wash-up dish from a hook on the wall, placing it on the table, a tin tray beside it. Homey smells of hot suds filled the air as Marelda scrubbed and cleaned, making a cheery clatter banging plates, cups, knives and forks down on the tin tray to drain. Greta took up a tea towel folded over a chair, thinking she'd better get used to her new life in a small grey house.

'Well, are you going to take it?' Marelda kept her head down, using elbow grease to remove a speck of rice off a plate.

'It's a cubbyhouse and no one can say any different.' Greta was going to say more but the honk of a horn and the sight of Mannie pulling up with Andy already out of the car was enough for her to fling down the tea towel. Apologising for her sudden departure, she ran across Marelda's yard, then turned back to yell, 'Thanks for everything, Marelda, and yes, we're taking it!' She sprinted up her own back steps two at a time.

Once again Greta felt that things were moving too fast. Thinking over the day's events she lay in the dark of the hotel bedroom, the racket of a Saturday night's drinking session floating up through the floorboards. Andy had been more than contrite about the length of time he and Mannie had been away, but his enthusiasm about the work ahead – starting Monday – and his meeting with the tobacco farmer Stone and his broken-down generator had taken the edge off his contrition. 'Funny sort of fellow,' Andy had mused. 'Shunted his wife back into the house when we arrived, and she tore up the stairs with devils snapping at her heels.'

Greta, not knowing why, said nothing to him about the snake.

In a way, it turned out to be a night of celebration. Just the two of them. After dinner Andy had suggested that they sit on the verandah, before leaving her with a promise that he'd be back in a few minutes. He returned with two glasses, a bottle of ice-cold champagne on a tray and something in a brown-paper packet. The champagne had come in his duffle bag all the way up from Sydney. 'I didna' know if I'd find it up here.' He had then handed her the package, screwed tightly at the top. 'For you, special price.'

She opened it and peered inside, bursting into laughter. 'Caviar and Sao biscuits! You're a clown, Andy Flight. No wonder I love you.'

The sound of a popping cork and champagne fizzing brought on, as it always did, a happy gaiety that went with the warm starry night. Once again, she'd decided not to spoil it all by telling Andy how she had found herself sitting in Marelda Larkin's kitchen. As they clinked their glasses, Andrew had declared it was a night of firsts for them. A house, a job and a Ford utility to get him there! The utility, on a use-now, pay-later basis, had her asking wouldn't Andy's new boss, one Mannie Coleman, provide the necessary transport?

What followed nearly wrecked for her a night of toasting their good fortune. Without her knowledge a deal had been made. 'Mannie,' he had explained, 'who knows everyone in every dale and field around, will find the work, and there's plenty of it. Tobacco farms going up all over. I repair whatever has to be fixed and get the use of the garage of course, rent-free. I get paid in full and he gets commission at a fair percentage.' Andy had finally convinced her that his deal with Mannie was the best option he could possibly hope for. 'This means in a way I'll be my own boss.' He was all for giving it a fighting chance.

The noise below was quietening down. Sleep for Greta still seemed far away. Andy had been so buoyant, so sure that the business, by word of mouth, could only grow and succeed. 'We canna' go wrong, lassie.'

Now he slept, his arm holding her close to him as she heard him murmur, 'I love you, my darlin'.' He was awake after all. She felt his hand stroke her hair and a kiss on her bare shoulder. 'Ah, don't fash y'self, lassie. Everything will be all right. Now go to sleep.'

CHAPTER ELEVEN

Riding a bicycle was supposed to be easy. But Greta found out that two gravel-rashed knees and a skinned elbow were the prerequisites for gaining a cycling diploma. It had taken her all of one weekend to complete a wobbly ride down the road between the backyard fence and the Larkins'. The first attempt had Relda holding her sides in chortling encouragement while the oldest lad, Spanner, pushed her off to a flying start. And fly Greta did – down a slight incline that ended in a confusion of spinning wheels, torn skirt and the first grazed knee. She won Spanner's admiration and complete capitulation when he saw how she untangled herself, ignored the dribble of blood down her shin and righted the bike, ready to begin again.

'Wait a mo, Mrs Flight. I'll start you off.'

'Like hell you will!'

But this time he held the back of the seat, keeping her steady and running alongside until she found her balance. After that, a determined weekend found her more or less proficient; diploma won.

In the flurry of setting up house, it had not taken long for Greta to realise the advantage of having her own transport. A mile and a half walk into town was not Greta's idea of having fun. As a practical solution, the bike was a success.

Whizzing along, as free as the breeze, had given her an unexpected sense of freedom. She was unaware that her frequent trips around Yunnabilla, hair radiant in the sunshine, long legs peddling, were cause for speculation. 'Already the husband has taken over Mannie Coleman's garage,' they said. From then on it hadn't take long for the citizens of Yunnabilla to compare notes on the Flights. They came from 'The South', that was for sure. Andrew was already known as 'the Scotch Pommy'. 'Jack Goodall walked out the day he walked into Mannie's office,' the word went around. 'Come out from England and knows it all,' said some, while others claimed that he was a dab hand with engines and why not give the poor bastard a fair go? As for the wife in her shorts and tops and those pyjamas she wears in the daytime, it might be all right for Cairns, but doesn't she own a decent dress, I ask you? Those on Greta's side, intrigued by her looks and going on the few glimpses of her they had seen, said, 'Relda Larkin thinks she's just lovely, and you know Relda. Can't pull the wool over her eyes.' And so it went on. Speculation it might be, but then came the day when Greta was ready to step out.

In the dressing-table mirror Greta gave herself a nod of approval; the aqua voile looked cool with its cape sleeves and pintucked bodice; the skirt flared just enough to flatter. There was one good reason why she was dressed up to the nines. Today would be, not counting Relda, the first time she would meet the ladies of the town. There had been a note inside the letterbox – an invitation to attend a card afternoon. No riding a bike in this outfit, and for the occasion Andy and the ute were taking her to town.

There was no denying the admiration in Mannie's eyes when she and Andrew walked into his office.

'Strike a light, Andy, you sure know how to pick 'em.' It was impossible to take offence for the candid compliment. It appeared that Mannie was taking a trip somewhere. Beside him was a cane and leather suitcase, a rifle case and a large packing case held fast with wire bands.

Answering her unspoken question he told her that he was going away for a few days. He tapped the side of his nose as if conveying a secret to be shared only between the three of them. 'Off to New Guinea.' She was surprised that New Guinea could be visited in just a few days.

After buying furniture and purchasing a gramophone and the bicycle, their funds were getting low. Up to date no money had exchanged hands and the Stone's generator was taking longer to get the kinks out of it than Andrew had supposed. Somehow Greta didn't like the idea of Mannie scarpering around the wilds of New Guinea when he should be drumming up business for the Flights.

As if he knew exactly what she was thinking, Andy led her over to the side door which gave a full view of the garage's interior. 'Take note of what's in there, Mrs Flight.' Inside the garage stood a gleaming dismantled Buick, its innards strewn around and a large delivery van needing urgent attention, with the addition of a newly appointed mechanic on hand to help out. With Mannie standing not a foot away from them and the gawking newcomer in grease-stained overalls nearly as close, Andrew gave her a bear hug and kiss with the threat that if she insisted on looking so gorgeous a man should close up shop and announce that business was over for the day.

'And you're an idiot, Andy Flight!' But she couldn't hide the pleasure of feeling his arms around her, even if he did smell of oil and petrol, with a bit of sweat thrown in for good measure. In a funny way, what pleased her just as much was the sight of not one but two motors in the garage. 'We're going to be flat-out for the next week or two,' he said, giving her an extra squeeze, adding with satisfaction that the truck was the property of Molloy & Co, and a contract was signed to keep the vehicle in good running order – indefinitely.

For Greta this was the best news as far as the business was concerned. Molloy & Co was the largest and the busiest store in town. 'We Stock Everything From Tractors to Hair Pins' was their proud boast. In her opinion the 'We Stock Everything' bit included the frowsiest of fashions this side of Bullamakanka. But no one could deny it was a solid business that paid up without a quibble on the presentation of a bill; a bonus not to be ignored. With another kiss, this time more of a peck, Greta gave a cheeky wave and left them ready to stage her first official appearance – and perhaps the most important one she had ever made – before the ladies of Yunnabilla.

Somehow, the School of Arts Hall reminded Greta of the Bohemian Club in Sydney. There was a stage instead of a dais, and the same unpainted timber walls were decorated with tired paper streamers as if someone had overlooked the fact that Christmas and New Year had arrived and passed by three months ago. Card tables, already occupied, were scattered over the bare floorboards and the subdued murmur of card players accompanied the click and clack of mahjong pieces in fierce battle in one corner of the room. Undaunted by the concentration and the hush of the ladies in the hall, cheerful chatter from the adjacent annexe overrode any objections to noise, and the rattle of cups and saucers announced that afternoon tea as promised would be served on time. Near the door two women sat at a table cluttered with tickets, a cash box and a few small packages wrapped in bright tissue paper.

Their smiles were friendly enough as one took Greta's silver coin, the entry fee as printed on the board outside, while the other handed her a lucky door number.

'You're new here, aren't you, Mrs . . . ?'

'Flight. Greta Flight.'

She knew that every pintuck was under scrutiny, and two pairs of eyes travelled all the way down to the flared skirt, silk stockinged legs and to her three-inch high heels. She smiled down on them, confident in knowing that aqua was her colour and no one could fault the style. As always, Greta made a strong impression. Most of it favourable.

'Lovely of you to come. Oh, and I'm Poppy Griffen.' This from the younger woman. 'We can always do with another someone to make up a four.' A perky, pretty face splashed with freckles looked up at her. 'What's your favourite? Contract or auction?'

Greta was caught off-balance. What on earth was the woman talking about? It was easy to see that she was expected to have the right answers. She took a wild stab and hoped for the best. 'Auction, of course.' Life was an auction, anyway.

'Wonderful!' Poppy Griffen beamed. 'You'll be at my table and by the look of it, you're the last one to arrive. We can close shop for the day.' Greta had heard those same words spoken not more than fifteen minutes ago but the connotations were miles apart.

For the first time the older woman spoke up, not bothering to hide her derision at the idea of auction bridge. 'I play contract myself,' she sniffed. 'Auction is for babies and dunderheads.'

'And contract is for cheats,' Poppy snapped. 'I prefer a bit of a gamble myself. And if you don't mind, I'll take Mrs Flight to *my* table for introductions.' All Greta wanted to do was to make an escape but Poppy had sprung up and was already ushering her towards turned heads, curious stares and card games deferred while first impressions were cemented into Yunnabilla's psyche for an indefinite time.

It was the few sniggers, clearly audible, that unnerved her.

'Don't take any notice of the old cows.' It was only a whisper as Greta felt herself led not towards any table but to the kitchen. For the first time she saw a familiar face. Marelda Larkin came towards her with Poppy still in tow.

'Relda,' Poppy called, 'can you get soap, hot water and a clean dishrag? Look at the poor love.' Before Greta could utter a word, she felt herself turned around, her back towards Relda, and heard her giving a cluck. It was a peculiar blend of sympathy and suppressed humour.

'Oh, Greta. That husband of yours.'

'What the hell are you talking about, Relda?'

By now it was clear to see the concern on Poppy's face. 'You'll know once you get that dress off.' Numbed into submission, Greta was hurried behind a partition that hid her from view.

Once the dress was off it didn't take long to discover the trouble. Planted on the back of the dress was the grease-blackened imprint of two hands – large hands that could only belong to a man.

'Andy!' At that moment Greta could have killed him. Tears prickled her eyes as Marelda, still clucking, carried the aqua voile garment away, saying it would all come out in the wash. In spite of the embarrassment she couldn't help thinking that the satin and lace-trimmed petticoat and matching scanties were the prettiest that Anthony Horderns' had to offer. No one would dare snigger at *them*.

It was a case then for Greta to disappear and be grateful for a burgeoning friendship with Poppy. 'We'll go back to my place,' Poppy insisted, 'and see what can be found in the wardrobe.' She was smuggled out the back door in a wrap-around overall belonging to one of the kitchen ladies, as they called themselves.

Once at Poppy's, she held out a pretty floral georgette dress, all flounces with puffed sleeves. 'Not quite your style.' There was a touch of apology in her voice. 'And I'm not as tall as you, but at least you'll be respectable enough to get home.' Her eyes twinkled. 'And I'd not care to be that husband of yours when he arrives!'

All Greta could think of was the sight of those two black hands. One hand in the small of her back was one thing; the other hand was enough to make a girl blush. There it was for all the world the to see: dobbed fair-square, exactly in the place where her bum should be when wearing her lovely, smart, beautiful aqua dress. She could cry tears of blood!

And what the hell was auction and contract all about? Instinct told her Poppy had made a shrewd guess that Greta Flight knew bugger-all about bridge!

As the town's lone taxi drove her home, Greta heaved a sigh. So much for meeting the respectable ladies of Yunnabilla . . .

After Mannie had headed off to New Guinea, Greta, without a word to anyone, put a sign in the estate agent's window, announcing that Mrs Greta Flight was ready to give dancing lessons, ballet, tap and jazz at her home, five shillings for a morning's lesson. Bookings could be made courtesy of Coleman's office. A surprised Andrew deemed that Mannie should at least be given the opportunity to agree or disagree on his return. He succumbed when Greta said it was one way she could meet a few mothers apart from weekly card parties. And when, she asked Andrew, was Mannie coming back?

After the fiasco of her first attempt at making herself known she had vowed never to set foot inside the School of Arts again. Her only entertainment up to date was morning tea with Relda, and if she kept gutsing on her gigantic scones slathered with butter and her tomato and ginger jam, she wouldn't be able to get though the back door. Since Spanner Larkin had shown her the swimming hole only a bicycle ride away from the house, she had been able to at least exercise and limber up enough to keep herself supple. Of course, she could do that in the house but it was not half the fun with sweat running down her legs and the chances of Relda coming up the back stairs with a cake hot out of the oven.

'This way, Andy darling, I'll have women coming to *me*.' Careful not to get greased up again, she kept a small distance away from him. 'My kind of women who want the best for their kids. Give them a bit of class.'

'Whoa, lass. Don't let anyone hear you say that.'

Ignoring the advice, she went on. 'And the money will come in handy, even if it's just to buy gramophone records.' She didn't remind Andy that the Buick, repaired and delivered in pristine condition, had not yet been paid for.

'Not a soul. Not a plurry soul.'

'Who?' Andrew's voice was vague enough for Greta to know that his thoughts were miles away. London? she often wondered.

'Not one answer to that sign I put up three weeks ago. Doesn't anyone want their kids to learn how to dance in this place? Is it just pig shooting for the boys and marriage and babies for the girls?' Greta flung a starched and perfectly ironed cloth over the kitchen table. She had surprised herself by taking to her new role in life with gusto and some enjoyment. Even she and the Victor stove were coming to terms.

'Give them time, sweetheart. They could be a wee bit on the shy side.'

'Shy side!'

'If you think about it, that sign in Mannie's window tells all the world that you're a dancer. You're different, my darlin' – thank God for that. It will be a while for folk to take to the idea.'

Knives hit bread-and-butter plates with a clatter. 'If that's the case, I should have included belly dancing at special prices! I dunno . . .'

Andy was sitting on the back step, plucking and tuning the fiddle, melodies going through his mind, and trying to brush away thoughts of unpaid bills and the altercations between himself and the new man Mannie had introduced into the garage. Things were not working out as they should.

Although there was work and plenty of it, the money wasn't coming in. Two farms in two weeks he had been called out to. He hadn't mentioned the fact to Greta that the promise of payment would eventuate – if the rains came. If . . . . How many ifs? But how can you refuse a man when his crop is thirsting with a creek not that far away and forty-gallon drums to fill standing beside it, waiting? Waiting for a truck made useless, the engine butchered by ignorance; its owner trying to save a shilling by fixing it himself. Andrew mended the truck.

Another farm, and now that their tractor was up and going, a promise was made in concrete of payment after the tobacco sales were over. A tobacco sale, Andrew now realised, that had come and gone. A call to eat was a pleasant distraction from the worries building up to a heavy ache in his head; an irritation to be ignored.

Greta found herself adopting the ways of the town. The midday meal was 'dinner', hot if Andy was home, and in the evening, salad and cold meats that the locals called tea. For Greta, the kitchen was a much different haven than on the first visit. When she had finally confessed to Andy about the snake and how she had crept down the back stairs, in her own words, a complete mumbling mess, it had taken ages for her to walk into the kitchen without having a good look up at the rafters. The memory of the drama that followed still gave her shudders.

A set of red canisters stood at attention on the shelf above the stove. Curtains with a pattern of red apples adorned the one window that overlooked a paddock, the home of a billy goat and his entourage of six nannies. As Marelda had prophesied, the family had grown and three kids now gambolled over the paddock. Marelda had nearly spoiled the picture of proud parenthood by saying, 'You can't beat young nanny goat for a good roast dinner!'

Andrew reached for a slice of cake. 'Seed cake! And where is the good Scot lady who gave you the recipe?'

'Dear good Aussie Marelda, that's wot.'

Andrew cut himself another slice. 'By the way, for a bit of a change we're having dinner with the Colemans on Sunday. Mannie's back and we think its time to have a try-out together. There's a football game coming up. If a three-piece band is waiting to play a wee tune, an evening of dance is sure to follow. Like the idea?'

'Love it!' Keeping it to herself, Greta hoped they would make enough money to pay Mannie the rent owed.

CHAPTER TWELVE

Mannie Coleman's house was a surprise; his wife was a surprise; and his farm exceeded all expectations.

Following his instructions on how to get there, they drove the several miles out of town through scatty thirsty bushland interspersed with giant anthills, strangely beautiful with their spires and crenulations. A wooden bridge crossed a whisper of a creek more sand than water, and bottlebrush-shaded pools were alive with the rainbow flashes of kingfishers. The dry air smelt of a gravel-cleansed river somewhere out of sight.

The track, more than a road, opened up to reveal some acres of waist-high tobacco leaf, surrounding a house with wide verandahs and a double staircase. A short driveway lined with oleanders gave out a sweet welcome. Mannie waited until the utility came to a stop, and coming down the stairs, greeted Andrew with a handshake and a kiss for Greta. He seemed genuinely pleased to see them.

'You made it! Not hard to find,' he tossed over his shoulder as they walked up the stairs, and on reaching the verandah he paused, hands planted firmly on the railings. 'Well, what do you think about it?' There was no doubting the pride of ownership in his voice. The vista from where they stood was of green to golden tobacco fields. There was a barn-like structure that Mannie called a curing shed. 'You could call it the most important piece of equipment in the place. I'll show you later on,' he promised. He pointed out a clump of banana and mango trees vying for attention near the tank stands at the side of the house. 'Mangoes nearly finished but remind me to give you some bananas before you leave. Now it's time to meet the wife.'

Placing himself between the two of them, his arms resting on their shoulders, he guided them into the house. There was an involuntary gasp from Greta, and Andrew came to a full stop. It was a large room halved by a decorative timbered arch leading into the dining area. Greta had never seen anything quite like it. It was a triumph of the exotic, blending in with pieces of furniture that must have been fashioned by a creative and exceptional craftsman. Easy chairs of cane and seagrass gave a light touch to the elegance of more formal lounging chairs and a richly carved monk's bench. Wooden sculptures of weird, unfamiliar beings that came from New Guinea, Mannie explained, loitered behind a jardinière of a graceful devil palm. But the most astonishing addition to the room was a baby grand piano with stacked music sheets on a stool beside it.

'Come in, come in!' A lilting voice with the merest hint of an accent preceded a woman who, with floured hands, came towards them. 'Ah! My hands.' She gave them a hasty wipe on her apron. 'Blame the knishes and stuffed monkeys! They are very delicious.' Greta could only assume that stuffed monkeys were some unknown Yunnabilla delicacy, and hoped for the best.

Mrs Coleman was tiny. Deep-brown eyes alight with welcome

darted between Greta and Andrew. 'Forgive my husband. He forgets manners, so I'll introduce myself. I'm Leila. My mother says it means tulip.' She shrugged. 'Maybe. I don't know.' She wiped her hands once more on the apron and folded Greta's hands into her own. 'I am so happy to see you.' She turned to Mannie. 'Silly man . . . You did not tell them!' She then looked down at Greta's sandals. 'No hat and such beautiful shoes. Husband, you know how hot it is outside.'

'I was coming to it, I was coming to it.'

Were they going to eat alfresco? Perhaps in the deep shade of the mango trees . . . But the idea soon abated as Mannie, already on the move, was taking them outside to show them what a real tobacco farm was all about. Leila's voice followed them. 'Wait! Wait!' She dashed out of sight and was back in seconds with a straw hat, which she handed to Greta. 'You must wear it – your lovely complexion.' Then she turned back to Mannie with a warning. 'And do not be late for the food I make.'

'Not for the world, my dear.'

They walked between rows of lush plants admiring the breadth, height and health of them while Greta silently cursed the hot, brown soil filtering through her toes and open sandals. Remembering the snake, it seemed that every time she wore the damn things it was one more step towards ruining them! Even so, what Mannie had to say was more than interesting.

Dry farming, he called it, and he thanked his lucky stars that a river ran close by.

'Dry farming?' Andrew was intrigued. 'I've never heard of it.'

'Then I'll tell you.' Pleased to have a willing audience, he went on. Out of politeness Greta stifled a groan, keeping her thoughts to herself.

Mannie told them that river water was tanked and trucked up to the farm. 'I've two good men working for me here, tough bastards, but they know how to put their backs into it.' He explained how each tender seedling was watered cup by precious cup as the truck slowly went down the rows. Farmers less well off or devoid of a creek paid for water, and if not lucky enough to own a truck they borrowed or begged for a horse to pull a sledge up and down between the rows.

Mannie pointed to the barn-like structure they'd seen from the verandah. 'You must see this – it's a sight to soothe a worried farmer's breast.' Mannie led them across the bone-dry earth, aware he was on centre stage. 'Now to the hub of the whole business that can make or break a man.' With the air of a humble cleric unlocking the entrance to Westminster Abbey, he almost reverently opened the door. They were assailed by the rich, heady aroma of tobacco leaf while, on what seemed tier upon tier, hanging like ragged curtains, were tobacco leaves pale gold to burnt umber. In case the smell and slow curing escaped, Mannie closed the door. 'Not a trace of cut worm or frog eye disease to be seen. It'll bring in top price.' More hope than certainty told a wilting Greta that the inspection and lecturing tour was coming to an end.

'Ah, yes.' Mannie held up a finger. 'One more thing.' He pointed out a barbed-wire fence surrounding a small area of seedlings. 'My babies. Experimental, of course. But could earn me a fortune. Who knows?' Beside an improvised gate of wood and wire was a wheelbarrow filled with what appeared to be squares of paper.

Mannie took up a handful. 'Ah, yes,' he said again, giving a surprised Andrew the squares, 'thought you wouldn't mind giving a hand; sun does horrible things to young plants.' He pressed more squares into Greta's hand. 'Leila usually helps but she wants to do you proud.' Handing out another pile all around, he went on. 'With the three of us it can be done in no time at all. Then dinner.' Full of exuberance, he rattled off the menu waiting for them. 'Chicken, fish from the river, vegetables from the garden, Tsimmes and more. My mouth waters thinking of it!'

Struck dumb, Greta watched while Mannie explained what had to be done. Paper squares were placed over each seedling and pinned down with a scoop of soft dirt. That bloody Mannie! I should have known better! Greta thought. Furious, she waited for Andy to object but his shoulders were shaking with ill-concealed laughter.

'Och, ye're a lad, Mannie. I'll give a hand. But Greta? Ye canna expect —'

It was Mannie's shrug and the raised eyebrow that stung. 'Oh, can't she!' Greta snapped, and was the first to bend down to cover a seedling. She had three plants completed before the men began. Bugger the fingernails! she muttered as she tamped down the soil. For more than an hour they toiled under a sun that seemed to get hotter by the minute, Greta staying ahead, determined not to be outclassed. Her hands were a mess but her body from cycling and swimming was dancing fit. She'd show 'em. The pair of them! Two more rows to go and Greta allowed Andrew to catch up while Mannie forged ahead.

'How are ye going, my bonny darling?'

'I'm fine, m' bonny lad.' Her voice was astringent with sarcasm.

'Talk about singing for your supper and Mannie and his missus taking the encores for granted. You get no favours for nothing around here.' Getting that off her chest, the anger subsided a little. 'It's out of here the moment that last scrawny tobacco plant is covered. Okay?'

'Couldn't agree more, but for one thing.'

'What, for crikey's sake?'

'The orchestra. The try-out. Remember?' Andrew continued, forever polite. 'I suppose you cannot blame the wife for Mannie's tricks.'

'Humph!' Greta continued on in silence. 'But she knew about it.'

'And she gave you a hat.'

For no reason at all Greta felt her lips begin to twitch. Conned well and truly! One more row to go; Mannie nearing the end of his.

'Well, that dinner better be bloody good – I'm starving!'

Leila had met them at the door with towels and directions to showers upstairs and down. There was perfumed soap and talcum for Greta and an unopened packet of Lifebuoy soap for Andy with the promise that their clothes would be dusted off. 'That is all I can do, my friends. But you will feel much better.'

All was forgiven when Greta saw the table. Shades of Sydney and its grand hotels – silver service at its best. A damask cloth, cutlery gleaming, wineglasses sparkling, and a mammoth crystal bowl as a table centre heaped with fruits that could only be found in the tropics. A lazy overhead fan cooled the room. Tureens and covered bowls gave promise of sumptuous satisfaction. Everything about the table was in keeping with the first impressions gained when the Flights had walked into the house.

Before they were seated a tall, well-built man came in from the kitchen. It looked as if he'd been sampling some of Leila's cooking as he wiped crumbs from his lips with a folded handkerchief as pristine as the cream Tussore silk suit he wore. Not young, he had a thick brush of grey hair and although he walked with the aid of a cane, he was handsome enough to turn a woman's head.

'Mannie, old chap.' His voice was resonant and assured. 'Give me Leila just for a day and I'll leave you everything in my will. What a cook! I envy you.'

Mannie beamed as much as for the compliments to his wife as he did for the added pleasure of the man's presence. He turned to Andrew and Greta. 'Let me introduce you to Dr David Pedersen, an old and good friend.'

The doctor shook Andrew's hand, took one good look at Greta and with supreme confidence took up her hand. '*Enchanté*, Madam,' he said as he bent and kissed it. Greta took it all in her stride. It was not the first time her hand had been kissed by strangers, but even so, before Pedersen had straightened she and Andrew exchanged glances with more amusement than anything else.

Six sat at the table – the Colemans, the Flights, the doctor and a young girl of about seventeen, pretty in a quiet sort of way, who Leila introduced as Dorothy Stone.

'Dorothy helps out sometimes.' When the girl left on a small errand to the kitchen, Leila quickly explained that Dorothy was the Stone's foster-daughter.

'She's a good kid,' Mannie butted in. 'Do anything for Leila and me. She's an extra hand in the fields when needed. We pay fair wages, of course.' He looked slightly apologetic. 'At least that gives her money she can call her own. Poor girl.'

Greta felt Andrew's nudge and heard his murmur, 'Poor girl, right enough.' She knew that she'd hear more about Dorothy when they were by themselves.

In spite of the heat, the tureen of chicken soup, herbed and fragrant, was voted by the doctor as the best he'd ever tasted, helping himself to a second serving and another glass of sherry. Andrew and Mannie were quick to follow but content to leave the sherry alone. A smiling Dorothy brought in a fine baked dish of freshly caught river perch.

'Practically hooked it at the back gate,' said Mannie as he portioned helpings onto the warmed plates.

'I love the way Mrs Coleman cooks fish. It's so juicy and nice.' They were the first words uttered by the girl, who then blushed at her own temerity.

With more than one glass of the Colemans' imported wine combined with the soup, fish and a strudel with pastry ready to float away, Greta felt a need to burst into song. It was time for them to start the proposed 'try-out' she warned herself, before they all crashed to the floor in a heap. David Pedersen looked close enough to it and who wouldn't be, after finishing off a full bottle of burgundy alone, not counting the chablis . . .

Dorothy was left to clear the table, and although Greta felt a twinge of guilt at the thought of the stacked dirty dishes in the kitchen, she didn't feel guilty enough to offer a hand. This first practice was not only a 'try-out' but a test in itself to discover if the four of them were compatible enough, not only musically but emotionally. Andrew would never be a problem. As for Mannie, he thought he was the top dog of everything, no matter what. It was Leila Greta wondered about. A quick glimpse of the music stacked on the piano stool told her that it wasn't for dancing a quick step or a gypsy tap. Even the fact that Mannie had spoken of playing for the local hop didn't necessarily give her confidence. A one-off practice was hardly enough for the standard Greta expected of herself, let alone the others. Her heart began racing. It was no different from the countless other times she had stood in the wings ready to give an audience her very best, and an audience of only one made little difference. Already, the doctor had settled himself comfortably on a settee with his hooded eyes closing for sleep.

Leila was seated at the piano, her husband standing by, softly fingering scales on a brightly shining piano accordion, perfectly at ease. Andrew plucked a few strings, and tried out notes with the bow while Leila, to Greta's relief, tossed a few sheets of music aside to expose a thick album of well-known and popular songs.

'I know what Mannie and I like to play,' Leila said, looking up to Andrew, 'but yourself, you must have favourites? Tell me, and we'll see what we can find. I see also that you have not brought anything with you.' She looked around the room and gave a small shrug. 'No music stand, no music. You must be very clever.'

'I travel light.'

'And you, Greta. You travel light also?'

'As far as a song goes, yes. But I'm selective. Count opera as out. Blues and jazz in. Anything from a music-hall ditty to silver screen hits and the latest of Bing Crosby. You play it and I can sing it.' Feeling more confident, she added, 'And by the way, shouldn't we work out a program? Or do you have more or less the same program at every engagement?'

'More or less the same.' Mannie pushed his glasses closer to his eyes. 'Get 'em started on a good old-fashioned waltz, then a quick step. Nothing like a quick step to bring out a sweat and loosen up the joints.'

If it had been an afternoon of surprises for the Flights, there was one surprise left for the Colemans. It didn't matter what Leila and Mannie played, Andrew followed and the result more than delighted them. Even the doctor sat up straight and sober enough to give the trio his full attention with a clap and a 'Bravo!' in the right places.

Greta had felt uneasy on seeing Leila's music and had wondered how a classical pianist would fit in, but on hearing her first few notes and chords she relaxed. Leila might be topnotch on the highbrow stuff, but her renditions of popular music were as brilliant as her cooking. The stuffed monkeys – morsels of peel and ground almonds wrapped in butter-rich pastry – brought in with the coffee were the final proof.

While they rehearsed, Greta was content for the while to watch and listen. They had all agreed that she should restrict her singing to chosen pieces for a bigger impact on the dancers. Already they had heard her go through several popular Tin Pan Alley songs and, combined with Andrew's playing, they had Mannie announcing that Yunnabilla folk were in for the thrill of their miserable lives.

'It can only be concluded,' he chortled, 'that the Riverbank Players are in for engagements galore!' He declared that Andrew and Greta Flight's arrival was an event, more than a case of simply shifting house.

'Husband! Why must you exaggerate so? You will embarrass them for certain.'

Leila didn't know Greta. Praise was enjoyed to the full and taken in her stride. As for the Riverbank Players, it was the first time she or anyone else, she guessed, had heard of the title. But what the heck – let Mannie have his way. The name had a good ring to it.

Before goodbyes, Leila asked Andrew if he would accompany her on a piece that she and Mannie loved. There was a touch of shyness in her voice. He gave her a smile.

'Would be a pleasure, Leila. And what's this we must play together?'

Leila sorted through the music she had cast aside earlier. 'Ah, it is here.'

Andrew thumbed through the sheets and gave a slow whistle. 'Och, it's a while since I attempted this one. But we'll give it a try.'

Although Greta had never heard the melody before, she gave herself up to an exquisite flow of rippling arpeggios, her heart bursting with pride as her man gentled the music along with the tiny woman. It was a sound that made the heart ache. Never would she tire of watching him with violin tucked firmly beneath his chin or the fluid movements of his body in response to the music he played. It was the concentration, the absorbed expression that sometimes – only sometimes – was broken by a wink as if reminding her that his thoughts were reaching out to include her in the melodic magic of the moment.

And he did.

It was enough to set up a turmoil of longing . . . A longing that coursed through her body only to be satisfied when they lay again in each other's arms. Even then, when they were in bed together she didn't ask him the name of the music he and Leila had played. It was not important. Just to hear it had been enough.

CHAPTER THIRTEEN

Moonlight streamed across the bed. In sleep, Greta rolled over, an arm reaching out for Andrew. She felt the emptiness on his side of the bed, the sheets cool as if he'd not lain there for quite a while. Possibly outside having a wee, she thought sleepily, and now half-awake waited his return. Minutes passed. Too long out there. She reached for the torch on the bedside table, although the moonlight should have been enough. Not a sound outside – not even the oom-oom of the mopoke that often disturbed her dreams. Andrew was not outside or in the lav.

'Andy!' Her voice grew anxious. 'Andy?'

Not a sound.

Nights were getting cool and she shivered. Where was he? The beam of the torch needled every shadow, sprayed light over the woodheap. Greta, more puzzled than alarmed, went around the house to the front and found him. He was sitting on the steps.

'Andy!' Relieved, she stood before him, waiting for some explanation, the torch shining in his face. He blinked but that was the only response. 'Andy?' She tried controlling the tremor in her voice.

'What's wrong? Tell me.'

Before she touched him, she could feel the heat. He was burning up. 'My God! Quick! Let me get you inside.' He was a dead
weight as she half-dragged him into the house and back to bed.
Dawn was breaking and still he burned in spite of cold water packs
that she applied to his face and body. She had to get to a doctor
and quickly, but how to leave him? She'd get Marelda. She ran out
of the house.

Waking up Spanner to run for the doctor, Marelda had rushed out
to Greta's frantic call and in minutes was standing by Greta's side,
her bulk a shield against panic and fear. Still in a nightdress, her
homely face showed concern. 'It's the fever! The fires of hell have
got him. I've never felt anyone so hot.'

Together they sponged him over and over again, fanning him,
forcing aspirin between clenched teeth, and coercing him to take
drop by drop a herbal mixture of Marelda's brewing that seemed
to have little effect.

It felt like forever until they heard a car pull up near the back
gate, but not before Spanner hurried in to say that the regular doctor couldn't come and he had to get Dr Pedersen instead.

Marelda gave a humph of disgust. 'That drunk! Still, I suppose he's better than nothing,' she said, just as David Pedersen
came through the door, brushed and shaved as if attending a social
function.

He gave Greta a brief nod, strode over to the bed, placed a hand
on the sick man's forehead and with the other felt for a pulse in
Andrew's throat.

'Has this happened before?'

'I – I don't know. Maybe . . .' Greta floundered, trying to make sense of it all, aware of Pedersen's shrewd gaze and that he was making guesses of his own.

'Has he lived in the tropics? Cairns? New Guinea? Singapore? Some place like that?'

'I – I'm not sure. Well, yes. But before I knew him.'

'Hmm.' Without further probing, he went on. 'Never mind. Quinine. Do you have it?'

'No.'

'Has he?'

'I don't think so.' If he did, she knew little about it.

'Just as well I have.' Pedersen opened a Gladstone bag and produced a number of small envelopes, handing them over to Greta. 'You'll need these until you can get to the chemist. That's about as much as you can do with malaria, and I'm suspecting that's what it is. Meanwhile, depending on how bad the attack, we just have to wait.'

Malaria! She'd heard of it and knew what Pedersen meant by waiting. Sweat it out – get rid of it! It was a fever that could boil the blood, so she'd been told. An old wives' tale?

David Pedersen seemed to have more success than Greta and Marelda in getting medicine between Andrew's closed lips. He stood for moments looking down on the heated body as if waiting for some immediate result. Finally, he looked over to Greta standing rigid on the other side of the bed.

'Get wet towels, ring 'em out and cover him. All over.' He acknowledged Marelda standing in the doorway. 'Hello there, Mrs Larkin. You've both done well. Now how about you ladies making us all a cup of tea and a piece of toast? I'll stay with Andy for a while, and no,' as Greta began objecting, 'you'll have enough nursing to do when the fever breaks – *before* it breaks – and believe me, it will.'

Midafternoon, and still Andrew burned. The doctor had promised to return. Before leaving he told Greta that he'd taken a blood sample to send south. 'We'll just see what we're dealing with.' Keeping up with the fanning, changing nearly dry towels for wet, she wondered just what David Pedersen had thought on discovering how little she knew about Andrew's condition. Then there was Marelda who had also witnessed her professed ignorance. Marelda would have made a few guesses of her own, of that she was sure.

Into the third day of Andrew's fever an exhausted Greta thanked her lucky stars for a neighbour like Marelda Larkin. Taking turns at nursing Andrew, she had organised her own busy domestic affairs to fit in around it and was bossy enough to succeed in having Greta snatch a few hours of much-needed sleep.

Day four, and the malaria showed no signs of abating. David Pedersen's visits were now more frequent. On the second night, smelling of whisky, but sober faced, he had kept close watch over Andrew himself, ignoring the babbled mutterings of a fevered brain. 'Keep up the fanning and wet towels,' he had ordered. Before he left the sickroom he had promised Greta that Andy would recover.

Greta found his promise hard to believe.

'Time for some shut eye, Greta.' Relda clomped up the back steps, her arms loaded with cleanly laundered sheets and a covered dish. 'Spanner brought home some nice meaty pork bones from the factory. Makes lovely soup.'

Greta sagged into a chair. 'He's no different, Relda. How can a body take so much? Maybe another doctor . . .'

'Don't even think of it. I've changed my mind about that man. No other doctor could do more. If he says your Andy'll get better, he will!' She thumped her chest. 'I feel it right here,' she said, then tapping her head, 'and here. Now, the kids are doing their homework and Spanner's seeing that they don't get up to mischief. I'd like to see you eat up that soup and get a bit of sleep.' By now Greta was sleeping in the second bedroom, and for once she didn't argue.

Deep, dreamless sleep. A hand gently shook her shoulder and Greta was instantly wide awake, heart hammering.

'What's wrong? Tell me. What's wrong?'

'It's all right. But come and see.'

Marelda was standing beside the bed, the kitchen kerosene lamp in her other hand. Before Greta could be restrained she sprang out of bed, her stomach churning.

A candle's soft light was enough to see him look up at her. His smile was the ghost of the one that she knew and loved. The fever had broken! Tears flowed as she leant over to kiss him, afraid to hold him tight but she felt the slow steady beat of his heart against her cheek as she knelt beside the bed. She stroked his hand which felt a lot thinner than she remembered.

'Hello, my bonny darlin'.' His voice was a whisper. 'I'm here.'

CHAPTER FOURTEEN

Recovery was slow, with Andrew not strong enough to lift a pair of pliers. His usual buoyancy was replaced by a quiet facade of appreciation, if not resignation, that had Greta worried.

Days passed slowly in a routine that found him taking walks, enjoying the sunshine, and having long talks with Spanner, who often came to visit.

Although Dr Pedersen had told her that the blood tests revealed that Andrew had malaria, she couldn't help asking why the lethargy of convalescence was lasting so long. Four weeks had passed since the night she had found him sitting on the front steps.

'You're lucky to have him alive, with all his faculties. Malaria – a severe case – can affect the brain.' He took her hand. 'Be patient, Greta.'

She couldn't tell him that four weeks without Andy being able to work was a near disaster. Money for food and rent was close to the borderline, let alone a doctor's fee that must be paid. One day she had taken the ruby from its secret place in the hope that Mannie might find a buyer for it, or even want it himself. Knowing it was a talisman for Andy – heaven knows why – she gave up the idea before it really began.

Mannie never came to visit with empty hands. Fruit from the farm one day, a cooked leg of smoked mutton and a full tin of Leila's stuffed monkeys the next. And they weren't the only ones to help, Greta discovered. Yunnabilla looked after its own, newcomers included. Contributions mostly from vegetable plots and kitchen ovens found their way to the little grey house that stood alone. As for the Riverbank Players, Mannie had suggested that Leila and he would keep up the music for dances as they had always done, but perhaps Greta could lend her voice to round out the entertainment side of it? She agreed, with Relda Larkin offering to keep an eye on Andy if necessary. One occasional Saturday night of singing wouldn't pay the rent, Greta realised, but it would help. But another idea was taking over that could work out.

Once again a sign went up in Mannie's office window, this time with his permission.

ROOM TO LET – 10 shilling per week.
FULL BOARD – 30 shillings per week.
Enquiries: Coleman's office.

Greta, already anticipating Andy's objection to such an idea, planned ahead. No expert on preparing one of his favourites – plum duff cooked in a cloth – and having once tasted a magnificent portion from the Larkin's biggest saucepan, she decided to give it a go, trusting that Marelda would lend her the pot.

'Relda!' she called, before walking into the kitchen just in time to see her neighbour taking one of her famous fruit cakes (a must for the raffle on every card day) out of the oven. Relda looked flushed but triumphant. 'Good enough for the Cairns Show!' she gloated, tucking grey strands of sweaty hair into her bun. 'Not a crack on it.' She placed the fruit-filled marvel on the table. 'Looks cooked,' and from her bun withdrew an outsize hairpin and jabbed the cake all over. No point in feeling squeamish; it was laughable, really, considering Marelda's reputation as the best baker of cakes in the town. How many jabs to a cake? Greta wondered.

Satisfied that the hairpin came out clean without a trace of uncooked cake to mar it, Marelda nodded. 'Yep, done enough.' She now gave Greta her full attention. 'What can I do you for, dear? Andy orright?'

How could you not love the woman? Although Marelda offered to make the plum duff, Greta was determined to make it herself. And it had nothing to do with hairpins, was a half-guilty thought.

Ignoring budget concerns and armed with a grocery list, Greta cycled into town, the thought of a surprise dinner somehow giving her a lightness of heart – something she'd not experienced in weeks. She wondered if she could put a bottle of bubbly on tick at the pub (and the pub did sell it, she'd found out). She'd put aside the real reason for the dinner, but justified it by believing, and rightly so, that it could make a difference to Andy's recovery. An unexpected treat instead of an ordinary meal and the usual early bedtime routine would cheer him right up. She'd deal with objections of taking on boarders some other time.

Spanner Larkin came in on the act. He told her of a bloke he knew with some chooks, and when their egg-producing days were over, he sold them on the cheap.

'Get me one.' Greta was now no longer the thrifty housewife

but a spendthrift to the core, aware that poultry was a luxury to be eaten only at Christmas and Easter time. Used to seeing neatly tucked-in and dressed chickens in a Kings Cross butcher's shop, she was dismayed when Spanner produced a struggling hen in a hessian bag for her inspection.

'Nice and plump too, Mrs Flight.'

'But it's alive! It's got feathers!'

'Never mind about that. First thing to do is chop the old head off.'

Must everything be done with an axe? 'Not here!' she almost screeched.

Spanner, now understanding their neighbour more than Greta realised, gave a wicked chuckle. 'Behind the woodheap will do. Won't see it running around headless so much there.' She gave a small moan. 'Our woodheap, of course, Mrs Flight.'

'You're a bugger, Spanner.' Already she'd forgiven him.

Spanner, unseen somewhere in the Larkin's backyard, attended to the hen. But Greta couldn't close her ears to the squawking of the terrified bird or the screaming laughter of Marelda's excited brood. All Greta could do was to be thankful that Andrew, taking his usual afternoon rest, slept through the ruckus undisturbed.

Not long after Spanner presented her with what could only be called a noble bird. Plump and shiny, claws already demolished by a neighbour's dog and not one stray feather in sight. As he had done since Andrew's illness, Spanner chopped and filled her wood box before he left.

Now by herself, Greta stuffed the fowl, and everything that should be was in the oven in good time. Already, the cloth-bound pudding was gently bouncing in a perfect and proper simmer in the pot. Greta opened a bottle of Madeira, another favourite, and poured herself a glass. She deserved it!

With the afternoon waning, Andrew, awake and interested, appeared at the kitchen door. 'I smell a smell.'

Dressed in the backless sequined gown worn on the first night they'd met and wearing an apron, Greta swayed towards him. Andrew caught his breath at the loveliness of her but drew in his cheeks, raising a quizzical eyebrow. Although the lines that framed his lips were deeper and the nose more beaked on a thinner face, he almost looked like his old self again. In fact, Greta thought he looked devilishly handsome.

'And what's this?' He carefully noted the table with cutlery placed just so and the vase of honeysuckle and zinnias centred on a brightly checked tablecloth. Picking up the Madeira bottle, he asked if it was half-full or half-empty.

'I couldn't shay,' Greta giggled. 'You tell me, shailor boy.'

She pulled out a chair and invited him to sit, patting his shoulder and kissing the top of his head. 'Jus' call me Marelda Larkin.'

'Hardly.' By now he was grinning all over as he watched a slightly wobbly Greta head for the oven. Carefully she took out the bird, skin golden and crisp, and a memory of childhood came to his mind. '"There never was such a goose" my mother would say every Christmas without fail, and today there never was such a chook,' he said aloud.

'All compliments gratefully received,' beamed Greta, taking up a gleaming carving knife and fork.

'Whoa, there! Would you like me to carve?'

'I'm in perfeckly control.'

But Andrew had no need for concern as Greta cut slice after slice with all the expertise of any hotel cook. She had done herself proud, and the plum duff she produced to an astonished Andrew was perfect in every way, although she hiccupped an apology for the custard.

'Shorry, luvvie, but the custard's lumpy as a pickled walnut.'

Solemnly accepting the apology, Andy poured her another glass of champagne. The night turned into an occasion and for the first time since Andrew's malarial bout, Greta went back with him to the double bed.

Andrew swore it was the plum duff, hot or cold, that was the final cure for his malaise, and a week later Greta waved him off to work. Up to date no one had answered her ad for a boarder in Mannie's office window, and as Andrew had taken a turn for the better she'd told the estate agent to remove it before Andy stepped into the garage where Molloy & Co's truck waited for his attention.

It felt like a holiday when Marelda Larkin called over the fence to have a scone and a cuppa. It had been weeks since Greta had sat in the Larkin kitchen, hearing the gossip of the town – still about people she didn't know. The days were getting cooler, to her surprise, and a kitchen's warmth in early morning was welcome. She was on to her second scone when Spanner appeared with a load of neatly cut pieces for the wood box.

He was a tall young man, muscles hard from physical labour, with blue eyes like his mother. There was a bit of larrikin mischief about him, and it looked as if at some time or other his nose had come in contact with a well-aimed fist.

'Hello, Mrs Flight.' He poured himself a cup from the never-empty Larkin teapot.

'Not at work today, Spanner?'

'Factory closed down for a few days.' He didn't say why. But Spanner, who usually sat on the back steps to drink tea, seemed unwilling to leave, giving Greta a glance or two as if summoning up some sort of courage to speak. He sucked in his breath. 'Um, Mrs Flight . . .' Now having Greta's attention, he behaved as if he didn't know what to do with it. She was aware of a look, hard to decipher, that passed between mother and son. Intrigued, she waited for Spanner to carry on.

'Before Andy got sick, you went over to the Colemans' place, ay?'

'That's right.'

'Was Dorothy Stone there?'

'She was. You know her?'

'Yeah.' There was no display of embarrassment now. In fact he looked Greta straight in the eye. 'I know her, all right. And I want to marry her.'

Greta stared at him in genuine surprise. 'Marry her; she's a bit young, isn't she?'

'She's seventeen. Mum was married at that age.'

'It was different then,' Marelda butted in. 'She's a foster child, y'know. The Stones treat her like dirt, poor kid. Won't let her out of their sight unless she's loaned out as a skivvy or a workhorse for someone.' She vigorously buttered and jammed scones. 'Who wants some more?'

Now that he'd broached the subject, words spilled out of Spanner's mouth as though he expected Greta to do something about it, or just lend a sympathetic ear to hear his story. Spanner confessed he'd been more than attracted to Dorothy since the first time he'd seen her with the Stones at the church bazaar. He described her as a pretty and sweet girl who was, at a guess, about fifteen years old at the time. At first the Stones had proudly introduced her around as their dear little foster girl, bringing her along whenever they came to town. As time went by Dorothy was gradually left at home and nothing was heard or seen of her until the day Spanner, when helping out on a friend's tobacco farm, found her working in the field beside him.

'I was surprised, I can tell you. And I was pretty pleased to see her. For a week we worked together and I guess we started to get a bit keen on each other.'

Girls often worked on their parents' or neighbours' farms, especially when the tobacco was ready to be picked and sorted, and at the time he didn't give a lot of thought to her being there. At the end of the week when he asked if she'd like to go to the pictures, her reaction he told Greta, could only be called weird.

'She started crying, an' ran off to the washhouse. There was nothing I could do. I had a few tools to pick up, and by the time I got there I found her bike gone. She had scarpered off without a word.'

Spanner found out why soon enough. His mates knew all about Dorothy Stone. Their advice was to keep well away from her. Old Stone ruled his house with an iron fist and threatened to use it on anyone who dared put as much as a hand on the foster girl's arm.

Marelda had to put her own spoke into Spanner's wheel. 'He could've spoken to me – but what son talks to his mum about his latest heartthrob? I knew that the poor kid was only a dogsbody for the Stones. It's common knowledge at the card club. They'll send her off to anyone to do anything and the old man pockets the wages.'

'I know, Mum.' Spanner's expression was more sad than annoyed. 'So you've said before.'

Guilt swarmed over Greta as she remembered how Dorothy was left in the Colemans' kitchen after lunch that day without an offer to help from herself or anyone else. Ignorance of the girl's situation was no excuse. Even when she had brought in the coffee and biscuits she had been practically ignored, although invited to sit and listen once the washing-up had been done. Without a warning Greta felt that somehow she was now involved in Spanner's problems. 'But Spanner,' curiosity had her asking, 'it sounds to me as if you've had more than one chance to see her.'

'Thanks to me mates, Mrs Flight. Once they knew how I felt, seriously felt about Dorothy, they'd let me know if they'd seen her working somewhere. I'd go along and do the ride home with her – or as far she'd let me, anyway. She worked at the bacon factory for a couple of weeks, that helped.' He gave Greta a shy, sheepish smile. 'We have ways of getting together. Not too often, ay? But it's been enough to know how we feel.'

Marelda with tight lips thumped over the floor to shove a few pieces of wood into the stove. 'He won't listen. That Stone is a dangerous old git and D.O.R.O.T.H.Y. spells *Trouble*. Mark my words!' But she hadn't finished with Spanner yet. 'Marriage, he says! And I say, How's that possible when you can count on two hands the times they've really met?' She shot her son a dark look. 'That's what he tells me, anyway.'

As someone who knew that three days was sometimes long

enough to experience deep feelings, or, as Spanner called it, to be 'keen' on each other, Greta thought it would be a good idea to leave. She was certain that Marelda already expected her full support in denouncing a foolhardy Spanner, and she knew she couldn't do that. Fortunately she soon found a good excuse to leave.

Even Marelda was intrigued enough by the interruption to bring her railings over Spanner to a halt. Approaching on a bicycle that appeared far too small for the stout body and short muscular legs, they saw through the window the rider stop outside Greta's backyard. The way he settled his bike against the fence hinted at a fussiness of nature that seemed to match his round face and the clerical collar beneath it.

'It's Reverend Baker – what's he doing here?'

'Only one way to find out,' said Greta, as she made her escape.

'Mrs Flight, Reverend Baker's the name, and I apologise. Should have introduced myself weeks ago – or months? Time flies so quickly.' All this was said before Greta had time to open the gate.

'Er – how do you do, Reverend.' Feeling a little disturbed as to why a minister should be following her across the yard and being excruciatingly proper (as she later reported to Andy), she invited him inside. Moving closer to the back stairs she suddenly remembered the unwashed breakfast dishes still stacked on the kitchen table. Damn, she thought, why couldn't he have come to the front door?

Greta flashed him a smile. 'So hot in the kitchen,' she said and did a sudden about-turn, walking briskly around the side of the house. She practically bundled Reverend Baker into the sitting room and as soon as the minister was seated, 'A cup of tea,' she asked brightly, putting off the real questions buzzing around in her head. Did he know anything about her and Andy's circumstances, and that the title 'Mrs' Flight' was nothing but a sham?

'Tea! Ah, yes. That would be welcome. Quite chilly outside, don't you agree?' She felt that he was fully aware of dirty dishes and would have been more comfortable sitting in a warm kitchen. 'However, Mrs Flight, first things first. You must be wondering why I'm here without invitation.'

You could say that again, she thought, wishing he'd get on with it.

'You are a dancer, I believe, as well as a singer.'

Her heart thumped. Gawd, he does know all about me! 'You know . . . ?' Her voice was a whisper.

'Well, of course.' His expression was bland. 'Your notice for pupils in Mannie Coleman's window.' He gave a high, excited laugh. 'Need I say more?'

Relief swept over her. She had momentarily forgotten about the ad. Always at the back of her mind, their flight out of Sydney was an itching reminder that there might come a day of humiliation and exposure. Andy's naval desertion or their quasi-marriage didn't seem to worry him, but then didn't every woman say that men were different? Thoughts flashed though her mind even as the Reverend was speaking.

'I realise, dear lady, I am asking a lot of you on such a short acquaintance, but the church is in desperate need of funding, and I've a little idea that could work – with your cooperation, of course.'

'My cooperation?'

'How do you like the thought of putting on a concert?'

'A concert!' She bolted away from the suggestion. How could she explain to the Reverend in all his innocence that his idea of her running a concert was a laughable joke? Performers didn't come out of thin air and the town, as far as she knew, lacked any talent good enough to put on any sort of a show, except for Mannie and Leila, of course.

'For a start, Reverend, a concert means singers, acts – even dancers . . . And as far as dancers go,' Greta allowed herself a short laugh, 'I've had not one answer to that little notice in Mannie's window.'

'I have a feeling, Mrs Flight, that the situation could be altered somewhat.' He smirked. 'I could help there.' He seemed to forget about her offer of tea. 'Of course you know Poppy Griffen.' He had to be aware of the fiasco at the card afternoon. Her cheeks grew hot, but he seemed not to notice her embarrassment. 'She told me of her intention to bring her little girl along for lessons.'

'One little girl hardly makes for a concert.'

'Well, we're not talking about tomorrow, Mrs Flight.' And as if he had read her thoughts, followed on by saying that there *was* talent enough in the town. 'You'd be surprised.' What he had to say next, though, floored her. 'Used to be in theatrics myself before changing jobs.' Her heart slipped again as he gave her a smile that could only be described as conspiratorial. 'Of course, I haven't mentioned the fact since coming north. The professional stage, as we know it —'

'*We?*'

He ignored the interruption. '— in a small town like this, even today, can be looked on with suspicion and disapproval, but an amateur presentation with local performers is another matter. And with some of their own in our little show, I think it can be done.' *Was he already counting on her to agree?* 'You *will* do it for us, won't you?' It sounded like an order, not a request. Just how much did he know about them? About her? She wasn't going to ask and he wasn't going to tell, but the whole business to her smelt like a mild form of blackmail.

He left with Greta promising that she would think about it, depending on her eventually getting enough dance pupils.

'I'm sure you will, Mrs Flight, and in time, between us, we'll put on an event that the town will never forget.'

As Greta watched him ride away, exhilaration at the thought of stage work worthy of her own talents surged through her, combined with a strange apprehension that somehow the Reverend Baker had her well and truly over a barrel!

Andy's reaction to her news that night was no more than expected. He was delighted for her. It was a grand idea, and after next Saturday night she'd have the ladies bringing their little darlings to her in droves.

'And why after Saturday night?'

'Because, my lassie, the Riverbank Players are ready to roll.'

'But we've only had one rehearsal!' She was serving up cottage pie, another of Andy's favourites beside porridge – at any time of the day or night.

'Mannie and I've been having a few practises on the sly.'

'Business a bit quiet around town?' she couldn't help herself asking.

He took some time to answer. 'You can say a bit. Of course there *is* the truck.'

There was not much point in saying more. The newspaper up from Cairns said it for her. More unemployed men were arriving from the south searching for work, and employment for the towns-folk was dwindling away. No one had to tell her that many of the local farms – especially those without a good water supply – were going down.

'Well!' With an effort she brought the brightness back into her voice. 'Saturday night it is.' Popping her own dinner into the oven, she went to the front room and rummaged through their small stack of records. The strains of 'Ain't She Sweet' accompanied her back to the kitchen.

'Enough Madeira left over for a tot or two, darling.' She held the bottle up to the light. 'Just enough to wish the Riverbank Players well. Now let's eat, drink and get merry!'

CHAPTER FIFTEEN

It appeared that the visit from Reverend Baker was all that was needed. The next day not one car rolled up to the front of the grey house but two. The first was no other than Poppy Griffen. The sound of a motor brought Greta to the verandah and down to the gate before Poppy had stepped out of the car, helping a diminutive copy of herself to alight. The child wore what was the height of fashion for little girls all over the world: a Shirley Temple dress. It was a spotted organza confection with a black-velvet bow and puffed sleeves.

'This is Annabelle, your first pupil!' The child could have been no more than four years old but the bobbing bow she gave Greta had her smiling back, already bewitched. As she ushered them inside, Poppy paused, touching Greta's arm. 'I know – I —' There was a slight blush of discomfort to her cheeks. 'I should have visited before, even if only to thank you for returning the dress, but things got in the way and with your husband not well . . .'

'Yes, you were out at the time I came.' Greta didn't add to Poppy's discomfort by saying that she had returned the dress weeks ago. But never mind, she had brought the child along, her first pupil – even if it had taken some encouragement from the pulpit. More students were bound to follow.

Greta felt as if she was playing ladies, and to her quiet amusement there was a full cake tin of Leila's stuffed monkeys on hand. As she poured tea, a picture came to mind of Flossie's reaction to such domesticity and she reminded herself that she must write to her soon.

Not wasting time, and just in case Poppy changed her mind, Greta began the first lesson. Annabelle, apart from being a little dear, was a natural. In no time Greta had the gramophone on, teaching her a simple routine that had the mother singing praises of her darling's talents and of Greta's brilliance as a teacher.

With another blush, this time because of shyness, Poppy confessed that she had always wanted to be a dancer.

'No reason why you can't be. Right now!' It was a dare that had Poppy looking over her shoulder as if the Reverend was standing behind her.

'Oh, I can't! What would people say?' Then, in a rush, 'I'd love to, but I *am* a married woman, as you know.'

'The town can't be *that* wowserish.' Greta was already miles ahead with the idea of a mother-and-daughter act for the concert if it ever happened. She took the needle-holder off the gramophone, grinning. 'C'mon! Be a devil. We'll start with a few limbering-up exercises. Marvellous for the figure.'

Time flew with laughter, groans from Poppy and shrieks of delight from Annabelle. Poppy, dress hiked up to the thighs and halfway down to the floor in an awkward version of the splits, was immobilised by a knock.

'Mrs Lockard!'

Standing on the verandah was a tall, well-groomed woman who, at a glance, would never wear a Molloy & Co garment and would also never be called anything else but 'Mrs Lockard'. Wife of the manager of the most important bank in the district, she carried her role with dignity and a touch of tongue-in-cheek humour. Greta, on the point of explosion herself, guessed that Mrs Lockard was making a supreme effort to maintain that dignity as an embarrassed Poppy scrambled to her feet.

'Greta, this is Mrs Lockard.' Poppy's flustered introduction was hampered by an attempt to remove every crease from a dress that portrayed an afternoon of riotous behaviour. There was no need for the introduction; Greta knew Mrs Lockard on sight.

'Come in, come in,' she called and, banking on that sense of humour, couldn't help adding, 'join in the fun.'

'Not quite dressed for it, I'm afraid, and please forgive the intrusion.' There came a surprising look of discomfort. 'Although we haven't met, Mrs Flight, I do have someone with me who would love to "join in the fun".' Without warning she turned, then hurried back to the large handsome vehicle parked beside Poppy's more modest car.

She stood awhile at the car window before opening the door, making what seemed to be nods of encouragement to the person inside and at the same time pointing to the house. At first there was no response, yet she still waited. Finally, a young girl stepped out of the car. From where Greta stood it was apparent that she was perhaps fifteen or sixteen, and more striking than pretty. Long straight hair, black and glossy in the sun, gave an elegance to her poise as she glided, more than walked, towards the house. What a showgirl she would make! was Greta's instant thought.

Before the pair had reached the verandah Greta heard Poppy mutter, 'It's Lorraine . . .' in a tone more questioning than informing. Grave of face, the girl stood near the open front door as if reluctant to move an inch inside. Mrs Lockard sighed and walked over to Greta.

'Please, Mrs Flight.' Her fine eyes were suddenly sad. 'Come, meet my daughter Lorraine – I know she wants to meet you.' She then turned and took hold of the girl's hand, silently mouthing the word, 'Greta', followed by a fluttering of hands. She began the same way as before, 'Greta', and added the word, 'dance'.

'You must by now realise Lorraine is a deaf mute.' She gave a thin smile. 'Yes, my girl is deaf and dumb. And, Mrs Flight, I have the strongest feeling that you'll be able to do something for her. Teach her to dance.'

'I could certainly teach her ballroom, a man leading her . . .' But Mrs Lockard was already shaking her head.

'I don't mean to offend, but that is not what we want. Not at all. Aren't there some things she can learn? Jigs, even the tap dancing we see all the time in those pictures from Hollywood?'

Greta felt helpless, confronted by the hope in Mrs Lockard's voice. How could the girl, lovely as she was, be taught to dance? Without hearing, how could she possibly keep in time to the sound of unheard music with its rhythms pulsing and driving a body to fly? Sure, she could be taught the steps, but what a parody to the joy, the liberation that dancing gave . . . The thought, the picture of her dancing in quietness, was a sad reality that had Greta shaking her head.

'I'm truly sorry, Mrs Lockard, but —'

'But of course you can.' Mrs Lockard was on firm ground,

refusing to take no for an answer.

The record on the gramophone was slurring to a standstill then slurred up again to full pitch with Poppy at the rescue, giving the machine's handle a vigorous wind as if life depended on it.

'My qualifications don't cover —'

'I'm sure they do. Perhaps just simple steps that she could do with the other pupils.' Mrs Lockard shot a glance over to Poppy. 'Like Mrs Griffen for instance.' Not saying a word, Poppy gave the impression of a butterfly caught in a net.

'Mrs Lockard, have you any idea how frustrated your daughter could feel trying to keep up with the class? That's if I get more than young Annabelle attending.'

'You will, I'm sure of that, now you've made a start.'

Greta had the distinct impression that Mrs Lockard knew all about Reverend Baker's idea of a concert, and was ready to coerce her into having Lorraine somehow involved.

'I don't – I'm not sure that it would work.'

Mrs Lockard suddenly dropped the pose of lady of the manor and a pleading look came into her eyes. 'We could just try . . . couldn't we?'

Greta felt herself slipping into some sort of an agreement. 'Yes, I suppose we could.' Gawd, Aggie, what had she let herself in for? she wondered, regretting the day she'd placed that notice in Mannie's office window.

Poppy Griffen's aches and pains after the first work-outs with Greta had ceased weeks ago. No longer did she groan like her husband after a game of football that weekend after weekend was played when the season was in full swing. No longer was she compelled to sit in stands and outdoor benches in chilly weather watching a game that bored her to sobs. Greta Flight had changed all that. Her husband's outrage when first he heard she had started lessons had soon changed with his appreciation of her improved curves, a seemingly renewed zest for life – not to mention lust in the bedroom.

Poppy never told Greta why after that day at the School of Arts she had not followed up on their meeting, which had held all the signs of a friendship waiting to begin. She could never explain the true reasons why not a soul had initially responded to Greta's notice about dancing lessons – something that would have added to the town's enjoyment as a community.

The day after the notice went up, the usual Friday night euchre party at the School of Arts was buzzing with supposition and excitement. Ethel Rourke, the most vocal of all the card players put together, had said, 'Not only a singer but a dancer! On the stage, I'd make a bet. Knew there was something funny about her the moment she walked into the tearooms that day. A right proper hussy in those shorts. And him such a lovely man.'

Some thought that Ethel had no cause to talk; didn't she give the glad eyes to every man who stepped foot into the tearoom for a cup of tea and a scone?

Poppy was told about it the next day and of the stand-up toe-to-toe fighting words Relda Larkin had with Ethel when she heard her running Greta down. Marelda said, and many others at the time agreed, that since the Flights had arrived, bringing their talent to the Riverbank Players with a singer like Greta and a violinist like Andrew, the town had something to be proud of. The Yunnabilla matrons (except those who obeyed the elders of a church forbidding lipstick, pictures on a Saturday, hair waves and anything else enjoyable), greeted the idea with enthusiasm. Quite a few were ready to sign up their children for dance lessons straightaway.

It was the talk that had followed that put a stop to the classes before they had a chance to begin. It started with a word here, a word there, innuendo on top of innuendo that Greta Flight had been nothing but a 'fancy girl' before she married Andrew Flight. What's more, she had been seen – a married woman, mind you – swimming alone with Spanner Larkin, doing strange thing with her arms and legs and him lounging there not a yard away! Ducking and diving and you can guess the rest. And not only Spanner Larkin; what about that tippler Dr Pedersen? They'd been seen sitting on her verandah with glasses and a bottle of who-knows-what while that poor husband was working on a farm somewhere. Disgusting! It was no place for innocent children.

'Young Spanner, ay?' chortled the regulars of the Victoria hotel, 'getting in for his chop while the Pom's away. Ah . . . that's our boy!'

It went on and on, with only a few in the town believing it all. But rumours are rumours, and for Poppy Griffen, with an accountant husband in business, it wasn't wise to go against supposed general opinion. But with a lack of titbits and for want of refuelling, the gossip dwindled away and commonsense took over. So, kicking herself for being a pasty-faced fool and not once visiting Greta during Andrew's illness, she dressed in her best and with Annabelle in tow had driven off to the little grey house, as Greta called it.

The arrival of Mrs Lockard, though, had come as a complete

surprise. Once the bank manager's wife (the only title some gave her) accepted the idea of a dancing school, it put a final end to the ugly stories blighting Yunnabilla. Her patronage was the catalyst to Greta's growing business.

Poppy did a back bend in slow motion, then straightened and finished off the day's exercises by sinking to the floor in a perfect and graceful execution of the splits.

CHAPTER SIXTEEN

Midwinter and Greta, ignorant of northern weather, found it hard to believe that the heat, humidity and wet of summer were gone. Even the locals were shaking their heads over rain that had been too scattered and inconsistent to soak the canefields on the coast and the tobacco fields on the highland's dry belt.

She revelled in the cooler daytime air, the sparkling hours of sunshine, and had been astonished to find one morning that a bucket of water left on the tank stand was covered by a thin layer of ice.

They had made a few good friends over the months and there were now eight paying pupils for Greta's dance school, not counting a couple of unpaying ones that included the Larkin girl. Most Saturday nights found the locals and out-of-towners swaying, twirling and stomping to the beat of the Riverbank Players: lancers, gypsy tap, waltzes, old-time favourites that vied in popularity with New Vogue, Yunnabilla style. If the business between Mannie and Andrew was less than it should be, never mind. And thank the Lord for Molloy & Co's delivery truck, which always seemed to be breaking down. Andrew could not believe that a business like Molloy & Co depended on what he called an outmoded wreck. False economy, he called it, and Greta kept her fingers crossed that their idea of economy would stay exactly as it was.

With tongue clenched between her teeth, and hips swaying to a record of Paul Whiteman's music, Greta's floured fingers worked out the intricacies of twisting savoury dough into acceptable cheese straws.

'We'll call it dinner tonight,' she had informed Andrew. 'David Pederson is coming and we'll do it posh, canapés with whatever and let's hope it's bubbly he's bringing before we dine on a Café Romarna special – spaghetti *not* out of a tin.'

David was always welcome and mere acquaintance had blossomed over the months into friendship; especially enjoyed by the Flights who appreciated his dry wit and conversation that didn't include the price of tobacco leaf and the vagaries of weather and commerce. Andrew's full recovery was always a good excuse for celebrations, no matter how modest. With wine (hopefully), good food and David Pederson's company, Greta knew that the night held a promise of success.

Pederson did bring wine, not 'bubbly', as Greta had hoped for, but a rich red brew from his own cellar. Andrew suspected that, apart from the Colemans, the doctor had the only cellar worth speaking of in Yunnabilla.

Greta glowed in self-satisfaction. The bolognaise had gone down a treat and high praises came from the men over the poached figs (from the Colemans' farm), with its servings of caramelised

Nestlé's cream. Head slightly on the swim, as she described it, she savoured a golden sweet liquor that David had also produced, waiving aside their protests. 'A suitable ending to such perfection,' he'd insisted.

The three of them lazed contentedly in the sitting room's sea-grass chairs, listening to the crooner Bing Crosby wondering 'How deep is the ocean', with Greta joining in, wanting to know 'How high is the sky.' As the record ended, Greta gave a shiver. 'Apart from Bing Crosby, that song gives me goose pimples.' She shot a look over at Andrew, eyes half-closed, and then stood up, arms outstretched. 'We should be dancing, husband; put Bing on again.'

Pederson watched as they danced. Oblivious to his gaze, it was more like an embrace in a secret world where he had no part to play. He watched as the woman, glorious in lamp light, hair cascading over her shoulders, bent to the man holding her close. Again he felt the intruder. More than once on seeing them together he had sensed a union both rich and rare that nothing could tear apart. Quietly he sat until the record ended, taking the spell with it, and the dancers broke apart. David gave a soft cough looking down at his watch. 'Time I went, good people,' he said, starting to rise.

'Bloody hell, you're not, Pederson. Ye haven't heard the newest acquisition yet!' Andrew was already putting another record on the turntable, grinning as if the interlude just witnessed had never occurred. Pederson could have sworn that the Flights were good and ready for bed.

But no, Paul Whiteman and his band were suddenly in full swing with Andrew, violin tucked under his chin, adlibbing, going his own way without a care in the world, sweeping his audience along with him. Gaiety filled the small room as Andrew played and Greta danced alone, shoes kicked off under the settee, pirouetting through the house from kitchen to the verandah. Again and again the gramophone was wound up until in the end player and dancer collapsed to 'Bravo!'s and applause by their audience of one. Hours of talk, music and laughter melted and slipped by until close to three, when they agreed with some reluctance that the party was over.

Slightly impaired, the Flights bundled the doctor into his smart shining Daimler and under the crisp, starry night with arms around each other, they waved the weaving car off.

'Och, what a night.' Andrew gave Greta a hug. 'Doesn'a happen too often, eh, bonny dearr?'

'It happens every night and day, you idiot.'

He kissed her for that.

It was too late for bed, Andrew announced as they returned to the kitchen, the room still warm from the stove's glowing coals. In loving companionship they made toast and fresh tea and watched dawn cast a latticework of scarlet and gold over the morning sky.

Saturday dancing lessons were over and it was warm enough for Greta to put on swimming togs under her dress, throw a towel over her shoulders and take her bicycle out of the shed. Time enough for a quick swim down at the waterhole before the day ended. She couldn't get there quickly enough, and already in her imagination she lay under the riverbank bottlebrush, the current flowing over her skin and through her hair. The sound of a car brought on a frown.

'Damn!' Leaning the bike against the fence, she waited for

David Pedersen to drive up to the front gate. 'David! Two visits in a week . . . And you, you naughty man, what have you there?'

'A small thirst quencher, my dear. And have you any of those cheese straws left over from the other night?'

They sat on the verandah, David with a glass of brandy in his hand and for Greta a sweet, hot drink of a new product that she'd seen and bought in town. The look and smell of the condensed milky beverage brought a pained expression to the doctor's face.

'Must you drink that in my presence, Greta?'

'It's coffee.'

'Absolute rotgut.'

'And you should talk!' Unabashed and making noises of supreme satisfaction, Greta refused to be disturbed by David Pederson's disapproval.

'How's Andrew keeping?' The sudden change in the light bantering between them made her heart trip. It was clear to see that David Pederson had not just come over for an afternoon chat.

'Well, you saw him a few nights ago.'

'You would let me know if anything goes wrong, wouldn't you, Greta?'

'I said he's fine.'

'You said nothing at all. You didn't even answer my question.'

'Well he's good! Better! A hundred per cent. Happy?'

'If you are.'

She noticed a slight trembling as he lifted the glass to his lips. She wasn't surprised – Dr Pederson had not held a scalpel in his hand for years. But his eyes were searching, the gaze steady, as if he knew about last night and that she was on the brink of confessing a concern.

'Well, there *is* something.' She tried to laugh it off. 'I suppose it's a something nothing. But last night when Andy came home, he just seemed a little – a little vague. He sat on the back steps for a good half hour. Didn't say much, and that's not like him either.'

'Did you speak to him about it?'

'Well, no. I just felt that he wouldn't have answered. I didn't think it was a good idea at the time.'

'Perhaps you are right.'

How could she repeat the strangeness of Andy's words when he finally spoke? He had walked over to the table and picked up one of the apples in the fruit bowl. It was a large red delicious – the only kind that seemed to be sold in the town. He had held it in his palm as if judging the weight of it. 'Can ye see anything?' he'd said.

'No, I —'

'Look, woman! But don't touch it,' he had warned her sharply.

'What *are* you talking about, Andy?'

He had smelt it and then shaken his head, eyes narrowing, steely grey, while in confusion Greta watched him, and as if it was made of glass, he carefully placed the apple to the side. 'I'll return it tomorrow. They canna' do that to us.' That was all he had to say. No more explanations. Nothing. In silence he had eaten his meal, then without another word had gone to bed while she sat at the kitchen table alone, wondering and remembering David's words, 'You're lucky he's alive – malaria can affect the brain.' He had been in deep sleep when she finally joined him but not before she'd thrown every piece of fruit in the bowl over the back fence for the goats to eat.

His arms were around her the instant he'd awakened, stroking her hair and whispering endearments; hot words that had aroused.

'Good morning, Mrs Flight. If it's Saturday, I claim my dues. Lie still, my sweet, while I take them.' Their lovemaking as the sun came up was all the sweeter for Greta having him back again. She hadn't dared ask about the strange mood that he'd brought home with him the night before. Better to act as if nothing had happened. It might never happen again.

A pat on the shoulder brought her back to the verandah and David, who was calmly eating through the last of the cheese straws. 'This vagueness you're talking about. Happen often?' His eyes were enquiring, even shrewd, as he studied her. There came a distinct feeling that he knew she was keeping the full truth from him. A feeling of shame swept over her. David *is* Andy's doctor. A good doctor, and she would insult him by not revealing Andy's actions of last night.

'David, there is something else.'

Without interruption she spoke of the bizarre behaviour she had witnessed, feeling the weight of fear and anxiety leaving her while David listened to the end. Drained, she leant back into her chair.

'Now you have the full story. All of it.'

David nodded. 'I suspected as much. Cerebral malaria – thank God he came through with flying colours.'

'It could return, though . . .'

'With luck it may never be as bad as that again. He could have sweated it right out of his system. It happens.' David poured himself another drink. 'If this vagueness, as you call it, returns, I want you to tell me. Malaria can do funny things to its victims. Especially the virulent kind as Andrew had. What about worries – any that you know of?'

'No more than anyone else around here.'

It was not a question that Pederson was in the habit of asking.

'Hmm. By the way, where is he?'

'He'll be home soon. It's Irish stew tonight; like to stay?' She tried to sound enthusiastic, but she'd had enough of Dr David Pederson for one day.

'You're tempting me, but no.' He stood up, head poised as if listening, a slow smile curving his lips. 'Well, now. Marelda's in for a surprise.' His smile broadened at the faint sound of a man singing. The song grew louder and the words more distinct as the singer weaved into view.

Good Lord above
Send down a dove
With wings as sharp as razors
To cut off the lugs
Of the wicked mugs
Who slash the poor man's wages.

'Never thought I'd hear those lines again,' Greta murmured, remembering the disappointment of Cairns.

'It's Biff Larkin's homecoming ditty when he's in his cups, and a signal for Marelda to hide the cash in hand until he sobers up. Otherwise . . .' He left it up for Greta to guess the rest.

Even from where she was standing, Greta could see that Larkin was a man no one would dare raise a fist to. Pick and shovel work had broadened his back and shoulders, and his imposing girth spoke of years spent in a hotel bar room. As they watched, Larkin stopped short of coming closer to the house. He stood for a while as if wondering where his steps had taken him, then did a sharp right-hand turn and with obvious effort walked in a straight line towards Marelda's back gate. 'Relda! Put another spud in the pot, y' old man's come home for a decent feed!'

Intrigued as to how Marelda would react to the bellowing command, Greta shooshed Pederson down the verandah steps. 'Bye, David, can't miss out on this!'

Like any village gossip, she hurried to the back door in time to see the husband struggling with the looped wire that opened the gate and Marelda flying across the yard with the Larkin brood only inches away from her apron strings. 'Let me open it, y' silly muggins.' It was obvious that Marelda was more than pleased to put another spud in the pot and that drunk or sober, her man was home. There was a happy clamouring from the Larkins as they escorted father and husband into the house.

Absorbed in the homecoming they failed to notice Spanner, with Dorothy Stone perched on the crossbar of his bike, riding into view. Arriving at the open gate he stopped, one foot touching the ground for balance, allowing Dorothy to alight.

For some reason he seemed reluctant to join in the family celebrations and Greta, recalling the castigations that Marelda heaped on Spanner whenever he mentioned the girl, was not surprised. Even so, she was puzzled. Spanner of all people knew what the farmer Stone was like concerning his foster-daughter, and Marelda for one wouldn't appreciate an irate father turning up at the door with a shotgun as he'd been known to do.

The light was fading and still they stood there, as if waiting for the ruckus inside the house to quieten. Spanner put his arm around Dorothy's shoulder, but instead of taking her through the gate he crossed the road, walking towards Greta's own backyard.

'Mrs Flight,' he called softly, 'are y' home?'

'Nowhere else, Spanner.' She moved to the top of the stairs so he could see her.

'Is Andy there?'

'Will be soon.'

'Can I – we – come in?' Without waiting for an answer, he led Dorothy towards the steps. The sight of the girl's tear-swollen face had Greta running down to meet them. There was no need to ask the cause as they gentled the girl up the stairs.

Tears were one thing, but the way Dorothy had stumbled into the kitchen and the look of grim concern on Spanner's face as he helped her to a chair told Greta that it was more than tears that had him defying Stone's threats and rages.

'Spanner, what's happened?'

'Just undo them buttons, Mrs Flight,' he pointed to the shirt dress that Dorothy was wearing, 'and see for yourself. I'll wait outside.'

Intuition made her half aware of what to expect as she carefully undid the two top buttons. 'You poor little love!'

Dorothy, now limp, arms hanging down each side, made no attempt to stop Greta's dismayed inspection. Bruises disfigured her budding breasts and by the look of it the girl had been beaten severely. Without giving it a thought, Greta helped her off the chair and led her into the single bedroom.

'Spanner!' she called out. 'A basin of cold water. There's a jug in the ice chest and a sponge in the bathroom.' By now Greta had removed Dorothy's dress and from the raised welts from back to buttock and a patch of broken skin, it was obvious to see that a razor strop had been used. When some of the red heat had been sponged away and aspros and glasses of water had done their work, Greta found Spanner still waiting in the kitchen.

'Well.' Greta poured out a measure from the bottle of brandy that David Pederson had left behind, handing it to Spanner. 'You'd better have this. By the look of it, you need it.'

'I'll kill the mongrel.' His throat worked as if struggling against tears, and his blue eyes, so like his mother's, clouded with anger. 'He's found out about us. Nuff said. I found her crouching in the grass outside the bacon factory. Don't ask me how she managed to get there.' A sob escaped him. 'Black and blue. I could string him up for that!'

'A fat lot of good that will do you. We'll have to think up something better than that.' There was no thought of sending Dorothy back to the farm and with her on the bed in the single room, Greta was already up to her neck in Spanner's mire, *and with Andy due home any minute.* Greta couldn't help thinking Spanner should thank Lady Luck that the Riverbank Players had the Saturday night off, owing to the takeover of the School of Arts Hall by visiting missionaries.

'Spanner, what do you intend doing?'

'I – I don't know. I'll think of something.' He downed the brandy and shuddered. 'Orr! How do they drink the stuff? Puts the teeth on edge, but thanks,' he said, handing the glass back to Greta.

It was dark enough for her to light up the kitchen lamp, the busyness with the wick giving her time to work out the next move. Carefully she fitted the globe into place, then turned up the flame.

'You know he'll be looking for her, and he could have a fairly good idea where she might be.'

'I was hoping that Mum . . . She does have a soft spot for Dorrie —'

'Oh, Lordy, Lordy. Hope springs eternal.'

'No, I mean it. Once Mum sees those bruises . . .'

As the words lay between them, the homecoming beep of the utility horn announced that Andy had arrived. He was soon taking the back steps two at a time.

'I smell a smell, m' bonny —' He stopped in his stride. 'Spanner!'

Before anything else could be said, Greta was bundling Spanner out the door. 'You'd better warn Marelda and your dad to expect a visitor!' It wasn't the wisest thing to do, but she felt it was better that Spanner stay out of sight when she gave Andy the news about the unannounced guest in the second bedroom.

CHAPTER SEVENTEEN

'I see you have something to tell me.' As if unconcerned, Andrew strolled over to the stove, lifted the lid off a saucepan and gave an appreciative sniff. 'Something's happened. A problem?'

'Well, yes, there is . . . sort of.'

As the 'problem' in question was now in the deep sleep of exhaustion, Greta could see no point in delaying the evening meal; it was easy enough to dish up and eat while she recounted Spanner's plea for help. Andy kept shaking his head in disbelief over her description of the welts and bruising, and sympathy overflowed as she told of Spanner finding Dorothy crouched in the grass outside the bacon factory. 'Like some sick young animal, poor kid.'

Andrew pushed his plate aside. 'Sorry, love, but I have no stomach for it.' It was understandable, for she herself had only picked at her food.

Brooding, Andy remained still, head bent over crossed arms resting on the table while fear plucked at Greta's heart. Was there going to be a repeat of last night's silence? Of Andy's strange words that had made no sense? Anger flooded her. Blast Spanner and his troubles. Why dump them on her doorstep? And why wasn't he over here to take the girl off their hands? She leapt out of her chair to look outside, anxious, and wondering just what was going on next door. Everything seemed unnaturally quiet, from the silence in her own kitchen to the silence of the black night, although there was lamplight shining in the Larkins' house.

'Then the poor lass must stay here.' His voice was strong and confident enough to make her jump. She turned to find Andy spearing a dumpling and slathering it with gravy as if the afternoon's complications and perplexities had never existed. 'But for how long? Tha's something else. You agree?'

'Of course. We – all of us will work something out, but Spanner should be here.' She went to the door again in time to witness Marelda carrying a hurricane lamp, followed by Biff and Spanner leaving the house. She could hear Marelda ordering her brood to get into bed. 'We're only over the road, and I want no fightin', no sneakin' outside to stickybeak, and if I hear as much of a whisper or a fart, *look out*! Greta and Andy, do yer mind? We're comin' over. Things have gotta be talked about.'

'You can say that again,' replied Greta under her breath, clearing away plates to make room for the Larkin invasion.

Greta had never considered Marelda as slender, although she wasn't grossly overweight either; she had the comfortable look of a country woman who'd never dream of a day without morning and afternoon tea with a scone or a slab of Kentish cake. Spanner, comfortable in a Jacky Howe and with youthful, smooth muscles, was a good head taller than Marelda, but could never match his father in corpulence and height. The trio gave the Flights an impressive picture of family solidarity.

'Mr Flight and Missus, Biff's the name and Relda's told me all about you and all of it good.' Looking completely sober, his boom bounced off the walls, somehow making the roomy kitchen appear much smaller. 'Spanner seems to 'ave done the wrong thing dumping young Dorrie in yer lap. Sorry about that. We've come to take her off yer hands.'

Greta, acting out the Yunnabilla code of offering a cup of tea to anyone placing a foot inside the door, handed around cups of the steaming brew with she and Andy in tandem saying that Spanner had made the right move . . . for the time being.

'The poor wee thing canna' be sent back to that house.'

'And if we report it, and we should —'

'For Christ's sake, Mum, what are y' talking about?'

'Shut up and let me finish.' As if biding for time, Marelda spooned four teaspoons of sugar into her cup. 'The girl's underage for one thing. Report the beating and she'll be shoved quick smart into another foster home.'

'Don't you think I know that?' Desperation roughened Spanner's voice. 'We've got to hide her!'

'Not in our house, and how many times do I have to say it? We've got the kids to think about, and don't you believe that Stone doesn't know where Dorrie is. Biff!' Marelda turned on a silent husband. 'Don't just sit there, say something! What are we going to do?'

'How the hell should I know? I don't know!' Biff's thump on the table rattled cups in their saucers. 'But I know what I'll do if he comes round here.'

'Only thing for Dorrie and me is to shoot through. Get out of the place.'

'With an underage girl?' Marelda shot back. 'And have the police chasing after you? Is that what you want?'

Greta felt that all this had been said over and over again in the Larkin kitchen and had taken them nowhere. Any minute Dorothy could wake up and her appearance would do nothing to calm the overwrought atmosphere of the room. And what about Andy? Why should Andy be badgered? Worry. Wasn't that what David had been probing her about? But Andy seemed to be taking things calmly, standing at ease against the washing-up bench, his pipe tobacco pungent enough to kill a mossie stone dead, as she had told him more than once.

'Verbal ping-pong. Tha's all ye are on about.' Andrew's voice held the ring of authority that stopped the Larkins in their tracks. Greta, about to pour out a second round of tea, blinked, teapot held high. 'However,' removing the pipe from his mouth and using the stem as a pointer to emphasise what he was about to say, 'I have a plan. It could work. Spanner, I've heard you want to marry this young lady. Right?'

'More than anything, even if it's just to get her away from that bastard.'

'That sounds more like pity to me.' Andrew was shaking his head. 'It has to be more than that. Do you love her? *Really* love her – adore her?'

'Course I do.' Beneath his tan Spanner's cheeks darkened.

'Well, laddie, let us all hear you say it.'

'I love her, and yeah, I guess I adore her. She's a beaut kid.' Warming to the idea, he finished off with something he'd heard in a song. 'I'd walk a million miles for her Andy, honest.' Speechless, mother and father listened, open-mouthed. Such endearments and wild statements had never in their years together passed their own lips. Andrew, seemingly satisfied, turned his attention to the pair. 'And if it can be done – a marriage, I'm talking about – as Spanner's parents, would you go along with it? A legal marriage would certainly protect Dorothy from the wrath of that maniac.'

Greta had to hide a grin and a sent a wink of encouragement over the heads of the Larkins. It was again the Andy in Mannie's office conning himself into a job on the first day they had landed in Yunnabilla. It was a good act that had the Larkins thirsting for more.

'Well, put it down to happenchance,' Andrew carried on, 'but this weekend David Pederson is entertaining some nobs – old friends – from Townsville and Cairns. A soirée, as he calls it. A small peccadillo.' He sucked in his cheeks and with a raise of an eyebrow included them all in an ironic dismissal of the doctor's term of speech. 'But we'll allow him that. He's a good chap as well as a friend.' Another round of the pipe stem demanded their full attention. Andrew was enjoying himself. 'Now, among this select gathering is a magistrate – David told me this himself – from Cairns. Too late to barge in now, but magistrates can marry people, if the circumstances warrant it. Young lads and lasses for one thing, especially if the girl is expecting.' He gave Spanner a glare of picaroon intensity. 'She's not, is she?'

'No! I – we – I've never touched her. Not that way.' Blushing, Spanner raked fingers through his hair, but it was easy to see the hope in his eyes. 'You mean a magistrate could marry us?'

'Aye.'

'But there's none here.'

'Not here. In Cairns, as I have said.'

Andrew glanced at the kitchen clock, mentally ticking off the hours to complete the rest of his scheming. 'For a start, Dorothy stays here. No one need know.' He shot a look of enquiry over to Biff and Marelda. 'The bains. Are they in the picture?'

Biff shook his head. 'No. Don't think so. Marelda shunted them outside as soon as Spanner turned up. Knew something was wrong, but.' Biff's answer had the gruffness of a man realising that matters had passed out of his hands and he was incapable of snatching them back. Andrew was the pacemaker and Biff was aware that all he could do was follow.

'Good.' Andrew nodded, satisfied. 'They don't need to know. We'll keep it that way.'

At that moment Dorothy walked into the room. Her tears had dried, and to Greta's surprise and admiration, she looked quietly composed. She acknowledged the Larkins with a faint shy smile as Spanner sprang up, putting his arms around her, but noticing a slight wince of pain he let her go, contrition written all over his face.

'It's all right, Spanner.' Carefully she sat on his offered chair, winced again but remained sitting at an odd angle.

'I've been awake for a good while. Listening to you all.' She turned to Marelda. 'I'm sorry, Mrs Larkin – I —'

'Don't say anything, Dorothy. What's done is done. And we Larkins stick together. And by the looks of it, you'll be one of us before long.' Marelda fumbled in her apron pocket and produced a crumpled handkerchief in response to tears brimming in Dorothy's eyes. 'Now, now, m' girl, don't start bawling.' She sniffed and blew her own nose before handing the handkerchief over. 'Wipe them tears and get back to bed. Yer in no state to be sittin' up and you can listen to what's going on just as good lying down. Spanner,' she ordered, happy to be in charge, if only momentarily, 'see that she lies down and come straight back here. Don't worry, love, it'll be all good news in the morning.' Her looks were fierce, challenging them to contradict her. 'I hope,' she finished under her breath.

They talked late into the night with Andrew mostly leading the way. Only one person should be informed, he insisted, and that was David Pederson. Although they knew he was entertaining the magistrate from Cairns, they thought it politic to wait until the weekend was over. The possibility that David might refuse to help never entered Greta's or Andrew's head. They reasoned that the doctor would want to examine Dorothy's injuries before informing the magistrate, by phone they presumed, of the situation. If a marriage was agreed upon sight unseen, arrangements could be made so that on arrival in Cairns the two could be married without unnecessary delays. Biff Larkin's triumph came when he confided, to Marelda's astonishment, that he had a nest egg in the bank in case he dropped dead, and a will to go with it. 'Wasn't goin' to leave you and the kids high and dry, Relda; y' old man don't booze the lot all of the time.' There was more than enough, he told them, to get Spanner and 'Dorrie' to Brisbane. At the suggestion that work could be found there, Spanner cried him down.

'No need to go that far, Dad, it's up to Dorrie anyway. I reckon I'll find something in Cairns and if I don't we'll come back here. I can get a job anytime at the bacon factory.'

Greta had a strong feeling that Dorothy would be only too pleased to put a thousand miles between her and Farmer Stone.

Thinking of that long journey now more than twelve months behind her, and recalling the laughter, the hope and ardour that accompanied them every mile of the way, she was startled to hear Andy say, 'Greta can go with them.'

'You've done enough already, and —'

'No, Marelda, you've got the bains to think about. Don't forget all this is on the hush-hush. Ye'll make a gossip all over town if you disappear for a day or two with Spanner missing as well and Stone kicking up a stink – ye can count on it. As for the young lass, we'll keep her out of sight. Whether she is here or there, who would know? And as Greta intends going to Cairns in the next few days,' he tapped his nose Mannie Coleman-style, 'on business, of course . . .'

Greta had to bite her tongue. It was the first she'd heard about it.

At sun-up Stone was hammering at the door of the Larkins' front verandah. 'Spanner Larkin! Yer thieving bastard, where's Dorothy? Dorothy!' His bawling command had dogs barking and a few of the curious abandoned a Sunday sleep-in and strolled to their front fences so as not to miss out on what promised to be a good belt-up between young Spanner and Mad Hatter Stone. The sudden appearance of the smallest Larkin hanging over the verandah railings seemed to be the only result of his yammering.

'Where is she, you young whelp?'

It was enough to send the youngster scuttling off around the side verandah to a safer place and to send Stone hurtling along the front fence to the back of the house followed by his truck-driving wife, the truck belching fumes in cadence with Stone's fury. He stopped in mid-stride, ran over to the truck and through the cabin window hauled out a shotgun. Still baying for Spanner's blood, he wrenched at the gate and was halfway up the yard when the back door of Marelda's kitchen burst open.

Like some behemoth, Biff Larkin lumbered down the steps to meet him, bare-chested and in his pyjama pants. Stone, with sinews of wire and an evil temper that could give him the strength of four men when aroused, stood his ground.

'She's here, I know.' Nostrils were distended with his heavy breathing.

'Who are y' talkin' about?' Biff scratched a hairy belly.

'You know who I'm talking about – my daughter!'

'Not here, she ain't.'

'An' tell that God-rotting son of yours to come out here and face me like the thieving cur he is!'

'Spanner's at the factory where he should be. Extra shift.'

'Yer lying!' Stone was wild-eyed and trembling with rage. 'I'm tellin' you, Larkin, hand that whore of a daughter over, or I'll get the police.'

'I said she's not here.' There was menace in Biff's rumbling denial. He took a step closer to the man, ignoring the gun. 'I'll say it again, she's not here and nobody calls Biff Larkin a liar. You bring in the police if you want to, but if you, you mongrel dog, set foot inside this yard again with a gun, I'll break the bloody thing and shove it up yer jack as far as it'll go!'

By now Marelda, petrified and surrounded by her offspring, stood witness as Biff closed the distance between himself and the farmer. He broke into a bellowing run so fleet of foot it gave Stone no chance to either raise the gun or defend himself.

To the crack of a massive fist on jawbone, Stone catapulted backwards into the air and fell a good yard away from Biff's feet. It was over in seconds and, not pausing for breath, the big man picked up the inert farmer, flung him over his shoulder, picked up the gun, striding out of the yard to the truck and a fearful wife. He hurled the gun into the back tray, flung open the door and dumped Stone onto the seat. 'Take him home, Mrs Stone. He won't be pullin' weeds for a while, I reckon.'

CHAPTER EIGHTEEN

No one awake could have missed hearing the ruckus exploding over the Larkin house that morning and Greta, keeping out of sight, had seen and heard it all the moment the truck had driven around the corner. With Andy and Dorothy still asleep she had crept into the kitchen. Now sitting alone, drinking morning coffee, her mind was in a tumble over the night and morning events. She had no desire to go to Cairns as nursemaid; but there was no doubt that if the man found his foster charge she'd end up as mincemeat.

'Have they gone?' Dorothy was peering out from the short hall-way. 'I heard the truck coming up . . . then him . . . I've been hiding under the bed.'

Pity at the sight of the frightened face and a body wracked with trembling made Greta's mind up for her. She'd chaperone the pair right to the magistrate's door, that's for sure! Holding out her hand, she replied, 'Yes, they've gone. Now come and sit down – if you can.' With the picture of Biff bundling the farmer into his truck stamped in her memory, she gave Dorothy a wide grin. 'You won't see him for a good while, if ever. Biff landed him one. A corker!

Never seen the likes of it. Now what would you like? Tea, coffee, some toast, nice and buttery?'

Andrew, standing in the spot that Dorothy had just vacated, rubbed his hands together. 'Ah, toast and tea. Just what the doctor ordered. And talking of doctors, young lady,' he was the warm rock that Dorothy could lean against, 'we'll get David to come over and look at those bruises tomorrow, eh?'

In a piccaninny dawn they had caught the four-thirty motor and – hallelujah, Greta had breathed – with not a soul that counted in sight. David Pederson had words to say that he should have been called earlier, and had taken only seconds to examine the abused, tender skin. 'I'll get in touch with Harry straight-away and see what can be done.' Andrew had gone back to town with him and returned in less than an hour with news that the magistrate, friend Harry, would perform the ceremony in Cairns without delay. So far, so good.

As the morning sun gilded the distant sea and flooded the patchwork quilt of cane farms with light far below, Greta wondered how Dorothy was coping with the bounce and rattle of the rail-motor. It seemed that nothing, not even discomfort, could erase the sheen of happiness and excitement on the girl's face as she gripped Spanner's hand, as if never to let him go. They had hurtled passed the Barron Falls and were now halfway down the gorge.

On arrival at the station it was only Greta who was given more than a second glance in the business of catching trains and pur-chasing tickets for the sunshine route to Brisbane. Counting their lucky stars, Spanner noted there was not one familiar face in the railmotor's return to the Tablelands. 'Not long to go now, lovey; two o'clock and we'll be able call you Mrs Larkin, ay?'

Pretending it was spring, the clouds over the sea port were rain-free, and a breeze frolicking along the streets kept the humidity at bay. After the quiet of Yunnabilla the bustle in the main street gave Greta a lift of unexpected pleasure, and a surprising number of fashionably dressed matrons and office girls had Greta for the first time in her life feeling that corn cobs were growing out of her ears. Soon fix that up, she promised herself, as she ushered Dorothy into what appeared to be the most exclusive dress shop in town.

'The prettiest dress you can buy and things to go with it. Isn't that what Biff told us to do?' Dorothy, stunned by the array of satins, flowing silks, gay cottons and flowered hats, could only nod. Biff had also insisted, in spite of protestations from Spanner, that a honeymoon should be spent at Green Island in a shack belonging to a fishing mate. Greta could only send blessings to the man who wouldn't take no for an answer. Outfitting Dorothy was going to be a piece of very enjoyable cake!

The girl stood before the full-length mirror in the hotel room and saw a young woman in a floral georgette dress that flattered and clung to rounded hips, her legs shapely in silk stockings and smart court shoes. On the bed was a wide-brimmed, creamy French straw hat and matching gloves. She turned around, looking over her shoulder, admiring.

'It's lovely, Greta.' Pain and fear for the moment were banished. 'Can't believe its me.'

'All you need now is a tiny bit of lippy and rouge – not much,' she said as Dorothy drew back. 'Just a little, trust me.' Dorothy pulled a face under the onslaught of the snow-down powder puff, then submitted happily while Greta, with a fairy's touch, applied the rouge to the smooth and lightly tanned cheeks. She went carefully with the pink lipstick. 'Now the hat.' Placing it at just the right angle on Dorothy's sun-bleached hair, she stood back to view her handiwork with satisfaction. 'Perfect! Take another look at yourself.'

Dorothy was bubbling with delight. 'What's Spanner going to say, ay?'

'All he has to say for the moment is "I do". The rest will come later.' Greta looked down at her watch, her voice brisk now that all preparations were completed. 'Time to move, Dorrie. Spanner and Sam will be waiting at the courthouse. You've got time to be five minutes late.' She gave Dorothy a wink. 'That's the bride's prerogative, wouldn't y' say?'

It wasn't often that Greta Flight didn't give herself the once-over from head to toe before going out. A quick glance in the mirror was all she allowed herself as they left the room, but it was time enough to see that the new American rose voile suited her down to the ground.

Sam Riding, on short notice by a telegram from Yunnabilla, had met them outside the Railway Hotel. That he'd be coerced into acting as witness to a wedding was the last thing he imagined. Although Spanner was a stranger, he happily took the young man under his wing with instructions from Greta to fit him up right and proper with a jacket, trousers and a decent tie.

Years ago Sam had cast off the usual serge suit favoured by most males for important occasions, swearing that a coat in this bloody heat was madness. Now he stood with Spanner, his white shirt and collar starched and as pristine as the Japanese laundry could make it. In concession to the importance of the day, he wore a tie. As the two women approached, each man in his own way greeted them. Sam, thinking that Greta was the most gorgeous woman he had ever had the good fortune to meet, grinned from ear to ear. 'Greta, you scrub up bloody beautiful.' Spanner, standing straight with pride and love, quietly took Dorothy's hand and together they lead the way into the courthouse.

The ceremony was simple as it was short, played out in a room richly lined with rainforest timbers to match the silky oak desk and chairs, a draped Union Jack and a framed print of King George the room's only decoration. But it was enough for submerged longings to remind Greta that marriage for her was a remote possibility. As the couple took their vows, she visualised their life together, wherever they would find themselves. There would be happiness and children to seal their union, something that must never happen for her and Andy, she acknowledged with a pang. What a start in life it would be for their poor little bastard child if people found out its parents weren't married! And what about Andy's other child – boy or girl? At least that baby was legitimate . . .

Annoyed with herself, Greta brushed away all sad and lonely thoughts, giving full attention to the finale of the drama that had had its beginnings in Yunnabilla: a good, sweet girl on the threshold of a brand-new life with a strong and loving man beside her. A fitting end to the story.

They stood on the wharf, watching and waiting until the small boat for Green Island reached the channel that would shepherd it through Trinity Inlet.

'First things first.' Sam Riding tugged off his tie and shoved it into his pocket. 'Don't ask me to do that again – the tie, I mean.'

Greta had already removed her hat, hair ruffled by a breeze coming in with the tide, but the sun was biting her back. There had been no time for celebrations. On leaving the courthouse it had been a rush for the newlyweds to get down to the boat.

'What I need now is a good cold beer and to get my feet out of these spikes.'

'Well, how about putting them under one of those comfortable cane-chair jobs they have at Hides Hotel? Not my usual watering hole,' he hastily assured Greta. 'The old Railway or the Barbary Coast does me.'

'Whatever you say, and lead on, Macduff!'

After an early rise and twelve hours of high activity, Greta felt she deserved a break and the idea of sitting in the coolness of Hides Hotel, swapping the news with Sam, held great appeal. First stop was at the post office, though, to send a cryptic telegram to Andy: DONE. HOME TOMORROW. LOVE.

Punkahs cooled the air and stirred the potted palms of the lounge as Greta sipped her second beer with relish. 'Umm . . . icy cold, just how I like it.' She told Sam that the ladies' closets – and that's all you could describe them as – of the Yunnabilla hotels discouraged a person to even poke their nose through the door. 'And you're called a fancy girl if you're seen there more than once in a month! I dunno . . .'

'Not thinking you'd like to live here, ay?' Sam felt in his glory sitting with the best looker in town. 'As I've said, the *Pelican* is just about ready to take off again.'

'Don't even think about it, Sam. In spite of my moaning and groaning, Yunnabilla isn't all that bad. The dancing school is doing well. Ten pupils now and you know all about the Riverbank Players.' There had been a three-way sharing of news between Andy, Mannie and Sam over the past twelve months.

'Andy and Mannie, ay? Thought they'd find things in common.' As if he had engendered the whole friendship, Sam looked hugely pleased with himself. 'And what did he think about this little caper we've just gone through?'

'Mannie? Doesn't even know I'm here. Although it doesn't matter now.' She also couldn't help feeling pleased with herself.

Giving a comfortable belch as he took Greta's empty glass, Sam asked, 'Another?'

'I've had enough, thanks all the same.'

'Good. I was only being polite.' There was a sudden change in Sam's benign demeanour. 'I know you think I'm an old political ratbag, and the way things are going I've got good reason to be. But before I start, tell me —' He pinned her with eyes both keen and questing, '— and don't bugger me around, Greta. How's business?'

It was the second time she'd been asked the same question in so many days. 'Good. Fine.' Her voice was sharp and to the point.

'I'm talking more about Andy. Mannie always has a finger in more than one pie. But from what I gather farmers – tobacco farmers – around your way are pulling up stakes. Ready to move.'

'Well, Andy's getting enough to make out.'

'Getting paid for it?'

'Sam!' She'd bet two quid that Mannie had been keeping Sam up to date. 'I suppose you've heard about the pumpkins.' She referred to a heap that had been dumped in their backyard to clear a debt. Sam Riding dropped the subject.

'Sorry, Greta, none of my business. I know you think I'm too fond of opening my big mouth and, by the way, I'm no Commie either.' Before going on, he reached out for the tobacco tin on the table, lifted the lid with his thumb, then thinking better of it, put it back into his pocket. 'Look . . . The ute's just around the corner and I'm asking you to come along with an open heart and mind. I've got a little job to do and something to show you. Won't take up an hour of your time.'

'You want me to see the *Pelican,* don't you?' In spite of the seriousness on Sam's face she deliberately kept up the pretence of amusement, already guessing that the *Pelican* was far from his mind. A quick roll in the hay? It was a fleeting thought, instantly dismissed. Not likely. Not Sam. But there was something about the look he gave her that showed a different side to him, and there was only one way to find out.

'Now you've got me interested. Sure, I'll come along.'

'Here we are.' Sam cut the motor. They were the first words either of them had spoken since leaving the town. The utility was parked beside what appeared to be a large, loosely fenced area enclosing, as far as she could make out, sheds and a grandstand. Puzzled, Greta looked around her. If it wasn't for high-heel shoes and an afternoon sun sending down a final blowtorch of heat, they could have walked the distance Sam had driven. Shouts of a football being kicked around came from a schoolyard behind her, and a few little girls played hopscotch in front of a small extension that looked like a general store, attached to a house and a garden of ferns and palms.

'Well, I'm waiting. What am I supposed to see that's so important?' Against the hot leather of the seat she felt an irritation of stickiness and the itch of prickly heat began to burn. Wishing she hadn't agreed to Sam's mysterious invitation and the accompanying silence of the drive, she was ready to be driven straight back to her hotel room for a shower and a cup of tea. Sam stood at the open door of the car. 'C'mon, this won't take long,' he said, holding out one hand for her to step down. The other gripped a pine delivery box balanced on his shoulder. She could only surmise that it had been stored in the back tray of the utility. No sooner had her feet touched the ground than Sam was off, heading towards the park's entrance toting what she now realised was, by the bottle of tomato sauce on top, a box of groceries, and leaving her to follow.

I'm mad, completely mad! was the grumbling thought as she caught up with him.

Once inside the park all that Greta could see was an expanse of dirt and scattered weeds and grasses and the grandstand with a row of dilapidated open-sided sheds to the side. As they approached the buildings she noticed for the first time a man squatting beside a tripod and a large blackened billy can over a small fire. Gypsies was her first impression, but as she and Sam drew nearer it seemed to be the signal for a group of men to appear from out of the sheds and for the squatting man to rise to his feet. He ambled over to meet them.

'G'day, Sam.' The greeting was polite but his eyes were on the cardboard box. 'Thanks, mate,' he said, lifting it off Sam's shoulders. It hurt to look at him and she had to turn her eyes away. Never had she seen such pitiful gratitude. That he was past pride was easy to see and she wondered if he had the strength to take hold of the heavy load. By now the others had come to lend a hand and although some were sinewy skin and bone, none were as poorly emaciated as the man someone called Clarrie.

A jolt of remembrance took her back to the scattering of men they had seen from the train with the sugarcane closing over them. The police on the hunt. The unemployed. A rag-bag flotsam with sagging trousers held up by rope and sweat-stained belts, coats on thin shoulders that once would have sat snugly on their beef-fed muscles and brawn. Was this the end of endurance? The end of the line?

She could only guess at the hopeless state that the 'Great Depression', as it was now called, caused. Newspapers wrote of the desperation, the reliance on soup kitchens and hand-outs, of wives and children left behind while their men tramped the roads in search of work, shunted from one town to the next for ration coupons worth a meagre six shillings a week, and the sad rest of it. Distance had muted the reality of the disaster and somehow people in towns like Yunnabilla with friends and families close at hand seemed to survive – at least for the moment, was Greta's uneasy thought.

Snatches of conversation drifted like the smoke from the camp fire around her head as the men shared out the food or consigned it to the community chest, as they did with the side of bacon, the tomato sauce and the porridge. Tins of baked beans, flour and at least a good four pounds of sausages, tea and sugar, plum jam and rice – and smiles broadened when at the very last, tins of tobacco and cigarette papers were handed around.

'About how many men camping in the grounds now?' Sam was asking.

'Close to fifty, last count – not all here at the moment but more are on the way. Just nowhere else to go, mate.' Greta heard an ironic half-laugh. 'Word has it that the good folk of Cairns want to get rid of us, pronto. Clean up the grounds.' He spoke of a meeting held and the council's promise that shelter would be found with camp stretchers and showers. To Greta the man speaking looked hardly different from the others. The same eyes sunken by hope long lost, the narrow gutted thinness of deprivation. He was called Joe. Nothing else.

'What about the Tablelands?'

'Not a hope in hell. They don't like to see us around —' He broke off with a fit of coughing and hawked up a gobbet of phlegm, rubbing it into the dust with his shoe. Breathless and wheezing, he carried on. 'No,' he repeated, 'won't have nothin' to do with us, and if there are any jobs to be had, wandering bludgers, as they call us, aren't welcome.'

A huddle, talking softly, were pointed out. 'They arrived yesterday. Seems like they were pulled off the train comin' down and tossed into the quod.' Surprised, Greta heard Joe laugh again but this time with real humour. 'Bloody policeman and his missus came good, but. Dished out goat stew and bread and fruit cake. Sent the fellas on their way the next morning with a timetable and where's the best place to get aboard!'

'So they're not all bastards, ay?'

'Few and far between, mate.'

The pavilion was casting long shadows over the grounds and although Greta had been acknowledged with a few nods, a kerosene box was produced to sit on and Sam had introduced her to the man called Joe, she had more or less been ignored in the business of dealing with the gift of groceries.

By popular vote the sausages were soon sizzling in a pan as black as the billy can and the smell of good beef and fat was a signal and magnet for the men to gather. In no time there were at least twenty of them grinning and joking around the camp fire, all in agreement that Sam Riding was a good sort of a bloke and by the look of his lady, a lucky one as well. Emerging from under the grandstand a man arrived with a battered saucepan of boiled potatoes. 'Cleaned up under a house and not only potatoes but she gave me this.' From behind his back he produced a cake popping with sultanas.

'What a ripper,' came from a lad no more than sixteen.

The sun had gone down and all that was left were a sky and clouds flushed with gold. Greta felt she was ready to sag into a heap as a tin plate with a sausage and half a potato was offered. 'No butter for the spud like at home but it's pretty good.' It was the boy whose eyes had rounded at the sight of the cake. She shook her head, smiling, the lump in her throat so big that it hurt. 'Seeing that it's all mine, I'm giving it to you.'

'Honest?' At her nod he wolfed it down, leaving her to wonder how far away the home was that had butter on spuds.

If Sam had brought her along to pull the heart strings, he'd succeeded. She couldn't take any more. The proof of poverty and desperation, of thin lips grinning at the thought of one lousy sausage and a potato, crowded out every happy image of the hours past. Yunnabilla and Andy seemed so far away and all she wanted was to feel his arms holding her, his kisses blotting out the memory of faces taut with hardship and hunger. Feeling relieved, she saw Sam was ready to go and was making his way towards her.

'Now for the real reason why I wanted you here, Greta Flight. How about something to cheer up the lads and only you can do it.'

'Oh no, Sam.' Her refusal was quietly vehement. 'I couldn't. Look at them, the poor sods. Do you think any of them would like some stranger cavorting around, singing love songs that would only emphasise what they've lost? This isn't the time or place. No!'

It was like he'd never heard her as he took his mouth organ from a trouser pocket and slid down a wild arpeggio and back again, slapped the harmonica on an open palm and hauled a protesting Greta to her feet.

'Workers! Comrades! Lend me your ears, and mates, you'll never regret it.' Greta, feeling like a fool, stood helpless, her hand lost in Sam's sweaty grip. 'At great expense and for your entertainment I have brought along with me none other than Greta Flight, the songbird of Yunnabilla's Riverbank Players. We're going to play a few old songs. Join in, yer know the words. Nothing like a good old sing-song to digest the sausages, ay?' Without a yeah or nay, harmonica to mouth, hands cuddling the small instrument, Sam ripped into 'Pack Up Your Troubles'. There was nothing Greta could do. Taking a deep breath, she matched Sam for speed and, hands palm up and fingers wiggling, the invitation was there for all to join in. The song ended.

Not a taker. Not a peep.

They stood or squatted on the ground in a stolid circle of silence. Greta gave Sam the nod to begin again. Damn it, no one was going to act like a stunned mullet when Greta Osborne of the Coconut

Grove Club sang! Sam struck up once more, beginning with the first notes of 'It's a Long Way to Tipperary'. Not to be beaten, Greta sang, marching to the beat, and threaded her way through the gathering, suddenly grateful for the lone voice that piped up to join her. It was the lad who'd offered her the sausage. She broke off the song, eyes dancing. 'Sure,' she addressed him aloud, 'and yer dear old muther must have come from the Emerald Isle. Am I right now?' There were a few chuckles as the boy grinned and nodded. She went on with the song. A tenor sang in harmony and another leant his voice to the old well-loved air. The ice was broken.

From then on one song turned into another. The park rang with lusty voices, the night deepened and the camp fire became embers.

'Time to put the old mouth organ away for another day, Comrades.'

'Just one more song!' they chorused. A piece of wood, fence paling, it looked like, was thrown on the fire and sparks flew high as the harmonica's sweet vibrato floated over the silent men once more while Greta, with all her heart, sang the haunting melody and words wistful with longing:

Keep the home fires burning
While your hearts are yearning
Though the boys are far away
They dream of home.
There's a silver lining
Through the dark clouds shining
Turn the dark clouds inside out
Till the boys come home.

Each to their own thoughts, the drive back to the hotel was as silent as the drive out had been. Greta's thoughts were with Spanner now and his wife, facing life without work but full of confidence that his old job would be waiting there for him – if and when they returned to Yunnabilla. Maybe. But the bacon factory could close down. Already the sawmill had been putting men off. And Andy? Unease skulked in dark corners ready to pounce. There was no denial that farm repairs had slowed down; the garage not that much better. But between this and that she reminded herself they were making do. One big job could be just around the corner.

'Here we are, Greta.' The same words said not so many hours ago but a world of difference separated them. Grateful for Sam's offered hand, she stepped down and eased footsore toes out of her shoes, slumping against the utility door. 'Sam, old pal, what a day.'

'You did a great job out there. Thanks a bloody million, Greta.' Reluctant for it to all end, he remembered that a snatched sandwich was all he had eaten since meeting Greta outside the Railway Hotel. 'When did you last eat?'

'About a hundred years ago.'

'There's not a bad café down the road. How does a feed of fish and chips sound?'

'If it was truffles and quail I'd have to say no. Sorry, old friend, but all I can think of now is a shower and bed. You're a darling, and I love you.' She leant over and kissed his cheek. 'But I'm buggered.'

As Greta reached the hotel door, Sam caught up with her. 'Now that the *Pelican* is in shape or just about, tell Andy that the offer still holds.'

With fingers crossed, she told him that she would.

CHAPTER NINETEEN

'Girls! Pixilated penguins could do it better. Watch me! *Again!*'

Greta marched over to the gramophone and placed the tone arm into its cradle before giving enough exasperated turns of the handle to set records spinning out the window. Ten enthusiastic dancers from little Annabelle up to her mother Poppy gave Greta their adored attention. Except for Poppy, each and every one of them wished that one day, by some miracle, they would look as lovely, have legs as shapely and dance as *marvellously* as Greta of the Flight Academy of Dance.

'Follow me. First the shuffle. One! Two! Three! Four! Box step. Don't look at your feet, Elsie, and chin up. *You've got it! Good girl!* Again! *Five, six, seven, eight!*' A sulky breeze did little to obliter-ate the smell of the schoolroom – stale sandwiches and smelly socks – as Greta followed every step of the simple routine to its end. 'And how do we finish the afternoon's lesson?'

'Cartwheels and splits!' The students squealed as they tossed aside their heavy tap shoes. The sight of bouncing bows and bloomers, flying legs and leaps executed with such enthusiasm brought a smile of approval to Greta's face.

'Perfect. Give yourself a clap.' Greta clapped with them. 'Now for lemonade. Icy cold.'

Some thought it was the best part of lessons when Greta, now no longer the teacher, sat with them talking and teasing, including them in her adult world as a friend. They absorbed her with their eyes, while she, combating the heat, had a wet folded handtowel around her neck, removing it, flapping it and patting her face for a few seconds, the smell of eau de cologne water a refreshment. To them her ways were different. She talked differently and every movement and gesture was something to relay to friends agog for the latest detail. By word of mouth, the Flight Academy of Dance was a growing success.

A surreptitious peek at the kitchen clock told Greta that in another ten minutes she could call it a day. The river and a swim were all she could think about: a delicious hour to herself and a choice between bottlebrush shade or rapids turning rock pools into a bubble bath.

Dancing class over and the house still, Greta hummed to herself as she washed lemonade glasses. Life wasn't too bad in Yunnabilla after all. It had been weeks since the last scrap of rumour had died a natural death, the most outlandish being that she and Spanner Larkin had eloped. The perpetrator of that was none other than Ethel Rourke, who swore she saw them out of her bedroom window catching the night-goods train. Dorothy Stone never rated a mention in that one. The true elopement of Spanner and Dorothy sizzled over the town for days when first revealed, with a few chuckles about the king hit Biff Larkin doled out to that bastard Stone. 'That took the piss out of him,' was the consensus at every bar in town. Yeah . . . Life in Yunnabilla wasn't too bad after all.

A knock on the front door cut short her humming and a recognised voice had her placing a glass carefully on the draining tray so as not to clatter. Perhaps he'd go away if she pretended that no one was at home. Brisk steps coming around the side of the house squashed that idea.

Bugger!

Moving to the kitchen door, out of the corner of her eye Greta saw Marelda hanging out tea towels, taking it all in.

'Ah, Mrs Flight. I thought you might not have heard me.' Reverend Baker, moonface beaming, climbed the back stairs. Defeated, she stood aside as he reached the top step.

'This *is* a surprise,' she said pleasantly enough, hoping he'd notice the bathing towel, togs and shade hat on the table and make a quick exit. 'A cool drink?' she asked, feeling a smile setting like concrete on her face.

'Thank you.' He gave a fatuous chuckle. 'I've been told your chilli wine with lime is well worth the ride out here.' He settled himself comfortably into the offered chair while Greta tried not to grind her teeth. Obviously the Reverend was paying more than a social call.

'Delicious, Mrs Flight. Another, you ask? Yes, I don't mind if I do.' He finished off the second glass with hardly a pause, then removed a handkerchief from his coat sleeve to dab his lips. 'I must admit it's a while since we've spoken. But I do like to catch up with my parishioners when I can.'

What a lot of malarkey, Greta thought as she swept up the

empty glass and dropped it into the dish of still hot, soapy water. Parishioners we ain't!

'Apart from the success of the chilli wine, I believe the dancing academy is going ahead in leaps and bounds as I promised it would.' He waved a waggish finger. She could have bitten it off at the knuckle. He promised! How? In a sermon? *Thou must go and multiply a thousand-fold the attendance at the Flight Academy of Dance*? Now resigned to a lengthy discussion, Greta picked up her swimming gear and dumped it in full view on a chair and pulled one up for herself. 'Yes, Reverend Baker, I'm certainly happy about the way things are turning out.'

'And young Mrs Griffen is a star pupil, I believe.'

'You could call her that.'

'And Mrs Lockard?'

'Not quite the dancing type, I'm afraid.'

'The daughter?'

'She's going okay.' Greta was beginning to wonder if she was expected to give a run-down on everyone in the class. He certainly had the local gossip down pat. There was one thing Greta was certain of: Mrs Lockard would be keeping the progress of Lorraine to herself. Even Poppy had no idea of the private lessons she was giving the deaf girl, although Greta guessed it wouldn't be long before someone found out about it. Realising they were circling around each other with words and fed up with the nonsense of it, Greta fixed him with a steady gaze.

'Let's start off with a bit of honesty, Reverend; you're not here for a friendly chit chat. It's about a concert, isn't it?' It was a flat statement, delivered without a smile.

'Then I'll come straight out with it, Mrs Flight,' he countered.

'It certainly is. And for a good cause.' But he couldn't help himself. 'And as to our little secret . . .'

'Didn't know we had one.' Her belly was a tangled knot.

'I think you know what I mean.' He paused, his glance more mischievous than sly. 'You and I and the *wicked, wicked stage.*'

'Not much of a secret.' Her relief was exquisite.

'In Yunnabilla it has to be.'

'Oh, I see.' She gave him her sucked-in-cheek look. 'We're talking from a wowser's point of view. I'm well and truly used to that.'

'It can make life very uncomfortable.'

As if to change the subject, a dreamy look of remembrance crossed the round face of the minister. 'Ah yes . . . the stage. The gaiety, the acts, and there's one I'll never forget.' He sighed with the sigh of the lovesick. 'I only saw her the once. A youngster, you might say, but what a talent.' The façade of love lost was replaced by a repeat of the mischievous gaze. 'Often wondered what happened to her.'

'And you think she might have been me?' Greta gave him the benefit of a laugh. 'I'll admit I've been in the odd this and that; mostly amateur stuff, of course. But you're barking up the wrong tree there, Rev. Never in my life have I had the good fortune to hit the boards with you. And what's your speciality? You never told me. Anyway, let's get down to the real business of the visit, eh?'

She still couldn't dismiss the idea that somehow the good Reverend Baker still had a few little surprises up his sleeve for her. The theatrical crowd kept close company and news travelled fast. Talk about unlucky . . . A stagestruck cleric in Yunnabilla, of all places!

Greta found it surprisingly easy to discuss a future concert with the minister. It could be done, she told him, and suggested that auditions of a sort should take place after Baker told her of a lad who could imitate Bing Crosby in song, and an Irish tenor whose rendition of 'Underneath the Arches' and 'Danny Boy' could bring tears to a mother's eye. Not very complicated routines for the ballet, she told him, but with the right costumes and a bit of razzle dazzle, it would bring the house down. While she talked, ideas flowed and excitement grew at the idea of a show Yunnabilla would never forget.

It could be done!

In her mind the Riverbank Players could be split into solo acts. Mannie, a gypsy king, playing wild tunes on the accordion; Leila with one of her classical pieces that could stun an audience into submission; while her Andy could make the heart beat and the toes tap with music never heard before in the tobacco town. Not forgetting Poppy and Annabelle in a mother-and-daughter act and of course her own students for the chorus line.

'But there's one thing, Rev, I'd like to suggest. A concert on the School of Arts stage?' Greta the professional shook a wise head. 'Too large, for a start; everyone would get lost on it. Nothing like a too-big stage to wreck a performance.'

'You're not suggesting the church hall. I don't think —'

'That's not what I'm getting at. How do you like the idea of a cabaret? Tables and chairs. A more intimate production.' Already she had him in the palm of her hand. 'Mannie Coleman walking around the tables with his accordion,' she giggled, 'making eyes at the ladies, like Ethel Rourke for one.'

Reverend Baker tried to smother a laugh. 'Don't even think of it, Mrs Flight, but I like the suggestion. A cabaret, eh?' He rolled the idea of it around his tongue. 'Yes, I think we've the makings of a sell-out show.' He paused, tapping a finger on pursed lips. 'At the moment, this little idea of mine, the concert – cabaret – has not been discussed with the ladies of the guild. I thought I should wait until we worked out some plan. Like a cabaret, for instance. Your idea of course,' he amended hastily.

'Of course.' The comment was as dry as a sucked olive seed. 'However, Rev, you tell your ladies about it all.' Greta, with one eye on the clock, stood up. 'I better get a wriggle on – we're playing tonight and Andy'll be home soon. Of course, this matter must be talked over with him. I never do a thing without advice from my husband.' She tried not to smile at the touch of wifely piety in her voice. Did he know the truth about Andy and herself? Did he have old friends still doing the rounds? Sydney friends? What the hell. The thought of a concert or cabaret made her toes itch in anticipation.

As Reverend Baker pedalled off, she realised that whatever the minister knew – or thought he knew – about them, his lips were sealed. He was as keen as she was to make it all come together. If the whole project was a financial success, there was no way in the world he would taint the good reputation that she and Andrew were slowly building up. There would be no announcement from the pulpit that the Flights were living in *mortal sin*!

The sight of Andy in the utility driving home filled her with warm expectation. Thoughts of a swim dismissed, she hurried into the bedroom and rifled through a dressing-table drawer. 'Ah.' Her eyes closed as she sniffed at the tablet of soap. 'Magnolia – gorgeous.' It was a perfume that sent Andy wild. Footsteps sounded on the verandah as she made a quick dash for the bathroom and dived through the door.

'Greta?'

She dumped her clothes in a corner, turned the shower on full blast and began soaping herself. 'I'm here!' Waves of perfume filled the tiny tin-lined room with the scent of magnolia. With a bit of luck he might join her. Time for a quickie before they dressed. After hours spent with the Reverend Baker, she was ready to have a good-looking man – a real man – make up for it.

CHAPTER TWENTY

Marelda heard shrieks of laughter from the grey house and knew it wasn't the time for her to find out just what the Reverend Baker and Greta had been up to. Not only that, but she had news about Spanner and Dorrie. It was the same old story repeated over and over in the newspapers. No work. Nothing. With Cairns running down to a standstill, Dorothy was reluctant to return to Yunnabilla, not that Marelda could blame her. The surprise was that before their money ran out the couple was going south and Spanner was thinking about joining the navy. At least it's work, Dorothy wrote, before sending Marelda her love.

With twilight falling, heavy drops of rain pitted the dust in Marelda's yard. She stood at the back door, enjoying the wet smell of it, and the lamplight glowing from the Flights' kitchen. She was busting to tell them about Spanner, but then remembered it was Saturday. Tonight Greta would be singing with the Riverbank Players at the School of Arts and a euchre tournament was on as well. Greta and euchre was a heady mixture that Marelda found hard to resist, making up her mind to beg a lift into town with them.

She heard laughter again. They're always laughing, she said to herself, and blessed the day the Flights, from out of nowhere, turned up with Mannie Coleman at the front gate of the house across the road.

The Saturday-night hop at the School of Arts was in full swing. Married couples on the floor, children pushing each other around the hall, and the flirting girls of Yunnabilla in full evening dress made by their mothers, danced until rivulets of perspiration ran down their legs. Single lads and men (if their wives allowed them) sneaked outdoors for a thirst-quencher brought from the nearest pub, one eye out for the sergeant who usually, for convenience sake, found other things to do when the Riverbank Players performed.

A good takings was assured for the night, bolstered by a truckload of enthusiastic revellers from Dimbulah way. Greta, taking a break, was dancing a complicated quickstep with a newcomer to the town, a schoolteacher who already had the unmarried in a fluster of hopeful expectation. Although she adored Andy's attempts to tread the light fantastic, she was in the arms of an expert, and blissfully unaware of whispers and half-envious looks as she was guided unerringly into a pivot that whirled them with speed around the hall. She hadn't enjoyed a dance so much since Fanny was a girl. The music stopped, she caught Andy's eye up on the stage and blew a kiss, ready for the next round to begin. A tap, so the MC announced, and she was surprised to hear her partner ask, what the hell a tap was. 'Are we supposed to twinkle-toe our way like Fred Astaire across the room?'

'You must be joking, and careful now, you could lose me to Doc

207

Pedersen. A tap on the shoulder is all that's needed for a lady to have a change of partners,' she said, as she saw David thread his way towards them. But someone else arrived first and with her eyes still on the doctor it wasn't until she felt a hard, tight grip around her waist that she realised at once that she was in trouble. Already the schoolteacher, not wasting time, was dancing with someone else, David not to be seen. The music began and dancers moved. No one noticed as Stone pushed her towards the door.

'You thought you'd get away with it, did yer?'

The menace in his voice had her heart jerking out of control. She felt the hot breath of the farmer only inches away from her face. Better to ignore him than cause a fuss, and she turned her head away from a face twisted in hate.

'Yeah.' He tightened the grip that left her fighting for breath. 'Had her hidden all the time while I was knocked silly by that gorilla Larkin.' Fury was getting the better of him and his voice grew louder while dancers stopped or drew aside, uncertain what to do. Drink had nothing to do with his rage and she looked into the eyes of a man completely and murderously sober. Frightened now, she struggled to loosen a hold that felt like an iron bar encircling her body. Then there was a shout from the stage, the music stopped and Andy was down the steps in two strides, pounding towards her as the dancers parted, giving him room. Sickened, Greta knew he was no match for the enraged farmer. She felt herself hit the floor as Stone dropped her.

'Come and get what's owing to you, you Pommy interfering shit!'

Andy, getting closer to the flailing swings, propped. He ducked, and head down, ran full bore into Stone. The two men fell to the ground, Stone on top, his hands around Andrew's throat, screaming retribution. By now more than one was coming to the rescue, prising the two men apart. It took three to heave the struggling man out the door with threats that if he didn't leave, they'd do him in, well and bloody truly. With Stone out of the way, Andrew helped a dazed and winded Greta to her feet.

'Oh, my love, are ye hurt?'

'No, of course not.' She dusted herself down. 'And before the hall turns into a free-for-all, let's get on the stage, quick time.' Already another two were grappling by the door, as if infected by Stone's vitriol, and Mannie and Leila were playing as if their lives depended on it. The whole episode would not have taken up five minutes, and with the orchestra swinging along and Greta launching into 'California, Here I Come', Yunnabilla, accustomed to the occasional joust, went on enjoying themselves.

But Greta couldn't.

She had glimpsed evil, inches from her face, and it terrified her. The song came to an end and, taking a bow to a spontaneity of clapping, she caught her breath as a jagged pain raced through her shoulder. She could thank Stone for that. The evening dragged on, and avoiding Andy's worried glances, she sang as if in music she could wipe out the hurt and memory of the night.

It was nearly half-past three after a late end to the night, for the music hadn't stopped – wasn't allowed to stop – until well after one. They were now in the kitchen, with Greta sitting upright in a chair while Andrew alternated between a cold pack of iced water for Greta's shoulder and gentle massage. 'Och, it was a stupid thing to do.'

'Attacking that man with a head butt?'

'That's not what I mean. The whole business of it. I didn'a real-ise that we were dealing with a madman.' His voice was gruff with emotion as he noticed her hands tightly clenched to control their trembling. 'We – I – shouldn'a have let you get involved.'

'And miss out going to Cairns? Bloody nonsense.' She tossed his concern aside. 'Between the two of us we saved a young girl from a miserable hell and you know it, Andrew Flight. Anyway, there's nothing like turning on a good old stoush to liven things up.'

Greta deliberately kept it light. There was no way she was going to let on how much Stone had frightened her. Andrew didn't know that after singing 'California' she had crept out to the back of the hall, sick and dizzy, wanting to bring up the bile that the farmer had left behind him. How many times would the same thing happen again? Although Mannie had assured her that the sergeant had already warned Stone to stay away from the Flights or find himself in the Stewart Creek lock-up, Greta wasn't so sure.

'How how does it feel now?' Andy removed the cold pack and began kneading her shoulder and neck again. The shoulder had been given a painful wrench; the result of her fall on the dance floor.

'Not too bad at all. Only did this to get your full and loving attention.'

'Ye'll have that till the day I die.'

'Umm, nearly makes it all worthwhile.' Greta raised her face to him, eyes glowing. 'You know I love you.'

'Sometimes I think ye're a right proper fool, Mrs Flight.' With expertise he had fashioned a sling out of a tea towel, good enough to support her arm. He helped her off the chair, but before she could take a step he swiftly gathered her up and carried her down the hall. Rain that had held off throughout the night spattered heavy drops on the roof and a cool breeze swept through the house. Carefully and slowly, so as not to hurt, he removed her dress and lace brassiere then eased her down on the bed. Rain enclosed the house with drums of sound drowning out the rooster's crow of early dawn as Andrew walked over to close the window. Coming back to her, he smiled in the darkness.

Greta was asleep.

A cup of tea and a thin slice of bread and butter in bed on a Sunday morning was one small luxury never taken for granted. Greta breathed in the fragrance of orange pekoe. Always stored in an airtight caddy, it was a weekend treat courtesy of Sam Riding, delivered by the postman. Somehow he had found out that the tea leaf, never available on their side of Capricorn, was a favourite blend. Andrew had given a Mannie Coleman-style tap on the nose when it had arrived. 'Fallen off the deck of the *Manunda*, I'd take a guess.' Blue-grey eyes glinting, his sly grin ended in a laugh. He handed her the steaming cup. 'How are things this morning?'

'Nothing that a swim, a kiss and a cuddle won't cure.'

'Not a cuddle until David Pedersen sees that shoulder.'

'Like we're made of money?'

There was no need to explain the tongue-in-cheek comment. They both knew that David had done enough. His bill for Andrew's fever, a ridiculously small amount, had been settled right away but his generosity had made them cautious and reluctant to take what they felt were favours. People in Yunnabilla had to be on the point of dying before a private doctor was called in. The hospital was free and good enough for most. Greta patted the side of the bed. 'Sit down – I've something to tell you.' She was ready to amuse him with Reverend Baker's agreement to a cabaret. 'But not until the good ladies of the guild give consent, naturally.'

Andrew drew back in mock horror. 'A cabaret! What a decadence! Do you really mean to turn the good ladies of the guild inside out and upside down?' His grin widened. 'Och, what a besom of a woman – and what a marvellous idea.' He then suggested that they drive over to the Colemans. 'That way,' he said, an expert in hooking up brassieres, as Greta had long-ago noted, 'we'll give them the good news before anyone else does.'

The road to Colemans' farm ran parallel with the railway going north, then branched off through the bush with its eruption of peaked anthills, the ironbark and stringybark trunks still wet and glistening from the night's downpour. Down a road, more of a mud slick than the usual dusty track, the utility lurched and skidded until it reached the creek that Mannie depended on to keep his tobacco leaf and crops alive. In spite of rain, the log bridge that he had built was intact as the creek burbled not more than twelve inches beneath it. Andy gave his usual three warning honks of the horn, announcing their approach. He eased the utility into a lower gear as it threatened to slide sideways into the creek. He shook his head. 'I can never understand these people. First there's Molloy's clapped-out truck, and Mannie builds a wee footbridge – tha's all ye can call it – and leaves it at that. Not guid enough.' Glad to be at the end of a bumpy ride, Greta kept silent. It was Andy's mantra every time they visited the Colemans.

Once over the bridge, the view of the property opened up before them. There were the tobacco fields on all sides, a paddock of cotton at an experimental stage, as Mannie had once explained, then the oleanders, pink and cream, hugging the drive until it reached the timber house ready to impress with its curved double staircase leading up to the wide verandah. Mannie, in his usual spot whenever a motor sounded up the drive, gave a wave as he came down to greet them, and was ready with a helping hand for Greta, her arm still in the sling.

'We thought you'd be taking it easy today. The pair of you.' He gave Greta a look of honest sympathy. 'As Mamma Coleman used to say, it's never the bad deeds that get you into trouble; nine times out of ten it's the good ones.' He stepped back to give her a second glance. 'And looking at you, she was right.' As an afterthought he added, 'She was never wrong, either, come to think of it.'

Leila was now running down the steps. 'Welcome, welcome! And Mannie, why must you talk down here? Bring the poor girl upstairs – oh, it's so hot – come on, come on!' No sooner were they on the verandah than Mannie was sent off for cool drinks.

Greta was thankful as she sank into the offered seagrass armchair, plump with a generous supply of cushions, for the drive had been more uncomfortable than she was ready to admit. The shade of the wide, sloping roof and a breeze up from the creek was a blessing, and the Colemans never disappointed. Although it had been only a few hours since they had last parted company, the pleasure they evinced was genuine. Greta and Andrew had deliberately kept their visit for the afternoon, making sure that Mannie and Leila had eaten their midday meal before turning up.

'Not that I'd mind helping out with a few farm chores around the place,' Greta said in a half joke, not forgetting how Mannie had tricked them into covering tobacco plants – nor forgetting the sumptuous meal that had followed. Between them they had decided that Mannie had put them though some kind of a test; as to why remained a mystery. Funny beggar, Andy had said more than once, for many visits and meals had followed after that first day. But covering tobacco plants was never mentioned again.

It seemed that Leila and Mannie had been expecting visitors for in no time Mannie returned toting out beer and 'for the ladies', a tangy concoction of crushed pineapple, pomegranate and lime made with the help of a newly purchased fruit squeegee-crusher, as he described it, 'and never seen up here before', with the pride of a coup accomplished.

From a jug he filled Greta's glass and stepped back while she took a sip. 'Well, what do you think?' Anxiously he watched while she drained the glass.

'You've a winner there, Mannie. Delish!'

If the drinks weren't enough, Leila appeared with a tablecloth and began setting up with knives and forks, brushing aside Greta's remonstrations.

'Of course you must eat with us.' A terrine, a salad of tomatoes and cucumber and pickled onions appeared like magic from Leila's kitchen. 'We've been waiting for you.'

'And that's the biggest porky I've heard this week,' Greta laughed, helping herself to olives and a slice of Leila's homemade bread. 'But ask me, how can I resist that meat loaf?'

Chairs were pulled up and Leila began cutting slices of the admired terrine as Andrew eased himself away from the verandah railing.

'We didn'a come to break bread with you . . .' He sat down

and held out a plate, his eyes gleaming with the anticipation of a hungry man. 'But don't mind if I do. Not only that, we've something to tell.'

'Not about Stone, I hope.' Mannie's face darkened in a way they'd never seen before.

'Forget about last night.' Andrew took a quick slurp of his beer. 'For the moment, anyway. No, something else that's going to take that look off your face. Greta will tell you all about it.'

News about the proposed cabaret and the ideas Greta outlined were met with full approval. The thought of it gave spice to their meal and soon Leila was thinking costumes: 'Mosquito net, that's what we need. Many yards of it, and I'll dye it. Yes!' She gave two quick claps of her hand. 'The colour of watermelons. Beautiful skirts I will make also.' She sucked in a breath. 'And the ballet will hold them up like so.' Leila sprang up and paraded, arms outstretched, humming to the tune of 'Red Sails in the Sunset', one of the songs already on the program. Mannie, king of the gypsies, accordion in his arms, was already trying out melodies with a gypsy feel to them, and Greta, one hand on her hip, swayed to 'Dark Eyes', singing with a passion as if the camp fires were burning and the plywood caravan painted yellow was half hidden beneath the trees.

As their enthusiasm came in waves around his shoulders, Andrew could only be pleased. Talking of the cabaret, and in the company of the Colemans, Greta seemed to have put the ugliness of the previous night out of her mind, for the present. Although she had tried to hide her distress, taking the view that 'the show must go on', he had also pretended to go along with it. Any suggestion that they should go home early and allow Mannie and Leila to carry on had been met with a stubborn refusal to leave the hall. He would have had to tie her down and carry her out by force to have his way. As they had played one interminable dance after another, so successful had she been in disguising the pain of her shoulder, it was only on their arrival home that he realised how badly she'd been hurt in the fracas.

Once again, he wondered if he had wrecked Greta's life completely. Never mind about his own. Was his love – their love – enough to keep them reaching for the next good day? He had been so certain, so sure of himself, that the plans he'd made should by now be nearing completion. Things had started off well in his dealings with Mannie. But the garage was just holding its own against bills for engine parts that were mounting up, as were his own unpaid accounts for work done.

The humiliation of the payment in pumpkins was hard to forget. Poor bloody new chum. It had been the town joke of the week. Then there was losing business to Grimshaw's workshop while he'd made a slow recovery after his illness. That too had come as a shock. Three years or more since the last malarial bout, this time was the severest. His failure to provide, though not entirely his fault, had led him down a path of self-recriminations ending in his confrontation with Stone.

He went over the night again. The image of Greta struggling in Stone's arms. There had been murder in his blood when he had charged the bastard, and he recalled the cringe he had felt as Stone was carried off while he lay there as useless as a castrated eunuch.

'Andy, why the silence? You've hardly said a word.' He was suddenly the centre of their attention and receiving a slightly wary look from Greta, as if she was trying to read his mind.

'With all the blether goin' on, a man canna' get a word in edge-ways!' Andrew left the table, his mind racing to hide his seeming lack of interest, and he opened the violin case resting on a chair. 'So far we have gypsies, beautiful girls of the ballet, and someone who sings 'Danny Boy' enough to bring on tears.' He gave them a droll raise of the eyebrows. 'The Irish love it.' The lines around his lips deepened, his eyes half-closed in thought. 'I didn'a bring one with me,' he said, his Scottish burr thickening, 'but do ye think we might get a kilt in Yunnabilla? There's nothing like a true Scot with his fiddle to warm the cockles and set the feet tapping. What d' ye think?'

He tucked the violin under his chin and swept the bow across the strings. Body swaying and bending, he quickly filled their ears with a manic, breath-gasping jig. Unable to resist the rhythm and its wild, rollicking invitation to the dance, Mannie gave a whoop and Leila joined him in a good imitation of the highland fling. Greta went to join them but stopped as a knife tore through her shoulder. 'Uh!' She gave a grunt of pain. 'I forget. Don't ask me to do cartwheels in the next twenty-four hours.'

Between talk and drinking Leila's excellent coffee, finishing off the olives, and the advantage of allowing a chap called Eggie Barton – completely unknown to the Flights – to play the jew's harp, Mannie swung doubt into favour. 'Not only is Eggie good with the damned thing,' he told them in all seriousness, 'he comes from a family of seventeen, with the rest of the Barton horde scattered over the district. If its funds the Reverend wants, the Bartons will supply a good percentage of it. That is *if* he's on the program, of course.'

Afternoon was soon closing down with a silent curtain of flying foxes drawn over the sky. Rosellas were making sleepy chitterlings in the mango trees and Leila was giving an invitation to stay for another feast. But it was time to go, and although the day had ended without another drop of rain, Andy wasn't sure of the gripping power of the tyres in the darkness and slippery mud.

'Anyway, I think its time to have a rehearsal in the bothy of the Flights, and I'll cook you up a meal like we've never had before.'

'Porridge. He makes honest work of it, salty and stiff enough to stand a spoon in it.' Greta was laughed down the stairs as a nagging witch while Andrew protested that his curry – a secret recipe from the Rajah of Ballyhoo's kitchen – would transport them on a magic carpet to the Taj Mahal itself.

As they drove along the bush track, just as greasy as before, Greta found herself dozing in spite of a dull ache more or less subdued by aspirins and the brandy Mannie had insisted she take before leaving. Andy's question had her suddenly wide awake.

'So you don't think we should pull up the anchor and try for another harbour?'

'Are you serious? You've a romantic way of putting it, Andrew Flight, but it sounds to me like "let's call it quits and clear out".'

'Sam's made an offer. The *Pelican* —'

'He never gives up, does he? And what about the cabaret? Are you telling me that this afternoon has been all a waste of time?'

'Not entirely. But after last night —'

'Ah! I thought there was something. You weren't giving a thought about the cabaret while we were blethering – your word for it – all over the place, were you? In spite of that bastard, we're staying right here!' Greta said firmly.

Headlights encased a world of silent tree trunks and sharp

shadows. A small creature scurried across the road to the sanctuary of the grass.

'Cairns . . .' Greta eased her shoulder into a more comfortable position. 'You know how I feel about that place. I'll never forget their faces – poor hungry souls!'

'He shouldn't have taken you there.' Andrew could not shake off the guilt that had plagued him throughout the day.

'I'm glad he did. For once I forgave him his preaching. It made me understand just what's going on. Made me realise just how lucky I am.' She patted his thigh, warm against hers. 'Never mind about last night. Yunnabilla is a good place to live in and I'm thanking you, Andy Flight, my wish, wish, wish,' – it was an endearment her grandmother had used – 'for bringing me here.' She gave his thigh another pat and, contented, rested her head against him, eyes closed.

CHAPTER TWENTY-ONE

Sam Riding pulled a hatch cover over the ice box he'd installed on the back deck of the *Pelican* and patted it for luck. 'A few days out and one good catch should fill you up to the gills, me beauty, and it'll be goodbye to lumping down at the wharf.' Well satisfied, he sat down on the ice box, and rolled and lit a cigarette.

The first drag was deep and comforting, the smoke drifting lazily through his lips. It had been hard long yakka and more than he could afford restoring the *Pelican* back to life; her wounds had been deep. But now she rocked gently at low tide, the smell of new paint overriding the fetid odour of steaming mud and rubbish on the exposed banks of Alligator Creek – a heady aroma that spoke of boats and freedom to the man lying at ease on the ice box. Clicking and clacking, the soldier crabs and hidden creatures of the mud soothed as he dreamt of fecund reefs delivering up coral trout, cod, parrot fish, trevally, sea brim and crayfish to the depths of his ice box.

Deciding that a wheelhouse was more comfortable than a boarding-house room, he now lived on the *Pelican* while still working on the wharves and, as he described it, pouring money into a large hole in the creek.

He had given up the idea of Andy Flight coming on board. There had been no mention of it by letter or word since Greta had gone back to Yunnabilla. It was now up to him to pick out which poor sod from the park could serve as deckhand. If all went well, lots could be drawn for the next and succeeding trips out. That would go a long way in helping to bring a bit of cheer, cash and a feed of fish to the men at Parramatta Park. Sam tossed the remains of his smoke over the side, and from the wheelhouse brought out the usual contribution of groceries and smokes for the men camping there.

Numbers had increased since the night Greta had sung for them. Now the men themselves held nightly concerts around the camp fire, singing and reciting the poems of Patterson and Lawson. They played mouth organs and jew's harps, and songs were sung to the clacking of spoons.

Hefting groceries shoulder-high, he was greeted by men mostly in good spirits while a few with a sliding gaze were still unprepared to accept the generosity of Sam's good heart. But there was something different about the park camp this time. Something Sam could not put a finger on. Although he was given the usual welcome by those who knew him, there was a feeling of unease as men grouped and talked quietly among themselves. A shaking of heads and a stray oath now and then surfaced into the air. Outside a shed graced with the title of Poultry Pavilion, a man wrapped barbed wire around a chunk of wood while another hammered a nail into a broken fence paling.

'What the hell?' Sam lowered the groceries onto a makeshift table. A short man, who once could have been described as stocky, peeled away from the nearest group with an outstretched hand. His trousers, worn and baggy, hung from his hips without a belt.

'Good ter see you, mate.'

'This don't look right, Chas. What's up?'

'It's not good, Sam. In fact it's bloody disgraceful. They want us out.'

'Who?'

'Who do y' think? The blustering, pontificating council and the fine, noble citizens of Cairns. That's who.' Chas gave his trousers a much-needed hitch and mumbled in disgust that some bastard had pinched his belt. 'We've tried to do it right with a proper com-mittee – president and secretary, the lot – talking to 'em and that got us bloody nowhere.'

'But you did that weeks ago.'

'Yair, weeks ago. Been about three meetings since then and always the same. Sweet bugger all.' Chas scratched his chest and his groin as if bitten by an infestation of fleas. 'A man's fuckin' raw. Haven't had a proper bath in weeks. That's another thing we were promised, showers. And now it's get out or look out. Seems they want to put an agricultural show on while we sleep God knows where.' He gave a laugh without mirth. 'Oh yes, we've got friends all right – word's been goin' round that the Returned Soldiers' League and the Micks were told from the pulpit to "get down and do over the unemployed".' He gave himself another vigorous scratching. 'Man should've stayed in Innisfail. They treat you decent down there.'

He spoke of a council that had built shelters and of the levy and contributions from the canecutters who had partly financed the project. 'Anyway.' His voice was gruff with determination. 'We're not leaving, mate, there's just no place to go to.'

'So you're planning to keep the home fires burning with waddies and nulla nullas?' Sam shook his head sadly. 'Not a hope, Comrade, not a hope.'

'Maybe. And maybe a bit of a dust-up makes men feel like men again instead of undernourished, grovelling dogs.'

'Would the fellas mind if I went down and had a word with 'em?' Sam nodded towards the poultry pavilion.

'Nah.' Chas gave his trousers another hitch. ''S' matter of fact, I'll come with yer.'

As they approached the pavilion – merely a shed with a roof and sagging timbers – the usual greeting between the men was missing until one of them broke a growing and uncomfortable silence. It was the same man Sam had seen twining barbed wire around the waddy. It was out of sight.

'Hello, Sam. The name's Arty. Have you come to report on the nefarious deeds of the Reds as we're all called around here?'

'Report? Come off it, Comrade. Just havin' a look around.'

The man gave a sweeping bow. 'Be our guest and enter the Palace 'Orrible.'

Sam didn't accept the offer. From where he stood it was easy to see the flotsam of men who'd been 'on the track', perhaps for years. Benches held rolled-up blankets thin and stained from many nights sleeping on the side of a road. There were Salvation Army giveaway shirts and trousers, neatly folded; blackened billy cans and fry pans and a few tattered books that had been swapped and read over and over by camp fires. Poor and mean possessions of men who had proudly followed their chosen path of butcher and baker, shearer and ringer, academic and carpenter, but now all existed under the one heading of 'the unemployed'.

At the far end of the shed was a battered tin wash tub with a bucket beside it and in the dim light a man could be seen, pale and slight, taking a bath. Arty allowed himself a smile. 'We take it in turns.' But his smile was short-lived. 'There's a strong chance the water will be turned off any day. Thank Christ there are tanks full enough to keep us going.'

Anything Sam thought he may have said to the men outside stayed concealed behind closed lips.

By now others had joined him and while Sam listened to them, guts churning with sympathy, instinct told him to take the *Pelican* and get far away from what he feared was going to be a disaster for the men of Parramatta Park. But Sam Riding had never in his life shied away from injustice or a good fight. Thinking of the canecutters in Innisfail, he decided that he could go a long way in getting funds from his workmates on the wharf for some sort of shelter. He gave a goodbye salute and left them talking and sharing out the contents of the cardboard carton.

Chas caught up with him. 'I'll walk down to the ute with you.'

Sam placed his hand on the shorter man's shoulder, his face set in earnest lines. 'Listen, Comrade, be careful. By the talk I've heard the fellas are reaching the end of their tether. You too, by the sound of it. I've got an idea. Let the fellas down at the wharf work something out. We won't let you down. You don't want a war on your hands that you haven't a hope in hell of winning.'

'Well, it mightn't come to that. There's another meeting tomorrow. Who knows . . . the buggers might have had a change of heart.'

'Here.' Sam took off his belt and shoved it into Chas's hand. 'A bloke's gotta keep his strides up.' He pretended not to notice the man's tears as he walked off without a word. Sam gave his trousers a hitch, then whistling off-key to the tune of 'Good Lord Above', he cranked up the utility and headed down to the wharves.

CHAPTER TWENTY-TWO

Giving up trying to sweep out a kitchen and wash the breakfast dishes with one hand, Greta, still in pyjamas, was ready to give Marelda a yell to say she was coming over for a cuppa. She didn't have to yell, for halfway across the yard, Marelda was doing the yelling for her.

'Hello, love, didn't see you yesterday – oh, y' arm's in a sling! That rotten Stone, we saw it all from the card room.' Marelda was ready to cluck and sympathise while sitting in full view, bloomers around her ankles, on the Larkins' dunny. It was a habit that Greta had tried to ignore, just as Marelda ignored the hints that sensible conversation was impossible under such conditions. Greta had tried various ways to discourage her: pretending not to hear, making a dash for her own lavatory, concealed by the honeysuckle vine. That move, as she had reported to Andy, seemed in Relda's thinking a cosy invitation to shout unseen over the ether about the doings and latest peccadilloes of Yunnabilla. What was amazing was that Marelda – who everyone knew and respected – got away with it.

Greta did a quick turn around and dashed up the back stairs. 'Later, Relda.'

The Larkin dunny door slammed shut but in a flash opened again with Marelda bloomered and respectable, hurrying across the road, taking only seconds to burst into Greta's kitchen.

'Quick, luv,' she panted, 'Mrs Lockard's on her way. And by the look of it, y' haven't done the dishes yet.' She dumped toast-spackled plates into the washing-up basin, pouring in hot water from the kettle. 'Saw her coming when I was sitting on the lavvie. I've got a good view there, right down to the sawmill. She'll be here any minute!'

The torrent of words above the clattering of dishes had a mesmerising effect on Greta. She seemed incapable of moving. Marelda gave her a quick look over. 'Stay here,' came her excited command. 'I'll get your clothes and help y' dress. Got to look respec'ful for the bank manager's wife, ay?' As an afterthought, 'Is the bed made? Don't worry, I'll do it.' She was back in no time, scanties and beach pyjamas flung over her arm. 'A tidy kitchen,' she said, hooking Greta into her brassiere, 'and the bed made up has a house all set and ready for visitors. Especially for Her Highness Mrs Joyce Lockard.'

Greta, allowing herself to be buttoned into and brushed down, suddenly came alive. 'And here's me without a skerrick of lippy and rouge. Hold the fort, Relda!' she yelled, skidding down the hallway. 'And a million thanks!'

Mrs Lockard wasn't the only one in the car. Greta, now sufficiently 'respec'ful', to Marelda's satisfaction, saw Reverend Baker standing by, ready to help Mrs Lockard out of her gleaming sedan. Unseen behind the sitting-room curtains Greta waited for them to announce their presence. She wasn't ready to stand on the verandah as if in expectation of early morning visitors. 'Hell's wheels,' she had protested to Marelda, 'it's only ten o'clock!' although she had a good idea of why they were there.

As usual Mrs Lockard looked as if she was ready for any occasion that warranted her being at her proper best. The cream linen skirt had hardly a crease, and teamed with a matching silk shirt, tan polished brogues and an important-looking leather handbag, she gave the impression that business before pleasure was on the agenda. The only concession to a more casual approach for a morning visit was the absence of a hat, although not a wisp of hair escaped the restrictions of finger waves.

Greta smoothed down her beach pyjamas with their sunburst of flowers against the dark-green shimmer of milanese, the wide, flared pants silky and cool against her thighs. She'd lost count of the times she had worn them but knew she was a match in style with Mrs Lockard any old time, even if she was sporting a sling.

Knocking on the front verandah brought her to the door.

'Mrs Lockard and the Rev,' Greta said, ignoring the woman's surprise, if not disapproval of her casual reference to the minister. 'Come in – and I've a fair idea what brings you over here so *early* in the day.' She managed to plump up one of the cushions on the settee, but discarded a further attempt with a shrug. 'Make yourself comfortable, please.'

Mrs Lockard was the first to speak. 'My dear, I can see you've been hurt. I am so sorry. That dreadful man. But I'm not going to mention anything about the brawling that went on.'

Brawling . . . was she hinting that somehow it was all Andy's fault? Greta felt herself bristle, but kept her mouth shut. She wasn't in the mood for explanations but sat back, ready to hear the woman out. 'However, we have more pleasant things to talk about, don't you agree, Reverend?'

'Most certainly.' He beamed, his face a pink moon. 'As you can guess, Greta – ah, Mrs Flight – a meeting of the guild was held, and as our president,' his eyes moved to Mrs Lockard, 'this good lady sitting beside me, is happy to announce that the show – I mean, cabaret – will go on.' He gave the impression of standing up and taking a bow.

'As I thought it would.' Greta nodded. There was a faint clinking of china coming from the kitchen. 'Tea?' she asked brightly.

'Wouldn't dream of it.' Mrs Lockard shook her head. 'Not with a sling on your arm.'

'Don't give it a thought.' Greta gave an airy wave of dismissal. 'Marelda's helping out, the darling.' Greta guessed that her neighbour had no intention of leaving the house until she knew the whys and wherefores of the morning visit and she was only too happy to allow her to take over the kitchen.

Greta herself opened up discussions with an enthusiastic outline of the planning progress made with Andy and the Colemans. 'I know I should have waited for the outcome of the guild meeting, Rev, but that's me – jump into things feet first and hope for the best. I didn't think you'd mind. Forgiven?'

Mrs Lockard had her fountain pen and pad at the ready for a report to the guild about Greta's suggestions, and on the whole approved of what she was hearing. Outlay for costumes, she told Greta, would be at a minimum, as the ladies of the guild, dressmakers all, would make them.

'Of course, it is obvious that you are experienced in this sort of thing,' Mrs Lockard said, pen poised, ready to hear a full account of Greta's expertise in organising stage productions while Greta, with a feeling of sailing close to the wind, avoided Reverend Baker's eyes.

'I can dance and I can sing, and that's just about it. But I do know a cabaret is easier than a full concert to tackle.' She gave an unconcerned shrug. 'No background or props to worry about; lighting not a problem with everything at floor level . . . Perhaps a dais for the orchestra and the MC. Just the thing for amateurs – and that includes me, Mrs Lockard, to tackle. Right, Rev?' She threw out a challenge and at the same time wondered what Marelda was doing in the kitchen. Oh, for a cup of tea! Her mouth was as dry as yesterday's bread. With relief she heard Marelda thumping up the hall.

'Here we are.' Greta did a double take to see Marelda wheel in a traymobile. It was obvious that she'd made a raid on her own house and, never with an empty cake tin in sight, she had brought over a plate piled high with Anzac biscuits and a tray of daintily cut tomato sandwiches. Marelda Larkin, Queen of the card-afternoon teas, knew how to do things.

Acting hostess, she poured tea, handed out sandwiches and in payment for services rendered, brought out a chair from the kitchen and plonked herself down. She was not going to miss out on another thing. 'A cabaret, ay?' She included them all in her warm smile, eyes bright-blue as glass buttons. 'Now, that's what I call a bit of class. Another sandwich, Reverend?'

Morning tea over, Mrs Lockard tossed the first hand grenade into Greta's lap. 'Of course you'll be having Lorraine in the ballet.'

Reverend Baker was suddenly looking anxious.

'Mrs Lockard, I —'

'It's been wonderful the way you've brought her on. She's so much brighter and I have you to thank.' Mrs Lockard's mask of habitual calm had dropped. Naked pleading was in her eyes, shocking Greta into utter panic and a confusion of sadness for the woman. What Lorraine's mother wanted would be impossible for her to carry out. In set routines the girl was always more than a shade behind, but desperate to please; a matter of small importance in the confines of Greta's sitting room or verandah. Although Lorraine danced around the house, deaf to any music, for hours, step perfect, according to her mother, dancing in public with the ballet could end in a calamity for Lorraine and the chorus line.

It had been months since Greta had felt a real need for a cigarette. 'Mrs Lockard, please understand. I don't feel that I can do justice to Lorraine's love of dance. Even before I began teaching her in private it was an embarrassment for her trying to keep up with the other girls. Young things can be cruel at times and I was afraid that teasing – not by all, of course – but even one unkind or derisive look could have brought on too much hurt for her to take.'

By the stony look on Mrs Lockard's face, Greta could see she was getting nowhere. She took a deep breath. 'In fact, I've never mentioned this before but I was relieved when you had your daughter take private lessons.' She was ready to explain that the extra lessons gave Lorraine a good start before the usual Saturday class began, but she was cut short.

'I see, Mrs Flight.' Pad and fountain pen were disappearing into the maw of the large leather handbag. Greta sat back into the chair. Her shoulder ached, her head throbbed. Bugger the cabaret and bugger them! Ignoring a tinge of regret about the way things were turning out, she was ready to call it a day.

'Mrs Lockard, dear Mrs Lockard!' The Reverend was springing to his feet. 'I'm sure something can be done about this, some
compromise . . .'

'Tell me, Reverend – I'm willing to listen. But it doesn't alter
the fact that Greta – Mrs Flight – has found it an onerous task to
teach my girl a few miserable dance steps.'

'*Mrs Lockard!*' Marelda Larkin bounced off her chair, chest
heaving. 'You don't know what y' talking about. I've seen this dear
girl sweating pounds off trying to teach your daughter them steps
over and over again. An' Lorraine, the poor little thing, like one of
them water spiders, sliding all over the place – every which way. No
idea of what's playing on the gramophone. I've seen Greta writing
down pictures and thumping her feet down so hard til they just
about fell off so Lorraine could feel the beat, as it's called.' Marelda
was breathing hard, hands on hips. 'So don't let me hear about it
being some onerous thing – whatever that means – because it don't
sound nice to me. And Greta doesn't deserve it!' She sat down with
a thump. 'Anyway, who'd like a pot of fresh tea?' she said, glaring,
daring anyone to refuse.

Out came the fountain pen and pad again. 'That would be very
nice, thank you, Marelda.' It was an unusually meek reply for Mrs
Lockard, but Greta could have sworn that the bank manager's wife
was working hard not to smile.

'Greta, forgive me. We'll not talk about this again.' She took out
a handkerchief and dabbed her lips and forehead. 'I have to admit
it will be hard trying to explain things – about the cabaret – once
Lorraine knows about it all.'

Greta held up a hand. 'Hang on a moment, Mrs Lockard. As
Rev says, compromise, and compromise I will. And Relda, love,

could you get me a couple of Aspros, and more tea would go down a treat. Now, Mrs Lockard —'

'Call me Joyce, please.'

Reverend Baker choked on an Anzac.

'It's Joyce, then.' Not a smile exchanged, but Greta's tawny eyes looked straight into Mrs Lockard's dark brown in silent recognition that some sort of a pact had been made. 'Now.' Greta paused for effect, her timing perfect. 'How about we have Lorraine do a solo?'

'A what?' The impact of Greta's words had Joyce Lockard catching her breath and hope returning to her eyes. 'You must be joking. No – no, I have to believe you. A solo . . .' Her composure completely crumbled.

'Yes, that's what I said, a solo. It can be done. And Lorraine is capable of doing it. But first I have to talk it over with Andy.' Headache forgotten, shoulder ignored, she clapped her forehead with her free hand. 'What am I talking about? Of course Andy will do it. It's right up his alley. Now, this is how we'll go about it, and thank my lucky stars it's a cabaret. Easy, breezy.'

She had the three of them on the edge of their seats as she went on to explain. Lorraine would be taught a series of steps, count by count, melding into yet another set, then gliding into a graceful slow routine while counting in her head every movement as she swayed between tables, smiling and beautiful. It could be in the gypsy number with Mannie playing softly in the background. But Andrew, already familiar, as Greta assured them, by practising with Lorraine himself, would provide the music. He would follow and accompany the dancer, watching out for any unexpected change of rhythm, adjusting his playing to suit the dance. 'It could be done,'

Greta told them, wondering what she was letting herself in for and improvising as she went along. Warming to the idea, she jumped out of the chair, pacing up and down the room, her actions painting a vivid picture of the proposed performance, enveloping them all with a vivacity that brought a brightness to the room.

'Got it!' Greta snapped her fingers. 'Joyce, you say you've seen her dancing around the house. I've only seen it once but the style, the movements, are Isadora Duncan to a tee,' she described, wondering if the mother knew anything about the outrageous free-living dancer who once had all of Europe clamouring for more. 'It was the day,' Greta went on, holding Joyce Lockard in the palm of her hand, 'Lorraine had kept up with the girls – it didn't happen often – but that day she was right up there with them.' She remembered how Lorraine, after the other girls had gone, whirled around the house to her own beat in a wild and glorious display of leaps and pirouettes that had left her swamped with pity for the deaf girl; a raw talent going nowhere.

'She'll be our star!' Greta couldn't resist throwing in a bit of skite for the benefit of Reverend Baker and the bank manager's wife. 'That's how we'll do it. An Isadora Duncan mix with a touch of modern interpretative movement.' *A few miserable dance steps, indeed, Mrs Wife of the Bank Manager!* 'It'll be hard work for the girl, though,' Greta carried on, and a gawd-awful time for me, she thought to herself. 'But never mind,' she assured the woman, 'it will be done.' The look on Joyce Lockard's face wiped away any misgivings. Lorraine would work her guts out to be a success, Greta knew that without telling.

After the second cup of tea, Mrs Lockard put pen and pad away and rose to her feet. 'Well, Reverend, we must be off.' There was no gushing, no display of gratitude now; full composure had returned. 'Lorraine, no doubt, will be pleased by the outcome of our arrangements. But there is one important thing not yet discussed. When, Greta, do you think this cabaret can be done?'

'I suppose that's up to you and the Rev. Not forgetting the ladies' guild, of course.' The touch of acid in her tone brought a grin to Marelda's face and an exchange of glances between the Reverend and Joyce Lockard.

'Well . . .' Reverend Baker, who throughout the morning had had little to say, pursed his lips. 'Christmas is getting close —'

'Close all right, we're into October now.'

'Ah, yes. Christmas. We were wondering if —' He paused, finger tapping his lips and taking a breath, rushed on. 'Could it be possible? Just a suggestion, of course. A few carols, perhaps?'

'For a cabaret? Come off it, Rev; you should know better than that,' Greta said, stopping herself from adding, 'for a professional', and for their benefit she did a shimmy and a shake. 'Cabaret is party time! Don't you agree?'

'Of course. Just an idea.' He retreated behind confusion.

'Christmas, eh? Doesn't leave much time,' Greta said firmly. 'What have we got. Nine? Ten weeks, starting from scratch? I don't know . . .' Her mind was racing. They had no idea of what had to be done. Her heart was in a state of palpitation at the thought of high kicks and music, lighting, costumes and song, not forgetting the applause. If Greta Flight née Osborne was going to put on a show, it was going to be a damn good one, that's for sure!

They stood there, waiting for an answer.

'As I've just said, ten weeks from scratch.' Marelda was stacking cups and saucers on the traymobile, making a neat pile of leftover biscuits and fluffing up cushions. It was plain to see she wasn't leaving, not even into the kitchen. In the built-up heat of mid-day the iron roof's crackling only emphasised Greta's silence, and cicadas in the grass vied with the plaintive bleating and baas of goats as they waited for Greta's daily offering of vegetable scraps. Expression neutral, her gaze was non-committal while Baker and Mrs Lockard held their breath.

'December, you say.' Deciding she had teased them enough, she gave them a grin and a nod. 'Why not give it a try? If we pull together, we can put on a show that'll be the talk of the Tablelands and right up to the tip of Cape York.'

Greta told herself she was stark-raving mad as she ushered the relieved pair to her front gate.

CHAPTER TWENTY-THREE

Poinciana trees splashed orange and scarlet blossoms over Yunnabilla with careless flamboyance, broadcasting that winter's 'dry' was nearly over and summer rains were not far away. Days were getting warm to hot. Tobacco farmers stood at their gates and the doors of their curing barns overlooking fields of tobacco, watching the sky for early cloud bursts and hoping that the drought of the last seasons was over. They prayed that summer's monsoons would drench the earth just enough for crops to flourish and mature, to be picked and cured, free from fungus and bug. They wondered if the last loan from the bank would cover a few Christmas presents for the kids and a new battery for the truck. Everyone, rain or sunshine, drought or cyclone, was ready to throw caution to the wind and go to Yunnabilla for the cabaret.

The town heaved with excitement, the Great Depression was put aside to worry over another day. It was early December and Christmas was just around the corner. Molloy & Co had a nativity scene in one window while the other flaunted a tree dotted with cotton balls and paper chains, displaying celluloid dolls and golliwogs, and surrounded by tins of fancy biscuits that few could afford. Paying homage to a magnificent cut-glass decanter filled with Piver's Princess quality cologne, satin-lined boxes of lesser brands were distributed carefully around its base. Over the town hung a rich aroma of freshly baked fruit cakes, and cloth-bound plum puddings tied to verandah rafters swung in the breeze. Marelda Larkin's giant hairpins were working overtime as she prodded and tested mince tartlets by the dozen for the CWA's street stall. The women of the association were all out to take advantage of the increase in population on the day of the cabaret.

A week to go, and the School of Arts was unrecognisable with full-length mirrors draped with red velvet, tables gay with cretonne covers and touches of the Sydney Bohemian Club were seen in the candles and their wax dribbling down the sides of lager bottles.

Centre of all the jollity, the small grey house had its rooms stretched to capacity with precious costumes courtesy of the ladies' guild and Leila Coleman. It was a beehive of comings and goings – visits welcome and some not so welcome. The gramophone didn't stop while Greta, with hardly a twinge in her shoulder, pruned and cut, exhorted and praised.

Light footsteps hurried through the front gate and onto the verandah. 'Hoo-oo, Greta, here they are.' Poppy Griffen, carrying a clean hessian sugar bag, poked her head around the sitting-room door. 'Will I put them on the kitchen table?'

Paul Whiteman's 'Strike Up the Band' had come to an abrupt stop as did the sound of tapping feet. Greta, her hair piled high on her head for comfort, had her usual wet barber's towel draped around her neck. 'Can hardly wait to see them. Girls,' she said to the ballet of six, 'take a break, there's lemonade out on the verandah.' Six hot steaming pupils of differing years flopped down on the floor, mopping shiny faces. Except for the gramophone, the room was bare of furniture. The seagrass sofa, chairs and cushions were now stacked in one of Marelda's spare rooms.

Greta followed Poppy to the kitchen and, not waiting, took a peek into the sack. 'Marvellous. You're a genius, Poppy.'

One by one, six papier mâché hats were placed side by side on the table. Painted pink, bright and shiny with Taubman's enamel, the cunning upturned brims had a delighted Greta already trying one on at a cheeky angle. 'They'll go perfectly with the "I'll Never Say Never" number. Here, put one on, I want to see how it looks.'

Poppy, who was lead dancer in the chorus line, was happy to oblige. They looked each other over, chuckling in agreement. Greta began singing the first line of the song with its catchy tune. Poppy picked up the second line and without pause both of them fell into step with the well-rehearsed routine. In seconds the ballet girls hearing the song were into the kitchen trying on hats and joining in. They romped around the table, up the hall giggling and singing the words learnt off by heart; a prelude of what was to come on the night of the cabaret. On reaching the sitting room and end of the song, the ballet fell into each others' arms, laughing and puffing, confident that they would do the Flight Academy proud. Greta had opened up a new world for them. It was something that they would never forget, they had told each other over and over again.

Greta herself could not have felt more pleased. Everything was going to plan. Between them, she and Andy had worked wonders with Lorraine and her solo, knowing that the girl was going to enchant them all. Her mother, tight-lipped and proud, had worked like a Trojan with the guild ladies, proof seen in the costumes hanging in the spare room. Mannie and his gypsies would create magic in the tarted-up School of Arts and the ballet had surpassed themselves. The weeks had been so flat out, so absorbing, there had been hardly a moment left to talk the day over. Not that Andy minded, immersed as he was in playing for and coaching the deaf girl. Rehearsals with the Riverbank Players and keeping the garage and repair work up to date (and, as usual, only being paid for half of it) had kept him busy. After an evening meal of sorts, the Flights discovered that bed was for sleeping in only, with one of them out to it before the lamps had been blown out. Both agreed they were having the time of their lives.

When all this is over, Greta promised herself, she and Andy would pull down the blinds, put out the 'Not at home' sign, picnic by the river and make love in the moonlight. There was a lot of catching up to do.

She was ready to wrap up a successful day of rehearsing. Poppy had left and it was only a matter of sending the rest on their way, elated and glowing from her praise of a job well done. As the last girl mounted her bicycle, giving a wave goodbye, Greta gave an inward groan. Joyce Lockard pulled up, making a much-too-late visit. As she slammed the car door Greta felt a ripple of unease. Joyce never slammed car doors, and as she approached it was obvious her usual calm had been left somewhere behind.

'I've come to collect the costumes. We've got time.'

'Time for what?'

'To make petticoats!'

She brushed a stunned Greta aside, going straight into the single bedroom and before she could be stopped, was tearing the 'Red Sails in the Sunset' costumes off their hangers.

'Joyce! What the hell are you doing?' Greta grabbed one before it was flung over the woman's arm. She was shocked to see tears of what appeared to be anger in Joyce's eyes.

'The guild – and that means the church, the congregation – is banning the cabaret. That means half the town will stay at home. Not the Catholics, naturally, and the Reverend is nearly out of his mind.'

'For God's sake, Joyce.' Greta pushed her down on the bed. 'Take it easy. Now what's wrong? Tell me.' Greta carefully removed the garments off Joyce's arm.

'They were seen drying on your line.'

'Of course they were – Leila and I had just finished dying them. The Sunset sequence has been her baby all along – even the making of the costumes she trusted to no one else.' Greta held a rose-sequined skirt up for inspection. 'Leila's done a wonderful job on them. Gorgeous, aren't they?'

'Some of the ladies don't think so.'

'What? I can't believe this.'

'The women feel they are far too immodest, too provocative. You can see their legs —'

'That's the idea. It's mosquito net.'

'I've talked myself hoarse.' Mrs Lockard's voice vibrated with emotion. 'I can't shift them, and the black satin shorts for "Never Again . . ."'

'Yes?'

'Thinking things over, for goodness' sake, they want skirts to cover the knees.'

'I see. As for "Red Sails",' Greta's tone was silky, eyes narrowed, 'petticoats . . . Is that what we're talking about?'

'Yes.' Mrs Lockard's reply was a whisper. 'And there is time to run them up.'

'Over my dead body. Showing their legs?' Greta's red enamelled nails raked through her hair. 'What's wrong with that? Anyway, that's how I want it.' She started pinning the skirts back on hangers. 'And that's the way it's going to be! For gosh sakes, Joyce, you approved of them yourself.'

'I know, but I'm not the only member of the guild.'

'Bollocks!'

'Greta, there's no getting around it. I'm sorry. I understand how you feel, but —'

'But bloody nothing!' Greta was breathing fire. 'Here we are, less than a week away. Everyone, and that includes you, Joyce, have been working like the furies to get things done. Someone is behind all this and I'd like to know who.'

'No one really, but some of the ladies feel uncomfortable. In their words, they say it's too much like Hollywood pictures on the screen. Like actresses . . .'

'Yair, like young Annabelle Griffen dressed up as Shirley Temple singing "On the Good Ship Lollipop". Oh, for gawd sake, Joyce!'

'Well, I'm afraid that's how has to be. A total ban.'

'Wowsers and illiterates, the lot of them,' Greta shot back, remembering an outraged mother cancelling lessons because she'd found her precious daughter delighting the lads next door by doing cartwheels in the backyard. 'Right!' Furious, Greta hurled caution out the window. 'You do what you like but as far as I'm concerned I won't be singing or dancing a step. You can kiss goodbye to the Riverbank Players *and* the props *and* the gypsy caravan *and* the mirrors supplied by Leila from heaven knows where, but I can tell you right now, as far as I'm concerned, run the damn thing yourselves. Including the Rev and his precious ladies' guild!' But Greta still had one ace up her sleeve and was ready to have a last try. 'And what about Lorraine, the loveliest gypsy that has ever trod the boards? How are you going to explain all this to her?'

'I've no idea.' Joyce Lockard's sigh did nothing to help the way Greta felt. 'But I'm not surprised by your reaction.'

Throwing Lorraine into her face was a rotten thing to do. Mean as the devil, was the only way to describe it. But she had to put up some sort of a fight. Not for herself, but for the girls. She thought of the joy and laughter that had rung through the house not a half hour ago. Her pupils. Every one of them over the weeks had put their heart and soul into what promised to be a near-professional performance. She couldn't let them down.

Joyce, giving up, sighed again. 'Now I've spoken to you I'll try to have the guild change its mind over the matter. What you have said,' and being the bank manager's wife, she raised a cool eyebrow, 'and *threatened*,' she paused only for a second, 'might have some effect.'

'You mean it should do the trick, eh?' It was more bravado than being cocky.

'You may put it that way.' Now composed, as if something had already been worked out, she got off the bed to leave the room. Without hat or gloves to bother about, Joyce wasted no time with goodbyes. 'I'll let you know what has been decided upon tomorrow. First thing.'

As she drove off, Greta knew that now she'd given Joyce Lockard an ultimatum for the guild to chew over, the battle was half won. Let the bank manager's wife do a lot of sweet talkin', she told herself, confident that the show would go on.

By the clock in the kitchen it was four in the afternoon and Andrew, with an out-of-town job, would not be home until six. The swimming hole beckoned. She dashed into the bathroom and in seconds togs were wrenched off a hook and pulled over thighs and hips. She dropped a house dress over her head and in minutes the bike was out of the shed and Greta, hair flying loose and free and legs pumping, peddled towards the river. An hour lolling in currents warmed by the day's hot sun would smooth away every niggle and prickle that had scratched at her sanity over the last hour. Damn the ladies' guild!

There was a small stand of bottlebrush not far off the riverbank making a narrow, gentle channel where Greta floated, smelling the honey sweetness of blossoms that tickled her face. Head half covered by water, all sound blocked out, she lay in a dream, cares leaching away and carried downstream by the river.

Tonight, there was nothing to do. Nothing planned. It would be a quiet time. Andy all to herself and no last-minute intrusions like a visit (though usually welcome) from David Pedersen, who'd been standing on the sidelines, fascinated by the glamour and glitz ready to hit the tobacco town. He had not been seen for days. It was reported that he'd gone to spend time at a farm owned by a 'health crank' who was into raw vegetables and that, somewhere near Millaa Millaa. 'Helps him to give up the booze for a while', was the general opinion, although he had left a note for Andy at the garage, giving an assurance that he'd be back in time for the cabaret.

Time to go home. Slipping her dress over wet togs and feeling cool and refreshed, Greta left her solitude behind. There was a climb on leaving the river, for in the past, rain and flood had scoured and washed away the riverbank, leaving behind deep gullies and crevasses, making shelter for goats and the odd cow that wandered down to drink. It was a place of rock and steep red soil banks. Greta never brought her bike down to the water's edge but left it high above; it was much easier to climb up and down unhampered by handle bars, pedals and wheels.

She hadn't realised she'd dropped her sandshoes in a small puddle before taking her swim. Now they were wet, and bindy eyes in the grass and the band of scree and gravel before she reached the soft dirt of the gullies could hurt. Always careful of her dancing feet, she slipped the wet sandshoes on and made for the path that led upwards to town and her bicycle. She soon discovered she had done the wrong thing. One second she was upright, the next sliding off a barely concealed rock. She crashed to the ground.

Bugger! Bugger!

The wind was knocked out of her but as she sat up she swore again. There was only one cow down by the river and only one cow pat left behind, and yet she had to fall smack bang into it! Her dress and arm were covered with the still-warm droppings. No use cursing, she told herself, thanking her lucky stars that nothing worse had happened. No ankle twists or sprains and her back felt fine, so she returned to the river and began washing the dung and dirt away. It was harder to clean her dress and as there seemed to be no one around to laugh or report, she waded into the river again, dress, togs and all. It was there that she discovered a not-so large cut above the elbow. It was bleeding, but not profusely. Nothing to worry about, and remembering that only a few weeks ago she couldn't lift her shoulder, Greta congratulated herself that all was well. Something for her and Andy to laugh about over dinner. Apart from the session with Joyce Lockard, the day hadn't been so bad after all. Sopping wet, Greta mounted her bike and peddled for home, a shower and dry clothes.

'You've hurt yourself.' Concern crossed Andrew's face at the sight of Greta sitting at the kitchen table, her arm resting beside a basin of water while she dab-dried the cut on her arm with a ball of cotton wool. A bottle of iodine stood near at hand.

'You're just in time to give first aid.' She held up her face for a kiss, then indicated a rolled-up bandage. 'A little deeper than I thought. A silly accident in the only cow pat down by the river and I had to slide right into it.' She reached for another ball of wool and doused it with iodine.

'What are ye doing lass?' he said as he watched her quickly place it over the wound. 'It's going to hurt like hell.' He squeezed her hand hard.

'Not if —' she gasped, gritting her teeth, '— if you do it fast enough. Now, quick! Bandage it!' Firmly and expertly, Andrew bandaged the arm.

'How's that?'

'Feeling better by the second. With no air on it, it doesn't take long to settle down.'

'What you need, my girl, is a good, solid slug.' He rummaged through the Gladstone bag that held lunch and the odd tools he carried 'just in case'. 'And I've got just the thing.' He held up a strangely shaped bottle for her inspection.

'Sherry?' she asked, intrigued.

'Far from it, sweetheart. Mountain juice – the best – to slip down the throat like fire and numb your brain.' He made a pretence of studying a crudely made label. 'The contents of this bottle are guaranteed to stop sore legs and arms, weakness of knees and bad, peculiar dreams.'

'Stop it, you idiot.' In spite of the iodine and a slight soreness, Greta found herself giggling. 'Now what's this all about?'

'Today, I've been up yon mountain,' he replied, referring to a mountain range twenty-odd miles away and a picturesque backdrop to the town. 'But wonders of wonders, it was cash on the knocker to fix a wee problem that was holding up production.' He had a pirate's grin and the devil in his eyes as he dived into the bag again and brought out a fan of pound notes. 'Thirty quid, and what do ye think of that?'

Greta's jaw dropped. 'Gawd, Aggie! Have you robbed a bank?'

'No, just an appreciative customer with a productive farm who knows a thing or two in the making of a good drop.' Andrew opened the bottle and gave a sniff. 'Good, all right.' He reached for glasses on the open dresser and poured out a measure for Greta and himself. 'Drink up, lass, while I do something for our dinner. What have we got?'

'Snags in the ice chest and eggs,' said Greta.

'And potatoes for stovies?' Andrew peered into a food cupboard. 'Just enough.' He spoke as an expert.

Cheap and filling, stovies was a Scottish dish of potatoes, onions and good beef dripping fried and turned over repeatedly in a saucepan, the end result a tasty pot of potatoes flecked with crisps of brown. It was a favourite in the Flight household and, more importantly, for Greta a satisfying meal when funds were low.

While Andrew cooked, Greta related – between sips of a spirit that warmed and kept her floating – the fracas between herself and Joyce Lockard. 'But it'll be okay. I know it will – I hope.' She poured herself another finger and held up the glass to where the last of the sunlight was streaming through the window. 'Golden. That's what it is. What do you call it?' She sipped again. 'Correction. What does *he* call it?' Another sip trickled down her throat.

Andrew flipped over more potato and onion and added another piece of dripping. 'I don't think he's got around to that. You give it a name.'

'"Greta's Gold". How does that sound?' Still floating, she got up and slid her arms around his waist. 'Everything is nearly done. Coming to a head, you might say.'

'I hope you're referring to the cabaret.'

'Maybe.' Her hands gave his belly a light tickle. 'Guess what?' Tickling fingers crept lower. 'Nothing to do and all night to do it in.'

'Nothing? Careful now, or I'll burn the stovies.'

'Don't let me stop you.' She pressed herself against him and gave a little wriggle, delighted at his response. Sausages in a blue haze sizzled in the pan.

'Och, ye're a besom of a woman.'

'I know.' Slowly she began to unbutton his trousers. 'How're the sausages coming along?' She pulled up his shirt and, planting kisses on the small of his back, her teasing fingers danced up and down.

'Now ye're in trouble!' The frying pan was pulled away from the direct heat, the pot of stovies followed. He turned on her, his arms gripping her tight, his kisses hard and demanding. He lifted her off her feet and even in his desire was careful of the bandaged arm. 'No dinner for you tonight, lass!' He carried her unprotesting out of the kitchen.

CHAPTER TWENTY-FOUR

Greta was well prepared for an early-morning visit: a batch of scones cooling under a clean tea towel, cups and saucers on a tray (borrowed from Relda) and a full kettle steaming on the stove. She was ready and waiting for the Reverend and Joyce Lockard to appear. Good news or bad? It depended on the influence Joyce really had over the guild; and the picture of Reverend Baker trying to convince a bunch of sanctimonious prudes that he condoned a bit of a leg show would have had her doubled over if it wasn't so serious. She had a feeling that the Rev probably would have kept well out of the way while all the chit chat was going on.

Close to eleven and still not a sign of Joyce Lockard's royal coach, as Greta liked to call it. Twelve o'clock and she sat by herself in the kitchen eating scones and drinking tinned milk coffee. She couldn't believe that Joyce would fail to talk the guild around, and she would not have hesitated to inform her of their decision straightaway. Few had telephones in Yunnabilla and perhaps not everyone had been contacted when Joyce had returned to town. Because of that, the meeting could have made a late start with the ladies now talking their heads off. It was easy to picture.

As she sat there drinking the coffee that David Pedersen always teased her about, 'filthy stuff' as he called it, a moment of concern passed over her. David had attended the 'drying out' farm as the locals called it more frequently over recent months. He would then show up with clear eyes and his limp less pronounced, declaring that after one hour under the 'health crank's' hands a miracle had been performed. But it never lasted long.

The afternoon wore on and there was still no sign of the bank manager's wife. After all the activity of the past weeks and the drama of yesterday, Greta suddenly found a vacuum that was hard to fill. There was Andy's thirty pounds still lying on the kitchen dresser and she couldn't leave the house to spend it.

Under the table was a drawer that held cutlery and odd bits and pieces. She scrabbled around for a pencil, found one and took out a writing pad. Time, she decided, to make a Christmas wish list – and topping the list was the two weeks' rent owing to Mannie. Give him another week, she thought, and he'll be asking for it; never admitting that he owned the place. Greta was sure of that. Thirty quid, she gloated, and some to spare for a few luxuries and a decent present for Andy.

Slowly she realised that something else was taking place in her mind. She was once again the housewife. But over recent weeks the old Greta Osborne had returned. Flight's Academy had never done that for her. Always she had looked on it as a business. Enjoyable. But not quite the same as a live performance to set the toes tingling and the blood racing. She went through all that had been accomplished over the time. The planning, the auditions, the rehearsals, the laughs and the tears (not on her part) – she had loved every minute of it. Even the altercations of yesterday and the mewlings of the guild had had its moments. Righteous indignation, she discovered, could have its own satisfaction; sometimes it even brought results. She couldn't guess what was going on in the church hall; if all went well there would be a final dress rehearsal in the School of Arts tomorrow night. By next Sunday it would be all over.

Mrs Lockard finally arrived midafternoon, a smile wiping away any hint of tension on her face. The car door slammed and before she reached the gate, called out, 'We've won! Greta, we've won!'

Over tea (she refused the milk coffee) and cold scones, she admitted that the last few hours had been some of the most awkward she had spent in her life.

'What about yesterday?'

'Yesterday?' Mrs Lockard held out her cup to be topped up. 'A mere bagatelle, my dear.' The atmosphere was so relaxed, so cosy, that Greta could have sworn the banker's wife was ready to slip off her shoes and wriggle her toes under the table. The woman had done a real turn-around. A picture of affability.

Greta listened amazed as Joyce Lockard told her the full story. The town had suddenly found itself divided. The majority, adamant on having a good time and a night out, were up against those who prophesied that a cabaret with young women and children flaunting themselves would be a slur on the town's respectability. Apparently it had been building up since the day Greta had hung out the net skirts on the clothesline to dry. Initially, not that many worried about the few who objected. But the small circle of good wives, church goers all, had made enough ruckus for the guild to let down the moat bridge and declare a truce. The costumes would be altered.

'And that brings us up to yesterday, Greta. I'm not denying that

I was extremely upset but deep down I was hoping for a positive reaction from you. And you gave it to me. Once I told the guild about you stripping the School of Arts bare – taking the orchestra off the program – well . . . they began to realise how a storm in a teacup could lose us more money than we could possibly make in a year of fêtes, street stalls and a mountain of lamingtons. Not counting Marelda Larkin's fruit cakes. Well, commonsense ruled the day. A vote was taken to ignore the few malcontents – troublemakers, I'd call them – and their objections. The costumes stay as they are!'

Joyce Lockard stood up, brushing crumbs off her skirt. 'And you, Greta, have done wonders in every way. Most of the guild ladies would agree with me there. Now, before I outstay my welcome, I've taxed you enough over the last twenty-four hours, but thank you again from Lorraine and myself, and we'll see you at the dress rehearsal tomorrow night.' She began walking towards the sitting room, then stopped and turned. 'Of course I noticed the bandage. Not too serious, I hope?'

'Nothing to worry about.' But the day had been more stressful than Greta was ready to admit. Her arm felt sore and the too many scones with butter and jam had left her feeling queasy. 'Cows and their poo . . .' she said to herself as she waved Mrs Lockard off.

It was during the night she found herself wide awake with pain and throbbing. Her arm felt on fire. Not waking Andy, she stumbled down the hall into the kitchen. Although the fire in the stove had settled down to ash, the water in the kettle was hot enough to bathe the soreness away and a couple of Aspros would do the rest. Seated by the table and careful not to hurt, she peeled away the bandage revealing a slight swelling and redness, although the wound did look a little smaller than yesterday. Water for Greta was the panacea for all troubles, imagined or real. Warm and soft, it trickled through her fingers. By the light of the kerosene lamp turned low, and with the soft ticking of the kitchen clock for company, the throbbing began to subside. She found herself nodding off, the water cooling, and she dabbed the wound dry, trying to rebind the cut as neatly as Andy had done. Nearly an hour passed and, feeling slightly woozy, she climbed back into bed. Andy still slept on undisturbed.

Five o'clock and the alarm shrilled in Andrew's ear. Lying there half asleep, he went over the day ahead. First of all Molloy & Co's truck was waiting for its weekly tune up. He then remembered the thirty pounds of yesterday. He had been overpaid and well he knew it. In fact, he had raised objections when the notes had been pressed into his hand. 'It is nothing. Just a little thing, between you and me, eh, my friend?' He had found it easy to understand such unusual generosity, not forgetting Greta's Gold – 'For your beautiful lady.' There had been a breakdown in a vital part of machinery – a small private production concerning malt and juniper berries – while bottles stood empty and orders for Christmas cheer were waiting to be honoured.

Greta lay quiet and still on her side of the bed. She too had a busy day ahead and a full dress rehearsal before it all ended. Pride swelled through him. What a woman she was. Directing, overseeing every detail of the cabaret . . . her enthusiasm had been inspiring. She had sailed through every hazard, every problem, so sure of herself that the cast had followed through without question, surprised at their own capabilities as she brought out every skerrick of talent they might possess. It was her triumph.

He moved over to kiss her awake, surprised that she still slept.

'Andy, a blanket. It's cold. So cold.'

He sprang up on an elbow, wide awake. Greta's eyes were glazed and to his horror she began shaking, her teeth chattering. Rushing out of bed, he hauled two blankets out of a drawer that had been stored away. As he wrapped them around her, he caught a glimpse of an arm bloated and scarlet-hot above the bandages, but still Greta shivered. From the wardrobe he grabbed a coat, tossing it over the blankets. By now her eyes were half closed and showing only the whites. Bursts of fear exploded through him as he pulled trousers over his pyjama pants. How can a woman feel cold enough to shake a bed while her body burns with God knows what?

He gave thanks that he'd brought the utility home. The hospital was all he could think about and how long it would take to get her there. Through the silent main street the motor driven to its capacity roared through the morning, tyres screeching around a corner and down the side street leading to the hospital. Greta, now only half conscious, was snatched up in his arms and, racing down a path and up wide shallow stairs, he pounded down the verandah towards a single light in one of the wards.

'I need a doctor,' he shouted, 'for Christ's sake help us – I think my wife's dying!'

'Quiet! We've sick people here.' An irate nurse appeared at the ward's door, sponge in hand and carrying a towel. If her words were sharp, one look at the distraught man was enough for her to hurry over. 'It's Mr Flight!'

'Her arm.' Andrew tore the blanket aside, revealing Greta's arm

that seemed more swollen than ever. One startled look was all that
was needed.

'Sister!' she called out. 'Quickly!'

A young woman, starched stiff in posture and uniform, came
out ready to chastise a stranger who dared upset the smooth running of making the sick comfortable and scrubbed clean. 'This is
not the time of day —'

'Stop you're blethering, madam. My wife is ill. I feel the heat
of her asking for help.'

She studied the swollen arm and felt it with a cool hand. 'Nurse.'
Her voice was even and calm. 'Don't go looking for a wards man.
Get a trolley and hurry! Take her to A2. I'll follow in a minute.'

As Greta was wheeled along the verandah Andrew kept by her
side, not letting go of a hand that felt as if it had been scalded by
boiling water. It was wet, yet it burned. She was taken into a ward
of six beds made up with precision neatness, only one of them
occupied.

'Can you help me get her on the bed?' the nurse asked him.
'But first we get rid of these.' Andrew was handed the coat, and
the nurse, as young and slight as she was, without fuss removed
the blankets that he had wrapped so tightly around Greta's body.
The movement seemed to have some effect, for Greta opened her
eyes and managed a weak smile and a hello.

'Can you sit up, Mrs Flight?'

'Of course she canna' sit up!' Unthinking, Andrew elbowed the
nurse aside, lifted Greta off the trolley and placed her down on a
bedsheet starched with hospital discipline. It was enough to bring
on another bout of shivers, not quite as violent as the first. Andrew
threw the coat over her. 'Wher'r is the sister? The doctor?'

255

The nurse had had enough and in one movement swished a curtain screen around the bed. 'Mr Flight, the sister won't be long. It would be better if you wait outside.' A fleeting look of pity passed like a shadow over her face. 'For the moment, anyhow.' Footsteps were heard coming along the verandah. 'And here she is.'

She was known as Sister Barry, and one of the few fully trained nurses in town. Her walk was brisk and full of purpose, undaunted by an obvious confrontation waiting for her outside ward A2. She had seen the man before. Many times. There was hardly a dance in Yunnabilla she missed. The Andrew Flight she knew was completely different from the frantic husband waiting outside the ward. Thoughts were fleeting as she approached him. When Andrew Flight played his violin with Mannie and Leila on Saturday nights, there was only one word to describe it: Romantic. Romance now was nowhere to be seen in the wild-eyed man with trousers over pyjamas, bare feet and his fair hair askew. Such a shame. But one glance told her how dangerously ill the woman in A2 was. The Flights. The perfect pair – so much in love and so happy to let everyone see it. She drew herself up, ready for conflict.

'Mr Flight.' Sister Barry looked down without expression at the hand clutching her arm. 'There is no point in me talking to you now.'

'My wife!'

'Yes, I understand. However you must allow me to see her before I speak to you.'

'But the doctor . . . where is he?' The hand still gripped her arm.

'He'll be here at eight.'

'What d' ye mean? For God's sake, woman, get him now!'

'He's sleeping.'

'Sleeping!'

'That's all I can say.'

A terrible mix of anger and fear engulfed him. He was aware that his voice could be heard throughout the small hospital, demanding and raging. The sister wrenched herself free and escaped into the ward.

'What is the meaning of all this?'

A woman, encased upright in a corset beneath her uniform, her veil in full sail, bore down on Andrew, ready to scupper him with the weight of rigid authority. 'How dare you —' She pulled up short on seeing who it was. 'It's you, Mr Flight.' Andy felt a moment of cynicism as the hospital's matron lowered her voice. 'I'm sure there is no need for you —'

'No need! My wife's nearly dying and your doctor is asleep.'

'That is correct. And although I don't think it *is* necessary to tell you why, he only went to bed an hour or two ago. An emergency. Now I think that is all you need to know.' She pointed to a long wooden bench lined up against the verandah railing. 'Take a seat. I shall go in and see what can be done.'

'I'm sorry.' Feeling powerless against such a regime of tradition and sterilised expertise, with effort Andrew calmed his voice. 'But could you please tell me what's wrong? Really wrong with her? It has to be her arm.'

'That is for the doctor to say.' He could see by her face there was no use in extracting more from her. Meanwhile Greta was in there, suffering and alone.

'She is in awful pain – can you give her something?'

'I'm afraid not. Not until the doctor —'

'*Fock the doctor!* I'll give her something myself!'

'Not in this hospital, you won't.'

With a groan Andrew buried his face in his hands. He knew they thought him a fool and this mad tirade against the hospital was getting him nowhere. He looked up and was surprised to see the matron still there. 'Mr Flight.' Her voice softened. 'At the moment we are doing all we can. Making her comfortable. Trying to lessen the fever. If there is any small improvement, I'll allow you in to see her. Be patient. Please.'

Eyes shut and her face taut with pain, Greta lay under the hospital blankets with a sheet neatly pulled up. Her arm, now a monstrous size, had been freshly bandaged. The nurse had done all the things that were thought necessary: temperature taken, sweat sponged away and a jug of water and a glass stood on a nearby locker.

Andrew had been sitting beside her for over an hour, stroking her forehead, murmuring his concern and love for her. By the ward clock, the doctor should be examining her in less than a half hour. Greta's eyes opened.

'What's today?'

'Still Thursday.'

'Dress rehearsal,' she murmured.

'Don't think about it, lass. We've cancelled it.'

'Bloody nonsense.' Her eyes closed again. 'The cabaret. Only two nights away.'

What was there to say?

He had telephoned Mannie, giving him the news. Though full

of solicitude, Mannie's reply had been typical. 'Ring me when the doctor comes and if the worse comes to the worse, we'll forget about the dress rehearsal. Not necessary. Everyone has things off pat. She could be home in a couple of days. If not, we'll manage without her.' It sounded so casually heartless that Andrew could have wrung his neck, and said so.

'Don't put your Scotch curses on me, Andy Flight – you know we can't let Greta down. It's a bloody shame, but as I said she could be home by Saturday. Now go back and stroke her head. And don't forget to give me a ring.'

'Here comes the doctor now.' Obeying the signal of the nurse drawing the screen around the bed, Andrew removed himself to wait outside on the verandah. Leaning against the railings, he had a full view of the ward and Greta's bed. The matron and a man in crisp white from shirt to shoes came out from a side verandah that had a sign tacked to a railing post pointing the way to 'Out Patients'. A bolt of anger rushed through him as he watched the pair walking without haste towards the ward where Greta waited for a doctor to prescribe something to relieve her pain – to make her well. As they approached, the matron hurried ahead towards the curtained bed, leaving the doctor to give Andrew a cursory, if not dismissive glance, before entering the ward.

In an agony of not knowing, the minutes dragged while the three of them, doctor, matron and sister, stayed unseen in a consultation in which he played no part. Why were they taking so long? He strained to translate and make some sense of the murmurs that occasionally escaped the confines of the screen and Greta's bed. A soft laugh reached his ears. What could be so amusing? Boiling in frustration, he fought every urge to go in, rip the curtain aside and ask why should anyone laugh? But he stayed where he was, not daring to make a move. He watched as the curtain finally parted. It was the doctor who walked towards him. He was not a young man, and before he spoke he gave Andrew the impression of testy impatience.

'You're the husband.'

'Aye, that I am.' And you damn well know I am!

'Your wife has a severe infection. It could get worse.' He tapped a stethoscope against his teeth, looking over Andrew's shoulder as if the view outside of mulberry trees and wattle would help in making some sort of decision.

'At the moment it's fluctuant —'

'What the hell does that mean?'

'Meaning —' His voice was tinged with veiled annoyance. '— there is a fluid centre behind the wound – quite deep – and we will try hot packs to bring it all to a head. Then we'll see what happens.' Above the bickering of mynah birds in the mulberry trees, a moan and a gasp of pain was clearly heard.

'Jesus, mon! Help her!'

'Take hold of yourself.' A cool hand restrained him. 'We are, Mr Flight. Give it time and your wife will be more comfortable.' The doctor released his hold. 'Now, go home.'

'Not until I've seen her.' The exasperated sigh was audible.

'Very well, but don't take too long.' He looked the bedraggled man over. 'You'll feel better after a shower and ask Matron if you need to know anything more.' With a nod he turned on his heel, leaving Andrew standing on the empty verandah.

Greta was awake, though drowsy. She took his hand. 'Cow's poo . . . Would you believe it? I'm sorry, darling.'

He choked down the lump in his throat, not bearing to look at

Greta's arm lying like a lump of wood on the bed. 'Oh God, what have I done to you?'

'Nothing to do with you.' With her free hand she stroked his face and gave a faint giggle. 'Oo-er, don' cha look a real proper git. Still in yer jammies.'

He bent over and kissed her cheek, not quite so hot, but still clammy. 'Did the doctor tell you about the hot packs and why?'

'Yes, he's told me. Its goodbye cabaret this time around, but you tell the crew to go ahead. Come Saturday, tell 'em from me to break a leg, ay?'

He ached for her. His darling girl . . . 'Without you? No! We can cancel.'

'Like hell. All that work for nothing? Poppy can take over. She knows what to do. You all know what to do.' Her voice slurred a little, her eyes closing. 'I love you, Andy. I'll be all right. Not to worry.'

He sat there, holding the other hand, not wanting to leave. She seemed asleep. Silently he laid it on the bed, ready to go, but her eyes opened again. They were bright and her voice clear as she said, 'Don't fash yoursel', laddie. I'll be okay.'

CHAPTER TWENTY-FIVE

They met in Mannie's office: Leila, Poppy, Mrs Lockard, Reverend Baker, the few guild ladies who could be contacted at short notice and anyone else involved that could come. Even the supper organiser, one Marelda Larkin, turned up. Andrew was not to be seen. It had not taken long for the news and possible cancellation of the cabaret to sweep though the town. Some wondered if they'd get their ticket money back or simply donate it to the church.

'Well, we've talked enough – any more suggestions before we take a vote on it?' Mannie shoved his glasses back up his nose. The office wasn't built for a soirée and the air was steamy, the atmosphere gloomy.

'Don't you think Mr Flight should have a vote?'

Mannie glared at the guild lady. 'I've said a dozen times that Andy doesn't give a rap about what's going to happen. It's in our hands. Do we or don't we? Remember it's just the rehearsal we're voting on. First things first.'

Joyce Lockard had felt like absenting herself altogether. It didn't matter what was decided: without Andrew, Lorraine would not be able to dance. The picture of her daughter's disappointment was an ache in her heart nearly impossible to hide, although Mannie had said that she could sit by the gypsy camp fire while he played.

Poppy Griffen, terrified at the thought of running and managing the show, put up her hand. 'Look, how many of us *know* just how we'll get on at the Arts Hall? We've never tried it out, and that is what a dress rehearsal's all about.' Her face was flushed as she tried to bolster up their enthusiasm, feeling her own flagging. Without Greta? It couldn't work, but it had to! 'If we *are* going to do it, I say a dress rehearsal tonight. I for one don't want to bumble around tables like an untrained seal. See how it works out.' She looked around her, trying to act and sound like Greta.

It must have worked. Every hand shot up in agreement, and word would be passed on to be at the hall by seven. Suddenly buoyed up by a decision made, all were ready to go and spread the news. The School of Arts doors would open on Saturday night, while Joyce Lockard inwardly shed tears, dreading what she had to say to Lorraine. It was then that Andrew Flight walked through the door. He waved aside questions and words of sympathy.

'I see you have decided. Good. Greta will be proud. It would break her heart if y' don't carry on.' He then told them of the prognosis, choosing to ignore the exchanged glances of people who most of their lives had lived in the tropics. A cut, a fever and a swelling; so often a dire result. 'I'm on my way back to the hospital now.' He then turned to Mannie. 'Is David Pedersen back yet?'

Mannie shrugged, shaking his head.

'Do ye know where this place is he's staying?'

'I've a fair idea.'

'There must be a phone number. Ring him. Tell him he's needed here.' Mannie was ready to say that the hospital staff would be doing their best, but the steel in Andrew's voice, and the grim authority of the man standing before him, was another side that Mannie knew little about.

'Right, Andy, as soon as everyone leaves.'

'One more thing before I go.' Andrew walked over and took Joyce Lockard's hand. 'Joyce. Tell your lass I'll be there for her on Saturday. I canna' make tonight but I'll be there Saturday.' He went on to say that it meant only a half hour absence at the most from the hospital.

David Pedersen cut his stay at the health farm short. The phone call from Mannie had shocked and frightened him. However hard he tried, he could not imagine a world without Greta. Seemingly to come from nowhere, without fanfare and without notice, the Flights' arrival in Yunnabilla had brought an enjoyment to his life he had no longer come to expect. Mannie and Leila filled a gap for which he was grateful, but he had discovered that with Greta and Andy around as well, pain and self-disgust diminished. They never made judgments; they accepted him for what he was: an alcoholic, a has-been, and a surgeon no longer able to hold a scalpel. Now, ladies who liked a bedside manner, coughs and colds and minor complaints (and little else) filled his days. He was a remittance man with more than enough to pay for the luxuries that had once been taken for granted, and still had enough left over to drink himself to death.

Without Greta's knowledge, she had changed all that. The health farm, for a start. It had been years since he had made a

genuine effort to curb his drinking. The first day he saw her at the
Colemans' farm her vivid beauty, her sparkle and her sometimes racy
talk mesmerised him as it obviously had Andrew. He knew there
was more to Andrew than the mechanic and the violinist. As for
Greta, he found it difficult to imagine her behind a counter selling
ladies' underwear or serving dinners in a hotel. She had more than
a voice and over recent weeks he had glimpsed a real professionalism, impossible for Greta to hide. He would be surprised if he was
the only one who thought so. She was clothed in a glamour rarely
seen in the North. And who, he had often wondered, was Netty?
In Andrew's malarial state, he'd mentioned the name more than
once. Intuition had prevented him from asking. Whatever Greta
and Andrew's past, his days had been all the richer for knowing
them.

He left the verdant greenery, the lakes and waterfalls, and the
banana plantations of the Tablelands. Yunnabilla, with its surrounds
of scattered bushland, anthills and tobacco crops, was only a couple of hours away. He drove along a road of dust and corrugations
thinking about them – her – and hoping to God that he'd arrive to
find her safe and improving. Somehow doubt kept darkening his
mind. He kept up a steady pace, the Daimler purring.

A bright, hot Saturday morning and Andrew's mind focused on the
hospital, having spent another sleepless night. The house kept to
its silence. No singing, no clattering in the kitchen. He pumped
up the primus to boil water for tea and spread marmalade on a
piece of bread. How long would David Pedersen take to arrive?
Last night Mannie had telephoned the hospital to say that David

was on his way. He gave a brief smile. The matron had not been amused discovering her office telephone had been used for a private conversation between himself and Mannie Coleman. She'd be less amused, Andrew admitted, if she had an inkling of what had been said.

When he had left the ward Greta was sleeping, the hot packs seeming to soothe; her arm still swollen but the throbbing momentarily eased. The night-duty nurse had been adamant that he should go home, making it plain that his presence hindered more than helped her patient to remain in a comfortable state. She had added that it might be an idea to cook a decent breakfast before he returned. Although Andrew had been offered meals in the hours he had sat beside Greta's bed, apart from tea and coffee he had accepted little else. The matron had deemed it a favour to ignore visiting hours and had given permission for Andrew to stay well over the allotted times.

By eight o'clock he was treading the hospital path, ready to make war if he was prevented from going into the ward. As he came closer to the building he was surprised to see the doctor already walking along the verandah towards the matron's office, his morning visit to Greta obviously earlier than usual.

He stopped on seeing Andrew. 'Mr Flight.' He motioned with his hand. 'Give me five minutes. Then see me in Matron's office.' It was a command more than an invitation. But Andrew had learnt that it was wise to hold his tongue when confronted with medical authority.

The five minutes crawled while Andrew paced up and down the path, ready to face whatever might be told or decided upon. Perhaps there was an improvement that had been impossible to imagine only yesterday. Greta was a strong and healthy woman in body and in mind. Surely that counted for something! But a growing dread, hard to define, kept surfacing and Andrew found himself hesitating – he didn't know why – to face that supercilious bastard (as he thought of him), waiting in the matron's office. He squared his shoulders and walked in.

Seated behind a desk, the doctor allowed Andrew a short nod and a slight indication of a smile. He motioned for him to take a chair and on doing so, leant back into his own as if ready to pass the time of day. It seemed as if he was taking measure of who would break the silence first.

Andrew waited.

'Well, Flight, as usual you're early. However, it's better that we talk now. And in here.'

'Talk about what?' Fear roiled inside him. 'My wife. How . . . I saw you walking away from the ward. Is everything all right?' Silently he cursed the man sitting there so cool and seemingly unperturbed.

'Your wife. Ah, yes. Things are not so good, I'm afraid. The hot packs are not working and a much more morbid condition has surfaced. Septicaemia. Nasty.'

'Septicaemia! What d' ye mean? Talk English, mon.'

'Blood poisoning. She'll be dead tomorrow. There – does that satisfy you?' Expressionless, the doctor allowed time for his prediction to sink in.

Livid, Andrew reeled back. His mind was blank, trying to control the terror threatening to erupt in bellows from his mouth. Iron naval discipline came to his aid and he stiffened, finding the strength to get to his feet, forcing the doctor to look up at him. His voice was low and steady. 'Well, what do you intend to do about it? There must be something.'

'I'm coming to that in a moment. Please sit down.' From a small stack of papers he pulled out a form and pushed it across the table. 'For you to sign, and yes, there is something that can be done. Amputation.'

'*NO!*'

'The arm must be removed.' The tone was dismissive, nearly insulting. 'It is the only way to save her.'

Andrew felt himself losing the little control he had gained. Not his Greta. Not his glorious wonderful girl! He had to fight for every lovely inch of her. 'For Christ's sake, stop shoving that bloody piece of paper at me! I'll not sign anything.'

'In that case we cannot operate.'

'You won't!' he roared. 'I'll not allow it.'

'And I'll not be responsible for your lack of cooperation. Every minute from now counts. She'll die. There is no doubt about that.' The doctor rose to his feet. 'Do you understand me?'

'I'll get a second opinion.' *Jesus, David, where are you?*

'From where?' He was arrogant in his knowledge that there were few to call on.

'Dr Pedersen.'

'You must be mad!' Equilibrium was fast disappearing.

'Not mad enough to allow her arm to be hacked off by an arrogant bastard of a doctor.'

'Get out of this office – now!'

'I'm not leaving until I get Pedersen's opinion.' Andrew raised his fist, then dropped it. 'Just bloody stay away from my wife!' He turned on his heel and strode down the verandah, determined not to take his eyes off Greta. The doctor followed, threatening to call the police, and neither of them saw the Daimler coming up the drive and David Pedersen alighting.

'Andy, wait!' David, hurrying as quickly as his limp allowed, called out again. 'Wait!' His command brought the two men to a halt. David climbed the shallow steps, first of all addressing the doctor. 'Hello there, Mark, I see you two have met.' It allowed time for each man to dampen his anger. 'I've heard the news. Bad business. And how is she keeping?' David then turned to Andrew. 'Andy, it's all right. Mark and I will work something out.'

'He's wants to amputate. I canna' . . .'

David gave an imperceptible shake of his head. His eyes spoke volumes to the distraught man. 'Consultation first, eh, Mark? I don't think Matron will mind if we use her office.' Turning to a nurse standing by, wide-eyed, he said, 'Do you think it's possible to rustle up something to drink? Coffee, if you have it. It's been a long drive. And one also for Mr Flight.' He squeezed Andrew's shoulder and, without another word, accompanied the rigid-faced doctor to Matron's office. Andrew, although desperate to see Greta, thought it better to keep out of sight, fearful of her seeing the despair that must be written on his face.

For a snail-paced half hour he sat outside the ward on the visitors' bench waiting for David and the hospital doctor to emerge from the office. From where Andrew was sitting he could see Greta's screened bed and the side window in the office, but it told him nothing. Obviously the two men were still seated and all he could do was wait, hoping and praying that by some miracle – and without the aid of a knife – his dearest would live. Every minute dragged.

Holding what appeared to be a large oval basin, a nurse, clever in the way of avoiding eye encounters and awkward questions, hurried past him. She entered a room close by and similar to matron's office at the other end of the verandah. In minutes she reappeared as a wards man with a trolley came towards them, and at her signal pushed it into the ward. Andrew sprang to his feet. Good God, was Greta going to be wheeled away without fuss, without explanation, to some operating theatre that was out of sight? Why had he expected more? Somehow his legs failed him. Not able to move, his eyes strained to where Greta was lying; the trolley was already behind the screen. He willed himself to do something – anything to avoid what was about to happen. Suddenly the curtains were whisked aside, the trolley, with Greta on it, was wheeled out, followed by the nurse who, on seeing Andrew, raised a hand as if to stop him, the smile of a coquette on her face. 'You men are all the same. Can't wait.'

Without time to be astonished, to smash her teeth down her throat, she was gone with the wards man and the trolley into the room where she had been before. Firmly shutting the door, there was only time for her to add, 'We won't be long, Mr Flight, then you can come in.' Not knowing and sick at heart, his legs finally betrayed him as he flopped down on the visitors' bench. He didn't hear Pedersen's cane tapping steadily down the verandah towards him.

'We've staved off the operation – for a while, at least.' David sat down beside him. 'Greta is now my patient. She's been moved into the ward where my private clients stay.' He nodded towards the still-closed door. 'More pleasant, for a start. Mark has agreed to what I want to do but doubts that it'll work. I'm inclined to differ.' David Pedersen stood up. 'Andrew, you must think this over.

There's a risk it won't work. If it doesn't, then even an amputation could be too late.'

He went on to explain what he intended to do: Greta's arm would be soaked in hot saline baths two hours on, two hours off, night and day. 'I've increased the morphine dosage. There's no need for her to be in such pain.' He nodded towards a nurse with Sister Barry, hurrying past. 'Starting from now.'

'Hot water and salt?' Andrew found it hard to believe that such a remedy could save an arm bursting with poison. 'It sounds so simple, David.' Forcing back tears, worry wracked his voice. 'But I canna' have her dead. And she wouldn't want to live without . . . Oh, I don't know!' He buried his head into his hands, but only for seconds, then stood up. 'But she'd want us to try the other way. Your way.'

'Whatever way, old chap, Greta would take it on the chin. Arm or no arm.' David was now even more serious. 'But what about you?'

'I want her well.' A hard sob escaped him. 'I want her alive and laughing.'

'In that case, I'll leave you here for a while.' David stifled a yawn. 'Then I'll be off and back later on.' He gave Andrew's shoulder a friendly squeeze. 'Buck up, Andy. We'll try. We'll damn well try, the both of us, to hear her laugh again.'

A night breeze trifled with the curtains in the quiet room. Greta slept, lying between clean sheets. Twice since he'd been sitting there, the sheets, sodden with sweat, had been changed. Two hours on, two hours off with the bathing, the staff meticulous in keeping the water in the basin at the desired heat while Greta's arm lay in there, inert. Once her eyes had opened and on seeing him, had given a dopey smile. 'Hello, love,' she whispered before dropping off again.

David Pedersen, an immaculate contrast in a grey suit to Andrew's open shirt tucked into drill khaki trousers, came into the room, his third visit in the day. Without a greeting he went straight over to the bed, read the report clipped to the end of it and felt Greta's forehead and her cheeks with the back of his hand.

Unable to wait for a verdict, Andrew sprung up. 'What do you think?'

'The same as I thought this morning. She's a very sick woman. Too early yet to judge.' His facade of professionalism altered, his expression sympathetic, yet troubled. 'By the way, here's your violin.'

'Ye don't think for a minute I'm leaving here!'

'I believe there was a promise made.'

'Ye must be daft to think I'll be going anywhere. I'm not leaving her.'

A look like he'd seen on the hospital doctor's face crossed Pedersen's own. 'Look, man. Be sensible. The cabaret is in full swing and getting encores. Supper's over and Mannie's gypsy act will soon begin. Go, and I promise I'll not leave Greta for a second.'

'I'm not going. An' tha's the end of it.'

'You're a five-minute drive away. Ten minutes with the young Lockard girl, not counting the encores, and it will be all over. Do it!' David found himself adding, 'Do it for Greta.'

The lines deepened around Andrew's mouth, his eyes grey and set narrow. He walked over to the window, looking into darkness, while Pedersen waited, wondering if he had gone too far. A nurse entered with a jug of water, steaming hot. As if she felt a tension between the doctor and the man standing by the window, she quickly poured it into the basin, tested the temperature with a thermometer, and gave the doctor a nod before leaving with speed. Greta stirred but did not wake. The morphine was doing its job.

Without a word, without a look, Andrew picked up the violin case and walked out of the room.

Mannie was standing with one foot on the stairs of the plywood yellow gypsy van, Lorraine sitting at his feet, a tambourine in her hand. He began walking around the tables, playing his version of what he called a gypsy tango, ignoring the spectacles sliding down his nose. He looked the part, dark eyes glinting, the red bandana knotted carelessly around his throat. It was his yellow satin shirt unbuttoned to the waist, exposing a hairy chest, that excited comment. There was no doubt about it. The cabaret was the most daring of entertainments that had ever hit the town. 'Red Sails in the Sunset' with the ballet in transparent glitter nearly stopped the show, but even that was outclassed by the 'I'll Never Say Never' number, with the tightest black satin shorts anyone had ever laid eyes on. The sight of those shapely – and not so shapely – legs had set the fellows whistling, and the younger women determined that if Greta Flight was going to put on another show, come hell or high water they'd be in it, and never mind what Dad said.

'Terrible shame about Greta, and as for Mannie Coleman wandering around the tables thinking he was flash in that outfit, well – enough said,' was the general opinion. Some wondered what Leila Coleman thought of it all, as he flirted and played his accordion to every woman within reach.

Mannie was in his element. Never had he played so well and

he knew the crowd was loving it. To make up for the absence of Andrew which had put a finish to young Lorraine's dance, other melodies of a gypsy theme were racing through his mind. Playing without stop, he sensed more than heard a slight commotion at the entrance of the hall. A soft clapping, a cheer here and there, and it was enough for him to stop.

The sweetest melancholy of sound flowed over the heads of the audience as Andrew threaded his way towards the gypsy van. The deaf girl gave the tambourine a tremolo of cymbals, standing up as if she could hear every note that Andrew played, her eyes never leaving his face. Mannie felt a tingle run down his spine as the violinist reached out and touched the deaf girl's hand. She swayed and slowly made her way down between the tables while Andrew, watching every move, followed, increasing and decreasing the tempo when needed. A collective gasp escaped as Lorraine, tables not a fingertip away, gave a sudden bound that carried her through the air only to land not a hair's breadth from where her mother sat. It was a spontaneous leap of joy that had the crowd clapping wildly. Every graceful bend, lovely twist and pirouette that had been practised time and time again with Greta were melded into a faultless combination of music and motion. For everyone it ended all too soon. Encores were called for but already the violin had been handed over to Mannie. The clapping died as Andrew walked back down between them all, hardly aware of the words of praise and encouragement as he left the hall.

CHAPTER TWENTY-SIX

Another night, another day, and no improvement after the next long night.

At sun-up, Andrew left the stretcher that had been brought into the hospital room for him. Hardly awake and not wanting to disturb the sedated Greta, he walked down the hospital path to the end of the drive. The sky in the east lightened and the air was filled with the smell of dew-moistened grass, but he could find no joy in it. Retracing his steps, his body heavy from lack of rest and with sleep-grit in his eyes, he trod quietly down the side of the verandah that led to the toilets and showers. A cold sluice refreshed him, and he decided he'd been out of the sick room long enough – longer than usual.

As he reached Greta's door a stench of putrefaction hit him. She lay in silence, eyes closed. Fear gripped him as he rushed over and saw the sheet where her arm lay was soaked in blood and pus. The smell made him gag as he fled outside, calling for a nurse. Sister Barry shot out of the ward opposite.

'What's wrong?'

'Something's happened!'

She pushed him aside and ran into the room. Following, he saw her stop short of the bed. 'What a bloody mess!' She didn't sound alarmed but turned back to him. 'Go and get a nurse.'

'What's wrong? What's happened?'

'It's come to a head. It's burst! Now go get that nurse!'

Arms braced on the verandah railing, the tears fell unheeded down his cheeks. She's going to live! She's going to live! He repeated it over and over to himself, hardly believing the truth of it.

Once again he was bundled outside by staff going in and out with hot water, clean bedding and bandages, and David Pedersen was suddenly beside him, materialising out of nowhere, and grinning with a faint smell of brandy on his breath. He felt a hearty clap on his back.

'We've done it, Andy; it's over. You'll be able to take her home in a few days.'

Thinking of the blood, the fevers, and how desperately ill she had been, he had to ask, 'So soon?'

'No question about it. The wound will have to be drained, of course. It'll seep for a time. But now the poison has gone and as I've said before, your Greta is a strong woman. Strong as Riley's bull. She'll heal – should heal – quickly. Believe me.'

Andrew would have believed the North Pole was joining up with the South Pole if David Pedersen had said so. He wanted to voice so much, but words weren't adequate to describe how he felt. How to thank the man gripping his hand?

'Andy, there is something I have to say. It's what I want you to do.'

'Anything.'

He was ready for the litany of instructions to be carried out for Greta's recovery: medication, perhaps even a private nurse, no matter what the cost. Nothing but the best for her. Mannie would know how to handle the sale of the ruby . . . Thoughts carcened through his head, then realising what David was saying, the simplicity of the proposed treatment stunned him.

'Vegetables, Andy, by the plateful. Twice a day. Potatoes, tomatoes, pumpkin, beans, everything – not forgetting the leafy greens. Rabbit food, as some like to call it. Marvellous stuff. Do what I say and you'll have your Greta fit and well in no time.'

A nurse approached. 'Mr Flight, you can go in now.' Still choking on words unspoken, Andrew followed the nurse into Greta's room. The doctor stood there for a while, pensive, alone. The uncertainty, doubts of ability and instinct and dread of the past four days were over. All quiet; order returned. David took one long look at the room where Greta lay, then, taking a firmer grip of his cane, limped along the verandah. The matron met him halfway.

'Congratulations, Doctor. You've worked a miracle.'

Still a little drowsy, she already looked different. There was peace in her sleepy smile and her arm, although bandaged, Andrew somehow felt or imagined didn't look quite as swollen. A nurse had brushed her hair and against her pallid skin it looked all the richer fanned out on the pillow. She was still the most beautiful woman he'd ever laid eyes on. Greta motioned him over.

'I've missed you. Come and give me a kiss.'

Two days passed and Greta was in no mood to tackle the plate of boiled cabbage, snake beans and the watery tastelessness of mashed pumpkin. She had picked the edges off a slice of roast beef and in a pique pushed the plate aside. 'David, I refuse to eat any more of it!'

'And you're the woman who drinks that travesty you call coffee!' He took sympathy on her. 'You'll find it different when you get home. To Marelda Larkin's outrage, I've been giving Andy lessons on how to steam a carrot or two.'

'So you're a cook now?'

'One of my talents for quite a while, courtesy of the health farm.'

'Oh, David, I'm sorry. But it's so hot; I'd give anything for a swim.' Greta gave a sigh of frustration. 'Christmas just around the corner and Marelda has to be fended off from making us a cake and pudding.' With her good arm she wrenched the pillow from under her head, and before David could stop her, gave it a few vicious whacks. 'There, that might cool it down a bit.' She leant forward. 'Put it back for me, will you?' As David was doing his best, she gave another sigh. 'Well, the Flight Academy won't be having its break-up party.'

'How sad for them.'

'Don't be funny. How long now before I can leave this damned room?'

'I'd say Saturday.'

Greta groaned. 'Gawd, Aggie, that's donkey ages away. How about Friday? I'm bored out of my mind.' Tears sprang into her eyes. 'Forgive me, David, but I want to go home.' She wondered if Andy would visit again after seeing her so early in the day. Only for a few minutes he was there before rushing off with a quick kiss goodbye. She understood why. Business already was at flagging point and the little there was had to be attended to. Five minutes later, the nurse had handed her a parcel wrapped in brown paper. 'Mr Flight left this for you. Said I wasn't to give it to you until you've had a sponge down.'

David Pederson crossed to the windows, poking his head outside. Greta was aware he'd been doing that ever since walking through the door.

'Are you expecting a patient or something?'

'No.' He sounded vague. 'Not quite.'

More than once she had seen him check his vest pocket watch. 'Shouldn't be long now.' As he spoke a faint sound came through the curtains. Greta sparked up, straining to hear. Andy, after all? was her happy thought as a nurse entered the room with a wheelchair.

'Visitors, Mrs Flight. Think you can manage the chair? If you're lucky you might be taken for a stroll down the drive.'

'Not in this heat, thank you very much. But the verandah will be wonderful – for a change. Anyway, who are they?'

'Wouldn't know.'

Ever since Greta's wits had returned and agony had eased to a bearable hurt, she was always groomed, ready to receive Andrew or anyone else who cared to visit. For a change she had asked the nurse to pin up her hair but the red-gold waves refused to be tamed and tendrils escaped. The silk apple-green and coffee lace bed jacket was cut for coolness. Andrew had left a note with the parcel. 'Especially sent up from Cairns for special occasions.' Between delight and surprise Greta had wondered how much it cost. Even so, she couldn't wait for him to see it on her, pleased that the visitors, whoever they were, would find her looking her best – under the circumstances, she told herself. Feeling wobbly, she left the bed with David standing by to help, and no sooner had she sat down than the nurse whisked her out of the room.

The sound she had heard was now unmistakable and growing louder. The chorus of 'I'll Never Say Never Again, Again' was coming from a large truck rolling up the hospital drive. It did a flourish of a turn, exposing Leila on the back playing a piano while Mannie in gypsy costume was already out of the truck to let down the tailgate.

With Poppy Griffen in the lead, the full ballet alighted one by one. Step perfect, pink hats shining in the sunlight, they trooped up the steps onto a now crowded verandah, dancing for Greta, the staff and the few patients that were there. They filled the afternoon with joy and good cheer. Matron ordered everyone to stand back as the girls tapped on the old floorboards, making a merry clatter, while Leila pounded away under the hot sun as Mannie played beside her, his fingers flying over the accordion keys. Children going home from school stopped, mouths agape at their view of the hospital verandah. Their shrill excitement added to the applause when the music ended. Happily for the audience there was more to come. The rendering by the Irish tenor of 'Danny Boy' caused one male patient to burst into nostalgic tears. 'Oh, it's a true Irish soul yer have to be,' he cried over and over.

From the moment the girls had left the truck and at the sight of Leila and Mannie giving their all to please and entertain, the lump in Greta's throat had refused to budge. If only Andy had been able to come. He must have known all about it; the cool of the apple-green bed jacket confirmed it.

As if that wasn't enough, Greta couldn't believe what she was hearing or seeing as Lorraine Lockard, accompanied by the strains of a violin, glided out of the matron's office with Andrew close behind. Although her dance was more constrained and shorter than it had been at the cabaret, it was enough when it ended to fill Greta with pride for the deaf girl.

What came next gave Sister Barry shivers and gooseflesh all over. She would never forget the look of love between the two as Andrew Flight bent down to kiss his wife's upturned face. A lingering, gentle kiss in front of everyone before he took up his violin again, and still with his eyes on her face, played some lovely melody she had never heard before.

More than once Sister Barry had tried to analyse what it was that not only her but half the women of the town saw in the man's looks. Greta could have told them in one word: Charisma. It was there in the blue-grey eyes that narrowed when absorbed; the deep lines around his full lips that came and went when he smiled. It was there in a hint of the devil-may-care look that could give a woman the flutters.

Not more than a half hour did the cabaret troop stay, but Greta's heart was full as they left her with kisses, hugs and good wishes for a speedy recovery. As they waved goodbye, Leila, still at the keys, played the current favourite, 'Now is the Hour', leaving Greta feeling belonging and accepted, more than she had ever felt in the town before. In no time at all she promised herself she'd be down at the river taking a swim, and the Flight Academy of Dance, with Poppy's help, would once again be in full swing, making another promise to herself that she'd eat those damned vegetables until they were sprouting out of her ears if that's what Dr David Pedersen wanted.

Patients were being ordered back to bed and she felt a kiss on the top of her head as the wheelchair began to move.

'Time for a rest, my bonny dearr.'

CHAPTER TWENTY-SEVEN

Six months since Christmas and Greta, radiant with health, completely ignored the ugly scar running jagged through the light tan of her arm. 'It's a war wound,' she had blithely announced; no one disagreed. She had even ordered her pupils to take a good look and get used to it. Which they did and, satisfied, never bothered about it again. Life, Greta had decided, was as normal and as pleasant as it could be in Yunnabilla.

Monday morning and Greta's clothesline, unlike Marelda's and most of the backyard lines in the town, was innocent of flapping sheets, pillow cases, tea towels and the rest of it. As far as Greta was concerned, Monday meant a catch up with the Cairns and Townsville newspapers that always arrived on an early goods train before dawn and were delivered by the youngest Larkin boy before breakfast. Marelda knew there was an invisible 'do not disturb' sign tacked to Greta's kitchen door when the papers arrived.

With the dishes cleared and washed (the only concession allowed to interrupt the morning), Greta opened up the paper. Her first reaction on seeing the headlines was one of disbelief.

MAYHEM AND VIOLENCE IN CAIRNS

80 injured, 8 detained in hospital

Yesterday morning the citizens of Cairns declared war on the
unemployed camping in the showgrounds of Parramatta Park.
Led by the mayor and encouraged by business to 'take on the
unemployed or not turn up for work on Monday', 500 people,
including police, aldermen and other worthy town folk gathered
inside the gates to oust the 100 men who had found shelter there.

With nowhere to go, it appears that the 'travelling
unemployed' had built a barricade of sorts between the cow
pens in defiance of a council order to quit the park. Arming
themselves with various homemade weapons, they declared they
would not be shifted unless provided with a roof over their heads
and wash facilities.

Greta tut-tutted her way through the report, thinking of the
travel-weary men she had sung to that day many months ago; dispir-
ited men who had reached the end of the line. She kept on reading.
'Previously, meetings had been held between spokesmen for the
campers and the aldermen, ending with promises to find decent
shelter for the unwanted visitors. So far this has not occurred.'

Over the evening meal Greta was surprised that Andy seemed
unaware of the incident. She began reading aloud to him as he sat
opposite at the kitchen table.

'Andy! This is important.'

'Go ahead. I'm listening.'

'Simmering resentments,' Greta read, 'finally erupted yesterday.
Bricks, concrete blocks, waddies, shovels and police batons were
freely used in the melee which resulted in a swift trouncing of the

unemployed. The three alleged ringleaders have been arrested for a variety of offences.'

It sounded like a bloody and brutal rout, and Greta wondered who the arrested men were. Could Sam Riding be one of them? Remembering her own encounter with the swagmen, she said, 'From what I saw at that park, I don't know how they found the strength to put up any sort of a fight.'

'Desperation can give a man the strength of ten.'

'It's Sam. I'm sure —'

'And I'm sure it's not for you to worry about.'

'I dunno . . .'

Andrew was still finding every day a win since Greta's recovery, and enjoyed the sight of her tucking into a mound of vegetables, with the steak minus kidney. 'That's for you only,' she had said, serving up, 'but don't ask me to like it.'

He got up to give himself a second helping, spooning more than one dumpling onto his plate. It was understandable that Greta was upset over the news, but there was good reason why he could not work up the sense of injustice the riot deserved. He had enough to worry about without concerning himself over a fracas in Cairns. Mannie's warning had come as a surprise to be thought about and perhaps worried over tomorrow. How would Greta handle it? he wondered. Possibly laugh and tell Mannie to go jump in the lake . . .

'Andy.' Greta was determined not to spoil a meal over what was happening in Cairns, giving him a look with a threat of mischief glinting her eyes. 'Know what I feel like?' She didn't wait for him to answer. 'Haven't had a taste or a sniff of it since that first night. Remember? I think we called it Greta's Gold. Any left?'

'I remember. It hasn't touched my lips since.'

'How about we have some?' Greta's question jolted him. What made her ask? Some premonition? Quickly thinking it over, he decided to mention the conversation he'd had with Mannie only that afternoon. The absurdity of it would go well with a glass of the stuff. His mind went back to the garage and Mannie's concern.

Mannie had strolled into the workshop and without preamble casually mentioned that Greta had told him about the man who gave Andy occasional jobs on a farm a good way from the town. She had apparently raved over the inordinate amount paid out for work completed. Long ago he and Mannie had decided, because of the mean pickings that their first arrangement produced, that he would go it alone, paying rent for the garage and the hire of the utility. But Andy had found himself asking Mannie if he'd regretted the cancelling of their previous arrangement.

'Hell, no.' Mannie's spectacles slid out of control by the vigorous shaking of his head. 'I'm just interested, that's all.' It seemed as if he wanted to say more, for his look of strange speculation had Andrew wondering. 'Greta didn't know his name.'

'You mean that you asked her?' Irritation prickled as if he'd sat on a patch of burrs. 'If it's *that* important, I'll give it to you. It's Castino.'

'You've been up to his bloody still, haven't you?' The sudden change in Mannie's face was remarkable. What before had seemed to be a casual curiosity was now one of almost comical consternation.

'Of course I've been up to the bloody still. So what?'

'So next time he wants a favour, tell him you're busy.'

'It's not a favour, mon, it's an honest day's work.'

'Honesty and Castino make strange bedfellows.' Mannie gave a shrug as he walked away. 'Just be careful, that's all I'm saying.'

But in five minutes he was back again. 'Have you ever heard mention of the Black Hand Gang?'

'Canna' say that I have.'

'You poor, ignorant Pommy bastard.'

'Well, don't walk off like that. Fill me in.'

Careful not to smear his shirt, Mannie moved away from a grease-stained bench, preferring to sit on the steps leading into the office. 'The Black Hand Gang,' he repeated, 'some Itite mob – Italians to you – round Innisfail way. Rumour is they've got the cane farmers down there by the short and curlies. Extortion, protection.' Mannie gave a shrug. 'Maybe, maybe not. Yunnabilla's a long way up the track from the coast and news like that moves slow, if at all.'

'And you're telling me that Castino could be —'

Mannie held up his hand. 'Might be. There have been whispers about him, even if he is a hardworking, God-fearing dago. Just be careful. That's all.'

Now, thinking over the afternoon's conversation, Andrew poured the golden liquid into two crystal liquor glasses, a Christmas gift from Leila and Mannie, deciding it was best not to say anything to Greta after all.

Andy was no fool. But right from the start he had accepted the Castino still without question. Illicit alcohol was a nothing business, more of a joke than anything else. Nearly every farm he'd been to in the district had its own 'ginger beer plant' – even pineapple champagne was sometimes the boast, and serious fermentation was often carried out on a good few farms in the district. He'd clear up the mystery with Mannie first thing in the morning.

———

Greta was squeezing lemons into a gallon-sized jug while the pile of juiceless halves grew higher on the bench. Every now and then she would pick up one of the discarded halves, examine it, then place the half on a bent elbow and give it a vigorous rub. Marelda, who had come over to discuss the goings on in Cairns, slowly shook her head. 'The things you do.'

'Marvellous for scraggy elbow skin, Relda. Feels nice too.' She handed one over to her neighbour. 'Go on, try it.'

'Too late for anything like that.' Marelda looked down at her arms, cross-hatched by years of tropical sun and neglect. 'I've a better plan for that peel. I'd crystallize them.'

It was Greta's turn to shake her head. 'The things you do.'

'And I reckon you spoil those girls rotten. Lemonade, no less!'

The Flight Academy School of Dance still served up lemonade after lessons. What had once been not more than ten glasses had now expanded to twenty. After the success of the cabaret the class had grown to twice the size. Greta sometimes found the more strenuous steps and routines still caused stabs in the arm, although not as bad as it once had been. Poppy sometimes stood in for her, refusing payment of any kind, but grateful that her Annabelle was showing a distinct talent for song and dance under Greta's tutelage.

'She'll walk the boards one day,' Greta had said, half in jest, and still joking told Poppy that soon she'd have to hire the School of Arts Hall for classes. 'The little grey house ain't got elastic walls.'

Money for rent and machine parts for garage repairs was still tight. But good rains had boosted the crops, and with the bacon factory open again, farmers found they had just enough to pay back the bank, and the townfolk themselves were not asking the butcher and baker to 'tick it up'. But more often than not, what was owing to Flight's garage by necessity came last on the list.

However, the Flights were managing. Just. The safe return of Greta into Andrew's arms was enough to keep their buoyancy on high and a certainty in line with the town's expectations that 'hard times' must soon come to an end – as long as the weather behaved.

Up to date there was an ongoing feud with David Pedersen, who was refusing to send in an account for his services and the private ward, while they were just as determined to settle up and get it over and done with. Already the ruby had come out of its hiding place, ready to be put to use.

Dancing class was nearing its end and the girls were having lemonade on the verandah. Greta was in a carefree state of mind. Not a twinge felt as she had tried out a few swift high kicks, then finishing off with a perfect exhibition of the splits. She loved everyone, even the funny little Henderson girl who in extremis wet her pants regularly. Greta had a store of 'cleans' just in case. But today, Greta thankfully noted, the child's bloomers were dry.

The little Henderson girl was the first to see it. 'Mrs Flight,' she chirruped, 'your car is coming down the road.' It had to be Andy, home early for a change. 'An' Mrs Flight, he's got someone with him.'

The students hoped he would pull up in front of the house where the class had grouped, spilling down the front steps with stickybeak eyes, the older girls dying to see Mr Flight close up, if only to say hello. But there was disappointment as they saw Andrew swing the utility around on three wheels and drive down the side of the house to the back gate. Greta, hoping she'd made a mistake, gave a hurried command for the girls to collect their things and leave, uncertain whether her eyes had deceived her.

From the kitchen she saw Andrew open the passenger door and assist a man out of the car. His forehead was bandaged and as he came closer she could see a dribble of blood down his cheek, the bandage dry and caked with it. A battered face that she barely recognised. Words she could hardly understand squeezed out between swollen lips. 'Betrayal, Greta. They let me down, the sods,' Sam Riding said, as Andrew helped him up the stairs.

CHAPTER TWENTY-EIGHT

Sam's story and explanation of his state was as shocking as it was unbelievable. In the Cairns riot he had been set upon by men whom he had thought of as mates. Men who had promised to give voice and support for the campers at Parramatta Park in their claim for shelter, as promised by the mayor and his aldermen.

'They didn't have a hope in hell of calling those bastards off. Five against one. And those who fell – kicked into submission. A young lad crying for mercy, that's what I saw, and that's when I stepped in and got the wrong end of a shovel over the head.' Bloodshot eyes turned to Andrew. 'Wouldn't have that flask of yours handy, would yer, Comrade?'

'Clean out of whisky, old chap. But a nip of Greta's Gold will help.' There was a tumbler half full on the table waiting for him. Sam drank it down in one gulp. He snorted and winced as the alcohol stung his lips. 'Not a bad drop,' he managed to say.

Already Greta was soaking the bandage, carefully removing it inch by inch while Sam talked. He couldn't stop. It seemed that every word he uttered diluted the poison of disbelief and hurt overwhelming him. 'Poor buggers, scattering everywhere, getting chased down the streets like criminals by those animals baying for blood. 'Orrible, it was. I'll never forget it as long as I live. And by the way . . .'

As the last of the bandage slipped off, Greta gasped and clapped a hand over Sam's ear. It seemed to be hanging by a thread. 'Andy, quick! Get David before the damn thing falls off!' One look at Sam's dripping ear had Andrew down the stairs and in seconds the utility at full speed was roaring towards town. Sam seemed to be unaware of the situation as Greta hastily rebandaged his ear. Greta's Gold and exhaustion were taking over. His speech was more slurred and his head was nodding. Greta dragged him out of the chair. 'C'mon mate, the doctor should be here any minute. You'll be okay, we'll see to that.'

Sam managed one more sentence as Greta with effort got him onto the single bed. 'Didn' finish tellin' yer, I'm wanted by the police. Supposed to be one of the ringleaders.' There was a parody of a laugh and Sam's eyes closed.

David Pedersen had wasted no time. As he came up the front steps Greta was thinking of another favour bestowed and a clandestine one at that. What would his reaction be once he learnt about Sam being wanted by the police? How would Andy and Mannie take it once they found out? According to Andy, Sam had turned up in Mannie's office earlier in the day, apologising for 'making an inconvenience' before collapsing onto the floor.

With Andrew standing by, the doctor studied the comatose man. Once the bandage was removed the ear flopped back towards the pillow. Pedersen gave a grunt, repositioned it and replaced the bandage.

'We'll stitch it up now while he's out to it. With luck it'll be all over by the time he opens his eyes.' He turned to Andrew. 'Get a chair and cover it. A clean tea towel will have to do. Bring it in here.' Catching Greta's eye while he opened his Gladstone bag, he added, 'I need a basin of hot water and soap on the kitchen table.' He followed as Greta hurried down the hall. David soaped and scrubbed every inch of skin up to the elbows, pausing only to ask if there was methylated spirits in the house. Wordless, Greta nodded.

'Good – we'll need it to clean up the area before we do anything. God knows where he's been lying.' He held Greta's gaze. 'And you should know where that can lead to. Big trouble, eh?' With instructions to bring more soap and hot water with her, he went back to Sam. One by one needles, rat-tooth forceps and black silk thread were laid out on the tea towel. He found time to grin.

'Always carry a sewing kit. Just in case.'

Sam didn't stir as his ear was scrubbed clean with the soapy water and a good swabbing of spirits. Satisfied that all was as ready as it could be, David Pedersen threaded the needle. 'Hmph . . . shame it's not sterile. Never mind. We'll do the best we can.'

While Sam slept a conference was held in the sitting room. It seemed to Greta that all had been worked out between Mannie and Andy even before Sam had set a foot inside the door. Sam would stay with the Flights until ready to go back to Cairns, Greta acting as nursemaid. With Sam's last words still ringing in her head, Greta listened, biding her time while Andy and Mannie, who had arrived not long after David had done his work, talked over a bottle of lager, cold from the ice chest. They were so sure that everything was cut and dried. Refusing a second glass, David Pedersen excused himself. 'I think not. However, I do have some paperwork to catch up on.'

Mannie gave a nod. 'Just let me know the cost, David. Sam's an old friend and I owe him more than one favour.'

'Then I'll say my goodbyes.'

Greta stopped him leaving with a hand on his arm. 'I think you better stay, David. There's something you should know. Sit down.'

Taking her time, Greta fixed Andy and Mannie with a stony stare. 'Before discussing anything more – that *is*, if there is anything more to discuss, you better listen. Sam's wanted by the police. He told me before he passed out. And that makes us, including you, David, accessories after the fact. Right?' Stunned, they heard Greta relate how Sam had told her of the police accusing him as being one of the ringleaders and a warrant was out for his arrest.

All previous plans went on hold. Mannie at once wanted to take Sam out to the farm, but David cautioned that it would be better if Sam could be left where he was for the night. He could be taken there tomorrow.

'Did anyone see him arrive?'

Mannie shook his head. 'I doubt it. He walked – staggered, I should say – into the office. Even Andy didn't see him come in. We thought it best to bring him straight here. He can leave for the farm first thing in the morning.'

'Someone might have seen him. But never mind.' David stood up. 'It's a risk that's already been taken and I have to go.' It had Greta thinking of Marelda, who didn't miss a thing.

Mannie's glasses went for a slide. 'Er – that paperwork you mentioned . . .'

'Nothing to do with this.' David's lips twitched. 'I'm keeping my thoughts to myself and my mouth shut. But I'll send that account off tomorrow, Mannie, never fear.'

'Everything's settled then.' Mannie, looking concerned, drained his glass, making signs that the meeting had come to an end. 'I'd better be off. Police!' He threw his hands in the air. 'Who wants them?'

Not five minutes after Mannie left, Sam made a wobbly entrance into the kitchen, waving aside their admonitions and advice about returning to the bed. He flopped into a chair, asking for water.

Now with a stitched ear and more rational, he insisted on telling them the story of the chase and rescue. He was hazy about some of it, but remembered being hit by the shovel, police chasing him up a street and being in real fear for his life. He couldn't tell how he came to be miles out of Cairns, halfway up the range and on the road leading to the hinterland. He had no idea who had bandaged his ear. 'Whoever it was, God bless 'em.' The Good Samaritan had also left him with a bottle of water and bread shoved into his pocket.

'Been half molo most of the time and keeping out of sight. Not even sure how I got this far.' Andrew sprang and caught him as he slumped forward. Between them they carried the man back to bed.

'What a turn-up,' was the only thing Greta could say as Andrew removed the man's boots and mud-caked trousers.

Frying up the last of the bacon for breakfast, Greta wondered why ever she had dared to believe that troubles – most of them, anyway – were behind her. Now, she found herself cooking up a meal for an injured Sam Riding, expecting the police to bang on the door any minute. At least Sam would be well and truly out of sight and safe on the Colemans' farm by mid-morning, she consoled herself, flopping over the four eggs sunny-side up.

As she was taking hot plates out of the oven, Andy could be heard coming down the hall. 'I smell a smell . . . Up and rise, Sam Riding, we're going for an early-morning drive.' As he walked into the kitchen Greta could see a touch of that piratical smile. It was as if nothing had happened the night before. The appearance of Sam Riding in danger of police arrest, the plans made to secrete him out of sight all amounted, by the look of Andy's cheerful demeanour, to be nothing more than a schoolboy frolic. He was enjoying every minute of it!

Never mind how she felt – stomach tied in knots and mouth as dry as a dusty broom. Even Sam, now he'd had a night's sleep and food in his belly, was a different person from the beaten and distressed man who had landed without warning in the kitchen yesterday. With a piece of toast Sam wiped up the last skerrick of egg yolk glued to his plate. 'Not only can she warble like a turtle dove but she can rustle up the best bacon and eggs I've ever tasted since the last time. Thanks a million, Greta.'

Andrew pushed himself away from the table, giving Greta a wink. 'Now that ye've finished with the compliments, Comrade, we have to move on before Marelda comes over here with a batch of scones.' Up from his chair, Sam rubbed hands together as if the pair of them were off to a scouts' jamboree. There was a peck on the cheek from Andrew and a two-fingered salute from Sam before they went, leaving behind nothing more than a cheery wave and dirty dishes. She was glad to see the last of them.

Men! I dunno . . .

It took only minutes for Marelda to walk up the steps as Andrew had foretold, not with scones but with one of Greta's favourites – Belgium tea cake, its top glistening with baked sugared apples and cinnamon.

'Seeing you had a visitor, it went into the oven before breakfast. Nothing like a nice piece of the old Belgium for morning tea.' She pretended surprise. 'But they've gone already!'

Even for freshly baked tea cake, Greta was not ready to sate Marelda's curiosity. 'Actually, he's a friend of Mannie's. Had a nasty accident.' She gave a casual shrug. 'Motor bikes. Always said they were dangerous things.' It was a lame sort of explanation thought up as she went along, and by the look on Marelda's face she wasn't believing one word of it.

'Hmm . . . Wonder they didn't take him to the hospital.'

Damn it! If Marelda didn't miss Sam and Andy's departure, she certainly couldn't have missed the dramatic arrival of David Pedersen as well. Greta, recalling her secret dash to Cairns with Dorothy Stone and Spanner, knew Larkin gratitude was a guarantee that Marelda could and would keep a serious confidence to herself.

Greta sighed in resignation. 'Wait until I clear the table, Relda, and I'll tell you all about it.'

Marelda, feverish to hear every word, wasn't ready to sit down and wait. 'I'll help yer!'

She relished every bit of Greta's tale of the night's events, sympathised in the right places and, as the wife of a hardworking fettler, deplored the fate of 'those poor men and their families left behind'.

Greta buttered another slice of tea cake. 'So, there you have it. Sam will stay out of sight until things settle down and it's Leila who'll be nursemaid instead of me – thank the Lord Harry for that!'

'Lovely woman, that Leila, and to think we couldn't take to her when she first turned up.'

'Turned up?'

'Yair, that's the very word.' Marelda settled her bulk more comfortably into the chair. 'Mannie went down south for a holiday, so he said, and no sooner down there than he was back with Leila. Couldn't speak a word of English and didn't see much of her, although every bazaar we had after that, she'd send in the loveliest things for it. Cakes —'

'Stuffed monkeys?'

'Yes, them too, and needlework. We'd seen nothing like it. There's hardly a house in Yunnabilla that hasn't got one of her cushions. Then, out of the blue . . .' Marelda gave a bemused shake of the head. 'The football club puts on a dance and not only is Mannie playing the accordion as usual but there's Leila, smart as paint, playing the piana, looking so neat and proud. Oh, she's a lovely woman all right. But it still took a while to get to know her.'

'Like it did with me, I guess.'

'Well, there are a few couples like that around here. Just turn up.' She gave Greta a piercing appraisal with her startling blue eyes. 'Makes you wonder . . .'

Sam Riding stayed a few days only with the Colemans. As Mannie reported to Andrew, he couldn't rest, hardly ate and spent his time mooching around the farm, moody and nearly unapproachable. The *Pelican* moored and vulnerable in Alligator Creek was a constant worry. He was convinced the police were tramping all over her or, worse still, she could be lying somewhere smashed and gutted in the mud. There was nothing Mannie could do but lend him enough to catch an early railmotor back to Cairns.

'Last words he said to me were that if he found her safe and sound he'd take her out right away and head north.' The day's quiet was broken by the snarling and yelping of a dog fight, the two making their own whirly-whirly in the dust outside. Andrew shut the garage door on the noise. Mannie in generous mood had raided his office drawer and held two filled glasses in his hand, offering one to Andy. 'Here's to Sam, me old mate.' He took a swig and gave a satisfactory shudder. 'Listening to him you'd think that boat of his was a woman. Besotted with it, he is.'

Following Mannie, Andrew held up his drink in a silent toast. He understood Sam Riding's misery. Mannie watched, wondering if he had caught a fleeting look of regret in Andrew's eye.

On the day the Flights had first walked into his office, like David Pedersen, Mannie Coleman had guessed there was more to Andrew than a man who knew all about spark plugs and played violin as a hobby. According to Sam, when he'd been offered the job as part skipper of the *Pelican* he had jumped in feet first at the idea. Greta was another piece of the puzzle: beautiful, talented – and the cabaret, as far as Mannie and Leila were concerned, had been a dead giveaway. Greta was a professional, no doubt about it! And the north had always been a place of refuge where anyone could melt into the humidity, taking their secrets with them, and the further north travelled, the less was asked about the past. It was

then up to the stranger to fit in one way or another. Mannie gave
a mental shrug as he swallowed the last of his whisky.

The three of them sat on the Flights' verandah: Mannie, Andrew and
David Pedersen. Before leaving, Greta had left a large jug of lime
squash – for the doctor, mainly – but as David had arrived armed
with gin and tonic the lime drink was treated as a supplement to an
afternoon of serious drinking. The mood was expansive and mellow,
their voices accompanied by the occasional plop of a ripe mango
in the backyard. Talk centred around Sam Riding and the *Pelican*,
now moored at Port Douglas, and already they had the boat sailing
further north, maybe as far as Portland Roads; a snug little outpost,
Mannie informed them, for a handful of miners and the occasional
fishing vessel escaping an over blustery sou' easter.

'Frontier territory, up there.' Andrew gently stuffed tobacco into
a pipe. They had to agree that Sam was already a forgotten man, for
the *Cairns Post* had triumphantly announced that every ringleader
of the riot had been caught and was now awaiting trial.

David poured himself another tot. 'The public and the papers
are losing interest. Stale news is bad news. Every day they seem
to giving more space to Hitler and those murderous thugs of his.
Making bonfires of books, razing retail stores – mainly owned by
the Jews . . .' There was a moment's pause as if to access opinion.
'And now rounding up poor bloody gypsies and anyone else they
have a hate against. God knows what they're doing with 'em all.'

A cloud of silence hung over the men. They had all read the
news and were aware of the escalating tensions that were enveloping Europe. Even the Great Depression was taking second place to

the ranting and ravings of one man and his henchmen in Germany. It was Mannie who joked them away from grave thoughts.

'Did that wife of yours make any sandwiches before she left? All this meat and no potatoes makes a man peckish.'

Now the proud possessor of a driving licence, an afternoon's chinwag between the Three Muskets, as Greta called them, was a good enough excuse to take the utility down to the river. But before leaving she had made enough curried egg sandwiches to feed a platoon instead of three men.

The swimming hole as usual was deserted. Once, she had secretly claimed it as her own personal pool and gave it the name of Bottlebrush Getaway, with a libation of dry sherry. She had often wondered at the lack of swimmers in the river, not counting the children; its serenity was rarely disturbed. Now that she could drive she had offered to take Marelda. The response had been for her neighbour to cackle with embarrassment, throw her apron over her head and say, 'I can't – everyone would talk!' (Though never mind about a gossip's broadcast while sitting on a dunny seat.) Greta gave up trying to work out the mores of Yunnabilla. Feeling as free as the kingfisher flashing blue through the bottlebrush, she opened the letter Andy had given her before she had left.

She sat on the bank, squishing her toes in river sand, soft water cooling her ankles as she read Flossie's letter. Her Sydney news was always a treat and a laugh to read. As her eyes travelled down the page a slight frown appeared. She read the page over again and feeling not as free as she had a moment before, carefully folded the missive and put it into her towel bag. Thoughtful, her mind going over her friend's news, she slid into the water. Sometimes Flossie's prattle should be taken with a grain of salt.

CHAPTER TWENTY-NINE

'Greta, darling! Greta Osborne!'

The voice echoed up and down the one main street of the town. She didn't have to turn around to see who it was. She'd know Eddie's voice if she heard it in the market place of Timbuktu. It was too late to shoot into Malloy's and keep out of sight. Already he was racing towards her like a lover screaming endearments, arms outstretched and Ethel Rourke's eyes bugged with astonishment on the other side of the street.

'Shut up, Eddie, for God's sake!' She tried not to clench her teeth, steering him into the store. 'It's Flight, now. Greta Flight.' It seemed as if he hadn't heard her.

'And why aren't we in America?' His voice, so loud, was an actor's production that could be heard clear up to the water tower.

'I told you to *shut up*. Quickly, behind here!' She thanked her stars that it was early morning and was grateful for Molloy & Co's recent addition to the store: a large bookshelf, newspaper and magazine rack. Impossible for anyone to see them from the footpath. She didn't doubt for a moment that Ethel Rourke was now hotfooting it across the street, on the twitch for more details. If Andrew showed up to collect payment as he often did on a Monday, the fat was truly in the fire. Bohemian Club Eddie would remember him only too well and would expect some sort of explanation. As it was, with a bit of luck maybe Ethel had not heard the surname 'Osborne', and the boisterous meeting between her and Eddie was just another thing to add to Greta Flight's list of sins. Eddie, of course, would not give a fig about she and Andy 'living in sin'. Acceptable to him, but not so in tight little Yunnabilla.

'Eddie, just keep quiet, will you, and listen. There's a little shop down the end of the street. Actually a fruit and vegie shop. But they do serve up a cup of tea. Coffee, if you want it. Go there and wait for me. I'll come down as soon as I can.' Greta stopped his protest with a hand over his mouth. 'I'll explain everything when I get there.' Then, for his benefit, she relaxed and gave him the smile that she'd been famous for in Sydney. 'And I am glad to see you. Believe me. Now scram!'

She gave him five minutes to get to the shop and was about to leave herself when Ethel Rourke ambushed her behind dress materials. 'Morning, Mrs Flight. You're out nice and early.' Was there too much emphasis on the Mrs Flight? Was the smile too sweet, when a sniff in passing was Ethel's usual greeting? From that first day in the railway tearoom Ethel Rourke had taken an instant dislike to her and she was never quite sure why.

'And the top of the morning to you, Ethel Rourke.'

Breezy was the only way to describe it as Greta swept by, sashaying out of the store. She wasted no time in slipping into the chemist shop two buildings down. Ethel was a slow mover and even if intent on nosing out more, Greta would have disappeared by the time she stepped outside. She hoped with a bit of luck that another early shopper would appear, as Ethel would be unable to resist relaying the extraordinary scene she had just witnessed. 'Greta Flight, no less, being embraced by a perfect stranger first thing in the morning in the main street of town!'

Greta had guessed right. Luck was on her side.

Taking a cautious look towards Malloy & Co, she saw the tea-room proprietor engaged in animated conversation with one of her card-playing cronies. Good! Let them gossip their heads off. In self-congratulation she took the side door that led to a lane not that far away from the back of the garage. She dismissed the idea of telling Andy about Eddie and warning him to keep out of sight – if he was there at all, and not on an outside job. Fingers crossed that he was away. Eddie's front cloth act could be discussed with him later on. Meanwhile, she advised herself, better not waste too much time or Eddie, tired of waiting, would go into one of the pubs and start asking about Greta Osborne. If he did, her reputation would be up for grabs. Apart from that, what on earth was he doing in Yunnabilla?

'So what in the blazes are you doing up here, Eddie?'

'Simple, my love. I could ask you the same question. But I won't.' Eddie was speaking in short bursts of excitement. 'You look marvellous. Absolutely *marvellous*. Can't wait to tell them down south.' Eddie flung himself into the back of the chair, a hand pressed to his chest. 'Jesus wept! What has happened to your arm?'

'It's a long story. But first things first.'

They sat in the dimness of stained dark-brown timbers. An

opened sack of potatoes with the dirt of a paddock still caking them stood against a small counter, their dusty smell vying with the pungency of a full stalk of overripe bananas swinging by a rope from the rafters overhead. As if an afterthought, two small tables with chairs were crammed into one corner. Greta had often wondered why the elderly shopkeepers had bothered, for few people came to sit there and drink tea. But schoolchildren daily took up the limited space at lunchtime for meat pies and the toffees produced in a kitchen tacked onto the back.

'Well, I'm waiting.' Greta poured herself a cup from a surprisingly handsome pewter coffee pot. 'What *are* you doing here?'

Flossie had been right after all. Eddie had disappeared from the Sydney scene and he confirmed the rumour that he'd partnered up with a talent scout for the Tivoli playhouse and a stage presentation of vaudeville as it used to be.

'Eddie! You and I both know vaudeville is dead.'

'I agree, with good old acts scattered over the country.' He sounded genuinely saddened. ' Half of the poor beggars making a miserly quid in a sideshow alley of some hillbilly turnout. Disaster, Greta. Pure disaster.'

'And where is this millionaire who has the cash for a full-blown production?'

'Just waiting, darling, with his big, fat cheque book. Waiting for us to get the acts together.' There was no mistaking the gleam of discovery in his eyes. 'We —'

'Who is we?'

'Bart, my partner. We came up here in the most gawd-awful railmotor – hours of torture, my love – on hearsay. Hearsay being that this funny little place had put on a cabaret. A *sparkling* cabaret.

Of course, we couldn't believe it, but leaving no stone unturned, we've arrived! Now all is understood. The cabaret! The sparkle! But no one spoke of our Greta.' For a moment he looked puzzled. 'Not a mention of Greta Osborne. And here she is! My God! Luck divine.'

'The name is Flight. *Mrs* Flight.' Greta's voice was as flat as a wooden bench.

'You're married! Who? When?'

'Eddie, listen.' Greta took his hand. Such short notice to work out what should be said and what to leave out. And where was this Bart? Obviously Ethel Rourke would have seen them arrive. They possibly had tea and scones at the station.

Shit!

She took a deep breath. 'Eddie, love. If you think anything of me at all, I want you to forget you ever saw me here. I know the last thing you'd want to do is hurt me. Give me pain.' Greta's eyes pleaded, taking on for all she was worth the role of a haunted woman.

Bewildered, Eddie was shaking his head. 'Of course not.'

'But in Yunnabilla I'm known as Mrs Flight – a widow, if you want to know.' Why was she lying? she asked herself. She didn't have to show a marriage certificate to Eddie or anyone else – but you never know. 'And under the circumstances,' she carried on, 'it was the best role for me to take. The arrival of a single woman – you've only got to see what sort of town it is – is always suspect, and I'm doing well with my little dancing school.' She made it sound like a nunnery. 'I wanted to forget all about Sydney and my dreams.'

'Greta, darling! Did the contract fall through?' Eddie was practically salivating.

'I don't want to talk about it.' Her sigh would have rung the heart of a Scrooge. Greta felt painted into a corner. Her and Andy's mad rush from Sydney had been unnecessary; she realised that now. In spite of Andy's assurances that deserting ship wasn't looked upon as a heinous crime, it hadn't quite convinced her. More for her sake than his, they decided a quick getaway was the sensible thing to do. Flossie was the one and only bohemian to know. 'By the way, when are you leaving?'

Eddie shot her a glance loaded with questions. 'Well, Gret, I don't know what the devil is going on but if nothing has surfaced in a town that's supposed to be crawling with talent, we're going back to civilisation this afternoon.'

Greta looked down at her watch. Eleven and the train left at two. Could she keep Eddie where he was sitting until then? 'What about Bart – where is he?'

'Holed up in some pub. I do the donkey work and he handles the admin side of it if I find anything worth finding. Are you sure —'

'No, Eddie. I've picked up the pieces. Better for them down south to think I'm in America than admit . . .' She heaved another sigh. 'Never mind what they think really . . .' She allowed her voice to fade before giving him her bravest smile. 'Forget about me, Eddie.' She paused, then rushed on. 'It's just wonderful seeing you after all this time. Now tell me all the news – the gossip. And you must try these pies. Best I've ever tasted.' She hoped that the only customers for the day would be the schoolkids at lunch time.

The last thing Greta said as Eddie left the fruit and vegetable shop full of meat pie and more cups of coffee than his stomach could handle, was 'Eddie, for cor' sake, don't even mention a Greta Osborne to that nosy parker in the tearooms. Remember, Mrs Flight is the name.'

The last thing Eddie said, leaving Greta to pay the bill, was 'Greta, my love, where is the closest bog? I'm busting for a piddle.'

In the hope that he could be trusted, Greta watched him lope with haste up the street. She made up her mind to write to Flossie, describing the last few hours. A bit of exaggeration here and there could turn the encounter into nothing more than the joke of the week. But Flossie would read between the lines and keep an eye on Eddie once he was in Sydney, for her sake. Eddie's gossiping and vaudeville bush telegraph could be as dangerous as Ethel Rourke at her best. It made Greta wonder just how many friends the Reverend Baker did have on the stage.

CHAPTER THIRTY

Leila, if possible, had surpassed herself to the full appreciation of her guests sitting around the dining table: David Pedersen, as usual giving fulsome praise to her efforts; Greta and Andrew; and Sister Barry. Since Greta's stay in hospital, the nurse had become a friend, and on Greta's suggestion that she be asked, Leila, always with an eye on a bit of matchmaking where the doctor was concerned, could only agree.

Although Greta and Andrew were regulars who enjoyed to 'break bread' with them, as Leila liked to call it, they both felt that this time there had been something more to the usually casual invitation; more formal this time, as Andy described it. Formal or not, Leila's food was anything but casual. The barramundi stuffed with herbs from her garden, the cabbage rolls – precisionally perfect and lying on a bed of mutton breast with potatoes crisp yet ready to melt in the mouth – all smacked of Leila giving her best to those she loved and admired.

Mavis Barry had never seen a table like it. Silver glowed and crystal winked under the tinkling beads and ruby glass of Mannie's latest purchase: a library lamp brought up from the south. Mavis watched as David helped himself from the centrepiece – the out-size cut-glass bowl, overflowing with tropical fruits, as always, a speciality in Mannie's orchard – and wondered if she dared follow David's lead. She'd heard about mangosteens and the strange exotics not only in Mannie's orchid but in the Chinese market gardens down by the river. Another glass of wine and she'd be game enough for anything.

Conversation over the meal had been mostly about the riot in Cairns and the ringleaders who were facing the upcoming trial. The latest news of Sam, who had been keeping in touch with Mannie, was that he intended taking the *Pelican* further north again, even as far as Thursday Island.

Mavis Barry's face brightened. 'Thursday Island. I've been offered a position there. I've been wondering —'

'Another world, Sister.' Mannie beamed, pleased to demonstrate his knowledge of the far-flung island. 'The Torres Strait. Nothing like it. I notice your interest in the masks. Beauties, aren't they?'

'From Thursday Island?'

'No, the other island, New Guinea – the big one to the north, more or less, and not that far away. Papua we mainly call it up here. Dutch to the north, but Australia now administers most of it. Took the rest of it from the Krauts during the war.'

'British, Australia . . .' David Pedersen cut in, 'Dutch and the Germans, then Australia again.' He concentrated on the removal of the last piece of shell from a lycee nut. 'Wouldn't be surprised if the savages who first owned it started jumping up and down to get it all back again. One day, it'll happen.'

'That I'd like to see.' There was disbelief in Mannie's voice.

'Meanwhile it's a fascinating place and ripe for the plucking. Carvings, masks, crocodiles – make a fortune selling tanned skins and what about the Star Mountains – who knows what's up there? Gold?' Mannie looked at every one of his guests as if waiting for an answer and not finding it, shook his head. 'Unexplored territory. Wild country.'

It now seemed that information about New Guinea had come to an end. Lately, wherever and whenever friends met, conversation eventually veered towards Europe, teetering on the brink of confla-gration. It was mainly 'men's talk' while the women remained silent. As it went on, more between Andrew and David, Greta caught a glance exchanged between the Colemans. Hard to decipher and only lasting seconds, it made her wonder.

'It is coffee time and for many slices of Doboz torte.' Leila smiled and stood up, waving an arm and hand towards the drawing room. 'Make yourself most comfortable. Then I shall play the piano and Greta must sing for us. You agree? And Andrew, you have brought along your violin. We play something together.'

Mavis Barry, enchanted with everything around her, felt as if she'd been transported into the middle of a Somerset Maugham short story. Like others who had visited the Colemans for the first time she was intrigued, nearly overwhelmed, by the rich strangeness of the large dining and drawing room: the grand piano, the monk's chest, the masks and artefacts seemingly imbedded into the walls, grinning and leering through the foliage of potted palms and ferns. But nothing jarred and in spite of the masks, everything melded into a picture of good taste and flair. Not out of place in such a setting was the sight of Greta in clinging emerald satin, her hair richly auburn (did she henna it?) under that amazing library light and Andrew so far removed from the frantic man on the hospital verandah. He stood no more than a touch away from Greta, his love achingly plain to see. It was enough to give her goose bumps.

Each minute that passed was a memory she'd never forget. The music, Greta's singing, and the regret that it all must end. It had been a surprise to find herself here and in such company in the first place, but the biggest surprise came at the end. They were saying their goodnights when Mannie took hold of Leila's hand. To Sister Barry's slight embarrassment and to Greta's astonishment, Mannie kissed his wife's palm. Public affection was a rare thing to be seen in Yunnabilla, weddings and funerals the exception.

'You have something to tell our guests?' By this time they were on the verandah and Leila's face was in shadows, as if she wanted it that way.

'Dear friends.' Her lips were smiling, her eyes sad. 'Tonight I say goodbye. My mother, my father in Poland, must come with me here. Before it is too late.'

In silence they heard of the parents who ran a small haberdashery shop in a village not far from Krakow. Poland wasn't Germany, as Leila explained, but even so she was worried. 'It is not good there. I feel it. Anything can happen. Mannie will stay here,' she told them, 'we must keep our business going and the farm for them to come to. To be safe.' There wasn't a need for her to add more. They understood.

Mannie closed shop the next day, taking Leila to Cairns to board the *Manunda* going south. In Sydney she'd leave on a P&O liner for the six-week sail to England and from there it was up to Leila to find her way to Poland. Yunnabilla, when they heard the news, could only wish her good luck, and chinwags over back fences noted that Mannie, to anyone's knowledge, had only closed the office door twice since the day he'd opened it: the first time to bring Leila back from somewhere south, and the second to take her off again.

The Riverbank Players still performed on Saturday nights with Andrew playing piano after revealing that he could tickle the ivories in emergencies. When Greta asked why he hadn't mentioned it before, Andrew had shrugged off the question by adding that he could also strum up a chord or two on the ukulele. This new information was accompanied with a squeeze on her bottom and that he only twangled a ukulele under a full moon. 'The river is a pleasant place . . .' he said, and left it at that.

In the weeks that followed Leila's leaving, there was something that concerned those who called Mannie a friend. Frequently taking advantage of an open invitation to eat with the Flights, he'd arrive with a bottle or two and a lighthearted relay of the day's events in and around the town. Business as usual, seemed to be his motto. It was his cavalier attitude, with Leila so far away and possibly in danger, that puzzled them, and from what they could gather letters from her were few and far between.

'I can't understand him,' Greta complained. They were standing at the gate waving Mannie off after a dinner of rib roast and steamed pudding. 'You'd think with us he'd be happy to talk about Leila. But we know nothing. He seems so confident that everything is all right. Bright and breezy, without a care in the world.'

'It could be a cover up.'

'Who knows? Not a frown, nothing. Only a word to say she's all right. It's getting an embarrassment to ask about her.'

'Well, he did have something for *us* to be pleased about, eh?'

'About Stone's farm up for sale?' Greta had to acknowledge

that Mannie's news – the reason that had brought him over – was
something that would have her walking on air for weeks. 'Can't
believe it. Touch wood!' It meant that a trip into town, her growing
fondness of Yunnabilla and her enjoyment of singing on a Saturday
night would never again be tainted with the fear of a chance meeting. A feeling of utter happiness swept over her. 'Quick,' she said,
'inside. Is there any of that Greta's Gold left? I feel a celebration
coming on!'

It was a fine Saturday morning and Andrew whistled as he carefully
steered the utility over a new deep rut in the road leading to the
Colemans' farm. There had been heavy rain in the early hours but
now the sky was clear, the anthills washed clean standing defiantly
red, rearing up from grasses creamed and flattened by last night's
deluge.

A mild rash of guilt would be appeased once he had seen and
spoken to Mannie. A small problem in one of the curing barns,
he'd been told, followed by assurances that there was 'no hurry,
roll up when you've got a bit of time', was enough for Andrew to
put the request on hold. Driving over the planks of the bridge now
slightly awash from the rain, he wondered, not for the first time,
why a mechanic was needed for a curing barn, but knowing the
man it was bound to be some cracked idea he had dreamt up in
bed during a sleepless night.

There was no sign of Mannie as he neared the house, which
was unusual for him. If he was out in a paddock or in the orchard,
instinct or excellent hearing would tell him a car was coming over
the bridge. Business or pleasure, he was always standing at the top

of the double stairs, beaming a welcome. One thing he could bet on: Mannie wouldn't be having a Saturday morning sleep-in.

Cutting the engine, Andrew waited. All he could see were empty tobacco fields, the workers gone home for the weekend. It was the silence that disturbed, as if every living thing was holding its breath in waiting. Waiting for what? No birdsong; even the mynahs were sulking in the mango trees and the one cicada's cackle only emphasised the quiet. Was Mannie ill? Had something happened during the night? An intruder? He left the car, treading the stairs lightly, already noting that Mannie's two cars were in their open-sided shelter. But still that unnatural hush all around him. With one foot on the verandah he could see into the house and was thankful that he had not called out. It was the sight of Mannie, close to the piano, that caused Andrew not to make another move. He was on his knees, his body curved in sheer despair as he rocked back and forth, his eyes closed, tears coursing down his cheeks and a prayer shawl over his shoulders.

It was tragedy surrounded by a sea of papers. Newspapers, *Smith's Weekly*, the *Herald*, papers garnered from every state, every city; some even printed in foreign places. Magazines. *The Bulletin* and others of the same ilk – anything he could get his hands on. Printed commentaries large or small that could tell him about events in Europe. Following Leila's journey night by night and day by day, praying that she could find a way through neutral paths to safety. How many hours had the husband scanned so many words that more often than not only increased the heartache of not knowing?

Had word come through of a dreadful calamity concerning Leila? Andrew knew he was only guessing, although he felt that weeks of concealed strain could account for Mannie's state. Whatever the trouble, surely they'd find out soon enough. He decided not to make his presence known – sometimes a man wants to be alone in his grief. Andrew turned away and quietly left the house. Tomorrow he'd return with Greta to see what could be done.

'I'll never forget it, Gret, Mannie in a tallith. The sadness . . .' Sombre-faced and as if he expected Greta to disappear, he cried, 'Come here!' Andrew clutched her to him, burying his face in her hair. She too clung to him, comforted by his warmth and strength, never believing for one moment that separation like the Colemans faced could happen to them.

'Whatever comes up, whatever we do,' she had to say, 'we'll do it together.'

As it was Saturday, they were expected to play at the School of Arts. 'Just you and me tonight, I'd say.' Andrew adjusted the cummerbund around his waist while Greta, in the green satin, rouged her cheeks. Only the piano, Andy and her. Greta hoped that the night wouldn't drag on. It all depended on a lorry load from Dimbulah turning up. If they were enjoying themselves they'd pay up freely for the night to go on.

The wings of crimson rosellas shredded the sunset, before settling down on nearby gum trees; raucous shrills petering out at the first sign of a star. Andrew and Greta had arrived early, intending to have a tryout before the ticket seller opened up shutters and turned on the lights. Their footsteps echoed around the hall as they walked towards the stage.

'Hey! What's the hurry?'

They wheeled as one to see Mannie, spruce and grinning, in a shirt starched stiff and ironed to a shine, his cummerbund tight and perfect. What was there to say? What could they say, as the three of them made for the side steps leading up to the stage. It was obvious by Mannie's appearance that Leila was somewhere, hopefully alive and well. What Andrew had witnessed would remain a secret between the two of them; Mannie none the wiser.

CHAPTER THIRTY-ONE

There was cause to feel good and happy. Greta hummed as she turned over her growing stack of records. Bing Crosby or Cab Calloway? Calloway won. Once 'Minnie the Moocher' started up she did a few perky box steps and a shuffle or two, experimenting in an impossible dance combination.

Reverend Baker paid an unexpected call, the outcome being that another concert might eventuate – 'If you can manage it, Greta, and how is the arm, by the way?' When she had replied that after nearly nine months it was doing fine he did have the grace to look mortified. Not once since the cabaret had he paid her a minute's visit and at times she had wondered if he did know anything about her true marital state. But he had turned up moonfaced and smiling, having the cheek to ask if she still made that delicious chilli wine. He was such a farce of a man that she had no trouble in pretending a welcome, apart from liking the idea of putting on another show.

Trying out a few routines wouldn't hurt, she told herself, doing another shuffle and ending with a heel clip. Time for a limber up or two down at the swimming hole. Maybe tomorrow. Meanwhile the afternoon was getting on and Andy would soon be home. Feeling carefree, she dropped mutton chops into a pan, her mind on chorus lines and individual acts. *Top Hat Revue!* She could see it all. Curtain parting on an empty stage except for a top hat eight, no, nine feet high! The Flight dancers, top hat, bow ties and cheeky tails appearing from behind it, tapping their way to the footlights. Perfect! Only the other night she'd seen Fred Astaire tripping the light fantastic across the screen. What a dancer! As the film was still on, she and Andrew would go again. Copy a few of those wonderful steps. Why not tonight?

Humming 'Top Hat, White Tie and Tails' she swayed to her own rhythm in front of the Victoria, flipping over chops and unaware that Andrew was coming up from behind, a grin on his face and a streak of grease down his cheek. He grabbed her. She gave a squeal.

'Gotcha, my sweetie!' He pulled her clear away from the stove.

'Get away, you! BO and grease – take a shower!' Laughing and struggling, she tried to free herself but holding her close, and sharing the greasy cheek with her, Andrew kissed the laughing generous mouth. 'It's a full moon tonight, m' bonny darlin', and I wash in the river. Get your togs. There's cold champagne in the ute, caviar if you want it and a ukulele. Don't ask me where they came from. I'm ready to twangle the whole night long.'

'Oo-er . . .'ow you go on.' Whatever Andy liked to call it, she was ready for a bit of twangling herself, her breath matching his as he kissed her again, short and fast.

Sensitive to every touch, not a word passed between them as they drove down to the river following a grass-covered track that hugged a bend and stopped where the sound of cataracts splashed and jostled over rocks close to the opposite bank. Nothing was left of the sun, only a soft haze beneath a sky turning indigo. They lay where casuarinas covered the sand, silvered by a rising moon, the river running velvet-smooth and black. Naked, not touching, they walked to the water's edge. He pressed her to him as slowly, face to face, his arms folding around her, and they glided into limpid shallows caressing the sand. Wet and warm. Muscles lithe and strong, she gloried in his weight upon her, breasts crushed beneath his ardour. He sucked water from the hollow of her neck, gloating in her beauty, hair fanning out dark, wet and lovely under moonlight. Drifting apart, they allowed the current to take them out and over to the other bank then sat together on a shelving rock. As he stroked her hair she leant against him, admiring his skin so fair and gleaming.

'Should never have left Scotland,' she murmured, 'no wonder you have a freckle or two.'

'And you shouldn'a look so gorgeous, all wet and glistening. A man canna' think straight with you so close.' Chuckling, he gave her a push, sending her splashing back into the river. As she rose up, spluttering, he dived in to join her. 'C'mon now, ye braw and beautiful lassie, over to the other side. There's champagne to drink and I've some news to tell you.' Laughing, he raced her across the river.

It was there as they sat together in the moonlight that Andrew gave her the news about Leila. With her parents and in the company of others escaping Germany, she was now safe in Switzerland. 'Mannie's handing around champagne as if he owned a private well of it in the backyard. Must have crates of it stashed out of sight for the happy occasion. The week Leila gets home he has invited the whole of Yunnabilla to a party.'

'Poor Leila!' Greta hoped that Mannie had already lined up the guild ladies to cater for such a celebration.

Not long after Reverend Baker's first visit he came again, this time with the bank manager's wife for company – and back up, Greta guessed. Joyce Lockard was not exactly a 'buddy buddy' as Greta had told Marelda, but something had cemented between them since the cabaret. Her appearance with the Reverend told Greta that she would give her support and assistance in every way. On the other hand, Joyce Lockard would fully expect Greta to find a place for her daughter some way or another in the concert. Unknown to Joyce, Greta had already taken up the challenge. Revues and showgirls went together and Lorraine's figure, looks and stature as a showgirl would add class to any song-and-dance act. She half expected Joyce to turn her idea down flat. But no, Mrs Lockard said why not, to Greta's relief. It meant hours saved in having to give Lorraine extra practises, allowing her time to concentrate on the other girls. All Lorraine would be expected to do was walk and pose, looking stunning and gorgeous. Even so, Greta wondered what the deaf girl would think about it. But that was something to worry over later on.

By now, knowing the two better than she had twelve months ago, Greta felt she was on firm ground. No nasty surprises like hiding legs beneath petticoats and anything else a few wowsers might dream up at the last minute. Experience, and with the success of the cabaret behind her, she was ready to give a definite yes to their proposal of a concert.

Time slipped pleasantly by, discussing, if tentatively, future meetings and plans until Mrs Lockard, pleased that first steps had been made to her satisfaction, picked up her leather handbag. Standing, she brushed imaginary cake crumbs off her impeccable skirt. Greta had only served coffee, silently punishing them for arriving, as they had once before, without warning. Relda and Poppy could pop in any time. Joyce Lockard and the Rev were a different matter.

Feeling smug and a little complacent, Greta walked them to the front gate. She'd certainly given them something to talk over at the next meeting of the ladies' guild. She watched as the Reverend held the car door open for Joyce to be seated. After she had settled herself, he looked back Greta's way as if something still had to be discussed and was contemplating if he should return. Greta swore under her breath. What was so important that it couldn't wait? She'd had enough of playing ladies, but Reverend Baker was trotting back.

'By the way, Greta, I saw a friend of mine a number of weeks ago.'

Her heart jumped before anything else was said. 'Oh?'

'Eddie Murray. Actor. Been around the ridges here and there, now and then.' He gave her a cherubic smile. 'It crossed my mind that you might know him.'

Had Eddie spilled the Greta Osborne beans? Or had he witnessed that ridiculous performance of Eddie's, as Ethel Rourke had? Had Ethel said something to the Rev? Questions rushed in a jumble as she forced herself to appear casually indifferent to his question. 'Eddie Murray? Nope, never heard of him.'

'Thought you might have bumped into him somewhere.'

If the Rev knew anything, racing thoughts told her, he's keeping it to himself – for the present. An impatient honk of Mrs Lockard's car horn saved her from answering as he sprinted as well as he could back to the car. As they drove off, it took her back to the first time he had come to the house and the faint – more a joke, if anything – feeling of mild blackmail she'd experienced when a concert had first been suggested. This time things were more serious. She could not ignore the possible consequences of Eddie's visit to Yunnabilla. Slowly mounting the steps of the grey house, she could feel her carefully built up respectability crumbling, and could already hear the whispers: 'They're not married, you know.'

It took a few days for Greta to talk herself out of worrying over innuendos and supposition. Bed made and kitchen tidy, she found it easy to have a bit of a giggle at the sight of Marelda enthroned, giving her offspring a verbal lashing over some misdeed.

Determined to push the Reverend and Eddie out of her mind on such a lovely morning, she'd do something with the cumquats Mannie had left. 'Ever try your hand at making jam, Greta? Wouldn't mind a pot if you succeed.' Trust Mannie! She wondered if she could entice Marelda over to give a hand at removing the pips. 'Oo-ah, ain't we getting domestic,' she sang to the tune of 'Top Hat', making up silly words as she went along. But Marelda beat her to it.

'Greta, love, got something for yer.'

'Not cumquats, I hope.' The Larkin tree was loaded.

Marelda was already in the kitchen clutching a large paper bag. 'Y' always complaining about the cock-ar-roaches. Nasty things, couldn't agree more. Well, we're goin' to fix 'em up right now. Charlie

Harris brought 'em up from Cairns.' She banged the bag down on the table.

It split open. Greta squealed. 'Ugh! What are they?'

Five toads, huge, fat and ugly, hopped in panic over and off the table, with Marelda after them.

'Quick – get something to put 'em in.'

'What?' Greta shrieked, scrabbling onto a chair. Marelda panting and laughing, held two of them in her hand. 'They won't hurt you.' Three, still at large, were hopping in every direction. 'Here, hold them. I'll get the rest.'

'Are you mad?'

Still wary but seeing the funny side of it, Greta edged on tippy toe and fled out to the tank stand for a bucket. Marelda, still laughing and belly jiggling, waited for her return. 'Hurry up, before they hop outside.'

Three toads, finding security up against the kitchen wall also waited, silent, yellow eyes open and looking fatly sleepy. Gingerly, the bucket was handed over and the two amphibians placed out of harm's way while Marelda made a careful start on the other three. It was all over in minutes. Marelda tried to catch her breath.

'Now you've seen them – harmless things.' Marelda peered into the tin bucket. 'They're putting them in the cane fields to eat bugs or something.' She took another peek. 'All there safe and sound. Just put 'em into the cupboard – they love the dark – bring them out at night and in the morning back into their sugar bag – got one? Then into the cupboard. You'll never be bothered with cockies again.' Grinning, Relda held out the bucket. 'Want them? I've got six of the ugly buggers myself.'

'Now you've got eleven.' Greta took a quick look and shuddered.

'Thanks all the same, Relda, but you can take them home. Then come back for a morning cup. After all that I need one!'

'Love to, but I gotta get cracking. Rent's overdue. Otherwise Mannie Coleman will be wanting to know why.'

Such a lovely morning, and she was going to make cumquat jam or bust! Shame her neighbour wasn't able to help, to advise and gossip, and she wondered at the same time if Marelda had heard anything about Eddie via Ethel Rourke.

Greta soon found that removing pips from citrus fruit was a task more than tedious. Soon absorbed, a careful eye on the bubbling contents in Marelda's preserving pan, she kept up the stirring on tenterhooks that she could spoil the lot. Clean glass jars waited in a row, a jug handy to fill them. Going on Relda's advice that cooked jam made plopping noises, Greta felt that the jam had plopped enough and picked up the jug.

'Oh, don't we make a pretty picture. All wifey-like.'

Greta turned, already feeling a curdling of juices in her stomach. Stone!

Drunk and evil, he was leaning against the door. 'Thought you'd get away with it, ay?' His lips twisted into a parody of a grin. 'Mrs Andrew Flight. Wot a laugh – what a joke. *Slut!* Heard the Pommy picked you up somewhere down south.'

'Get out!' Greta was paralysed with fear. '*Get out!*' She could have been screaming at a brick wall.

'We know all about you. Kicking up your legs and showing yer tits all over the place. I've made sure of that. I'll teach you to take my little girl away from me and the missus.'

'I said, *get out!*'

'Not till I've had my money's worth.' He flung some silver coins on the floor and took a step towards her. She could feel in frantic memory the steel trap of his arms at the dance hall . . . three men struggling to fling him out the door. She didn't stand a chance.

He took another step.

'I told you to get out!' To her ears her voice sounded high and reedy. Was he bluffing? What did he know – and how? Never taking her eyes off him, she still couldn't move, her feet nailed to the floor.

'Bitch! I'll fuck you into hell!'

Full of intent, he dived at her. Without realising the filled jug was in her hand, as his face loomed closer, Greta flung the boiling jam at him, splashing his face, arms and chest. Dripping and screaming, he stumbled out down the stairs and, finding the tank's tap, turned it on full blast, plunging his head and body under its stream. Every nerve in her body, her pounding heart told her to shut and lock the door, but she had to stay; to make sure there was no attempt to re-enter the house, front or back. Better to watch as he scraped the sticky mess off his chin and arms. She could have blinded him, but didn't care. Finally he shuffled across the yard, mouthing vile words hardly understood. She stood there watching while he scrambled into the truck, driving away out of her sight.

She found the strength to go down the stairs and fill a bucket up to the brim. Both doors, front and back, were locked. Sobbing and trembling, Greta sank down to the kitchen floor and on hands and knees, wiped up every trace of jam. What was left in the preserving pan she tipped over the fence. Let the goats eat it.

One thing for certain, Andy would not be told tonight – if ever. The Stones were selling their farm and were going away. At that moment she couldn't bear the thought of relating what had happened. To say anything – no matter what – to Andy could set in motion a violent confrontation between the two men: dragging her again through the filth of Stone's accusations.

CHAPTER THIRTY-TWO

A midday hush over the main street was not unusual between twelve and two on a weekday. By the time the sawmill hooter gave the knock-off signal, those who could went home for the midday meal and a somnolence settled over the town until the one o'clock hooter blasted its warning that life carries on.

Andrew always enjoyed the peace and quiet of the hour which sometimes stretched to more, while the town recovered from too many servings of hot meats and puddings, allowing the sandwich eaters to deal with any emergency. With Mannie entertaining business associates in one of the hotels, he enjoyed his solitude and the task of tuning an engine without interruptions. Although not hungry, he was aware of a growing thirst and, tossing the shifting spanner on an upturned oil drum, went outside to quench it.

Standing where the tank threw some shade and on his second mug of water, he took time off to admire a flood of Japanese honeysuckle pouring orange over a rusted shed, its blaze emphasising the heat of an unforgiving sun. Somewhere out of sight the 'marrrr' of a nanny goat with her kid hardly intruded on the stillness.

Before turning back to work, he filled to the top a chipped enamel basin and plunged his arms up to the elbows, splashing his face and head, revelling in the cool relief it gave him. Going back inside, he saw the silhouette of a man standing at the garage's front double doors. Although black and featureless against the outside glare, his stance was familiar and as he came closer, recognition instead of curiosity took place.

'Andino, my friend!' The man's face shone with exuberance and heat as he approached. 'A long time, no see.'

Andrew stepped back, avoiding an embrace from the outstretched arms. 'That's because I am a good mechanic, Mr Costina.'

'Call-a me Vince -Vincenzo. Yes, you are right – a good mechanic.' He gave Andrew's chest a prod with a stubby finger. 'And fix other things, eh?'

'You could say that.' Feeling that the man had more to say, Andrew waited.

'I like you, Andino.' The Italian looked around the garage as if assessing the worth of the galvanised walls, grease-stained benches, tools, discarded tyres and the innards that had been wrested out of a car's body in need of repair. 'Ver' good.' It sounded as if Costina was ready to buy him out. 'But *amico*,' he carried on, 'today no business. My wife she is making the spaghetti, speci-ial for you and my good friends from Babinda, and-a maybe Silkwood. You must come, eh? And your *señora*, of course.'

In spite of Mannie's warning, Andrew felt that there was no way of refusing the invitation, and what was the harm? Things had been quiet, especially with Leila gone, and with Greta refusing to attend any bridge afternoons and not playing tennis, the only social outing she had was singing with the Riverbank Players; hardly social for her. Food and wine with the Italianos, he reasoned, could turn into jolly good hoot for a summer's night.

Andrew extended an oil-stained paw. 'Right, Costina, we'll be there, and when?'

After Costina left, Andrew thought over the invitation. It was something that Greta would normally jump into feet first. Lately, he had to admit, she seemed pensive. Subdued, and during the night, restless in sleep. When he allowed himself to think about it, the guilt of dragging her up to the North was always there, ready to surface. At times he wondered if a hired detective could solve the mystery of Netty's disappearance. It could put an end to the life he and Greta had between them. But it could mean a return to England if there was a child involved. A detective . . . would the price of a Burmese ruby be enough to cover it? Perhaps.

Greta squeezed Andrew's hand. 'What a ding!' Her eyes were gleeful, her mouth parted in smiles as she took in the scene around her. It was fiesta and the air was sweet with the smell of the flowering Rangoon creeper and the rich aroma of spitted pork, of lamb and fruit and pastries. Wine by the gallon with not a pot of beer in sight.

It was Greta's night. Never at a loss for words when a beautiful woman was in sight, the men gathered around her and Greta, after the drought of few compliments (not counting Pedersen and Andrew), flirted outrageously as men vied for every dance while their women shrugged and talked among themselves. In a tarantella with a Lothario who was considered the best dancer among them, she was spun and twirled at dizzying speed; a laughing Venus egged on by bravos and whistles. Andrew, no match for the fleet-footed men who danced with her, was proudly content just to watch and adore.

'I've completely had it. What a night!' Relishing the breeze flowing through the utility as they drove along, Greta leant over to give Andrew a kiss. 'You didn't mind?'

'Mind?' he echoed. 'Mind having the most glorious creature beside me – well, most of the time – and the envy of every man there? Not bloody likely!'

'Weren't jealous?

'No.'

'Just a little bit?' she teased.

'Hush. You're talking too much.' Andrew grinned, the glow of the dashboard softly highlighting his profile. His answer, or lack of it, was enough.

Greta, completely relaxed, lifted her hair to the breeze. It had been a long time since she'd been belle of the ball and at a place so predominantly male. Yes, a long time, she thought, snuggling into Andy as he carefully handled the curves of the mountain road.

Once again, Andrew found himself wondering what was troubling Greta. It seemed that after the night with the Costinas the exuberance that she had brought home with her soon subsided.

The days passed as they always did, and the prospect of the Top Hat Revue and what it entailed failed to bring back her spark. He was not to know that 'the spark' dissipated at the sight of Reverend Baker every time he set foot inside the house with excuses that some small detail about the coming revue should be talked over. His talks were becoming more frequent and, for Greta, every smile or smirk the minister made held an undertow of a conspiracy imagined or otherwise to be shared. Ever since Eddie's appearance and Baker's shock announcement that he and Eddie were, if not friends, acquaintances, Andrew wasn't to know that Greta felt she was walking on splintered glass, waiting for blood to flow.

It was the first time he had ever felt any constraint between them. He hesitated to question too closely, but was prepared to wait it out, trusting that Greta would eventually confide in him. Who was he, he asked himself, to demand explanations, well aware of his own days – fewer now, thank Christ – when brown clouds covered the sun? Greta, without complaint, always waited it out.

The sight of Costina walking into the garage again wasn't welcome. Although he had never mentioned it to Greta – he had been reluctant to spoil her enjoyment of the night at the Costina farm – he had sensed an undercurrent of being included in some plan, in the glances and smiles that the men had given him while he stood in the shadows as Greta danced. It had caused discomfort; enough to keep his back pressed against the bulk of the Rangoon creeper.

'Andino!' As before, with arms outstretched, and with Andrew taking a backward step, Vincenzo Costina seemed not to notice the automatic rebuff. 'I have the good news for you, *amico*.'

'Aye?'

'You enjoy yourself at my pl-aice? The *vino* strong. Good, eh?' The Italian seemed pleased with himself as his fist lightly punched Andrew's arm.

'Aye . . .' It was time to lean against a shelf, arms crossed, as he listened to what Costina had to say.

'My friends like you ver' much. They 'ave many cars, not-a rub-bish cars.' Costina's bottom lip jutted with pride, looking at the one Andrew was working on with disdain. 'You will fix them. You work for us. We 'ave one for you to fix now! At my pl-aice.'

'Hey! Hey, wait a minute, mon. Nothing doing. I canna' drop everything right now and you know it.'

'Okay. We pay you good. My friend must go back to Babinda.' The bottom lip jutted more. His car —'

'I'm afraid not, Vince.' Andrew pointed to the vehicle he was repairing. 'He's a good customer. And while ye'rr here, I dinna' like people telling me what I must do. As far as I'm concerned in my business, it's first in, first served.'

Costina's brown eyes narrowed as Andrew, unsmiling, stood his ground. He didn't like the way things were turning out.

'I giv-a you one more time. Work for me – for us.'

'Who the hell is us?'

Costina shrugged. 'My friends. They like you. We pay you, *up front!*' He waved his hands, frustration ugly on his face. 'No tax . . . we don't cheat. Treat-a you well.'

'Sorry, mate – I work for myself.'

Costina's eyes travelled the garage, taking in the small evidence of a not-so busy enterprise. Tense, Andrew waited, remembering Mannie's warning. How long ago? The silence lay heavy in the overheated air and he wondered if he should order Costina out of the garage, deciding it politic to wait, hoping things would cool down. He knew by now who he was dealing with. Although the Black Hand Gang usually carried on business among the Italians themselves, there was little point in making enemies. Newspaper headlines of bombing and exhortations around the cane fields raced through his head, reminding himself again that, as far as he knew, the ordinary citizens of the cane-growing towns were exempt; hoping it to be true.

'Andino.' The jutting lip turned into a smile but the brown eyes looking at Andrew were flat, without expression. 'Forgeeve me. I did not mean to be the up-setter. I will go and perhaps we talk about this matter some other time, eh, *amico?*' He looked over the workshop again, making Andrew wonder if a bombing was in consideration. He was not far off. What Costina said next chilled his blood. A drop of cold sweat trickled down his spine.

'Your *señora*. What a beautiful lady.' He shook his head as if in admiration, but the flat gaze remained. 'Her arm is better now. I am pleased.' His voice was smooth as slime. 'You stop the doctor from cutting it off, eh?' *How did he know that?* The alleged report of dismembered hands nailed to Italian cane growers' doors tightened Andrew's innards into knots.

Tread lightly – keep the fear out of your voice. 'I think ye'd better go, Costina.' Andrew's breathing was steady as he turned his back on the man, lifted the bonnet of the car and carried on with his work, his mind racing as to how to remove Greta permanently and quickly out of Costina's sight.

CHAPTER THIRTY-THREE

A sou' easter and a following sea eased the *Pelican* onwards. At the wheel Andrew's heart lifted, feeling the engine chugging comfortably beneath his bare feet. A sea of splintered turquoise parted before the bow and the sight of Greta sunning full length up front filled his heart with deep and wonderful joy.

Expecting objections from Greta, even demanding questions as to why they should pull up stakes and suddenly quit Yunnabilla, their secretive departure had been surprisingly easy to arrange. It even came with a promise of better things to come as if it all were meant to be. Legs braced against an occasional roll, Andrew relived their flight from the moment Costina had left the garage. Mannie, still in his office and unaware of the words spoken between them, heard the news with equanimity and immediately began making plans.

'Escape – pleasure,' Mannie enthused, 'more than you can imagine, and of course not forgetting the business side of it. The three of us . . . You, me – over this side of the water to handle things – and Comrade Sam. Perfect!' He had slapped his thigh hard enough to dislodge his spectacles. His scheme for them without a by-your-leave was to join up with Sam, head for New Guinea and then sail along the coast to the Fly River and Kebai Island. 'Get in first, I'd say. Nothing to stop us from making a million. Well,' – he'd had the wit to correct himself – 'thousands. A good quid or two, anyway. See what you can do!' Andrew chuckled, shaking his head at the speed Mannie had taken to work out a bizarre – you had to call it that – future for the Flights. Trade! Oil! Crocodile skins! It soon overrode his own idea of taking Greta to Brisbane, a city he knew little about. He couldn't deny that Mannie's schemes were tempting, and all without Greta's knowledge at the time.

But now on the *Pelican* with Greta and Sam, sailing to the last outpost (as he thought of it) had been the ideal solution. A phone call to Sam at the Port Douglas post office had been all that was needed and his immediate response was to say '*Come aboard!*' loud enough to make Mannie's ears ring. The outcome had been a hectic midnight plunge with Mannie driving them down the mountain highway to Cairns, Andrew explaining to Greta on the way why they were quitting Yunnabilla. The hidden threat behind Costina's garage visit she had accepted without question.

Even so, Greta's enthusiasm for a change of scenery had been astonishing. The Top Hat Revue – 'Poppy can take over that if they must have a concert' – was dismissed with a toss of her head as she threw clothes into a port, understanding the reason for such haste and secrecy. She only stipulated that Marelda and David Pedersen must be told, as well as taking her records down to Poppy for safekeeping. 'I can send for them later,' she had told him. 'The only thing I regret is missing out on Leila's homecoming party.' It was only a small sigh, though, a faint uplift of the shoulders. 'Never mind.'

Whatever had been haunting Greta magically disappeared the moment she'd been told they were leaving Yunnabilla.

At dawn they were greeted by a delighted Sam Riding, freckled by the sun, and both ears in place. And now here they were.

With a bunting sea, a few puffy clouds in the sky and Sam's harmonica playing a reedy tune in the company of gulls wheeling around the stern, Andrew couldn't believe his luck. Already he had a sailor's affection for the FJX *Pelican*, a sturdy, wide-beamed vessel of just under forty feet. He acknowledged that Sam had done a good job of restoring the vandalism and had added a few improvements of his own. The fishermen of Alligator Creek had joked about Sam's idea of what a wheelhouse should be like. 'Yer never have an opening at the back of a wheelhouse. The side mate, the side; that's all yer need.' But Sam had gone his own way and the wheelhouse with its 'improvements' in Sam's way of thinking couldn't be better. The galley, if it could be called that, took up one side of the wheelhouse with its built-in cupboard and a benchtop wide and sturdy enough to support a screwed-down two-ring gas burner. 'That's all yer need to cook up a pan of fish and boil the kettle!'

Not quite like the Victor, was her thought as Sam, full of pride, showed Greta and Andrew cunning arrangements for storing and stacking. There was even a bookshelf making room for a cookbook among the few salt-stained copies of *Bulldog Drummond's Adventures*.

Greta had taken one look at the two bunks below deck and opted for sleeping on the hatch, which was large enough, the skipper had boasted, for a man to take a doze or sleep under the stars. Below decks was a lightweight mattress to be brought up if necessary for a softer sleep. They'd had four days of perfect weather and Greta's rest had been sweet. She accepted the fact that Sydney was only a memory, Yunnabilla just a stopover, and she sang into the wind, heart lifting with the waves, ready to face the next challenge as long as Andy was there beside her. Not one instant of regret or thought of what might have been; only excited anticipation of what was to come.

Hugging the coast, the *Pelican* anchored at nightfall. Each day more miles lay behind them with Port Moresby as their goal. Even so, there was time enough for idle wanderings on islands lush and green and on sands untouched, waiting for their footsteps. More often than not they abandoned the galley and rowed into inlets and shelving beaches, and by firelight savoured the smell of cooking fish that they had caught during the day. There were nights of singing to the accompaniment of harmonica and ukulele; a harmony of camaraderie between them.

Sam, throwing another piece of driftwood onto the fire, sniffed the air, appreciating the tang of salt and seagrass drying out at low tide. 'One of the cleanest stinks in the world, y' reckon?' Contented, he rolled a cigarette, handing the tobacco tin over to Andrew. 'Feel like a durry? Help yerself.'

'No, thanks.' Andrew tugged a pipe out of the pocket of his shorts. 'I'll stick with this tonight.'

'What about me?' Greta held out a hand.

'Oops, I forgot about the deckie.' Sam chuckled and ducked as if expecting a blow.

Greta had become an expert in the art of rolling her own, another newly discovered accomplishment like gutting and scaling fish; she was the best, it seemed, at catching them and cooking up a feed. Storms had been few and far between and when the men battled on a heaving deck Greta was at the ready with hot cocoa laced with rum when it was all over. Rowing the skiff she looked on as exercise. It was a life she had never thought of, even in her wildest dreams. What thrilled her most was the sight of Andy, surprisingly tanned, the days of introspection and silence diminishing. He was, like herself, exuberantly happy and gloriously fit. Making love sometimes on the hatch to Sam's explosive snores down below was spiced by the thought that he might appear, as he sometimes did, to cool off in the night air. Strangely enough, ardour was aroused only when opportunity reared its enticing head.

'I'd say it's Port Moresby the day after tomorrow. You agree, Samuel, old chap?'

'You could say that.'

Andrew knocked the dottle from his pipe, refilled and relit it with a smoking twig. He looked down on Greta, her head resting on his lap, hair heavy and cool slipping between his thighs. Thinking over the last few weeks he was amazed at how quickly she'd adapted to life on a small boat short on space and only roughly comfortable from a man's point of view. He had to admit that to some the word for it would be primitive. Each day he found himself loving her more than ever. He wondered sometimes if she would ever tell him why she had been so glad – it had been obvious – to leave Yunnabilla behind. Someday she'd tell him . . .

The velvet of night was thick with diamonds and the *Pelican* chugged through a sea devoid of a ripple; smooth and flat as a sliver of polished onyx. Sam was at the wheel, Andrew and Greta on the bow. Too hot for talking, breathing in air damp with humidity, lightning pulsed on the horizon with the promise of a storm.

Greta flapped a wet towel over her nearly naked body. Brassiere and scanties only, in deference to the heat. 'My dizzy aunt, is it always like this? And I thought Cairns' heat was tropical enough.'

'The doldrums, my beauty. That's what they call it, before the rains.'

'Bring on the rain, for gawd's sake! Buckets of it.'

After consultation, the three had decided that a straight final run through the night to Port Moresby was a reasonable idea. It seemed that the cooler weather had, with the rain birds, migrated south, and fresh water and supplies were running out. They all agreed that holidays were over and it was time to test their sea legs on dry land. Not, as the two men told Greta, that the venture could be called a trial of seamanship, congratulating themselves on a journey without serious crises. She dozed, too hot for sleep, drowsily aware that Andy had risen to his feet. His turn at the wheel.

A sudden thrill of the unknown surged through Greta. Papua was just over the horizon. To her it was a land of mystery, little heard of or thought about in the old days before meeting Andy. Now wide awake, senses alert, she sprang to her feet to savour it all; and as if in response a sea creature of size arced through the air, causing a fountain of silver phosphorous as it splashed back into the deep.

Another turnaround in life, she exalted, and whatever lay ahead she was ready to meet it full on . . .

CHAPTER THIRTY-FOUR

Sam wasn't happy to leave the *Pelican* anchored and unattended among the sailing craft of Port Moresby. The canoes with their high curved sails of plaited pandanus, stout and large enough to carry twenty men or more, lay still like black-winged moths scattered haphazardly over the harbour.

'Don't like leaving her anywhere alone, 'specially here.' Sam squinted against the glare that gave the water the sheen of pewter. 'Thievin' mongrels wherever yer go, and I'd say it's no different here.'

'Come on, old Comrade.' Andrew gave Sam's shoulder a slap. 'Where's that "every man is equal" attitude?'

'Gone mate, gone long ago. But you and Greta go ashore, have a good nosy round and line up provisions and water.'

In the time it took to row ashore it was plain to see that Port Moresby was a town of reasonable size. Houses nudging their way up the hillsides, tin sheds and what looked like stores scrambling for room closer to the shore. Under the watchful brown eyes of women and children, the skiff's rope was tied up to a coconut palm bending for their convenience over the shallows. The women, some bare from the waist up, others in Mother Hubbards, slowly gathered around, accompanying them up the sand to a dirt road that followed the curve of water leading to the town. A few of the older women, their heavy breasts restricted by strips of coloured cloth, gave shy smiles while pointing to what appeared to be a busy market under the shade of the heavy-leafed trees.

'A market! The fruit! Just look at it.' Greta picked up the golden globe of a paw paw and sniffed. 'And the pineapples! Never seen anything like it,' she said, amazed at the intricate hatching of the peeled flesh without one eye left behind to tease the tongue. She shook her head as some of the women, sitting cross-legged on the grass, pressed her to buy. 'We'll get some on the way back.' She wondered if she was understood.

'The *boong* closes down about twelve. So get what you can now and store it in the dingy. It won't be thieved.'

The accent spoke of an education in the best of public schools with the final shine and polish from a young ladies' establishment in Switzerland. She was as tall as Greta, a gypsy look to her, with eyes nearly as black as her hair, her face shaded by the large floppy brim of a sun hat; class and style personified. With a flash of even teeth she held out her hand, first to Greta. 'Sabrina Logan. Staying a while, I hope?' But her eyes were directed at Andrew.

Greta suppressed a giggle as Andy bent over her hand. '*Enchanté*, madam. Andrew Flight the name, and my wife Greta.'

Greta had seen these first encounters before, but Andrew's response, charming enough to win a heart, quickly dissipated Sabrina Logan's hopes as he made it plain that his own heart lay elsewhere.

Andy's hair, now sun-streaked, and eyes more grey (as if the tropic sun had bleached out the blue) were veiled, not giving anything away. Greta had to admit that he managed to carry off the wearing of his Bombay bloomers with flair, ridiculous looking as they were. His 'whites', as he always called them, were immaculate with a sailor's expert folding. Greta swelled with pride, pleased that instinct had told her to wear beach pyjamas instead of shorts. She agreed with herself that the Flights would have little trouble finding acceptance in this strange and exotic land.

'Of course you must allow me to take you to town,' Sabrina Logan was insisting. 'The car should be arriving any minute. We're eating at the hotel and Burns Philp is stocked up with fresh supplies including —' With a twist of her wrist, she gave a good imitation of holding a glass in her hand. 'It could end up a wicked afternoon – goidonk, goidonk – but fun. Of course you're invited. Coming?'

Before Greta had time to reply, Andy was shaking his head. 'Thank you, but no. We will take our time and walk. A guid way to get the feel of a place.'

'In this heat?' She stood back, blinking as if he might be an eccentric – even mad.

Andrew placed his arm over Greta's shoulder. 'We're used to it, eh, lass?'

By now a car, well used and dusty, had arrived, driven by a young man as immaculate as Andrew in whites. He leant over, opening the door, eyeing off the Flights at the same time. 'C'mon, Sabrina, we'll miss out on *kai* – it's roast pork and the fellas are hungry and waiting.'

Sabrina hesitated, turning back to Andrew. 'Sure you won't join us?'

'Another time perhaps.'

She shrugged, then signalled to a native in a lap-lap standing by with a push cart filled with fruit and vegetables. 'Asai! Take this to the house,' she said in pidgin, 'and don't go off chewing betel nut with that one talk I've seen hanging around, or else!' She turned back, as if reluctant to leave them there. It was Greta who now shook a head, and said to herself, 'On your way, lady,' not forgetting to give the young driver a Greta Osborne smile. 'Nice meeting you, Sabrina.'

Driving off, the car was soon engulfed in a red dust cloud, with the 'houseboy', as they heard Sabrina describe him, trotting behind with the loaded cart. As the dust settled, sympathy for the servant dissolved into laughter. Not so far away and no more than seconds after the car had left, he pushed the cart off the road. He didn't have long to wait. Promptly a young man joined him and beneath the spread of the poinciana's scarlet flowers and speckled shade, they set themselves comfortably on the grass and without preamble began rolling cigarettes – at least ten inches long – of newspaper and tobacco, black as sin. It was the first time and it wouldn't be the last that Greta smelt the heavy fumes of what seemed to be burnt treacle – to her, an unknown substance that Andrew called trade tobacco. Lounging against the tree trunk they chatted quietly, the pungency of tobacco smoke keeping marauding flies at bay.

'Now I've seen it all. Most of it in under an hour. What a place!'

'How about taking the good lady's advice? We'll buy some fruit and vegetables before they close shop, then back to the boat.' Andrew looked about him, his satisfaction of where the *Pelican* had brought them plain to see. 'How do you like it, Mrs Flight?'

'I love it!'

'Well, mad dogs and Englishmen go out in the midday sun, so they say, and that's not for us. Let's go back and cool off. We'll eat a pineapple and a passionfruit or two, then persuade Sam to come ashore. I don't think anyone around here is going to axe the old lady. She's not in Alligator Creek now.'

Sam agreed to leave the boat and the afternoon was busy. Three of the locals, stocky men with hair like helmets, strong and frizzy, had been hired as carriers to take stores to the *Pelican*, now tied up to the town's main wharf. Sam and his crew were lucky, the manager of Burns Philp had told them. They had arrived just in time to take advantage of what the supply vessel had brought in, its cargo still stacked high on the wharf.

Friendly and interested, and when told that they had the Fly River and Kebai Island in mind, his advice was to cover themselves for a few months instead of weeks. 'Buy up on tinned stuff, rice and powdered milk,' he said, and had asked Greta if she could turn her hand to making bread. 'It helps to eke things out. Not quite as bad as you might be thinking,' he added, seeing the expression on Greta's face, 'but sometimes arrivals are overdue up there and when goods already ordered have been delivered, you might find things a bit on the short side.'

He also advised that if they intended going upriver they should take a stock of tinned fish and meat for trade. 'Cloth, tin dishes and anything else that the villagers might find attractive and must possess. You never know what you could pick up along the way.'

They planned to catch a dawn tide, eager to sail further north. By the time everything was aboard, the sun was already sinking behind cumulous shot with gold and banking up with the promise of a storm.

Satisfied that everything was as shipshape as it could be, Sam flopped down on the hatch. 'Don't know about you two, but I'm buggered.' Not ready to admit it, but the Flights were too.

'Och, mon. Ye're getting old.'

'Maybe. But at the moment a cold sluice down and a beer – that's all I ask for.'

The ice box was now full to the brim with ice and fresh meats, its chill hopefully lasting for a good few days. The town, still unexplored, beckoned as lights flickered up the hillsides and brown women fished with handlines on the wharf. Nubile girls giggled and chattered, pretending that there wasn't a male in sight but blooming under the hot gaze of admiration from the young men passing by. The night air tantalised them with the smell of cooking fires, frangipani blooms and something rancid and unidentified.

'How about we celebrate?' Andrew was ready to take off. 'Our first port of call, and we've been working like dogs. Let's take a stroll and a look-see.'

'Got in before me, lover. I'm raring to go!'

Before they had left Port Douglas, Sam, on hearing that the Flights were joining him, had rigged up a bucket shower, easily dismantled, with Greta mainly in mind. 'Only when we're in port,' he had warned. 'At sea you wash in a bucket like the rest of us and get Andy to tip it over you when yer finish. I'll turn me back.' And he did. Now in the privacy of hessian walls on the back deck Greta had her shower and emerged fresh and shining and, as she said at times, 'Looking good and smellem sweet like Queen Victoria.' She had no idea where the saying came from.

The main street was as fascinating as the waterfront had been. Greta and Andrew had their share of curious stares, both from the locals and from the Europeans taking advantage of the cool night air. Most were Australian, by their accents, the males again dressed in whites, and in concession to the evening wearing ties and long trousers instead of shorts. It was the white women who earned a raise of Greta's eyebrow. It appeared that cigarettes were a fashion accessory, and handbags had been exchanged for packets of State Express, Capstan or the more expensive pack of the elegant Marcovitch Con Amore. She'd seen more than one in a woman's hand as they strolled along. Smoking in public! Not quite Yunnabilla, and even suburban Sydney might have frowned.

'D' ye feel like something cool to drink?'

They stood outside a hotel, a one-level establishment with floor-to-ceiling louvres ready to catch every breeze. The wide open slats were obviously the source of an evening's entertainment for those on the outside looking in. Greta had the distinct feeling that the Papuans watching, mainly women, knew the intimate details of every person seen in the large comfortable lounge and bar. Clearly heard male guffaws exploded from one group and a few couples danced to a gramophone record. The women, small in number compared to the men, were dressed mainly in evening dress, though a little out of fashion. There was an air of boisterous gaiety about the place that held instant appeal. Greta tucked her arm into Andy's. 'Do I feel like something cool to drink? You bet I do!'

Their entrance was noted with interest and all eyes, curious and some even calculating, swept over them. A closer look as they walked further inside told of an afternoon's heavy drinking by some of the men. Their whites weren't quite as white, crumpled shirts escaped from belted trousers, ties were askew and cigarette smoke hardly disguised the smell of sweat and booze. Greta, hair piled high on her head, her Fuji silk dress richly olive, had many a male envious of the tall, fair-headed man shepherding her towards the bar.

'Andrew! Greta!' Sabrina Logan burst from her own collection of aficionados like some exotic bloom, her black hair falling free to her shoulders. 'Had a feeling you'd turn up! What fun.' She pointed to the group she had left, two women seated and five men. 'Must join us. Dickie! Chairs, darling, chairs!' The young man appointed for the task leapt to his feet and nodded. But all he did was speak in a rapid dialect to one of the waiters, his lap-lap so stiffly ironed and starched it could have stood by itself upright on the floor.

Sabrina made a great show of enthusiastic welcome, introducing the Flights to all and relating how she had met the newcomers at the market. 'There they appeared from out of nowhere. Actually rowed ashore at full speed – goidonk, goidonk – smack bang into the middle – goidonk, goidonk – of the *boong*.' It seemed that 'goidonk' was an idiosyncrasy Sabrina used to emphasise and colour her speech, and she somehow managed to turn it into what sounded like sophisticated wit.

The seated women were polite but the barriers were too high for storming. Not wasting her time, Greta turned to the men, still standing as if waiting for permission to sit, noting that barriers didn't exist where they were concerned. She and Andy made a good team. While he would charm the ladies, in two minutes flat she'd have those rather attractive young fellas falling at her feet, she reckoned, in spite of Sabrina's goidonks. Introductions over, Andrew put his arm around Greta's waist. 'The first dance,' he whispered in her ear, 'may I? Before these hungry wolves carry you off.' He chuckled. 'I think, my bonny braw hen, ye're in for a busy night!'

After that, throughout a night of many gins and tonics and under the breeze of the ceiling *punkas*, the talk was of the price of *copra*, supposition about untamed and unknown territory, and more serious discussion of the impending war in Europe, while Greta danced the foxtrot, the quickstep and from old time to new vogue. Clumsy dancers and smooth gliding experts all had their turn. To the tune of every new record placed on the turntable, another partner was ready to take her in his arms. As she was for the umpteenth time guided around the floor, she found it was easy to guess that anyone, be she as cross-eyed as a hairy goat, would have her full share of the women-starved men begging for just one dance. A good ten to one, Greta reckoned, not able to refuse another waiting for his turn. She'd never seen anything like it. So many fellas, so few women!

Some whom she danced with were patrol officers in their early twenties to thirties, in Port Moresby on well-earned leave before returning again to trek mountain trails, ford rivers, duty bound and earnest. In parts it was a Stone Age territory, Greta and Andrew were made to understand, of warring tribes, 'paybacks', suspicion and rampant superstition. Office clerks, tradesmen, sun-toughened adventurers – 'Territorians' as they liked to call themselves – made a boisterous contrast to the more sedate plantation managers and their wives, turning the night for Greta into an exhilarating spiral of colourful exotica. Where have I been all my life? she asked herself.

As for Andy, she noticed that he was a part of an animated group breasting the bar, Sabrina and Dickie standing beside him.

He seemed so at ease, so attuned to the atmosphere around him. Did it bring back memories of nights in Singapore, in Bombay? It took Greta back to the first time they had met: the laughing and joking of another celebration in a Sydney mansion on a New Year's Eve. Suddenly, she felt alone and crossed the floor to join them, in time to see Sabrina closing in, her voice posh and husky as she looked up at Andy, an unlit cigarette in her hand. 'Light me, darling.' Greta also noticed the amused looks – another scalp for Sabrina's belt – exchanged between her admirers.

Not waiting to see the result, she turned on her heel and marched back to the young hopeful, still standing on the sidelines as if he knew she would return. His eyes brightened, and his grin was boyish as she held out her hand. 'You have to watch out for Sabby, Greta, or she'll hogtie that man of yours to a bed post.'

'Like hell, she will!'

Seething over the blatant invitation in Sabrina's smile and without trying to look, she saw the woman's cigarette was now well and truly alight. Andy? He was still there and Dickie nowhere to be seen. In sharp contrast to what she had been feeling not so long ago, she recognised for the first time since leaving Sydney an awareness of jealous mistrust. Come off it, Greta, she chided herself as she romped around the floor with her enthusiastic toe crusher. So he lit a cigarette. Big deal! Forget it!

But as the bar again came into view, Andy and Sabrina were suddenly missing. Despondency fell over her like a cloud. She shouldn't have danced so much – but then, he had never objected before, recalling her last fling at the Costinas' farm. He was proud of her and the way men flocked around her. Maybe tonight she'd had one dance too many, she told herself, looking over to the now momentarily deserted bar. She felt as if a dozen sighs were locked inside her heart, scarcely hearing the life history of her youthful partner. A hand tapped her shoulder.

'We sail at dawn, and the crew, including the deckhand, must be present.'

The sweet words washed over her like a balm. 'Aye, aye, Skipper.'

CHAPTER THIRTY-FIVE

Kebai Island

The three standing on the deck of the *Pelican* already knew that Kebai was an administrative centre and close enough to the Fly River for quick and easy penetration by boat into the mainland. It was a huge and lengthy waterway, allowing vessels and the government to service a native population of tribes and their village strongholds.

The Burns Philp manager in Port Moresby had given them a rundown on the area. They knew what to expect. Swamps, sago palm, rivers and yes, crocodiles aplenty. Trade the first source of income, crocodile skins a second choice. At the moment, as far as the *Pelican* crew and its skipper knew, their trip to Papua and its outcome had been a gamble. Success or failure? Who could tell.

'The Western District, eh?' Sam swept his binoculars over their first view of the island. With the charts that Mannie Coleman had pressed on them and that Andrew had made good use of, they made an easy time of it up the coast, and now here they were, the island not a stone's throw away. The *Pelican* was anchored well off-shore. Low tide had exposed a sheet of mud a good quarter-mile wide up to a shoreline protected by a wall of sturdy logs. 'Unless you want her lying on her side in mud we'll stay out here till there's enough water to row in for a look around.' Sam took a second sweep of the binoculars. 'Doesn't look halfway bad,' he said, handing them over to Andrew.

Even the mud held interest. Unlike the *lakatoi* canoes of Moresby, the outriggers strewn at ease over the foreshore were large enough to take a village to nowhere and back again. For added interest there seemed to be some altercation from the depths of one not that far away. A woman's voice, strident with anger in a language not understood, shrilled over the mud between it and the *Pelican*. A man appeared, leaping out of the canoe as though the devils of hell were after him. Dodging a well-aimed enamel pot, he fled with unknown curses burning his ears.

'We-ll now . . .' Drollery emphasised Andrew's amusement. 'A wee stramash! Outrigger domesticity reigns.'

Tall coconut palms reared above the spread of poincianas and bunched stands of mango trees. Already they had learnt that the Kiwais of the Western District were famous for their boat-building prowess; they could see the proof lying all about them. But a more intriguing sight was a dwelling standing alone on the shore. Built entirely of galvanised iron, its pitched roof was high enough to challenge the tallest palm. It had an annex to the side and even from the boat it was easy to make out wide thatched shutters serving as windows. 'It nearly looks like some kind of castle,' Greta mused, taking the glasses off Andrew for a better view. 'Well, not quite a castle, but looks important enough to be one.' Somehow the sight of it thrilled her. It was so different and in some tropical way personified everything that was and what she had heard about

Papua. The 'Cannibal Coast', someone at the Moresby hotel had called it. The incoming tide was now creeping with stealth around the *Pelican*'s hull. Not long to go, and they'd be ashore. Greta could hardly wait.

A man in starched khaki shorts, long hose to the knee, watched and waited as they rowed ashore. Under his gaze they secured the skiff and as they approached he came forward to meet them with an outstretched hand.

'Sam Riding? Andy Flight and Mrs Flight? We've been waiting for you. Arthur Mead's the name, of the Hotel Hibiscus – everything you "mead" we have got,' he said, shaking each hand in turn. 'Pleased to mead you.'

Gawd, Aggie! A backwoods comedian. Save us!

He was completely bald but made up for it with a ruff of a moustache, the tips waxed into submission. They could only hide their surprise and wait for enlightenment.

'Mannie's telegram – as you know, he pops over now and then – said you were coming.' He ushered them along the water-front. 'Hotel's not far away, beer's on ice and here —' He indicated with a wave of the hand a building further along the water front, again made of galvanised iron '— is my trading store. But we'll discuss all that later on.'

Although the day was nearly over, the heat was oppressive; the sun still burning through massed clouds hugging the island. Lining what was obviously the main road were a few shops, one slightly larger than the rest with the name Billy Fat & Co painted on the awning. For Greta a garage flaunting the one red and yellow petrol bowser it possessed held no interest, but the substantial Burns Philp store made it clear that here was the lifeblood of commerce in Kebai. From there the wide dirt road, straight as a ruler, carried on until it disappeared into bushland, leaving behind a huddle of grass huts and more mango trees.

'There's a convent not far from here,' Mead said, 'that's if you're a churchgoer, and of course Billy Fat's store.' He turned off the road into a lane shaded by mango trees, and grass thick and soft underfoot made walking easy. He gave them a stop sign. 'Welcome to the Hotel Hibiscus, the coolest place to wine and dine in the Territory.'

Thought had gone into making the place inviting. The hotel was a pleasing mixture of wood and bamboo interspersed with panels of woven grass. Bougainvilleas pink and purple clambered over the roof, and the wide wraparound verandah already had its share of drinkers out for a pre-dinner tipple, comfortable in planter chairs. It was obvious the hotel was named after the profusion of hibiscus making a hem of colour around the base of the building. Arthur led them up the shallow steps.

As before, the three were the centre of all eyes. It seemed that Arthur was an hospitable host not only because drinkers were money in the till, but a personal friend as he slapped this one on the shoulder, shook hands with another and bowed to the few women there. The newcomers were introduced as if their appearance must be of benefit to them all. Greta could only think of their unannounced arrival in Yunnabilla, of Mannie Coleman, and wondered where the catch was.

Apparently there was no catch; the arrival of the *Pelican* was a welcome addition to the few boats working out of the little port.

Before the night had ended Sam had hired out the boat for a tidy sum to take workers and timbers up the Fly River to a site where missionaries were waiting for a church and a school to be built.

Without too much trouble it seemed that the *Pelican* was soon in business, just as Mannie had foretold. There was to be no delay. All through the night Sam and Andrew worked tying down timbers and squeezing in yet another necessary item that could not be left behind. On Mead's suggestion they stocked up with pots and pans; ladies' shifts of garish colours; trade tobacco and newspapers for the making of cigarettes; rice and sugar – all of course, as Greta pointed out, from Arthur's trading store. 'The opportunity to get rid of it will arise up there, don't worry,' he had assured them. They found it impossible for Greta to accompany them. By the time the *Pelican* was loaded up, not even one of Marelda's cane toads could have been smuggled aboard.

As Andrew said goodbye on the rickety jetty Greta caught a gleam in his eyes, although he tried to hide it; the same gleam of anticipation that was there on the morning when he and Sam with his stitched ear had driven off to the Colemans' farm. At that moment she knew she was taking second place to this new *Boys' Own Adventure*. She stood with the Kiwai women, silently observing every move as she fought back tears, standing alone until the *Pelican* finally disappeared.

Never mind – it was a new start, she told herself, and she was ready to adventure on her own. First, back to the hotel where she had spent the night. Arthur – Arty, as most seemed to call him – had spoken of an empty house available: the old couple who owned it had retired to Queensland and it was for rent or sale. He had promised to take her there. Sitting on the hotel verandah with the geckos for company and a freshly squeezed lime squash to quench her thirst, she waited and hoped that the house at least had a stick of furniture in it, a chair and a bed to lie on. She sighed. Five days they expected to be away. Five days to find out, to learn who is who, and what in the hell was she going to do with herself?

Greta had been sitting on the verandah for over an hour without sight of Arthur Mead. Once he had flashed his head around the small reception room door, promising to return in a few minutes. At one stage she was ready to get up and walk out. But to where? A few early imbibers sat at the far end of the verandah, two men and a woman, their unabashed curiosity hidden under a façade of nods and smiles. It was the woman who made the first move to an introduction. Saying something to the men, she left her chair and strolled over, a tall glass of gin and tonic in her hand. It was her faint look of puzzlement that gave Greta a warning.

'I'm Louise Jackson.' She paused and, getting no response, carried on. 'I hope you don't mind me asking, but haven't we met before?'

'I very much doubt it.'

'I could have sworn . . .'

Such a friendly innocent question, but one that chipped off a shard of Greta's composure. She had never seen the woman in her life, but since Port Moresby she had quickly learnt that the Territory was not Yunnabilla. Most of the people she had met were transients; a cosmopolitan mix with some calling Sydney home. It was something she hadn't thought of. As for Andy, if the truth came out – and she had already thought about it a thousand times over – nothing much would be said. He'd be looked on as a bit of a dog – a lucky dog at that. But her? Sniggers behind her back, a wink between drunks. Still raw from her encounter with Stone, and even before they left Queensland she had decided to lie low. No singing out of the ordinary and certainly no solo dancing on tables. Yet already, here was a woman wondering if they had met. Had she met or seen Greta Osborne of the Coconut Grove? The Greta Osborne who should be in America, as reported in the entertainment section of the *Herald*? The woman was persistent and seemed reluctant to leave until Greta felt like yelling into the pleasant face looking down at her, *Yes, I'm not in bloody New York. I'm living in sin and I'm enjoying every minute of it, damn it!*

But of course, Greta kept her thoughts to herself. She returned the woman's smile and her invitation to join up with her two friends was met with a polite refusal. She wasn't prepared to meet anyone as yet.

'Ah!' Arthur Mead finally appeared. 'Apologies about the delay, Mrs Flight, but there's been a bit of a fracas in the kitchen. These *boongs* can't cook an egg without singeing it or wash a plate without smashing it.' He turned to Louise Jackson, still standing there. 'Sorry we can't join you, but Mrs Flight and I have a house to inspect.' Leading Greta away he turned to his three guests. 'By the way, you should stay for *kai*. Lamb and mint sauce on the menu, and Ammi cooks it to a tee.' Apparently happy to leave the lamb in the hands of a person who singed eggs, he led Greta down the hibiscus path.

They walked along the foreshore, the sea now a fraction below the barrier of upright logs. Another surge would have found it inching over the grass. With the Kiwai canoes free from the restrictions of a low tide, their full beauty of design and sail could be appreciated. A few, their sails unfurled, were winging out and away to open water. Each year, Arthur told her, there is a celebration and canoes from every river village come in to barter, boast, to show-off and sail – even to race. 'It's a lovely sight when they are all here. You've just missed it.'

'There's always a next time.'

As they passed Arthur's trade store Greta began to wonder just where he was taking her. They had walked by a few houses, uninteresting boxes of fibro and the ever-present galvanised iron. Native men and women walked by quietly, a few shy smiles, torpid if anything, leaving the laughter and shouts to the children scampering by. If anything, she was feeling pretty lethargic herself, wondering why she hadn't brought a hat.

So muggy hot . . .

In a way, and in addition to the sudden departure of the *Pelican*, she was mildly disappointed with this island of Kebai. Pleasant enough, but it could hardly be called a tropical paradise, although there was enough greenery around to give a false impression of coolness. The sea looked slightly murky compared to the turquoise and blue they had been sailing through, and last evening when they had come ashore there was no sand to speak of. You're judging without seeing it all, she told herself, and cheered up by thinking there must be some place, still unknown, where she could swim. Transport seemed to be just a few old trucks and utilities, making her realise that most of the population used their legs to get around. She wondered if it was possible to borrow or hire a bicycle. Somehow she doubted it.

Arthur's voice jolted her out of her reverie. 'Well, here we are, Mrs Flight. "Evenglow" is the name. They were a romantic old pair, for sure.'

It was *the* house they'd seen from the boat. Her house! It towered above her, silently inviting her to step inside. Her whole impression of the island changed as she walked across the road onto the mowed grass leading to a side door. By the steps stood an island girl, her grin as white as the loose-fitting dress she wore.

'Lo, Mrs Plight.'

'Nonee, your housegirl.'

Greta turned to Mead. 'I don't get it. It seems as if I was expected.' It was weird. Since they had arrived everything was too easy; too off pat. 'How did you know I would want the place?'

'How could you resist?' Arthur chuckled, looking pleased with himself. 'Luck, my dear, is working for you. Evenglow has been waiting. The old house has been empty for months. But when the owners left, dear friends of mine, I promised that no one would set a foot inside that door without my approval. Oh, yes,' he nodded, the waxed tips of his moustache upright in defiance of gravity, 'it could have been let ten times over but we're not having any boozers, flotsam or jetsam that float up here causing havoc. And they do, and they *can,* dear lady.' His little speech over, Arthur got down to business. 'Well, what do y' think? Twenty pounds a month and it's a bargain.'

Shades of Mannie Coleman.

It would cost nearly as much as the hotel would for a week. But they had to live somewhere. If Andy hated it, well, that remained to be seen.

'I'll take it.' Already entranced, Greta claimed the house for her own. Inside, it was nothing like anything she could imagine. The front room was enormous. Her assumption, because of its height, that the house was a two-level building had been a mistake. There was no second floor. No ceiling. But the room soared upwards, ending in a pitched roof high above her head. She had been right about the windows taking up the whole side of the front. Great sloping shutters of plaited grass propped aloft by strong poles framed a view of sea, the frieze of dark people walking along the shore, the canoes, all there like some gigantic painting for her own personal enjoyment.

Thankfully, Evenglow was furnished. Plaited mats of palm covered the floor. Large comfortable cotton-covered lounge chairs were made of bamboo and cane. A double bed and dressing table stood in the bedroom, and beyond that was a detached kitchen nearly as large as the front room. By the stance of the housegirl standing arms akimbo but still smiling at a long, scrubbed white table, the kitchen was her domain alone. Greta gave up. It was easy to see where she stood in the domestic scheme of things and by the sight of the wood stove, and feeling the heat of the iron roof overhead, she was happy to leave house chores – some of them, anyway – to this cheerful-looking young woman, Nonee.

Arthur was making signs to leave. 'Suggest you eat at the hotel until you get settled in. There are some provisions, kerosene for your lamps, etc. – Nonee will light up for you – and most of everything else you'll find at BP's. Any perishables can go into the hotel's cold room . . . At a minimal charge.' He again led her outside. 'Take a look around and while I'm at it, you'll come to no harm on Kebai Island. Safe as a jail. There's a small club not that far away.' He stood back, giving both sides of his moustache a twirl. 'This is a small place and by now there's not a soul, white or black, who doesn't know about your arrival.' He gave a wink. 'And the whites, may I say it, are dying to "mead" you.'

Gawd, Aggie, he couldn't help himself!

Half irritated by his jaunty air, she watched him striding off. Alone! But this time it really didn't matter. Time to learn just where the boundaries of the property began and ended. Part garden, partly a jungle of flowering trees, crotons and vines of honeysuckle and maiden's blush, criss-crossed by paths all giving, by the look of them, access to the sea front.

Imagination? She wasn't sure. But here the air seemed lighter, the breeze cooler. Relief more than anything seemed to be the feeling of the moment. A marvellous iron tropical palace that passed for a house, she gloated, and this gorgeous garden . . . it took all her will not to fling off her sandals and spin and pirouette over every inch of the magical grounds. Never mind the snakes, if there were any . . . Instead, with sandals still in place, she walked sedately up the three steps into the wide side door of the house. Once there, and not giving a toss who could hear or who could see, she let out a wild 'Whoopee!' Flinging herself down on a sofa beneath the window, Greta grinned. Life, ever since she had met Andy Flight, was full of surprises.

CHAPTER THIRTY-SIX

It was three days since the *Pelican* had left for the Fly River. Two days more to go and Greta, in hope that it could be sooner than later, usually kept a half eye directed towards the horizon. But a note had been delivered to say that everything was going all right, and Greta was told not to worry, not only by Arthur Mead but by the District Commissioner himself. On her second night she had been dining alone at the hotel when Arthur appeared. 'You've been invited by the boss himself to join his party,' the boss being the Commissioner of the Western District. He was a tall man and thin as if life in this part of the world had drained the juices out of him, leaving a parchment-lined face. His look of severity was saved by the candour of blue eyes and a wicked twinkle of humour. Greta liked him right from the start. She liked his wife, too: a plump, pretty woman who played her role as the leading lady of Kebai with unassuming charm.

After the frenetic night of Port Moresby, it didn't take long for Greta to realise that Kebai Island suffered a similar fate – women were few and far between. Here, in presence of the Commissioner, the talk although quieter was every bit as exotic, the anecdotes of the coast and hinterland just as wild and nearly as unbelievable.

She was amazed by the casual acceptance of drama and dangers that seemed to be a part of everyday living in Papua – not on Kebai, as she was assured by the Commissioner – and then was told of a mountain village raided for nothing more than the heads that the murderers had taken away with them. A patrol officer and a few native police searched for days and found the offenders who were now in the Kebai jailhouse. Talk swerved to the story of a gigantic bore that had recently killed a newcomer, whose half-eaten body had been found emerging from the mud and swamp of a tidal creek.

'Not the first time,' someone announced, 'and not the last.'

And Greta, who knew of pig hunts in the bush, chipped in. 'We mightn't go in for head hunters around Yunnabilla, but giant boars we've got. Some of the lads,' she continued, thinking of Spanner Larkin, 'keep the tusks —'

A roar of laughter stopped her and she felt a flush of annoyance. Trust her to put her foot in she didn't know what! But a frown from the Commissioner brought the hilarity to an abrupt halt.

'Excuse these barbarians, Mrs Flight. Let me explain.' The mild amusement in his voice took away the sting. 'This bore has more than a nasty bite.' He went on to explain how the treacherous clash of a full tide and the down current of the river like the Fly could spell disaster to a boat caught unawares. By the waves created, he told her, even a vessel of decent size is in trouble. 'Getting caught broadside, Mrs Flight, can mean the end of it.' She didn't care to ask how unaware a skipper had to be before inviting such trouble. But it seemed that the Commissioner had read her thoughts.

'I can see you are a little worried, Mrs Flight. Sensible men listen to the advice that is freely given around here. And from what I have already heard, the skipper of the *Pelican* and his mate did the right thing before leaving Kebai. I doubt if a bore would be of concern.'

From then on, conversation became even more polite. But then, Greta asked herself, who wouldn't be polite with the DC under your very nose?

In a short time she had already fallen into the way, as did everyone else after dinner at the hotel, of sitting, ears strained, to the cackling and scratching of the short-wave wireless reporting the overseas news. Lately, reports from London seemed more important than what was coming out of Australia. An end to the broadcast would bring on a spate of war talk followed by silences until someone would lighten the collective gloom by shouting drinks all round, and Europe would be forgotten for another few hours until the next evening broadcast.

The last night of sleeping alone . . . She lay in bed in the new house under a mosquito net with nothing covering her but a thin cotton sheet. Island rats scurried between the walls to the crazy tune of cackling geckos who spent the night gorging on insects. The five days had passed pleasantly enough, and she had acquired a surprising number of acquaintances. At the hotel there was always someone who seemed pleased to see her. She was rarely alone and had been invited to an afternoon tea that had turned out to be surprisingly pleasant. Can you imagine it, she had written to Flossie, me playing ladies with the Commissioner's wife and friends? Oo-er, 'ow we're comin' up in the world!

Greta had been grateful that few personal questions had been asked, not counting the safe enquiries on what she thought of Port Moresby and Kebai, and how did she like her new home? It had been a landmark for more years than some could remember, was the answer to her own queries about the house, and was told it had weathered cyclones, been a school for a while and even a temporary church. 'She's a grand old lady,' one elderly Territorian with a jangle of bracelets encircling her arm had said, and Greta could only agree. As for Nonee, she came from a village close to the settlement and had taken herself off to Evenglow, asking to be taught how to work and cook 'proper' in a house like a white lady, Greta learnt to the tune of the woman's many bracelets. 'Mrs Goodall, my dear, was only too happy to oblige.' The Goodalls had become fond of the girl but when the old couple were ready to return to Australia, Nonee refused to go with them. She had said that one day she would marry a rich Kiwai man, and nothing would persuade her otherwise. Greta was lucky to have her, was the opinion all round.

'Today's the day!'

Greta flew into the cubicle of the shower room, not unlike the tin-lined one of Yunnabilla, splashing herself from a full bucket of water that Nonee had left for her. There were another two waiting by for a final rinse. 'Nonee, I'm ready!' The housegirl was there in seconds. She picked up the bucket and began to pour, carefully at first to remove every bit of soap from Greta's hair, then over Greta's shoulders, allowing time for the suds to run away. 'Ready, Missus?'

'Yes, give me the lot!' Greta turned her back as Nonee whooshed the other bucket over her. Greta gasped, as the water, freshly filled from one of the tanks, was cold.

'Lovely!' She dabbed herself with a towel. 'And Nonee, forget about rinsing me tonight – my husband Andy will be pleased to oblige.' Without quite understanding, Nonee gave a squeal of laughter and scurried off.

In her imagination she could see the *Pelican* tying up to the jetty or, if the tide was high enough, the boat could take a scoot practically right up to Evenglow's front door. It had rained during the night – great torrents pounding on the roof, drowning out the noise of the geckos – stirring up a wind that lashed the palms, and at the end of it frogs in their multitudes had croaked a thanksgiving for the rain in all tongues.

The morning was deliciously cool and for once the sea was blue, a powdery blue Greta had to admit, for the waters around Kebai had kept to a sullen grey in response to the doldrums yet to break. But today the sky was clear and, for the moment, keeping the clouds at bay.

Whistling, for no one was going to prevent her from that, she bounced into the kitchen, appreciating the breakfast tray Nonee had prepared. A glass of mango juice, toast with not much more than anchovy paste to put on it and a pot of black tea; milk unavailable. As the manager in Port Moresby had warned, after everyone on the island had their orders filled, there was little to spare for newcomers. It had been starve to death or eat at the hotel. There was an order on the way, she'd been told; hopefully arriving soon.

There had been and still was little for Nonee to do, but it was made clear that the girl went with the house. She disapproved after the first night when Greta pulled up a bedsheet and plumped the pillows; she frowned when she was found lighting the primus for a cup of tea; and was deeply insulted when Greta went to one of the four tanks at the back of the house to fill up a bucket for a bath. A mixture of gestures, broken English and mime had made it clear that as far as Nonee was concerned, Greta was a hopeless and helpless white woman who needed Nonee to teach her what was what around the house. Small set routines were emerging, and so far, mainly through lack of provisions, there had been little scope for Nonee to cook a proper meal. Greta picked up the tray.

'Thanks, Nonee. And surprise, surprise. Could you light the stove? Tonight we might eat here. I'll be cook and bottle washer.' Sensing a mutiny, she hastened to add, 'And could you do the pudding and fruit salad? BP's has a pyramid of tinned cream. And would you mind getting what fruit you can from the market?' Partly mollified, Nonee nodded. Who could resist, when Greta turned on the full charm? Even Nonee was realising that this lady was a clever one. Not only clever, Nonee decided, she pretty. Fire hair, lips red and shiny and always laughing. Missus Greta was a good thing that happen. In her village Nonee was now the teller of stories; of the Missus Greta with the fire-hair and *purri purri* magic that had every man in Kebai wanting her. 'She whistles like a man does. Aiee! What a woman.' Nonee knew there would be more stories to tell when the man called Andy came to the house. Like Greta, she could hardly wait.

Greta stood in the doorway of the store. Yunnabilla's Molloy & Co was the Anthony Horderns' of the North compared to Burns Philp of Kebai Island, she decided. At least the thick concrete walls and floor kept the place cool. It was a good step above Arthur Mead's trade store with a few luxuries like face powder, some decent rolls of dress materials and 'Evening in Paris' perfume, two canteens of cutlery and one dinner set on the half-empty shelves. But Greta was told that once stocks arrived by the steamer she'd find a cornucopia of desirables undreamt of and hard to resist. By now, only after a few days, Greta was already a valued customer in the manager and assistant's eyes.

'Ah, Mrs Flight, what can we do for you?'

'I've heard you have a few chooks – poultry – in the cold room.'

'Did have, Mrs Flight, but right now I'd say they are stuffed and tied, ready for the DC's oven. There's an important dinner tonight. Government bods from Australia.'

'Damn! Not even one chook? A chicken?'

'Sorry.' Regret was eroding the manager's smile. His pet hate was disappointing a customer. He pointed out tins on a shelf. 'I already know you've got the tinned sausages. But what about a tin of Globe's ox tongue? It can be dressed up, you know.'

'Oh, gawd.'

'I'm afraid —'

'I did want something special. I thought – heard – but I guess I was wrong.' She hoped that the right expression was on her face: not too tragic, just a touch. She'd been told that occasionally BP's manager did carry an extra few items for emergencies and she was prepared to find out. 'I've an important dinner tonight myself. Andy'll be home.' She hoped she wasn't laying it on too thick. But by the look on his face it was working!

Not used to having the most beautiful woman he'd ever seen begging for favours, the manager found it too much to bear. He mentally threw up his hands in defeat. 'Well, Mrs Flight —'

'Call me Greta,' she purred.

'It was brought in this morning. You're lucky.' He turned on his heel and disappeared into the cold room. So he did have a couple of chooks stashed away after all!

When he returned she nearly fainted. It was monstrous, with feelers a foot long and what seemed like a score of waving legs, although its colours were lovely in bands of pink, blue and yellow, over an olive-green carapace.

'What is it? It's enormous!'

'A painted crayfish. Taste one of these and you'll never touch lobster again.'

Without thinking, Greta, in recognition of Nonee's untried and unknown expertise, was handing over the role of queen of the kitchen without a murmur. With a little tinge of nostalgia she remembered the day Spanner Larkin brought over a fowl in a heaving hessian bag.

'Have you a bag or something I can carry it home in?'

The manager looked slightly shocked. 'Mrs Flight, no way in the world! One of the boys will take it home for you.'

It cost a small fortune but the advance payment for the *Pelican's* services had been more than enough to cover unexpected expenses. Triumph lightened her steps, even if outside she felt she was fighting her way though a damp sea sponge. It's not hot, she repeated to herself, remembering an old saying, it's the humidity. Never mind. No sight of the boat as yet, and time enough to warn Nonee that the mother of all crayfish was on its way.

Fish gut trailed over the exposed rocks near the jetty. The stench was sending blowflies into a frenzy of gormandising, oblivious to the occasional wave of discouragement from a languid hand. It would be hours before the tide could take the mess and the smell out to sea. Fish jumped and flopped in baskets to be gutted on the spot for a ready buyer. At the smell and sight of it Greta decided that she'd go back to the house. She'd been too eager to catch a first glimpse of them from the jetty. It would be another good hour, she reckoned, before the *Pelican* would arrive, and there was a clear view of the sea and shore from the windows. Plenty of time to decide what to do once the boat was tied up or anchored, and the men ready to come ashore.

At first sighting, not long after she had presented the crayfish to Nonee, the *Pelican* had been just a speck on the horizon, nearly imagined, and a blink could make it disappear in the glare. It was a slow and steady approach of the graceful sloping bow and emerging wheelhouse; too far away to see the man she loved so deeply and the funny, lovable bloke who somehow had become tangled up in the fabric of their lives. As the vessel drew closer, she felt her heart skipping and at times beating its joy high in her throat. So much to tell, so much to show him . . . She waited and watched in a room filled with the scent of frangipani and the smoke of mosquito coils. Not long now . . .

Sam had been invited to stay but after exploring the house and garden, exchanging news, relating his and Andrew's amazement at the size of the mighty Fly River and of the success of their first trip, he had given a wink, saying that he also had a lady to look after; broad in the beam and frisky. But he promised that tomorrow, if asked again, he'd bring along the old harmonica and play a tune.

'Get that fiddle tuned up, Comrade, haven't heard it for a while.'
He had given a wave, then took one of the back paths that led to
the hotel. With all their talk of mission accomplished, Sam had
left it up to Andrew to tell Greta that the *Pelican* was leaving again
at first tide in the morning.

As if putting off the moment, Andrew, with an arm around
her waist, slowly mounted the steps. Inside, he held her at arm's
length. 'Let me look at you.' He touched her face, her hair, then
with a sound more harsh than anything else, pulled her towards
him. 'I've been waiting for this. *Dreaming* of this.' It was a savage
kiss of possession. He kissed her throat, his hands seeking, but
Greta pulled away.

'Not here,' she whispered, drawing his attention to a Kiwai
passing by the open door, 'and Nonee's working like crazy in the
kitchen.'

'Bugger!'

He gave her a grin more rueful than frustrated. 'I'd a had ye
down on the floor in seconds if ye hadn't stopped me. Och, what a
glory you are.' He gave her a swift kiss and a tongue lick. 'Now, the
bathroom.' He bent his head, sniffing an armpit. 'Phaw! I stink to
high heaven. You didn'a mention it.'

Together they dined by candlelight (a box of twelve discovered
in Arthur's trade store). She had placed them in every nook and
cranny she had been able to find. Nonee had thrown herself into
a frenzy of cooking and in a reversal of roles Greta was permitted
to make the fruit salad. From wherever Nonee had gleaned them,
tomatoes, now sliced thinly with onion, were swimming in vinegar.

There was tinned asparagus and a bowl of rice – there was always enough rice. Damper and the crayfish meat, white and glistening with lime juice, turned the meal into a gala affair.

The house was quiet as they sat at the small bamboo card table. Eating somehow embellished the mood between them, eyes absorbing every loved feature. Seductively her bare toes caressed first his ankle, then wandered to the knee, his shorts giving access to his thigh. He gave her a steady look. 'Do you want me to eat or ravish you now?'

'Fruit salad?' Her toes went higher.

'Och, ye're a besom of a women.' He grabbed her ankle. 'I'm warning you, Greta.'

Her body was pulsing. She picked up a piece of pineapple and, reaching over, placed it in his mouth. 'Sweet and juicy.' Then leaving the table she walked around the room and blew out the candles one by one, the two nearest the table the last to go out. She unbuttoned her blouse in the dark, then she bent over to kiss him, her breast teasing his mouth. He gasped and stood, every muscle taut, his thigh between her legs as he slowly eased her to the floor. She opened to him.

'Ravish me.'

CHAPTER THIRTY-SEVEN

Six months later, and once again Greta was on the jetty waving the *Pelican* off. This time it wasn't the usual Fly River run but across Queensland waters to Thursday Island, with a promise that it would return in a week. In all those months, she could count on one hand the times she had gone off with Sam and Andy. Not that they didn't want to have her – quite the opposite – but the deck was almost always loaded to the waterline with cargo. Privacy was one of the main deterrents, as far as she was concerned. There always seemed to be the odd man and sometimes a gaggle of women and children on the return to a riverbank village; often missionaries or Government officials, like now on their way to Thursday Island.

No use complaining, she sighed, as the last speck of the *Pelican* wavered under a heat haze and disappeared. She realised with pride that Andy was earning a small fortune compared to in Yunnabilla and on the mainland. He was in his element, with Sam happy to acknowledge that the three-way partnership, with Mannie working from the other end, was a winner; the debt of restoring the *Pelican* was behind him. Andy was now part-owner of the fishing boat, thanks to Mannie's interest-free loan – amazing for Mannie, Greta thought, without a shred of guilt. 'Give us a year and we won't be owing Mannie a brass farthing,' Andrew had assured her, at the same time voicing an opinion that with experience and newly found know-how, chances were that at the end of it they could be more than just well off.

She often recalled how Mannie's words at the time had sounded so outlandish; so bizarre. He had sworn that soon, if not now, crocodile skins from Papua would be in high demand. 'Rivers are crawling with 'em. And what woman doesn't want a crocodile-skin handbag, a man a crocodile briefcase? Answer me that.' Andy had been interested from the word go. When he was in port he spent much time with old hands, traders, crocodile shooters, asking questions, absorbing anything and everything they had to say.

As Greta walked back to Evenglow thinking everything over, she knew she should be as happy as a pig in mud. But not quite. There was no diminishing of her and Andy's ardour – she came alive when he was with her, that was for certain. Whatever it was, she just couldn't put a finger on it. Life in Kebai wasn't all that bad. There was a spring of fresh water about a mile down the foreshore, where someone thoughtful had built an enclosure with rocks to capture and hold the precious fluid. Sometimes it spilled over but the water, by some *purri purri*, Nonee said, was always fresh and sweet. Greta had no qualms joining in with the splashing and playing of the children. For some reason, the village women didn't take advantage of the place. Maybe *purri purri* kept them away, and often Greta was the only bather for days at a time. Now with the *Pelican* away, a week of boredom (mild boredom, she had to admit) and loneliness lay ahead. If only there was something she could find to do . . .

These were the times when she wanted to break out, roll up the curtain, high kick into a snappy routine and forget the idea of hiding behind the built up façade of Mrs Andrew Flight – 'such a nice woman' – and come out singing. For glory sakes, who could possibly know she was a true-blue de facto? How many Ethel Rourkes or Farmer Stones were there in Kebai?

Not wanting to return to an empty house, she took the path leading down to the local club, knowing there was usually someone there ready for a chat and a beer or two. It was a small building made ordinary with cream-painted fibro walls but saved from mediocrity by two pink acacia trees shading the path to the entrance. Inside was a well-stocked bar, ceiling *punkas* and a highly polished dance floor: the gathering place for patrol officers, skippers of various craft like the *Pelican* coming and going, the odd anthropologist and administration staff. A piano stood in a corner for any maestro to tinkle out a tune or sing a song.

The jocularity could be heard long before she reached the club grounds – surprisingly, for it wasn't that late in the day, giving little time for drinking to have reached its full potential. A beer, she decided, then a walk along the waterfront to the spring, intending to stop at the house and put on a suitable dress. Swimming *sans* bathers caused embarrassment; better, as Nonee had warned, to wear a dress – 'a beeg one'. So a dress it was, even if the loose cotton shift did blossom and balloon around her in the water at every move. Feeling more cheerful, she walked on a path pink with acacia blossoms but a voice inside the club brought her to an abrupt halt. Oh, no. Surely not!

'And there she was,' the voice said, 'sitting on his knees. In the nuddy, no less. Not a stitch on between them! Goidonk, goidonk!'

Another burst of male laughter. 'You can imagine what the gov thought about it. Scandal . . . Of course, she had to go. Sent back to *Orstralia* on the first available boat there was. A prostitute, no less. A gay girl!'

Greta's desire for a cold beer disappeared. It came as a shock to hear that voice again. And why in Kebai? Greta wondered. Business? Was there a husband lurking somewhere? A wedding ring on Sabrina's hand would have been noticed when they met in Port Moresby. Greta remembered those manicured hands so well: 'Light me, darling.'

Greta hesitated, wondering if it was better to go back to the house, but decided against it. So Sabrina was in Kebai. Impossible to ignore her presence, it was only a matter of time – a short time at that – and they would be meeting face to face. She took a deep breath. Get it over and done with, she thought, feeling pleased that she had dolled up to look her best for Andy's last kiss. Her entry was greeted with enthusiasm as Sabrina's coterie broke up.

'Greta! Someone for you to meet. C'mon, join us.' It was a good beginning. As she sashayed across the floor, Sabrina jumped up to meet her.

'Greta Flight! Fancy finding you here, of all places. I'm madly surprised. You look marvellous – sunburn and freckles completely erased. Clever you!' She led the way back to the group, sitting down and patting the spare chair beside her. 'You'll have to tell me all about it.'

'About it? About what?' Greta dazzled a smile as a frosted glass of gin and lime was thrust into her hand.

'About here, of course, and what you think of our funny little island.'

'You live here?'

'Darling, I work here! The Commissioner, bless him, can't do without me.' Sabrina placed cool long fingers on Greta's arm, her dark eyes studying, her lips smiling. 'But tell me. Where *is* that gorgeous man of yours?'

'Thursday Island. *Sorry* . . .' Tawny eyes challenged brown, and left it at that.

'Oh.' But Sabrina hadn't finished. 'Well, when he does get back you must come over for drinks and *kai*. Love to have you, and bring along Sam.' But what came next had Greta biting her tongue. Sabrina looked around, casting her net for attention. 'They were in Moresby, you know, just before I went on leave to Orstralia. And this Sam – deckhand, of course – you'll never believe it, calls anyone he meets *Comrade*! In *Moresby*! I ask you . . . Prostitutes and Commies all in one week!' There was a silence. Greta couldn't believe that this sophisticated woman could have made such a gaff.

Carefully she put her glass down on the table, rising to her feet. 'Thanks for the invite, Sabrina; we'll see. But now I've business to attend to,' (even if it was only to put an order in to BP's), 'and I'd best get it done.' Greta ignored the murmurs asking her to stay and the obvious disappointment in her leaving. But certainly not from Sabrina. Smoothing down her dress, Greta gave smiles all round. 'Bye fellas. See you all soon.' Timing her pause for effect, she stopped and turned back. 'By the way, Sabrina, Sam happens to be the *Pelican's* skipper. *I'm* the deckie.' Doing something she had never done in Kebai before, she gave them all a broad cheeky wink and left.

Let her 'goidonk' herself silly, Greta thought. I'm going for a swim.

The swim didn't happen. When she got back to the house, Arthur Mead was waiting for her, which was strange for at this time of the day he would normally be busy with luncheon, making sure that there was enough left over for the inevitable straggler. He had never completely recovered from the day when, in his absence, the bigwigs of a mining company had been hustled out hungry and hostile from the dining room by the waiter with, 'Food no got. Bye bye now.' Arthur that day came close to loosing his reputation of having everything you 'mead'.

'Ah, Greta – been waiting for you. Nonee ushered me in. Bright girl, that one. I have tried to prise her away from Evenglow more than once. Not a hope.'

'Didn't know you were a headhunter, Arthur. Wait until I leave.'

He looked startled. 'You're leaving?'

'Of course not. But would it make a difference?'

'Ah, it could . . . that's why I'm here. How would you like to help me out for a couple of weeks?'

'Help?'

'The hotel.' The cocky attitude was gone. Arthur Mead had the look of a desperate man. 'Just keep your eye on things.'

'Are you dingbats? Apart from the fact that Andy is only away for a week, I know damn all about running a pub.'

'I have to go – must go – to Port Moresby.' He didn't say why.

'Absolutely not. I —' She was ready to be knocked down by a feather. 'Surely someone else —'

'Most around here are tied up. Busy. As for the rest . . .' He spread his hands and shrugged. 'No more than a bunch of guzzlers. Wouldn't be a drop left by the time I got back.'

'What about asking one of the women? They seem to have plenty of time on their hands. Sabrina Logan, for instance.' She realised it was a stupid thing to say, and could have kicked herself.

'Sabrina? Too busy with Administration. Smart girl, that one. As for the others – you've seen 'em. Not quite up to this sort of thing.'

'Oh . . . So I am, am I?' Irritation swept over her. Was that the impression she had made in this mosquito-infested swamp? More at home pulling beers and breaking up the odd brawl than playing bridge with the ladies down at the club?

The hotel keeper put out a placating hand. 'Greta, I didn't mean it that way. I apologise, but you were the first to spring to mind with your sense of humour – you need it in this game – your commonsense and yes, your ability to take it on the chin. And you have – taken it on the chin, I mean – from the first day you arrived here. Left more or less sitting on the beach. You've been admired by more than one, I can tell you.' He dared to give her a knowing smirk. 'And it's not only the men I'm talking about.'

'Enough of the blarney. Anyway, I'm sorry Arthur, but no.' She was horrified to see his eyes fill with tears, then gulp them away.

'There is a good reason why I must go to Moresby. A steamer leaves Kebai tonight. I have to be on it.' Mead carried on to say that of late he had been off-colour and in a little pain. He had spoken to one of the missionary doctors returning from leave; a brief examination before going up river.

'He thinks it could be – maybe cancer.'

'Oh no!' All her sympathy went out to him.

'There's an excellent man down there who could tell me for sure. That's why all the rush. No time to arrange things. It may be something nothing . . . But I must find out.' Up to date the two had been standing, facing each other, but the emotion of such a confession must have taken more out of Mead than he was willing to admit. He sat down on the sofa and looked up at Greta. 'Well . . . ?' He pulled a small notebook out of his pocket. 'Look, everything is here.'

There was no doubt about him. Against her will, sarcasm surfaced. 'So all there is to know about running a hotel is in a notebook no larger than my hand? Didn't think it'd be so easy.'

'You'll do it?'

'Jeez, Arthur, you make it hard to refuse.'

He suggested that she go back with him to the hotel, take a look around, and unless she changed her mind she'd be introduced as 'boss lady' to the native staff. Before leaving, Mead asked her not to mention his reason for such a hasty departure.

'Keep it all to yourself. That's another reason why I asked you, for I know you will. I don't fancy clots sitting on my hotel verandah discussing my innards and taking bets on my chances of going to heaven or hell!'

Dinner on the night after Arthur Mead had left, was, as Greta wrote to Flossie the moment she'd arrived back at Evenglow,

> *one for the boys. There was I, standing at reception, splashed with Ashes of Roses, heart in my mouth hoping that the lamb wouldn't be served up bleeding, and not daring to check in the kitchen to see how things were shaping up. Word had got around that I was Arthur Mead's new 'boss lady' and they were coming in droves – well, practically – to case the joint and see if I was making a mess of things. Well, Flossie, this gal ain't no pushover.*

Except for the sugar bowls that had been filled with salt and
potatoes beautifully cut to the size of rolling dice swimming in a
dish of dripping (rescued just in time), everything went down a
treat. First day over. And you know what, Floss, it's not that bad at
all. See what tomorrow brings up.

    Love,

    Greta

There was someone else who'd have a bit of a giggle over the hotel news – even more than Flossie. Marelda Larkin. Greta could see her now, sitting on the back step, a cup of tea in her hand, a scone in the other. Greta picked up her pen again.

As life would have it, Greta had more than a fortnight in the Hibiscus Hotel. Word by a long cable relayed from Port Moresby told Greta that the *Pelican* was tied up to the jetty on Thursday Island; a slight engine mishap that would take time to repair. Not to worry. But she did worry. Missing Andy and finding herself unable to imagine what they were doing to fill in the time and how they were progressing, she lay awake in a lonely bed wondering how long it takes to fix an 'engine mishap', as Andy had described it. News from Arthur was just as unsatisfactory. The doctor was in Australia on leave, and Mead informed her over a telephone's scratchy reception that he was determined to wait for the GP's return. Both messages left Greta in a limbo of uncertainty that made her more determined not to let the hotelier down, count her blessings and look on everything that the island offered as an experience not to be missed.

CHAPTER THIRTY-EIGHT

No sign or word from Thursday Island, and it was three weeks since the *Pelican* had left Kebai. Greta found that a day at the Hibiscus could be exhausting. Although the house staff, gardeners and kitchen hands carried out their duties as written down in Arthur's notebook, there was still the odd domestic drama that could topsy-turvy a well-planned day. As for the head cook Armi, in spite of chatter and the hilarity of unknown jokes between the kitchen hands, he ran his domain without panic or theatrics, accepting Greta's presence with amiability, and recognising the growing rapport between them.

Dinner at the Hibiscus and Greta, still at her post, was mentally tapping an impatient foot and wishing that the lot still chatting at the corner table would think about others for a change. Tablecloths bar one had been removed, and the clink of dirty cutlery dumped onto to a tray signalled that the evening was nearing its end. The youngest waiter, a wilting hibiscus in his yellow frizzed hair, was opening louvers wide to remove the smell of tobacco.

Close to midnight. She smelt like a fried pork chop and

cooking fat from necessary sorties into the kitchen, with Armi feverish, 'cold sick' and dribbling. Eventually she had persuaded him to go home, sent for Nonee and between them had taken over the final preparations of baking a sucking pig and supervising the presentation of crayfish, reef fish, hibiscus and tropical fruits; a splendid table centre and one of Armi's specialities for important occasions. And an important occasion it had been in the feasting of an influx (for Kebai) of fact-finding reporters on the prowl for anything that might make headlines. The island was determined to do them proud.

Compliments when they left were embellished by generous libations courtesy of the hotel's cellar and were accompanied by more than one compliment to herself. Keeping in mind the 'Haven't we met before?' encounter of her second day on the island, Greta had deliberately kept away from probing eyes, worn the least of her smart things from an already scanty wardrobe, and kept lipstick, rouge and mascara to a minimum, but all to little effect. Male eyes just couldn't resist feasting on the curves, the red-gold hair pinned into a bun not severe enough to hold rebellious curls still trying to escape, and her smile, refusing to be restrained.

By now the sounds of the revelry going on at the club told her that the newsmen were being well entertained. In spite of tiredness there was satisfaction in a job well done and thank the Lord the stayers in the corner were getting ready to leave – Sabrina Logan among them. It wasn't hard to bump into Sabrina at the end of the day, either at the club or the hotel.

It was strange to think they had reached some sort of compromise, friendly enough; and if they happened to find themselves the only two around, conversation was on the same level and easy, with hardly a 'goidonk' in hearing. Sabrina, unusual for a woman, played an important role in Administration. She had a brain, was the consensus of those who knew her well. The gypsy, as Greta called her, was fun and clever, though she still intimated that Andrew was fair game. 'When he finally turns up, I'm warning you, Gret, I've got my eye on him.' Her audacity was breathtaking enough to be laughable and ignored, but for Greta there was a *maybe* attached to it.

'Greta, where have you been hiding? You've done a marvellous job. Dinner superb!' In a mist of Evening in Paris Sabrina stood back, an eyebrow arched. 'Experience always shows, doesn't it?' A sting in the tail, but Greta was expecting it. Another round to go before the gypsy left. 'Any word from that man of yours?'

As promised all day by rain-filled clouds, the first drops spattered the roof signalling a deluge was on its way. Now in a hurry, the party gave a goodnight with an invitation for Greta to join them at the club. What a laugh . . . Greta looked down at a grease spot small but noticeable on her dress. All she wanted to do was go home, take a bath – she'd stand out in the rain if was heavy enough – and wash her hair. Nonee had gone back to her village hours ago with a dillybag of leftover goodies to share up, but Greta knew that on arriving home, there would be a jug of freshly squeezed lime juice waiting in the cooler, buckets of fresh water in the shower room, clean jamas laid out and the mosquito net tucked firmly around the bed. Trust Nonee . . .

Mango trees blocked out the night sky and a great deal of the rain as Greta followed the beam of her torch down a now-familiar path to the house. Few passed her, for the black of night was filled with demons and those who ventured out were fools, the natives believed. Greta knew that even sensible Nonee was more than happy to be inside four walls after the sun had gone down. 'Magic no got for you pipple,' she had told Greta while informing her of the grizzly deeds devils committed on the unwary. Frogs celebrating the rain jumped out of her way until a staccato beat of a Kiwai drum splintered the quiet and obliterated the croaking. It was close enough to give her a nervous start and quicken her step. The sound grew louder and faster as she approached the house. Breaking free of the shadows, she realised the rain clouds had parted and a moon benign and mellow shone down, silvering a full tide and highlighting an outrigger of size; the source of the drum beats. Fireflies spun in a soft circle near her. She felt a fool, and cranky with herself. As for demons, the only ones around were of her own making.

Weary, she turned to Evenglow and was surprised to find it in darkness. Nonee always left a lighted lamp or three around the house, although she could see there was one alight in the bedroom. Perhaps the wind that came with the rain had blown the others out.

Cautiously as she went up the step, had she caught the sound of movement? There was no door to open, as the room was free of one. Heart rapidly pumping, she crept inside. Silence. A faint smell of trade tobacco?

'Gotcha, my bonny darlin'!'

A scream was smothered by kisses. To feel the strength of his arms again . . . to sink into the safety they gave her; troubles fading as passion grew. No time for words as they locked together. The staccato drum of the Kiwais slowed to a quieter throbbing as the rain beat down. It was Andrew who first pulled away.

'I canna' make love to you smelling like sweat and fish bait.' He heard her give a low chuckle.

'And I smell of pork chops and onions, so there's nothing to stop us.' She pulled him down, giving him her mouth, her body, her strong dancer legs gripping him. Nothing else was said until it was over.

Panting, they fell apart. 'About time, Andrew Flight. About bliddy time.'

Laughing, he jumped to his feet, holding out his hand and in one strong movement, yanked her off floor. 'Now for that bath – and who's going to soap and bucket who first?'

The rata-tat-ta rata-tat-ta of the Kiwai drum filled the rain-sweetened air.

At first Andrew did not take kindly to Greta working at the Hibiscus. Not wanting to spoil the homecoming, she had waited for morning to break the news. The usual sleep-in and lovemaking was abandoned as she tried to explain the situation. Dismayed, she had watched Andrew drag up the mosquito net and storm out of the house.

She sat at a breakfast table made up for two while a silent Nonee served tea and toast; the squeezed mango juice, Andy's favourite, went untouched. 'Nonee, go and tell Armi I'll be late.'

'Mister Andy not for breakfas'?'

'Who knows?' Greta was determined to wait it out. Apart from the *Pelican* there was nowhere for him to go. Pride would keep him away from the boat, Sam and the hotel. The club was still closed. It was a spat; nothing else. But his reaction to her news had been surprising.

An hour crawled by. She stood by the windows, wondering if

she should take a look-see along the foreshore, then spotted him walking slowly back. His face was unreadable, betraying nothing as he came in, standing so close that his breath brushed her cheek.

'Working at the hotel. Why, for God's sake?'

'As I was saying, before you tore out of the house, it's not for ever – I'm doing a favour, just a favour, until Arthur Mead gets back from Moresby. He —'

'To hell with Arthur Mead! If he wants to buggarise down in Moresby that's his affair. But I'll nae be having my wife —'

'Listen to me, Andy. Please!' It was hard to understand his anger.

'Listen to what?' Eyes of slate raked her up and down. 'For the first time since I dragged ye away from Sydney —'

'What the hell do you mean by *drag*?' She could have smacked him hard across the face. 'You make it sound as if you found me in the gutter!'

'Now, you're the one not listenin', woman. Och!' He ran a hand through his hair until it stood on end. 'Dinna' ye think it never leaves my mind how you came to me, gave your love to me without a promise, practically giving me the train fare? Now for once there *is* money, good money for us both to enjoy . . .' He shook his head in bewilderment. 'And you work in a hotel. *As a favour?* Ye hardly know the man!' His anger was abating but the puzzlement remained.

'Andy, love. Arthur could have cancer.'

'Oh . . .' He was caught off balance. 'Tha's bad . . .'

'He left in a frightened panic without finding alternative arrangements. The only one with practically nothing to do, and maybe trust, was me.'

'Hmph!'

Nonee, who would have heard it all, her large brown eyes looking from one to the other, padded silently across the room. She placed the morning coffee tray on a small cane table, then padded just as silently off. With the air growing lighter between them, Greta couldn't resist a giggle. 'House lady to a cook, six kitchen hands and four domestics; they don't have girls there. 'ouse lady. Little ol' me. Can you believe it?'

'No, I can't.' He sounded more grumpy than angry. 'But I dinna' care for it just the same.' As she pulled him down beside her on the lazy boy, he had to ask, 'How long, now?'

'Since we made love?' Greta ran a cool finger down his cheek, tracing the line beside his mouth and following the sensual curve of his lips. 'Forgiven?' she murmured softly then drew closer to nibble his ear.

'Och! Ye're a besom of a woman. Joking aside, when does Arthur come back?' The coffee was hot and Nonee knew how to make a delicious cup. Also there was plenty of the good stuff in the hotel kitchen and Andrew had no qualms about taking advantage of the situation.

Greta couldn't give him an answer. 'As soon as possible, I'm hoping.' She didn't add that she enjoyed it most of the time. Better than sitting around drinking morning tea or tossing off gin slings, a siesta in the afternoon and nights at the club for company. If there were questions to be answered, she had an important one to ask for herself.

'Andy, we've been here more than six months and I can count on one hand the times we've been truly together. When are you and Sam taking time off? And, better still, when can I come with you?' To soften her words this time, the finger ran over his hand, tickling his palm. 'I've seen nothing really since the day we arrived. I know this patch of dirt east, west, north and south, and there is not that much to see except the gorgeous view outside this window.' She gulped down the last of the coffee, wiping her mouth with the back of her hand. 'When you're gone, I'm lonely. Damn lonely!'

'I know, my love.' The look Andrew gave her was full of tenderness. 'But give me a year. Two. There are big things going on up here and the *Pelican* is and will be going flat out for a good time to come. Goods, machinery, building supplies . . . Never mind about shooting off the crocodile population which may come later. This way what we're doing is actually making a profit, and I've heard,' he spoke with a dreamer's enthusiasm, 'there's a good chance of buying into *copra* growing. Mannie – I don't know about Sam – would jump into hot porridge to be part of it. Can you imagine it? A plantation of coconuts, a great, cool house overlooking white beaches and coral lagoons . . .'

It was the Andy she remembered in Sydney telling her of the joys of going North: a paradise, he had called it. It was hard to think of Yunnabilla in that way.

But there was a promise extracted that she was sure he'd keep. Andrew said he knew of a small boat for hire. On the *Pelican's* next return, if Sam could be persuaded to take a break, he and Greta would explore a nearby river he'd been told about. 'We'll go up as far as we can. Two, maybe three, days. Just you and me.'

The Oriomo River, he called it: a paradise . . .

Loading up again. Two days in Kebai and in the morning the *Pelican* would be doing a round of the coastal villages with the usual supplies of rice, tinned fish and trade cloth. Time to make up for the slack of Thursday Island. There had been little chance for Greta and Andrew to see each other, although the coming separation was eased with the Oriomo trip a definite promise on the boat's return.

Andrew sat alone while Sam got hale and hearty at the bar. The club piano, out of tune, was playing its loudest and Greta danced with the fellow, a butterfly catcher, who had dined with Andy earlier that night at the hotel. A strange bod, was his impression, vague to a point of rudeness who had only brightened when catching glimpses of Greta doing her dutiful rounds of the tables. Did he liken her to one of his butterflies, exquisite, waiting to be caught in his net? Andrew grinned to himself. *Not a hope, laddie.*

With a burst of pride he thought of the way she had taken to the running of the Hibiscus. Admittedly, Mead had done a good job of it making her task easier. Excellent food, well-trained staff and a natural presiding over the enormous range in the kitchen, Greta had told him. But no matter how smooth the organising, crises happened in the best of hotels, and perhaps more often at the Hibiscus. The late arrival of a vessel with orders to fill could be chaotic. 'You'd never believe it. Completely out of tea,' Greta had said, turning the whole episode into a joke, 'and when it did finally arrive, tea no got but four crates of Russian caviar!' Fortunately for the Hibiscus there had been a wedding with people from all over the Territory attending, and caviar naturally was on the menu. Administration came to the rescue and did a swap. Tea for most of the caviar. 'I had fish eggs on toast for a week!' Greta had told him, producing a bowlful for lunch with champagne to wash it down. 'And it's still a delicious treat.'

What a lass! Sitting there watching her, happy, flirting, taking a quickstep in full stride with the butterfly man, he compared her to the other women in the room. As usual, none came near her for gaiety or the way she could broadcast to others her love of life. No wonder he adored her.

But one thing saddened him. Ever since their first day on the island, she had kept to her word. No one, to his knowledge, was aware of her talents; of Greta the songstress, Greta the dancer. No amount of persuasion could make her change her mind. He knew the reason. Once more he would try to make Greta understand that 'her secret', as she called it, didn't matter a jot up here. They weren't in Yunnabilla now. Some day he hoped he'd have her singing in this very club. Give him time. Someday . . .

'Andy Flight! You're back at last. Goidonk, goidonk. Greta has been pining, absolutely *pining* for you.' Sabrina Logan made a pretence of looking around. 'Where is she? At the hotel, I bet. *Always* at the hotel. I really think —'

Andrew, forever polite, rose to his feet. 'If you take another look, Sabrina —'

'You remember my name! I call that flattery.' She indicated that he be seated and snapped her fingers to a passing waiter. 'Boy! Another chair.'

'Flattery? Hardly. Greta told me you were here.' He paused, 'On the island.' His smile had an ironic twist. 'As I was going to say, take another look. You'll see her on the floor.' A waiter hurried over with a chair and Andrew, waiting for her to sit, asked, 'What are you drinking?'

'At the moment, not a drop.' With her eyes never leaving his face, she slowly sat down. 'We'll chat while your Greta dances the night away – they're still talking about it in Moresby. You don't?'

'Dance? I shuffle. I prefer to watch my beautiful wife.'

'Not getting far, am I?' she murmured, more amused than not. 'Early times . . .' She took a holder out of a beaded evening bag, slipped in a thin gold-tipped cigarette as black as her hair, then handed over a silver lighter, pressing it into Andrew's hand.

'Light me, darling.'

Light her! Greta fumed as they walked back to the house after the club had closed. Andrew was walking ahead with the torch, no room for two on the path. Light her . . . I'll light her at a bloody stake, given half the chance!

When the man who netted butterflies had brought her back to the table, seeing Sabrina there had startled her. Finding the two engrossed in conversation, the stink of that perfumed cigarette nearly knocking her over, she had taken a deep breath, telling anyone who cared to listen what a delight it was to find Sabrina Logan seated there. If Andy wasn't aware of the way she felt, there was no kidding Sabrina. She had oozed confidence, eyes glinting, blowing smoke rings and making plans for a dinner – 'An intimate foursome, darlings, including that hilarious skipper of yours, of course. Tomorrow night?'

For once Greta was pleased that the *Pelican* was leaving at first light.

CHAPTER THIRTY-NINE

By telegram from Port Moresby, Arthur was returning on the steamer *Waru* leaving that day for the Papuan Gulf and Kebai Island. On hearing the vessel's name from Greta, one stringy and dried-out ex-miner having his first rum for the day gave a bark of derision.

'The old *Waru*, ay? Means turtle in boong lingo, y' know, and turtle she is. Bloody milk run, that's about all she's good for.' He was happy to air his knowledge; an attempt to capture Greta's company even for a moment. 'Calls into every odd settlement on the way. Surprised, but . . . I thought she was on her way to Cairns. Going to be a troop ship. Rumours, ay?'

As far as Greta was concerned the *Waru's* arrival could mean tomorrow, maybe next week or the week after. If Arthur hadn't returned by the time the *Pelican* dropped anchor, too bad. Arthur could go to pot if Andy and Sam reached Kebai first. Lucky for him that Sam had taken on another job sending him and Andy further up the Fly. Further than they'd ever been before.

For once Greta hadn't been too disappointed. Let Sabrina cool her heels while she and Andy would be up the Oriomo making love, getting tipsy and ardent, alone and without a care. She had even heard that far enough away from the river's estuary the water was fresh and sweet. There had never been a sight of a saltie – 'yer know, a croc' – in years.

Every room at the hotel was filled with a rowdy, mostly happy, lot as diverse in size and character as to the reason why the hotel was their home for a week. Two school teachers, a couple of miners on exploration, the butterfly man Mr Simpson and a missionary intent of ridding the heathen of human skulls being the sole decoration of their long houses. 'Treasures of Satan!' he had roared one night just as dinner was ending.

Over a mug of tea Greta and Armi were discussing menus. Neither cook or houselady noticed the youngest houseboy standing nervously by the kitchen door. 'Lady boss.' Not wanting to interrupt, he waited a minute, then tried again. 'Armi.' As Greta and Armi had their backs to him his soft words went unheeded. A look of worry crossed his face and, squaring his shoulders, he came closer to the pair deep in conversation. He tapped Armi's shoulder. 'Armi.' As Armi turned he began talking rapidly in local dialect. Armi frowned, turning to Greta.

'This boy won't clean up number four room, missus.'

'Why not?' In her mind she could already see the mess. It happened sometimes. Too much grog, and a nasty job cleaning it up. One of the more disgusting sides of hotel life. But the butterfly collector who slept in number four usually kept to himself and was harmless. More likely it was one of the boisterous mob that drank too much on the verandah before dinner and after at the club.

'Why not?' Greta asked again, wondering if there was a girl in the bed, dismissing the idea at once. Simpson wasn't the type.

Armi looking uncomfortable and shrugged. 'He say *purri purri* there.'

'Hell!' A look Greta had seen before crossed the boy's face; a sullen closing down of all expression, of all communication. If she wasn't careful she could have a full-blown exodus on her hands. 'Armi, tell him, explain to him that we'll both go and clean the room. Tell him I will make the *purri purri* go away. I have special magic.'

Reluctantly, the houseboy followed her down the passageway with Armi close behind. Number four was shut. Was the occupant still in the room? Perhaps the *purri purri* had been only a ruse, an excuse to leave one bed unmade. Admittedly it had been a busy week. Greta knocked. No answer. She opened the door, expecting to see sight of early morning: a bed with tangled sheets, pillows damp with sweat, cloths and wet towels over the chair or on the floor in a heap waiting to be washed. But there was none of this as she walked into the room. The butterfly man was neat if nothing else. The pillow was plumped up, sheets neatly folded at the end of the bed and pyjama pants lying just so on the bottom sheet. The room was bare of clutter and stacked on the dressing table were the 'butterfly display boxes ready to be shipped down to the museum in Brisbane. How many butterflies can one catch in Papua? she wondered. She had seen him one morning on the side verandah carefully handling the delicate creatures, wincing at the numbers pinned down in the display cases.

She went over and stripped the bed. 'Come on,' came a cheerful command, 'we'll make the bed together.' The boy made no move and Armi's eyes were large and round as if he'd seen a 'debil debil' himself. 'What's wrong with the pair of you?' Greta marched over and grabbed the clean sheets from the house boy's arms. 'I'll make the damn thing up myself!' It was as she straightened the top sheet a feeling swept over her that all was not as it should be. There was a movement just out of eyesight; a strangeness that made her skin crawl. There it was again! It was then she spied a pillowcase on the floor. It was gently heaving. Another pillowcase beside it was also filled with some inert thing. A third was moving and through the mud-soiled pillowcase, cotton thin from a hundred washes, was the outline of a snake; a large one. Greta jumped, wordless, her eyes as large as Armi's. 'Mother of Jesus!' She scuttled backwards as she heard Armi say just one word, 'S-nake.'

Five pillowslips on the floor. She didn't even want to imagine their contents as she stood by the door. She'd kill the bastard! Usually out for the full day, she would have to wait until he came back for dinner.

'Ah, Mrs Flight. You've found the reptiles.'

Greta turned on him, steaming. 'Reptiles!' she yelled. 'What the blazes do you think y' doing – bringing snakes into the hotel. *Alive!*'

'Of course they are, Mrs Flight. They're for the museum. I was going to mention it.'

'*Mention it!*'

'Bought them from a collector yesterday. Wonderful specimens.'

'Get them out!' she screamed. '*OUT!*' She noticed that the other two, the houseboy and Armi, had escaped.

'Well, as matter of fact, I've arranged for that.'

How dare he be so calm as if there was nothing in those pillow-cases but duck feathers? Greta took a deep breath and straightened herself into a pose of dignified outrage. 'What arrangements? I trust they're immediate.'

'Er – not quite. I'm having crates made. Should be ready tomorrow.'

'I said get rid of them and I mean it, Mr Simpson. I'm not having the staff terrified silly.' Quite apart from me. Greta knew that the guests would treat it all as a joke – just up their alley. She could see it all. Drunk as fools and having bets on who would open the first pillowcase. She had visions of snakes slithering all over the hotel, let alone the garden.

Judging by the laughing and high cackling going on in the kitchen Greta guessed that already, with imagination and mime, the snakes had been dealt with by warriors brave, Armi and the houseboy: the fact that the man in room four could be seen toting the pillowcases out of sight didn't spoil the story. She'd swear over the days and weeks to come the story would do the rounds from village to village, growing more spectacular and improbable with the telling.

The incident had eaten into the morning's routine and the midday roast was still half raw in the oven, most likely. Not a good start. Greta hoped that the old theatrical saying 'Rotten in the morning, come good in the afternoon', would hold. She tried to still her trembling, the incident taking her back to the day Marelda axed the black snake in the backyard; the piece of flesh quivering on her sandal. Ugh!

Armi had worked some magic of his own and the noon meal, a leg of venison brought in the day before, was served up succulent and remarkably tender with potatoes and pumpkin and the usual tinned peas. It had come as a surprise to learn there were places not so far away where wild deer roamed.

'A delicious meal, Greta. You must be congratulated.' Out of politeness, Greta stopped by the table. It was Louise Jackson, the woman who had wondered if she had met her before. Although pleasant and friendly, Greta had made a point of not getting too close, trying to be somewhere else – nearly impossible – whenever Louise appeared in Kebai. Especially as Louise and her husband enjoyed the occasional meal at the Hibiscus. Still sitting, Louise dabbed her lips with a serviette before taking out a compact and lipstick while Greta searched for excuses to move on.

'Arthur has been so fortunate; you're an angel in disguise. But tell me, why *did* he leave in such a hurry? We're all wondering.' Her compliments were genuine, her curiosity obvious. 'You of all people must know.'

'He just said it was urgent, Louise, and I took him at his word. However, he did appear more than concerned. To be frank, I thought helping out could be fun.' She gave a comical lift to an eyebrow. 'And boy oh boy, it certainly has been. Wouldn't have missed it for quids.'

Question unanswered, Louise touched up her nose with the puff, snapped the compact shut and signalled to her husband, silent and waiting, that she was ready to leave.

'See you at the club. Picture night, don't forget.' She was referring to the weekly entertainment with a projector on the verge of collapse and films – predominantly cops, robbers and cowboys – sent up at random from Port Moresby. Louise had one more thing to add before giving a cheery wave. 'You must be pleased that Andrew's home. Saw the *Pelican* come in this morning.'

A good day after all!

Promising to be back for the evening meal, Greta took a quick look at herself in the Ladies' full-length mirror. Considering the turmoil of the morning she didn't look too bad. All she needed was a touch of lippy and a splash of Amber Rose cologne kept for emergencies in a drawer. He'd be at the house waiting. Goodbye hotel and hello Oriomo River!

As she reached the house the sight of the *Pelican* anchored and nodding gently at the sun gave her, as it always did, an excited surge of anticipation. He and Sam would have spent the morning washing down the deck, ridding the boat of accumulated smells. *Pelican* was a working boat and often would bring back with her entrenched odours of fish and grease, rotting bananas, decayed food left over from the hired crews' cooking pot, incessantly stewing with unknowns garnered from the river. Once in port, the vessel was scrubbed from bow to stern with phenol until all traces of crew and past cargoes (on one occasion the juices of crocodile skins that, unknown to Sam, had been badly salted) were swilled over the side and the *Pelican* left clean enough to invite the Administrator and his wife on board for drinks. Which of course, Greta having a bet with Andy, Sam never would.

But there was no sign of him when she walked into the front room. 'Andy!' No answer. Nonee appeared with a large manilla envelope in her hand. 'This for Mr Andy. From 'ministration.'

'Isn't he here?'

Nonee was shaking her head. 'He bin come and gone.'

'Oh . . .' Greta's surprise was mild. He must have gone to the hotel and they had crossed paths. 'Should I wait here?' she wondered aloud but decided against it. 'Look, Nonee, when he comes back here tell him I'm at the club. If I put a foot inside the Hibiscus I'll never get out again. Not until after dinner, anyway.' She checked her watch. 'It's three now. Dinner at six,' she said, glowing and thinking of the next few hours. Plenty of time for talks and anything else that might come up . . . She grinned at the double entendre, getting ready to leave.

'I give heem this one?' Nonee held up the envelope.

'No, I'll take it.' It felt heavy and important enough to arouse her curiosity.

Feeling light and happy, she took the cattle pad (as some called it) leading to the club, planning the night ahead. It had been a while since they had dined together at the Hotel Hibiscus. A bottle of Arthur's bubbly would go down well and who needs an excuse for a celebration?

Sam was at the bar with a band of cronies but Andy still nowhere in sight. She walked over and tapped the skipper on the shoulder, giving his cheek a peck. 'Hello, stranger – welcome back.' Sam swivelled around, the usual cheery smile missing from his face, looking uncomfortable more than anything else. Greta gave another look around the room. 'Andy not with you?'

'Ah . . . no, Gret.' It was easy to see his embarrassment growing by the second.

'Well . . .' Trying to make a joke of it, she peered over the bar top. 'Not there either.'

'To tell the truth, Greta, he's with the Administrator. He . . .' Taking a swig from his glass and giving his chin a good swipe with his hand, he added, 'They're talking business. Sort of.'

'Business? What sort of business? Anyway, you're the skipper – why Andy?'

Before answering, Sam took her by the elbow and led her away from the bar. 'Hush hush business, Greta, and Andy speaks the same language with these toffs —'

'Bloody nonsense!'

'No, Greta, it's not. Can't very well call the Gov Comrade, now, can I?'

She didn't believe Sam's explanation one bit. The whole thing reeked of conspiracy and the hurt was intense. Why wasn't Sam confiding in her? And why had Andy been in such a hurry to leave the house? It would have taken only minutes to pop into the hotel to explain what 'the business' was all about. She swallowed a lump springing unasked into her throat. It seemed that the whole island had known of the *Pelican*'s return while she was dealing with bloody snakes in Simpson's bedroom. Nevertheless Sam was keeping something of importance from her.

'Any idea when he'll be back?'

Sam's misery was plain to see on his sun-scorched face. 'Dunno. Sorry, Greta.' His face brightened. 'Can I get you something? Yer lookin' a bit hot. Lemon, lime and bitters?'

'A double scotch and dry more like it. And go easy on the dry.'

Should she leave or should she wait? With all this secrecy, would Andy go home? Maybe he'd want to talk things over with Sam. Tossing other options aside and feeling lousy, she decided to go back to the house. About to cancel the drink, she saw through the large open window the Administration sedan pull up outside. Andy stepped out, holding the car door open for a laughing Sabrina Logan to alight. Of course, the Administrator – and that damned woman swanning it around, possibly playing a part in whatever was going on! Sharing it with Andy. Feeling ousted, Greta watched as he politely ushered Sabrina into the clubroom. Thoughts of the Oriomo River faded from her mind. Andy couldn't look more pleased with himself; his expression bordered on smug satisfaction.

As if expecting to see Greta sitting there, he strode across the floor, leaving Sabrina to follow. He planted a kiss on her cheek. Nothing like his usual unabashed embrace in front of whoever when he returned from a trip.

Sabrina caught up. 'Greta, darling, we called at the house —' *Oh! did we?* '— and of course missed you. Goidonk, goidonk. Nonee told us where you were.' She sat down. 'Andy, would you mind? A very large g and t. Absolutely parched! What a morning!'

Andy, seemingly ready to oblige, went to the bar. The next thing Greta saw was him talking to Sam. Bloody hell! Why was she here? She'd give him the damned envelope but before leaving she had to say something to the gypsy. 'While Andy's not here, perhaps you can tell me, Sabrina – I won't ask Andy, he'll tell me himself – but what are you up to? What game are you playing?'

'I've told you what I'd like the game to be.' She hollowed her cheeks. 'But it's up to Andy, isn't it?'

Andy returned with the gin and tonic, a fresh scotch for Greta and a beer for himself. He sat down and held up his glass. 'To us.' He and Sabrina exchanged glances that told her nothing. By now Greta would lie dead in the street before she asked Andy to enlighten her about the morning. The next toast lifted her heart.

'Here's to the Oriomo, eh, lass?'

Sabrina gave her a look that could only be described as envious. Apparently it had not been that sort of morning after all. Greta then remembered the manilla envelope and took it from her handbag. 'This came for you.'

'Nonee said you had it.' He turned the envelope over, his expression halfway disinterested, slipping it into the jacket he was wearing. That was all he said about it, and Greta was determined not to ask. Sabrina got ready to leave.

'Have to go. You'll enjoy the river.' Another look passed between her and Andy before she left. It puzzled and disturbed Greta. Was this to be some sort of last farewell? A sop before an ending? No, she told herself, the Andy she knew wouldn't do it that way.

'Oh, by the way, Greta,' Sabrina called over her shoulder, 'word came through to the office that Arthur Mead will be back tomorrow.'

Not long after she had gone, Andy had excused himself, saying things must be discussed with Sam. An hour passed by and there was nothing for Greta to do but wait. Already she had sent word for Nonee to present herself to Armi. They worked well together and Greta was determined to sit it out, the whole night if necessary. Every now and then Andy returned with apologies and with a fresh something to wet her whistle. 'Shouldn'a be long, lass.' At least he hadn't forgotten about her altogether.

The afternoon dragged on, when suddenly general talk was silenced by someone yelling to shut up and listen. The clink of glasses was quietened, voices reduced to a hum. It was the late afternoon news, relayed from Moresby, and a very British voice announced that the day September 30th, 1938, was cause for celebration.

Prime Minister Chamberlain, after a conference with Adolf Hitler, had returned to London assuring British subjects that war was no longer a threat in spite of Germany mobilizing its military – for what? sceptics asked around the club. War talk as always waxed and waned until the next round of drinks, although lately discussions were getting longer and more heated. There were suppositions surfacing about Japan, referring as an example to the invasion of

China, but usually brushed aside by ridicule. From where Greta sat, Europe and Japan felt very far away. Let the world worry. She wouldn't. Tomorrow it was 'up the River Onions' for her and Andy. And blessed relief, he was now making his way towards her.

As the sun was setting, enamelling the horizon with a frieze of cloud and gold, and mosquitoes were getting hungry, the Flights strolled single file down the track. To heck with mysteries, Greta thought, humming to herself 'I'm in the Mood for Love'.

CHAPTER FORTY

'It's a very small boat,' Greta had commented at first sight. But never mind, it was theirs for a whole three days. It had a tiny box on deck that should not have been called a wheelhouse, steering wheel up front, a fold-back table and a narrow seat along one of the walls. And who cared if you had to sleep on the floor? At least it was clean.

Under the grand name of *Adventure Bound*, *Venture* for short, it chugged up the Oriomo River and except for a one-man canoe gliding by, there was not a soul in sight. The salt-mud smell of mangroves more than two hours behind them had been exchanged for the perfume of flower-endowed vines, their rich velvet of green draping the trees and shrubs with bunches of saffron blooms the size of a giant's fist. Paradise indeed, as it followed the *Venture's* course. Wavelets glitter-tipped by the sun parted as the little craft made its way upstream, nudging aside the odd carcass of a deer or a wild pig, bloated out of all recognition, on its way down to the sea.

Andrew nosed the little vessel into a dent in the river bank, flung a rope over a branch and secured it before he cut off the engine.

Complete quiet.

Ferns and palms crowding the bank were out-classed by the rampant and glorious D'Albertis vine, and although Greta's instinct was to touch and smell she had been warned before leaving not to go near it, the advice surprisingly coming from Sabrina herself.

'Hawaiian night, darling, goidonk goidonk, and some clown for a joke brought it along to decorate the club. Didn't tell us he'd used gloves to pick the damn things. He succeeded in putting one woman into hospital. Millions of hairy fluffy spines that burrow into the skin. Ghastly!'

Andrew, insisting it was Greta's holiday, pumped up the primus to boil water for tea. 'How long is it since ye've had a hot soaking bath, lass?'

'Lordy, am I that bad?'

'I'm nae talking about showers and buckets. A proper bath up to that lovely neck of yours.'

She shot him a puzzled glance, not sure of his meaning. 'Well, I suppose you could say Sydney. Certainly not in Yunnabilla. As for Kebai . . .'

His eyes were laughing as he pointed out a large forty-gallon drum taking up a good part of the aft deck. She had noticed it empty before the boat had puttered off and wondered about it.

'Take a look,' he invited her.

Still puzzled but cautious, it took her seven steps to see what he was talking about. The drum was filled with fresh water. It was warm and smelt of the river. In seconds Andrew's arms were around her, making a good job of unfastening the buttons of her blouse. For just a moment he cupped her breasts.

'Your bath is ready, Madam,' he said, handing her a fresh cake of soap. 'Cashmere Bouquet from the depths of Burns Philp's treasure trove and a large sponge from the blue waters of Greece. The manager said it went with the soap. Now in you go!'

Her skirt (never shorts in Kebai) dropped to the deck and as if Greta was a featherweight fourteen-year-old, she was lifted up and, laughing protests, helped into the drum.

Oh, the bliss of it! Andrew stood back, admiring his handiwork. 'My turn after you.'

Such luxury – she'd forgotten what a good soaking felt like. Not knowing anything about the workings of a boat, even one so small, she had to ask how did an empty forty-gallon drum become filled to the brim with river water?

Grinning, Andrew held up a hose. 'Ye dinn'a see it.' He explained enough to her satisfaction that water pumped up from the river could be channelled somehow into and through various stages to a hose resulting in her having a warm bath a hundred miles from nowhere (not counting Kebai), and there was her man bringing her what appeared to be something nice in a small glass. It looked familiar.

Taking a sip her eyes widened. 'It's Greta's Gold!'

'Aye. Couldn'a leave it behind.'

The golden fire trickled down her throat and with eyes closed she felt his hands slide down her body into the water, searching and arousing her, his tongue licking the sticky sweetness off her mouth. She gave a little moan. 'Not enough room, darling, for the two of us . . .'

'It will be all the better for the waiting.' He stepped back, eyes glinting, lips compressed. 'Take your time, my love.' Suddenly he stripped, stepped on the rail and dived into the river, taking passion with him.

'Andy!' He reappeared as quickly as he had dived in, shaking water from his hair. 'Crocodiles! For God's sake, get into the boat.'

Teasing her, he treaded water. 'Crocs? Not here, so I've been told.'

She didn't believe him, but remembering the glass and its precious drop still in her hand, she carefully placed it on the gunnels. 'Now, Flight, come up and get me out.' He had nearly spoilt it all.

Sun setting, they sat up on the forward deck, drinks in their hands, their backs against the wheelhouse. Hardly room enough for them to sit side by side. Flying foxes by their hundreds wheeled in a silent cloud high above them, taking off to unknown places; the river hushed as the light waned.

The day for Greta had been perfect, the pinpricks of Sabrina left behind. As for Andrew, she had deliberately kept questions at bay. Whatever it was he would tell her in good time, although a niggle remained, a sharp reminder when she allowed it to surface, of Sam's discomfort and the glances exchanged between Andy and the gypsy. She tried to put it out of her mind. This was an enchanted place, where even the usual invasion of mosquitoes was missing. They talked and shared the last of the Greta's Gold while Andrew spoke of his dream that one day they would find themselves on a plantation. There was money and more coming in, enough to give the wish serious thought. In harmony they watched the light fade from the sky.

Two days they had to explore the river and, making the most of it, they paid a visit to the people of a village where they saw grass houses on stilts stalking to the water's edge. A granny and a lad exchanged tins of peaches for several hands of ripening bananas and a mask like the ones in the Colemans' house. An hour further on, the river narrowed and an hour after that it turned into no more than a creek roofed by a tangle of brush. 'Time to turn back.' There was regret in Andrew's voice. 'There must be more of the river behind it. What a man needs here is a guid, sharp cane knife.'

'Thank the Lord you haven't. Let's turn around.' Greta shuddered, thinking of snakes, giant iguanas and maybe a roving crocodile. Up to date Andrew hadn't been able to persuade her to take a swim although he had while she held her breath.

Now they were tramping through waist-high grass that scratched and tiny insects crawled down Greta's sweat-clinging shirt. They were in search of an abandoned sawmill that Andrew had heard about. 'Who knows what we'll find there.'

'Diamonds?'

'Ye never know. But it's the finding, lass, tha's the fun of it.'

'Gawd, Aggie.' But she followed him as she always would, hot, sweaty, itchy and at the same time wondering what the devil was she doing there.

Not that far away from the river they saw it. Nothing but rusting machinery, hungry jungle and silence. A sad and derelict failure of someone's dreams. 'Let's go back,' Greta murmured.

The *Venture* was tied up to a decaying jetty and Andrew walked in front, ready to give a helping hand. Looking down, so as not to fall between the rotting planks, Greta screamed. 'Aah! Get them off!'

Andrew turned. 'Don't touch them!' he yelled, trying to stay her frantic hands brushing off a cluster of leeches. Black and bloated, they clung to her as blood dribbled down her legs. 'They canna' hurt you. We'll get them off. Just don't try.'

Sobbing more in disgust than fright, she held his hand and once aboard, kept still under instructions while every instinct clamoured to tear the loathsome things off. He snatched up a tin of matches near the primus and, striking one, held its flame close to the first leech. It dropped to the deck, leaving a tiny pinpoint of blood behind. Slowly and carefully he removed every one of the creatures, talking gently, explaining that pulling them off as she had wanted to could be dangerous. 'You nae want a head left under the skin. We've had enough of dangerous infections in this family.' The final leech dropped off, making a faint plop as it hit the deck.

As Andy had as many creatures happily syphoning away on his own legs, he found some difficulty in hitting the right spot with the little flame.

'Here!' Greta snatched the match tin away from his hand. 'Let me do it.' Grim-lipped, she removed every one off his legs. 'There! Now let's get out of here. But before we go I think I'll have that swim!'

As the second day ended and the leeches were nothing but a memory to laugh over, they tied up again to an overhanging tree where the river had widened to a lake-like beauty, its reflections enhanced by foliage and passing clouds. Sitting on the foredeck as they had done the night before, they drank the last of Greta's Gold.

'What a day,' she murmured.

He put an arm around her waist and gave her a hug. 'Aye. And there's more to come.' Andrew got to his feet. 'I'll be a moment.' He took her glass and went into the wheelhouse. When he returned he had the manilla envelope in his hand and gave it to her. 'Before you open it, I've something to say.'

Here it comes, Greta, m' girl . . . The picture had stayed of him and Sabrina laughing their way into the club. The glances between them had not been imagined after all. Now, instead of sitting by her side, he faced her, leaning back on an elbow.

'Greta, I think it's time we married.'

Through a daze she heard him ask if she would be his wife. 'I love you beyond words. You're my life; my other half. Will you be my lawful wife?'

Lawful wife. The sweet sound of it chimed and pealed through and about her head, lifting her thudding heart into a light and crazy happiness. Greta never gave a thought as to how it could happen. She didn't care. *It had to be right.* She gave a squeal of sheer delight and flung herself at him in an embrace that sent them nearly rolling off the tiny deck. 'Of course I will. Of course I will!'

In a delirium of ecstasy, Greta could hardly contain herself, the confines of the *Venture* hardly large enough on which to whirl around, hug and kiss him, making a complete idiot of herself with Andrew grinning like a fool and not a spare inch around to do the splits.

Later the manilla envelope was explained. It held papers that told of Andrew's divorce from Netty for desertion. Unknown to Greta and not wanting to raise hopes, he had given the ruby to Mannie, who had connections in the jewel trade, before leaving Yunnabilla. The resultant sale had given him a tidy sum to start with. Enquiries in England had produced enough evidence to prove that

Netty had deserted him and was last seen with a man unknown boarding a ship bound for Canada. No news of a child, but long ago Andrew had pushed aside the thoughts of maybe.

He also confessed to Greta that he and Sam had not been after all to the far reaches of the Fly River. They had been in Port Moresby where Andrew had to attend court and declare his case. Divorce granted. All over in so many minutes. It had been hard for him to believe.

Awash with relief and happiness, it was nearly as hard for Greta to believe what Andrew was saying. They were to be married! How many nights and days had she wished such a thing could happen? No more pretending – even to Andrew – that all was as it should be. Greta Osborne was going to be Mrs Andrew Flight at long last! Oh, the wonderful joy of it. How she loved and adored this man.

'We even made a small profit for going off-course. The bonniest piece of navigation I've ever done.' He referred to a handsome fee paid for the *Pelican* to ferry no less than five important (so it was said) politicians from Australia on a fact-finding mission. Andrew gave a quirky lift of an eyebrow, matching the sardonic gleam in his eyes. 'Three sleeping on the hatch and two below. Never learnt what they thought of the morning bucket brigade. But the porridge served with coconut milk was thick and good with plenty of sugar. Decent fellas, though. Not a complaint.'

'Gawd, luv a duck! There's no doubt about the pair of you.' She handed him a tin opener, plonking down five tins of food on the miniscule fold-back table. 'Tonight we dine like kings.' She couldn't help giving a little wriggle in her happiness. 'Ice, no got . . . so tinned everything it has to be. Asparagus and *red* salmon, served with a generous squeeze of lemon. Nonee's tomatoes and the *pièce de résistance*, Camp Pie, the very best of brands, pickled walnuts and onions.' She rummaged in the box they had brought with them. 'Oh, I forgot! Arnott's rose cream biscuits and – wait for it – quinces, tinned, and Nestlé cream. A feast. A celebration!'

He dropped the tin opener on the table and brought her close to him. 'Sounds wonderful, but must it be now?' His hands slid down her back, pressing himself into her. 'I know of a better way to celebrate.'

The tins were placed on the low seat lining the wall, the table hooked into its appointed place. The hurricane lamp was turned down to a glimmer as Andrew, piece by piece, removed Greta's clothing. 'Let me look at you.' Lightly he stroked her hair and brushed a curl away, touched her nose and kissed it. Slowly his hands followed the curve of her hips. They kissed again. The space was almost too small to lie on but they found it room enough . . .

Another day of drifting, making plans and making love went by. Already Greta knew that the Administrator would be happy to perform their marriage ceremony. Without a twinge she accepted that all arrangements had been made. Who could find fault in the surprise that Andrew had planned for her, even if the whole island by now knew that as a couple a marriage had yet to be performed? The Hibiscus had been warned by Sabrina to expect a wedding party in the very near future, so no wonder secrets had been shared between her, Andy and Sam. Greta, still in a joyous daze, remembered the look of envy she had caught on Sabrina's face. Even so, she told herself, you'll still have to watch her . . .

She settled her back against the wheelhouse. Tomorrow they would be back in Kebai and instead of feeling a little sad as she normally would, she was looking forward to a busy time. So much to do. Well, most of it had been done, Andy had told her. Would Burns Philp have anything like a yard of decent material that would make her a stylish dress? There was a woman who had been taught dressmaking by the convent nuns. Sometimes as a favour she would sew a dress to a pattern. Could a pattern be found at Beeps? There again it was a case of a lucky draw, but she'd see what a visit to the store would produce. Bouquets: hibiscus, frangipani? Could she get a pair of gloves from somewhere? What about a cake? She saw herself dressed up to the nines; Andy in his whites. What a pair they'd make. A willy-willy of happy thoughts whirled through her brain so at first she didn't hear the sound – a faint burr that suddenly exploded about her ears. It came from the river bank.

'What's that?' The noise was all around her.

'Insects.' Andrew was grinning, unperturbed. 'Heard it once before like that, only once, when we were up the Fly.' It was a noise that Greta could not describe; never heard before. Chittering, clicking, rasping, buzzing, thrumming – a cacophony of sound that merged into a vibrating whole from a myriad unseen, pulsating insects; an ovation to the coming night. The noise then stopped as suddenly as it began. The silence was complete. It had been too grand, too great, to follow it up with words. For minutes they sat there, half hoping for an encore until the chirrip-click of a lone gecko stowaway rang down the curtain. Greta sighed.

'Another wonderful day!'

CHAPTER FORTY-ONE

Not only Sabrina had known of Andrew's secret. From Port Moresby an urgent telegram had been sent to Flossie Stretton with instructions to send post haste an outfit that would please Greta and stun the ladies of Kebai. A response the next day had arrived with three words only: WACKO. WILL DO.

But a week had passed with no sign of Greta's wedding dress on the latest ship bringing up supplies. Another week to go and Andrew was getting anxious as Greta, locating the dressmaker and after turning Burns Philp inside-out, had found a roll of floral cotton, not quite her style, she said, but it would have to do. Arthur Mead had returned with the good news that all was well; his generosity spilled over in appreciation of Greta's good work and he promised them a feast, including caviar by the bucketful for the reception – *at half price.*

Never mind!

Kebai's social set, what there was of it, were ready to forgive the Flights for keeping them duped. Living together! How naughty of them. But they *are* a lovely couple . . . It all promised to be fun

and there wasn't much of *that* in Kebai! But with all the speculation and gossip over gins and tonics and the back-slapping at the
club bar, the afternoon news was never forgotten. In spite of Prime
Minister Chamberlain's assurances that all was well, already two
patrol officers and a married couple had left for 'Home', as they
fondly called England.

Their departure had left a sense of uneasiness in the small
white community. People were hungry for the latest news and
the late arrival of newspapers didn't help. The fear of an outright
war was growing and the marriage, the first to be conducted by an
Administrator in Kebai, lightened the sometimes sombre discussions at the club and hotel. Not that the spasmodic doom and
gloom affected Greta. She was in a dizzily happy flap. As for the
ladies of Kebai, delighted to get away from men's talk, there was an
unspoken competition as to who could put on the best afternoon
tea for '*dear* Greta'. Sabrina was invited, always welcome, even if
she *was* too fond of giving men the glad eye and 'goidonking' her
way through it all. Exciting times.

Andrew and Sam had left for a quick visit to the islands off the
coast, more as a look-see than anything. 'Never know what we can
pick up,' Sam enthused. 'Maybe some masks and carvings; Mannie
sold the last lot we sent over, and skulls. There's still a few around
and he's got a bloke – a Yank – who'll pay good money for 'em.'

'Nonee! Look at it. Look at it! She's gone berserk with the scissors.'
Greta was close to tears with frustration as she held up the dress.
'It was perfect at the last fitting. Too late to do anything about it
now. Even if Beeps still has any material left, I wouldn't allow that

woman to touch it with a ten-foot pole. Hell's bells! What a balls up!' The dress, made up to Greta's design, would have been fault-less but for a slash, although neatly mended, that marred the front from hem to hip.

'Maybe too much betel nut, heh?' Nonee dropped her eyes and shrugged before sauntering off. Another tale for the village storyteller.

'There's only one thing to do.' Greta grabbed her money purse and took off. She was certain that she could beg the use of a sewing machine from someone. Even the nuns might oblige, and if there was anything halfway interesting left in Burns Philp she'd have a go at making the damn thing up herself. Her first stop was at Arthur's trade store. It was full of locals, mainly women and children who studied her with curious eyes. There were some rolls of cotton, glaringly bright with flowers of unknown species, more suitable for Mother Hubbards than a wedding dress. Another smaller store reeking of trade tobacco sold nothing but gaily coloured tin dishes, billy cans and buckets, tinned fish and bags of rice.

Before entering Burns Philp's store, Greta paused, her eyes fol-lowing the road down to Billy Fat's shop. She had always intended going there but often found it too hot, and her shopping bag too heavy to warrant the effort. It was unusual for her not to have a stickybeak, but she had assumed it would just be a replica of Arthur Mead's store.

Two steps inside the dim interior of Billy Fat's emporium was a revelation. She had to call it that, for a treasure trove of goods were crammed into every corner and onto every shelf lining the walls. It was out of all proportion to the white population of the island. Hardly anything there to attract village customers. Who *were* his customers? she wondered. There were masks decorated with shells and feathers, masks of Chinese heroes and villains, carved not only from wood but ivory, ceramic pots and figurines, bamboo furniture and framed panels of silk. Not a roll of material in sight. A woman tottered out from behind a beaded curtain, her feet too tiny to support her weight. Dressed in black, her eyes nearly shut as she gave a gold-toothed smile. 'You look,' she fluted, 'you see, you buy.'

'Er . . . You haven't anything suitable, I suppose . . .' No harm in asking, Greta thought. But no, what's the point?

'You Flight lady?' Teeth flashed in a gilded smile and she put up a hand, jade bangles softly clicking. 'You wait.' She hurried as quickly as her tiny feet allowed through the beaded curtain. A good few minutes passed with no sign of the lady in black returning and Greta, in spite of the woman's strange disappearance, decided to come back some other time to look, see and buy. But before she could put a foot outside the door the curtain parted and the woman, under the weight of the load she was carrying, staggered in. Greta bounced over to help before the rolls slipped to the floor.

'So solly. So solly,' she lisped, dumping bundles of silk onto a lacquered table. 'You look. You see. You buy.'

Greta gasped. Unrolling before her eyes were rainbows of silk shimmering, slipping and sliding every which way to the floor.

'So beautiful . . . !' She fingered one piece after another. Silk embroidered with dragons, unimaginable birds, chrysanthemums of different hues . . . Impossible to choose, while at the same time wondering if the nuns could help out; her efforts at dressmaking too clumsy to even try. To be entertained at afternoon tea by the ladies of Kebai was one thing, but she shied away from the thought of asking favours. What to do?

As if she was reading her mind, the lady with the jade bangles flashed her golds again, and in a high voice spoke to the beaded curtain. In answer a slight young Chinese woman appeared with a tape measure in her hand.

Andrew, back with a day to spare, was devastated. The outfit from Flossie hadn't arrived and thinking of Greta's scant wardrobe, by now faded from constant wear and washings, he was dismayed that he could not give her something smart and new to wear. He had a fair idea what would be on offer in Kebai: bugger all.

But whatever Greta wore on her wedding day, his bonny lass would outshine them all. Greta, in Andrew's opinion, was the most desirable woman he had ever known, and by tomorrow afternoon she would be officially his forever.

Rain was bucketing down, the morning sun smothered by clouds and rising mists and the sea sullen as the *Pelican* swerved in response to a fitful wind.

'Not a bloody good day for it, Comrade.' Sam Riding swigged down his tea laced with rum.

'Well, as Greta says, rotten in the morning, come good in the afternoon. And mon, what an afternoon it will be.'

'Right from the start, I knew she was pure gold. And she's come through all this, now I know the full story, without a ring – in a way you'd call it that – on her finger.' Sam broke into a chuckle. 'Never forget that first day I met 'er. Didn't know what to think of me, that's for sure. But she came good, singing her heart out, me on the old mouth organ, you scratching away on the violin while that train rattled its way to Cairns. What a lady.'

'I'll drink to that.' Andrew picked up the rum bottle and poured a good measure into his tea.

Greta had ordered Andrew to sleep on the boat. 'You'll not see me until I walk onto that hotel verandah tomorrow! I've heard all about the wing-ding promised for tonight, so be on the watchout, knowing that lot. I don't want my man hung over before he says "I do".' With that she had shooshed them out of the house, adding a plea to the best man that he look after the bridegroom. Sam tried to follow instructions and although soused to the gills, way past midnight they both managed to row over to the *Pelican* and climb aboard without calamity.

To oblige, the rain had cleared and, sticking to tradition, Greta kept them all waiting for ten whole minutes. Andrew was the first to see her approaching, looking more beautiful and more colourful than the hibiscus lining the path. Her cheongsam of peacock blue and silver chrysanthemums had not been modified in any way, the side split exposed a perfect leg from ankle to thigh, long crystal earrings glittered in the sunlight, and her hair was piled high and burnished by the sun. It was a Greta Osborne entrance that had women gasping, the Administrator and his wife a little shocked but smiling, and from somewhere a male voice rumbled, heard by those around him, 'Lucky dog.'

With Sam and Sabrina as witnesses it was a service without homilies, but the warmth in the Administrator's voice told the gathering that the couple not only had his blessing, but his friendship as well.

It was brief, but vows according to the book were exchanged

and Greta heard the words she had longed for ever since the day they had boarded the train for the North. 'I take this woman . . .'

Except for the nuns and the Kiwais, all of Kebai came to the party. Arthur Mead had done his very best with what was available on such short notice. Greta gave Armi a wink as corks popped, beer frothed, and the kitchen staff-cum-waiters placed pots of caviar with wafer-thin croutons before the guests. It was the table centre that caused amazed comment. Armi had outdone himself: a magnificent creation of whole baked coral trout, crayfish, oysters adorned with orchids and the plumes of the bird of paradise a fountain of gold towering above it all. Sucking pig, venison, fried rice and salads of paw paw, pineapple and melon were made savoury by vinegar, salt and pepper. Shortbreads abounded (there was always enough tinned butter for shortbread) and Burns Philp had been skinned out of olives and gherkins.

For a wedding, speeches were few but as drinks were downed the few kept getting longer until the speaker was clapped or booed into silence. Appetites and thirsts were prodigious and the waiters kept busy. A final short speech by the Administrator wishing the couple good luck and happiness was the sign that he and his wife were ready to leave, but not before Armi, his black face split with a smile, carried in a wedding cake iced and as yellow as a Shell petrol bowser sprinkled in silver cachous. There were cheers of encouragement as the Flights cut the cake, egged on by the singing of 'For They are Jolly Good Fellows . . .'

'A little late, I know.' Andrew picked up his glass and, looking around, his eyes narrowed, the lines deep beside his lips only emphasising the smile when it came. More than one woman felt herself melting before it. 'I have a toast to make. It hasn'a been all roses for my lass since we've been together. At times the thorns have burrowed deep. However, together we've come through.' He then paused, looking down at her with a love that had some wishing and some envying. 'To my wife, Greta.'

A roar of approval, hands banged the long table, glasses clinked and Greta wanted to burst into tears. Glasses were filled again.

By now Arthur Mead was showing signs of disquiet. Dinner for the house guests was approaching and not everyone had sat down with the bride and groom. He began a half-serious protest when some prankster produced bows and arrows and fastened a large target to one of the verandah posts. 'All right, you lads, don't spoil the party. You can play your game at the club and lay your bets there and take those bows and arrows with you.' By now, with officialdom out of sight, the quieter contingent of Kebai thought it time to leave with the louder contingent wanting to stay. Greta, bubbling over with joy helped on by generous glasses of champagne, stood up.

'I cannot believe the height of those bows. I'm dying to see this game, as Arthur calls it – I'm one for the club!'

Her exuberance was contagious. 'Hear, hear! Goidonk, goidonk! Marvellous idea!'

Chairs were pushed back and, without warning, the men swarmed around. 'C'mon, Greta!' they cried, sweeping her up on their shoulders. They began marching out of the hotel and were quickly out of sight, leaving Sabrina and Andrew behind.

They stood up together, the last to go.

'I should have thanked you, Sabrina, while everyone was here. I'm sorry.' He was looking straight into her eyes. 'Ye've helped so much. Speeding things along. Arranging all this. How can a man thank you?'

'Easy, Andy Flight.' She suddenly came close, put her arms around his neck and planted a kiss on his lips, pressing close, then dropped her arms. 'That might be the last you'll ever get.' Her breathing was slow and steady. 'But don't count on it.'

He gave a slight shake of his head and stepped back to return the favour with a light kiss on her cheek. 'I have to settle all this up with Arthur.' He turned to find the hotelier at the reception door and wondered just how much he'd seen.

'My case – it's behind your desk.'

Arthur stepped aside. 'Help yourself. When's the *Pelican* off again?'

'Tomorrow. Medical supplies needed urgently at the mission.'

'Up the Fly?'

'Aye.'

Arthur showed mild surprise when he saw the shape of the case in Andrew's hand. 'A violin . . . You play it close to your chest, Flight.'

'No, under my chin.' Andrew's smile was as mild as Arthur's was surprised. 'Ye "mead" it at a wedding.' He chuckled at Mead's expression as he recognised himself. 'I'll fix you up for everything when we get back, Arthur, and thank you. Shouldn'a be long.'

The 'game', being who could hit a bullseye first, was the cause of high excitement at the club. It wasn't easy, as some were finding, arrows whizzing through the air, some to bury their heads into the timber, while another flew straight out a nearby window. There were no screams of pain outside so it was assumed that the arrow had fallen harmlessly to the ground. The target, large and pitted by numerous games played over the years, was hooked to the back wall, well away from most, although a few taking cheerful risks stood close to call out results. Greta, who thought she'd seen it all at the hotel, was appalled.

'Someone must get killed for sure.'

A roar went up as an arrow smacked the bullseye fair and square. Money passed hands and another arrow was imbedded into the back wall.

'They're mad!'

'It's nothing, darling – it's been going on forever, goidonk, goidonk.' Sabrina leant back in her chair, her eyes teasing. 'You and Andy not leaving yet?'

'No. There's something I want to do. It's a sort of surprise.'

'By the way, that cheongsam was an inspiration. Had every man panting.' Sabrina looked pointedly at Greta's leg. 'Still has.'

Sabrina and Louise Jackson with Greta, now deserted by the men, were sharing one of the club's cane tables under a ceiling fan. It was impossible to compete with the 'game'. Another intake of breath was heard as an arrow, aimed too high, hit the ceiling and ricocheted back to the thrower.

Greta waited. Any minute now . . . A strange mixture of excitement and nerves not felt for years stirred in her chest. Andy came over.

'Ready, Gret?'

She nodded.

Andrew went to the bar and spoke to the drink attendant who dived under the counter and brought up the violin case. She watched him go outside. Over the noise only she could hear him tuning up. Sabrina, not missing a thing, raised questioning eyebrows.

He then appeared by the open door, tucked the violin firmly under his chin and lifted the bow. The first note, broad and clear, soared over their heads. Absorbed as if no one was there, he launched into a jig – a lighthearted tune that tripped around the room, ensnaring attention as it went on its merry way. Too irresistible to ignore, Andrew netted them in one by one until all stood still gawking and astonished while he played on. Smiles broke out but they were silent as he weaved his magic to the end. Boots stamping floors, laughter, clapping and questions flew as to why he had never played at the club before. Andrew stopped the noise with an upraised hand.

'Ladies,' he said, bowing to the women, 'and gentlemen.' He strode over to Greta and taking her hand, kissed it before leading her to the centre of the floor. 'Let me introduce to you my songbird, Mrs Greta Flight, and tell us your favourite song.' There were puzzled glances as Andrew looked around, a neutral expression on his face, with Greta, trying to look serious, standing by. As there was no response to the invitation, he said, 'Very well, no takers, eh?' Once more he placed the violin under his chin and began the first notes of 'Smoke Gets in Your Eyes'. Although Greta hadn't sung to an audience in months, her notes were in perfect pitch, rich and pure. They were spellbound. When it ended the applause was wild.

'What about "Star Dust", Greta?' In the middle of the song Sam appeared, taking the harmonica from his trouser pocket and joining them. The bows and arrows were forgotten. Next, someone asked if they knew something lively. Greta was getting into her stride. 'How about "Top Hat, White Tie and Tails"?'

Sam swung into the catchy tune, Andrew picked it up and Greta belted it out. Feet were stamping – there had been nothing like it before in Kebai. For Greta it was like breaking out of the chains that had bound her tight for months. New songs, old melodies, inviting all to sing along with her, the old war songs of 1914 . . . The night sped on wings until Andy was ready to call it quits. 'The time has come, the rooster said —' a roar of hilarity greeted him, '— to carry my bonny sweet hen across the threshold.'

'That's the idea, mate!'

'Whacko the did! You little beauty!'

'Hey! We didn't see yer kiss the bride. How about it, ay?'

Ignoring the ribaldry, Andrew packed the violin in its case and handed it to Sam. 'Hold it, will you, Comrade?' He then turned on Greta, the devil in his eye. 'Come here, woman.' To protest was useless as he wrapped her in his arms and, bending over her to the delight of the watchful crowd, kissed her long and hard. Men grabbed their drinks and gulped them down before Andy's kiss could cause a mischief.

'Well!' That was about as much as Louise Jackson could say until she got her breath back. Sabrina's face was expressionless. The Flights didn't return to the table. Instead they left, arms around each other as 'good luck', and well wishes followed them on their way.

'Well!' Louise began again but this time had more to say. 'I *thought* I knew her. She's Greta Osborne! You know, the singer *and* dancer, if you go in for that sort of thing.'

'Never heard of her.' Sabrina sounded completely disinterested. 'I'm from Melbourne, remember?'

'You must have, Sabby. She is – or *was* – the rage of Sydney before she left for America. Wait a minute.' Louise frowned in puzzlement. 'What's she doing here, then?'

'She obviously likes Kebai – with Andy thrown in, of course – better than America.'

'Wait till I tell the girls!'

'You do that over your g and t's. But now I've got other things to do.' She rammed a cigarette into her holder, got up and sashayed across to the bar. Louise grinned as Sabrina closed in on the island's good-looking post master. She could almost hear her saying, 'Light me, darling.'

CHAPTER FORTY-TWO

While Andy and Sam had been up river, the military behemoth of Germany invaded Poland, and Great Britain wasted no time in declaring war. Her colonies, always faithful, followed suit. The news had been heard in every small outpost along the river with the speed of a rushing tide, and now the two men were on their way back to Kebai, in a lather to hear more.

It had been one of their most successful trips: five hundred American dollars for the safe delivery of crocodile skins to a buyer waiting in Kebai. A month had passed since Greta had waved goodbye from the jetty and both men were looking forward to her company and a night or two of music – now a regular happening – once they'd tied up.

They were a good hundred miles from the river's mouth and the *Pelican* was hitched up to a giant mangrove in a quiet stretch of the river, waiting for the tide to turn and the bore to come. Bores had been a regular thing since they had first ventured up the Fly River, and the *Pelican* could be depended to stay on an even keel meeting the onslaught head on. Still a couple of hours yet to wait, so they relaxed on the hatch, enjoying each other's company. Their regular helpers had already returned to their village, well rewarded in money and goods and taking with them the stench of the crocodile heads they'd bargained for and had boiled up in a forty-gallon drum on the back deck; a tasty snack.

Sam rolled himself a cigarette and handed the tobacco pouch over. 'Have a durry, Comrade. Settle yer nerves.'

'What nerves? Are ye daft?'

'Not daft by half of it, and I'm no dill either. You've been bloody edgy ever since we got news of the stoush over there.'

'Has it been that obvious?' Andrew sounded thoughtful.

'Like two pimples on a fancy girl's bum.'

'Sorry for that, mate.'

'No need to be. I've been giving it a lot of thought myself.' Sam looked across at the brown river, watching the canoes, nearly camouflaged, gliding beneath the dark shade of the mangroves. 'Whatever's happening over there, nothing will change here for the next hundred years. War is a million light years away and I bet the old girl will still be chugging up and down the river whatever happens. She's done well by us, Comrade.' He gave Andrew a look as if summing up the worth of him. From their first beer together at that railway siding, Sam Riding had taken to the tall Scot with his brogue and sometimes posh voice – strewth, how he could bung it on – a raw Scottish Pom with dreams in his eye and a dream woman to share his bed. But now he was nothing like the bloke he'd first set eyes on. Andy had changed, even looked different . . . close-cropped hair, the pale skin now lightly freckled, eyes steel hard and narrowed by the tropic glare. Hard yakka had developed the lighter frame into real muscle, so Sam thought; Andrew was now a man approved of and respected.

'Well, yer Scot bastard, are thoughts turning to home and duty? Now cough up, I'm willing to listen.' Sam could see his partner and the best mate he'd ever had taking off if the urge 'to do his bit' became too strong to ignore.

Andrew was shaking his head. 'Never back to England, mate, that's all behind me. Let's wait and see how things turn out. Early days yet.'

Not quite the answer Sam was hoping for. 'Y' know Arthur Mead is keen to buy us out.'

'That I know.'

Arthur Mead's offer had been discussed and dismissed more than once over tinned corned beef and warm beer while the river ran quiet and moths and mosquitoes suicided in a barrage of insect spray and smoking coils. Both men acknowledged without saying that war was a catalyst ready to turn things upside down.

Andrew gave a glance at the boat's clock. 'Should nae be long now. Give it another half hour.' He was referring to the bore. Sam cocked an ear and strolled to the rail, leaning out to have a better view downstream of the river. 'Think I can hear it. Earlier than we thought, though. Better start her up, ay?' He was slipping off the mooring lines, coiling up ropes and checking that anything loose was tied down. It was a procedure recommended, worked on and followed through ever since they had ventured into the Fly River. To stay where they were could endanger the boat on the off-chance of it being smashed against trees or mangroves as the expected volume of water flooded the nearby banks. Better to face it head-on in midstream as the tide rushed by. Andrew felt the engine throb beneath his feet as he swung the *Pelican* around to meet the bore, while Sam was aft, making sure for the umpteenth time that everything was as it should be.

Waiting, watching, practically drifting down with the still-placid current on its way to the sea. Already the bore was lumping a good way ahead but coming on at incredible speed, rearing at a height like a Bondi surf gone wild, jostling debris and ripped out trees ahead of it as if they were saplings. Andrew pushed the throttle forward. The *Pelican* bounded ahead, engine roaring, challenging its Goliath, crashing into the first wave. Bucketing and lurching under a wall of water that parted and fell away, the *Pelican* speared through it, emerging bow-high in triumph.

The second wave, not quite as savage, washed over the wheel-house, except for a sodden log that crashed down beside the deck then got caught up in the last surge again, disappearing out of sight. Adrenalin racing, Andrew pulled back the throttle. It was all over in minutes as the river settled down and continued on its way.

'As you've said before, she's a sweet little vessel.' Hearing no answer, he assumed that Sam, like a mother hen, was fussing around, inspecting any damage that the log might have caused. He looked over his shoulder to see if help was needed and frowned. The back deck appeared empty. 'Sam?' He took up a rope already attached to the nearest wheelhouse upright and looped it fast over one of the steering spokes, keeping the *Pelican* on a steady course. He covered the small cabin area in two strides.

'Sam!' No sign of him. 'Jesus! Where are you?'

Fear belted through him as he rushed to each gunnel, knowing in his heart Sam was not there. Where? How? Did the log smack down on him? Did he lose his balance? Overboard he would have been tossed and turned, helpless in the wrath of the bore. *Pelican's* engine roared again as it was turned back in a futile effort to find the skipper. He returned to where they had offloaded the helpers, the village not that far away. He knew their eyes would be better than his in finding Sam, alive or dead.

For hours they searched and probed creek and bank with no sign of Sam Riding. How far would the bore carry him before it levelled out, leaving him smashed and battered on the banks of some tidal creek or sago-covered swampland? Night was falling before the search was called off. For three more days Andrew looked and hoped without success. He reported the accident to the government station downriver at first chance, and canoes and a launch joined in the hunt until it was finally abandoned without a sign of the man.

Sam was gone.

Greta, standing on the foreshore in front of the house, waited until the *Pelican* anchored. A full-moon tide. Sam always preferred the anchor to tying up, the reason being, he'd once told her, that if a squall came up the boat would be swinging free instead of jammed under the ruddy jetty. Not only was *Pelican* anchored off shore, she was keeping company with the steamer *Waru*. Talk around town was that the *Waru* was heading south to bigger and brighter things. On such a lovely morning surrounded by the flapping sails of the big Kiwai canoes, the two vessels looked comfortably at home.

There was always the same thrill of pleasure to see their safe return with the usual cheerful wave from one or both of them. She could see Andy leave the wheelhouse to haul in the dingy trailing behind. Now only a matter of minutes after waiting more than a month to feel that first salty kiss planted on her lips. She watched as he climbed down into the skiff, untied the rope and started rowing. Sam wasn't with him. As he drew closer she felt trouble stirring in her bones. Did Sam have a fever or something?

Closing in, Andrew stopped rowing, the oars falling with a clatter into the skiff and him leaving them there, which was strange, for they were normally taken up to the house. He jumped out, imbedding the anchor into the strip of sand without a smile or a word, and began trudging towards her.

The shock was like a cattle prod when she first saw his face; taut and grim, lips drawn as if his smile had gone forever.

'Darling?' That was the only word she could find to say.

'Come up to the house.' He took her elbow and silently led her across the road. Nonee, who had just brought in a welcome-home iced lager with the usual morning coffee took one look at the pair, did a quick turnabout and fled into the kitchen.

Andrew eased Greta down on the lazy boy. 'Ye better sit down, love.' Then, without preamble, 'Sam's gone. Drowned. He's – he's —' The hard tone of his voice broke. 'Sam's dead.' Andrew picked up the opened lager bottle, put it to his lips, drinking it down without pause. He then poured himself a glass and one for Greta.

'We couldn'a find him – the bore – he just disappeared. He's gone, Greta, to God knows where.'

'No! It's not true!' Andy's words were a jumbled mess in her ears.

'It is, I'm afraid —'.

'How did – how could it happen? Where were you? What were you doing?'

He flinched as every question stung like a well-placed dart. 'At the wheel. Ye canna' leave it.'

'Why couldn't you —' She could feel angry despair like sour dough rising in her throat. Against Andy. Against the *Pelican*. He couldn't be gone! Not dear Sam; a quick memory of him toting groceries to the men of Parramatta Park flashed into her mind. Why? A good man no one could fault. She felt as if her heart was really breaking. 'He could be somewhere still. We need to search again. We'll find him!'

'He's not out there, Greta, believe me.'

Nonee's keening as she listened in gave truth to Andrew's words.

No sooner had the boat sailed in than word of the disaster, like the bore that killed Sam Riding, swept over the town, leaving a sad aftermath behind it. Sam had been well liked as a straight dealer and a good drinking partner, prone to livening things up on a dull day with his mouth organ.

As Greta heard every detail of the tragedy she realised that everything that could be done had been. They both felt the urge to go back to the *Pelican*. It was there that they would grieve and salute their old friend goodbye. It hurt, yet there was comfort to be had where the three of them had spent so many good days together. It was time for reminiscences, more of laughter than of tears, for Sam had left a legacy of happy memories behind him.

Late afternoon and a crowded dingy approached the boat with the full intention of conducting a wake for good old Sam. Andrew, hearing the noise, went out on deck, arms akimbo.

'We're here to toast the Comrade farewell, Andy.'

'It's a kind thought, gentlemen, but Greta and I have things to discuss.'

'Dry business discussing, Andy mate, dry business. But we've plenty with us to fix that up, ay?' A rope was thrown. It was caught and thrown back.

'We've plenty enough. Now bugger off!'

The hint was taken and the mourners made a noisy return to the jetty.

Greta and Andy talked far into the night; so much to go over. So much to work out. Flossie's letter that had finally arrived with Greta's wedding outfit. It had been full of good wishes and news of Sydney where men were falling over themselves to join up and some, for the first time in years, earning enough to support wife and family. Some of the old gang had answered a call for volunteers to entertain the troops. Flossie herself was already a war correspondent. *All those gorgeous men, lovey*, she wrote. *Can't wait!* Any day, she'd be leaving for overseas duty.

Too unsteady on her feet to climb into the dingy, and Andy no better, they decided to sleep on board for what was left of the night. On the hatch, as they so often had done.

Dawn had arrived unnoticed and by mid-morning the sky had a glare of tungsten steel. Every slap of a wavelet on the skiff was enough for Greta to wince and complain. Andy rowed, and nearing the shoreline they could see Arthur Mead waiting, shading his eye from the glare. In such a hurry to see them, careless of socks and shoes, he even came down and pulled the dingy into the shallows.

'Bad news, eh? Something like this hasn't happened for a while. The boat okay?'

Andrew knew what would be coming next. 'Later, mon. I've a horrible drouth. Ye'll see us later on.'

Greta, her tongue as dry as Andy's and with a raging head as well, completely ignored the man. Followed by a dour Scot, she walked across the short stretch of sand, homeward-bound.

Once bathed and sober, the Flights snacked on corned beef smothered in Gentleman's Pickles and homemade bread. The teapot had been filled for the second time. Andrew buttered his last slice of bread. 'Well, I suppose we better put Arthur out of his misery, eh?'

He was ready to tell Arthur that the *Pelican* was not for sale – not yet. A decision had been made that they would sail her to Cairns, following the coast via Thursday Island. What to do from there could be discussed with Mannie Coleman. Mannie was, after all, a sleeping partner. Andrew wondered if Mead had been told about the arrangement. He had a strong feeling that Mannie was ready to sell her.

'Is this the way you really want it?' Greta sighed, knowing that the old saying about heavy hearts was true.

Andy took her hand as if for assurance, then kissed it. 'It's the only way, Greta.'

'Even without Sam we could still make a go of it here. I'm not a bad deckie, y'know.'

'I know you're it. But the Fly River?' Andrew slowly shook his head. 'It's hard, wild country up there. Not only that, I wouldn'a have been with him for much longer. He knew it. The war has changed everything.'

'That's over there, not here.'

'I should be back at sea. Every able-bodied seaman will be needed.'

'You really want to go, don't you?' Quick resentment flared. 'We've only just got married! I've hardly had time to enjoy it.' How many times over the last hours had she said something like that, getting more drunk and frustrated as they had parried words far into the night.

'We'll make it a honeymoon to remember on our way back to Cairns,' Andrew promised. 'We'll make grand and beautiful love on every desert island we can find and swim in water the colour of gems. Just remember I love you with every fibre of my being.' But he could not erase the sadness in her eyes. 'Then, after the war, we'll be back and find the plantation tha's waiting for us.'

What can a girl do with a man like that? Greta wanted to know, thinking of the many women who, even now, were asking husbands, sons and lovers why must they fight a war in places they'd hardly heard about.

It wasn't fair.

CHAPTER FORTY-THREE

A thousand miles down the coast and Cairns was in sight.

It had been a bittersweet journey, their lovemaking a salve to the sometimes desperation of what might be. So many days of sunshine and laughter, finding themselves alone on sand spits and coral cays where the sound of seabirds' wails and cries vied with the sibilance of soft lapping waves. They were days when thoughts of what lay ahead didn't count. It seemed they were the only ones between the blue bowl of the sky and the ocean's depths. Greta had worked out long ago that sadness cannot be every moment of a day and night, just as a peak of happiness will subside waiting for the next burst of unbridled delight. With a bit of luck things balance out.

Now the buildings of Cairns could be plainly seen as they clustered around the waterfront, standing white against the green of foliage and the dark azure of the mountains. They were only minutes away. The *Pelican* was in the channel's last set of buoys, taking a careful course towards the wharf. Two figures left the shade of a holding shed. Greta snatched up the binoculars. 'There he is! And Leila's with him!' She handed them to Andrew before taking over the wheel. He stepped outside to give a wave that ended in a chuckle. 'Look at the pair of them – and there's Mannie's specs ready to fall off his nose. Get the lines ready, love, we're just about there and the old *Waru* is tied up and waiting.'

The last thing Greta wanted to see was the *Waru*. Already she knew why it was there. Still on a milk run but this time it was going to be a milk run from Sydney to Singapore with Andy on her. Cold comfort for Greta that Singapore was a long way away from Europe and the war, and that five days remained before Andy reported for duty on the *Waru*.

There were hugs and kisses between the women and a bois- terous 'Welcome back!' from Mannie, ready to drive them in his brand-new Daimler down to the Pacific Hotel. 'Best hotel in Cairns.' Already the Flights knew that the estate agent had a buyer for the *Pelican* – Arthur Mead's offer hadn't been enough. The wrench on leaving the little boat had been strong and Andrew hoped in his heart that the new owner would treat her well.

The past was dropping fast behind them.

No sooner had drinks been ordered than Greta made a phone call to Flossie. She knew what she had to do. Andy had agreed.

'Yunnabilla is only a day's drive away,' Mannie reminded them. 'You'll come up, of course, for old times' sake. Stay on the farm. The best place I know for serious discussion, eh?'

The fact that a room had been reserved in the hotel for them was something that Mannie and Leila ignored. The ceiling fans whirred overhead while Mannie adjusted his spectacles. 'For a start, Leila wants you to meet her mumma and poppa. What a story that is!' He leant over and gave Leila's cheek a kiss. 'She's a brave girl, my Leila. And you should see the welcome dinner she's planning.

The mumma has started already.' He pressed his point for 'serious discussion' by telling them that the time in Kebai had been well spent and with the sale of the *Pelican* a nice monetary result was there to be shared. 'That's another thing to work out. Fair's fair.'

Although Greta and Andrew would have preferred the last days to themselves, it was the sensible thing to do and to refuse the Colemans' offer would have been churlish and a disappointment to the generous couple. The Flights looked at each other, grinning. Greta squeezed Leila's hand.

'Why not?'

Yunnabilla looked just the same: sepia-toned with splashes of bougainvillea, its wild grasses still creamed and dried out by the sun. The farm looked no different and as strange as it seemed when they drove over the log bridge, Greta felt she was coming home. There had been a momentary pang when they drove past their little grey house; it looked empty and abandoned, its memories locked behind the front door.

Mannie still had the utility, which for the time she was there was Greta's to use. Andrew had no desire to visit the town. When Mannie gave him the news that had kept Yunnabilla enthralled for weeks, his objection to Greta catching up with friends in town faded away: Vincenzo Costina had disappeared after his house and sheds had been bombed out of existence (for reasons unknown), not long after they'd sailed north. Andrew wasn't at all surprised.

The first port of call as far as Greta was concerned was Marelda. Anticipation grew as she opened the back gate. Obviously Relda hadn't heard the utility arrive. It was the rich aroma floating out of the kitchen that told her she was home and busy. Greta walked up the kitchen steps, poking her head inside.

'Can I have a slice for morning tea?'

Marelda, testing a trio of fruit cakes with her reliable hairpin, looked up. 'I don't believe it!' Immediately she burst into tears. 'Oh, luvvie, I thought I'd never see you again!' Greta felt the warm big breasts pressed against her own in a hug. Marelda pushed her away. 'Now let's have a look at cher.' The hairpin was shoved back into its bun, the sniff wiped away on the hem of her apron. 'No different. The same Greta I knew before yer left. I've kept every letter I got, y' know, and gawd almighty, the things you and that husband of yours get up to. Tell me everything.'

Dismissing protests, Marelda began sifting flour, crumbling in her excellent rendered dripping, pouring in just the right amount of milk and in minutes a soft mound of scone dough was dumped on the table. 'Yer not leaving this house until we've had a cuppa and scones.'

They talked and talked. Marelda made tomato sandwiches. They finished off the scones. Greta joined the Larkin tribe, ecstatic to see her, for a rowdy midday dinner. Yunnabilla gossip was exchanged for the scandals of Kebai and beyond. A preserving jar of pastry shells – just for emergencies – was produced and filled with bush-lemon curd.

Wanting to relive it all over again, Greta described the wedding in Kebai, Marelda nodding and listening with a smile on her face.

'I knew yer wasn't, luv. Married, that is. Remember when Andy had that awful fever? He blabbed and babbled like a wounded bull. But y' secret was safe with me.' A wicked gleam came into her eyes. 'Just as well Ethel Rourke didn't nurse him, ay? She's still making goo-goo eyes at any strange man who happens to walk into the tearooms.'

With all the talk there was one piece of news that Greta waited for. Spanner and Dorothy. No mention of them. Ignoring some instinct that told her not to question, she had to ask. 'Spanner and Dorothy, Relda, how are they?'

'Spanner's in Perth. Might be goin' overseas, he reckons.'

'And Dorothy?'

'We don't talk about her.' The lines were bitter around the woman's mouth.

'What do you mean? What's happened?'

'Dorothy's back on the farm.'

Greta was bewildered. 'What farm are you talking about?' A trickle of alarm, she felt the hair rising on her arms. 'You can't be talking about the Stones. They sold —'

'That fell through. Money was the trouble.' As if a dam wall had broken, a flood of words, unstoppable, swept Greta into a strange world hard to believe or understand. Dry eyed, Marelda told of the sad business between her broken-hearted son and his wife. It seemed that after Spanner had joined the navy Dorothy came back to Yunnabilla. Not to the Larkins' house, but out to the Stones' farm.

'No one made her, Greta. No one. Not even Stone – as far as I know. She did come here trying to explain, and I couldn't believe it at the time. After all that was done for her. You, Dr Pedersen and Biff . . . she just gave it all away. She said she had to go back home. Home! To that beast and his missus. Said she missed them too much.'

Stunned, Greta couldn't move as Marelda stomped over to the

stove and poured boiling water onto fresh tea leaves. She came back, dumping the teapot on the table and getting clean cups. 'Worst part about it – she's havin' a baby. What d' yer think of that?'

'A grandchild – oh, Marelda.' The way things had gone, Marelda had little chance of ever holding it in her arms. 'With a baby, maybe Spanner could —'

'It's not his, Greta.' Marelda filled a cup, slopping tea into the saucer. 'It's Stone's.' Her face was without expression as she sipped her tea.

What sort of hold did that evil man have over his foster-daughter? The thought of Dorothy carrying the farmer's child was enough to make Greta's flesh crawl. What was there to say? What could she say? Especially as Marelda repeated again, 'We don't talk about her or that any more.'

Before the children came home from school Greta said goodbye. Keeping her pity and sympathy behind a smile, Greta swallowed tears as Marelda, giving her another hug, whispered, 'Now, don't go spoiling your holiday worrying over me. I've got more to do than worry meself over something I can't understand. Spanner will get over it, that I know.'

After the visit, Greta felt she had said her last goodbye to Yunnabilla. Time enough to greet the others who were attending the hello and farewell dinner at the Colemans' farm.

Leila, Mannie, Mumma and Poppa did the Flights proud. The wine, beer and tropical fruit juices to Mannie's recipe could have slaked a hundred thirsty throats throughout the night and into the next. Dishes were served up in never-ending courses. Since they had left, more library lights had been installed and the house glowed with the colour of jewels while breezes up from the creek made the hanging beads clink and tinkle even above the sound of the music and gaiety that vanquished any sad thoughts hanging around.

Everyone that Greta and Andrew knew and had formed friendships with had been asked to come along, which meant the whole cast of the cabaret and of the successful 'Top Hat' concert. Greta sang with them and although her high kicks since leaving had been few and far between, that night they were as high and free as Poppy Griffen's, now director of the Flight Academy of Dance.

Greta thought to herself that Captain David Pedersen in army uniform was by far (except for Andy) the most handsome man in the room. It was obvious Sister Mavis Barry thought so too. Were she and David . . . ? And if so, Greta wondered, did Mavis manage to keep David off the grog? She had noticed he was sticking to Mannie's fruit punch.

Cooling off on the verandah, Greta could hear Mannie and Andy giving a rousing production of gypsy music. Memories came with it of Lorraine dancing. She noticed that the girl had also left the room and was standing not so far away; quite still, as if every note was being absorbed into her skin. Could she be feeling, Greta wondered, some sort of rhythm, a vibration, something left over from the hours that she and Andy had practised with her? Thoughts were interrupted by the sound of David's cane.

'How are you keeping, Greta?' David sounded more solicitous than concerned. 'No need to ask about Andrew. He's exploding with good health.'

'So am I. I'm okay.' They were standing in darkness, away from the lamps. A cricket in tune with the night sang its song. David's cigarette in the short holder glowed as he sucked on it.

'I know Leila and Mannie would like you to stay with them while Andy is away. They would be company for you.'

'Nothing for me here, David. Better to be in Sydney where the *Waru* finishes its run after Singapore. At least I'll be down there when she berths. If at all . . .'

'Well, good luck, dear girl. But if ever you need —'

'Thanks, David. I'll remember that.' She leant over and kissed him on the lips. 'You've been nothing but a wonderful friend since the first day we met.' They heard laughter and applause. 'Better go inside. I have a feeling that the party's nearly over.'

His voice, tinged with amusement, followed her in. 'By the way, Greta, no one ever enlightened me. Who the hell is Netty? I've often wondered —'

'Just someone from the past, David . . .'

Who is Netty and where is Netty? Who bloody cares?

Andrew was looking for her, his eyes finding hers as she came into the room. 'Time to say our goodbyes, ay, lass?' Tomorrow they would be taking the railmotor down to Cairns, the *Waru* leaving the day after, Sydney-bound to pick up supplies for Singapore. Andy would be on deck as one of the crew.

Greta's rail journey south to meet up with Andy and the *Waru* in Sydney had been more or less uneventful, but crowded with thoughts of their reverse flight from Sydney to the North almost three years ago. The circle was closing and Greta felt as if she was living in the past, dredging up the sadness once felt when she thought he was leaving, never to return. No spick-and-span naval officer this time but seaman still, on a ship named after a turtle.

Flossie had given them the keys to her flat, refusing to take no for an answer. 'Enjoy the few days left to you. I'm bunking down with a friend.' Her wink and droll expression had left little to the imagination.

War or no war, Sydney had hardly changed, although uniforms were becoming a familiar sight. Kings Cross smelt deliciously of coffee and cream and the cooking of delectable fare: recipes handed down from mother to daughter from places with names that no one could pronounce. Displaced persons, they were called. Pawn shops displayed jewellery that had been smuggled out from the escape avenues of Spain and Switzerland and into Australia: family possessions worth more than the pittance they received from cunning buyers.

Their last morning together. In an hour the *Waru* would be throwing off her mooring lines. As if Andy had not a care in the world, he was tucking into porridge, salty and stiff enough to support a spoon standing upright. After carefully dabbing away the few tears shed out of sight, Greta made cocoa and took it to him. 'Just the way you like it, Skipper. A tot of rum and plenty of sugar.'

'Tha's my girl.' He pushed back his chair. 'Come here, me bonny darlin.' As if she were a child, he placed her on his lap. Smoothing down her hair, stroking the sadness away, his kisses were tender. 'Och, I love you, lass. Now give me that wonderful smile and I'll take it with me.'

Obeying, she ran a finger down the lines beside his mouth. 'And I'll keep these with me.'

A mournful warning was heard from a ship in a fog that had engulfed the harbour since early morning.

'Time to go,' he said briskly. Knowing better this time, Greta didn't suggest she go with him as she had before. A kiss, a last embrace, and Andy shouldered his sea bag. A wink caught and held in her heart, and he was out the door. Greta raced to the window and opened the shutters to mist and rain. He was standing there, ready to give her a wave before striding off.

As if timing it to the second, Flossie opened the door. 'C'mon, no time for tears – but there's plenty of time to get to the Heads!'

The two women raced down the stairs. A taxi was waiting for them. 'Watson Bay,' Flossie ordered. They were following a plan made out days ago. Greta hardly noticed the cannas in the median strip flaunting flames of fire from red to gold.

Flossie lit a cigarette and handed it over. 'Here, have this. It'll settle your nerves.'

It didn't take long to reach the Heads. The mist had cleared and waves bolstered by wild winds crashed and clawed at the cliffs. They stood there waiting, hair and skirts swirling and cheeks stinging, for salt was thick in the air.

Flossie, her voice shrill above the wind, cried, 'There she is!'

Greta snatched binoculars from a shopping bag, putting them to her eyes.

The *Waru* came into view, bucketing like she had never done before. Her decks were crammed with cargo and men, and as the vessel came closer Greta felt she could reach out and touch it. Andy was nowhere in sight. She expected this. He would be below decks in the engine room. Never mind. She was waving a farewell, come what may. 'Safe journey, my love. Come back soon.' Suddenly the wind won the battle and the clouds scattered. As the Waru went through the Heads, the sun came out.

An army camp in bushland, and the area fronting row upon row of army tents was packed. Men in uniform squatted on the ground, the luckier ones on benches they had commandeered from the mess. Officers sat on chairs nearest to the stage. The curtains were pulled tight. Excitement simmered over the buzz of talk and chiacking. An unseen piano started playing, inciting another burst of cheers and coo-ees. It came to a crescendo as the curtains parted, revealing only the pianist and his instrument on an empty stage. He gave a crash of thunderous chords and to the roar of more cheers and whistles a woman appeared. Her hair was long and swinging; her dress of clinging sequins as dazzling as her smile. The piano played the opening bars of 'Strike Up the Band'.

Greta Flight quickly got into her stride. The crowd couldn't get enough of her. 'Okay, boys, what would you like me to sing?' It was impossible to pick out a special request in all the clamouring noise. 'All right – I'll sing you one of my favourites.'

The crowd hushed as if they knew what was coming. Greta looked down to the upturned faces, then as if singing to each and every special one, the rich timbre of her voice swept over them.

We'll meet again,
Don't know where, don't know when,
But I know we'll meet again some sunny day . . .

EPILOGUE

The war had done little to change Kebai Island. Five rooms had been added to the Hibiscus Hotel, Arthur Mead's trade store still faced the waterfront and the frieze of brown people strolled along the foreshore as they had done forever and a day.

Administration had expanded in importance with its radio station and a small airstrip. The new jetty was longer to accommodate the flotilla that had grown, lured by the waters of the Papuan Gulf and the riches in crocodile skins – compliments of the Fly River and others that flowed through the swamps and mud of the hinterland.

Evenglow had still never been challenged by a taller building. It stood alone, lofty and grand, overlooking the bay. The woman stood admiring the view of the sailing outriggers and craft as she had done the first time she had set foot in the house.

Greta looked across to the grandfather clock that Mannie and Leila Coleman had sent over as a homecoming present nearly ten years ago, and checked the time. Any minute now it would strike three, but she decided against waking Andy. He had arrived in the early hours and now *Pelican 2* was anchored in deep water. For how long? A few days or, if lucky, Greta hoped, a week or two. It was not necessary now for Andy to take on every job that came along.

His salty kiss and sweaty hug still thrilled her as it had always done, lighting up the spark that dimmed while he was away. Thinking of a long-time promise that she'd find a paradise, Greta smiled. It had been found right here where she stood. It might not be the plantation they'd once dreamt about, but this funny little island had been good to both of them. They were content.

Children's laughter made her turn and smile. Outside Niah and her schoolmates were playing 'Catch me if you can'. Niah, with her red-gold hair and bonny ways, was a true Territorian, born in the Port Moresby Hospital and now seven years old.

As the clock struck three, Nonee brought a jug of lime juice and glasses on a tray and set it on the table. As if it was a signal, five girls bounced through the wide side door and disappeared to another part of the house. In no time they were back in matching blue shorts, white tops and tap shoes. Greta looked them over.

'Okay, girls. Don't forget, the nuns expect perfection from the Kebai School of Dance for the concert. Amy, Nicole, Bethany, Clare – and Niah, don't dawdle. Come on, limber up, girls. Stretch and bend . . .'

Minutes passed and, absorbed in their task, they never noticed the man entering and leaning against the door, his eyes on the woman he loved and the child he adored.

His mind went back to earlier days when he had first heard Greta's words in their little grey house: 'Come on, girls, follow me. Shuffle forward, back. *Five! Six! Seven! Eight!*'

Suddenly, sensing that he was watching, she looked over at him, not missing a beat. He gave a buccaneer's grin and a wink that took her right back to a New Year's Eve party many full moons ago.

Greta winked back.

ACKNOWLEDGEMENTS

As before, my dear family and good, true friends who have been with me all the way from page one to the end of the tale, you have my love and gratitude.

A huge thank you to grandsons Stephen and Brendan and friend Wes for recovering 85 000 words of the original manuscript that disappeared in a flash, thus saving me from heart failure; and to daughter Stella who advised me on the symptoms and the progression of infection.

For the help given in putting me right in all things nautical, thanks go to Bill Lewis of Brisbane, Brian Morrison of Plymouth, UK, and Peter Collins RAN, not forgetting George Craig of the *Janis B* who outwitted the recalcitrant tidal bores of the Fly River.

Gratitude to Doreen of E Street for the riotous hour when her hair design salon became a toe-tapping dance school, thus saving me from tripping over my two left writing feet.

A rich source of information freely given about the riot of 1932 came from the Cairns Historical Society, North Queensland. A sincere thank you to the volunteer staff for their unstinting help.

To fit in with narrative chronology I have deliberately put forward the date of the melee by around five years.

Selwa Anthony, agent and mentor, presented my story to Penguin and was canny enough to find the title *Burnt Sunshine* in all the many words written about Greta and Andy. Thank you, Selwa.

In conclusion I must acknowledge the pleasure I've had in working with and getting to know the folk of Penguin Group (Australia): Ali Watts, publisher, who gave me the happy news of *Burnt Sunshine*'s acceptance; designer Tony Palmer for the exciting cover; and Saskia Adams, editor and friend, for her patience and sensitive guidance throughout the long journey. I thank you all.

Subscribe to receive *read more*, your monthly newsletter from Penguin Australia. As a *read more* subscriber you'll receive sneak peeks of new books, be kept up to date with what's hot, have the opportunity to meet your favourite authors, download reading guides for your book club, receive special offers, be in the running to win exclusive subscriber-only prizes, plus much more.

Visit penguin.com.au to subscribe.